Dear Reader,

At Harlequin we have a long tradition of supporting causes women care about. The Harlequin More Than Words program, our primary philanthropic initiative, is dedicated to celebrating and rewarding ordinary women who make extraordinary contributions to their communities. Each year we ask our readers to submit a nomination for the Harlequin More Than Words award, from which we select five very deserving recipients.

We are pleased to present our five 2006 award recipients to you in our annual *More Than Words* anthology. These real-life heroines provide great inspiration to those they help and we hope, by sharing their stories with you here, that they will inspire you, too. With the help of some of our most acclaimed authors, the fictional stories inspired by the lives of our award recipients will warm your heart and nourish your soul. Susan Wiggs, Karen Harper, Kasey Michaels, Catherine Mann and Tori Carrington all donated their time and creativity to produce an entertaining and uplifting collection of novellas.
By purchasing this book, you are already making a difference—all proceeds will be reinvested in the Harlequin More Than Words program, further supporting causes that are of concern to women.

Please visit www.HarlequinMoreThanWords.com for more information, or to submit a nomination for next year's book.

Sincerely,

Donna Hayes
Publisher and CEO
Harlequin Enterprises

SUSAN WIGGS
KAREN HARPER
KASEY MICHAELS
CATHERINE MANN
TORI CARRINGTON

More Than Words

VOLUME 3

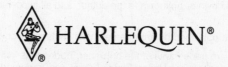

HARLEQUIN®

TORONTO • NEW YORK • LONDON
AMSTERDAM • PARIS • SYDNEY • HAMBURG
STOCKHOLM • ATHENS • TOKYO • MILAN • MADRID
PRAGUE • WARSAW • BUDAPEST • AUCKLAND

ISBN-13: 978-0-373-83658-1
ISBN-10: 0-373-83658-9

MORE THAN WORDS

CONTENTS

HOMECOMING SEASON   9
Susan Wiggs

FIND THE WAY   129
Karen Harper

HERE COME THE HEROES   219
Kasey Michaels

TOUCHED BY LOVE   313
Catherine Mann

A STITCH IN TIME   411
Tori Carrington

To my beautiful friend Shannon, a survivor

Seana O'Neill

Cottage Dreams

Cancer. It fractures the lives of families, can bring financial hardship, interrupts work schedules and taxes families emotionally.

Seana O'Neill knows from personal experience these intimate details of loss and distress after watching her mother and two uncles battle cancer. So, as she sat on her Haliburton, Ontario, cottage deck in 2002 an idea came to Seana that would not only change her life, but give hope and healing to hundreds of people living with the disease.

"It's not fair to just have this place sitting empty when it could be filled with people," she remembers saying of her cottage at the time.

It was Labor Day weekend and Seana was at a crossroads in her own life, not sure if she wanted to go back to her film career in Toronto. In the end, lifelong cottager Seana decided she would like to share her cottage with those who would not otherwise have the opportunity to get away. She was inspired to invite cancer survivors to her cottage when she wasn't there—and thought other cottagers might do the same.

She was right. The response to the idea was immediate and sparked the creation of Cottage Dreams. The registered charity connects cancer survivors and their families with donated cottages to help bring families back together, to recover, re-connect and rebuild their lives—all in a soothing natural setting.

In only one short year, Cottage Dreams went from idea to reality and placed its first six families. Today the cottage-lending program has grown to include over three hundred cottages across Ontario and has made more than one hundred placements.

"When you start something you really believe in, you do it because something is burning inside you," she says today. "I thought, 'I can't ignore this.'"

Nothing else like it

While the health care system provides patients with the support they need while in treatment, it stops when they finally walk out the doctor's door. Cancer survivors have to find a way to rebuild their lives. But it's not an easy task. A cancer diagnosis often brings financial hardship for patients and their families. Not able to work for lengthy periods, patients often find that a time away to heal and reflect is un-affordable.

This is when Seana and Cottage Dreams take over. The organization provides, at no cost, an opportunity to move on to emotional, spiritual and physical recovery. Whisked away to a natural setting, families are removed from the doctor appointments, hospital visits and other harsh and exhausting realities of their illness.

In other words, to speed healing there's nothing like listening to the gentle lap of the lake as your kids watch for falling stars.

Making a difference

Of course, Cottage Dreams is all about making wishes come true. And to hear the families tell it, Seana and her team do that and much more.

"Cottage Dreams has been a sense of new beginning for my family and me. After treatment was the perfect time to spend some quality time together and reconnect as a family," says one happy cottage visitor.

But the visitors are far from the only people to benefit from the program. Cottage owners who donate their properties also report positive benefits.

"To sum up my experience with Cottage Dreams—it made me feel good," says a donor.

Cottage Dreams makes Seana feel pretty good these days, too, although starting the project meant long hours, and trying to convince a few naysayers.

At the beginning, many of the people she spoke to asked Seana how Cottage Dreams would handle insurance, whether tax receipts would be issued and how Seana would choose the lucky families to stay at the cottages. But Seana wasn't worried. She soon talked to an insurance company, a cottage-rental agency and a lawyer. The rental agency and insurance company got on board almost right away and found innovative ways to ensure Cottage Dreams would be successful. Her lawyer, however, wasn't convinced.

"The lawyer said, 'It's going to cost you ten grand and I can't guarantee you anything. It probably won't fly,'" she says, pausing for a moment before continuing. "So I got another lawyer."

Her new lawyer is now sitting on Seana's board as chairperson.

Changing and growing

Seana's passion and commitment galvanize people. From the grassroots support of local families in cottage communities to major corporations, government and cancer research organizations, she's brought people closer. She says she's still amazed she was able to pull it together, but at the same time she had faith in her abilities to get the job done.

"I knew from the beginning that coordinating would be my strength. Also being a Virgo helps," she quips. "My mother would attest to that."

But running Cottage Dreams has meant changing and growing the organization so it reaches and helps as many people as possible. In the beginning, Cottage Dreams accepted only those in the recovery stage—within nine months of the treatment's completion.

After talking to other people who could use a week's respite, however, Cottage Dreams has extended its focus to include people in the middle of treatment and, in one case, a father of three young children who had an inoperable brain tumor. The doctors said if the man were placed within three months, he would still be well enough to enjoy himself.

"So we rush. Those people go to the top of the pile," Seana says.

Ask Seana what she's most amazed by, however, and she says she's been inspired by the inherent goodness in the people Cottage Dreams touches. One woman, a single mother undergoing chemotherapy, once told Seana to go ahead and give her space to someone else. "I'm sure there are more deserving people out there than me," the woman e-mailed Seana.

These are the lives Cottage Dreams strives to reach—not just in Ontario, but across Canada. Plans to expand nationwide by 2010 are under way.

"We're getting more families through the program, so we're getting more feedback. It really shows us we're making a difference," Seana says.

And Cottage Dreams is offering hope and respite, one cottage at a time.

For more information visit www.cottagedreams.org or write to Cottage Dreams, 33A Pine Avenue, P.O. Box 1300, Haliburton, Ontario K0M 1S0.

Acknowledgments

The author wishes to acknowledge the following individuals for their input and inspiration—the amazing Seana O'Neill and all the Cottage Dreams host families and guests, especially Phil Barley, Patty Varvouletos and Marie Stothart. Thanks to Marsha Zinberg of Harlequin for thinking of me.

SUSAN WIGGS

Homecoming Season

Susan Wiggs

"Your storytelling fills the little holes in my soul," wrote a reader of Susan Wiggs, and this comment perfectly captures what the author hopes to achieve with her novels. Susan, a former teacher, firmly believes that love can create a world in which all wounds are healed, and her award-winning tales of adventure and romance bear this out. Noted for their scenes of emotional truth, evoking both tears and laughter, her novels regularly appear on national bestseller lists. Susan lives with her family on an island in the Pacific Northwest, where she is working on her next book.

CHAPTER ONE

Miranda Sweeney's white paper gown rustled as she shifted her weight on the exam table and pulled the edges together to cover herself. "Just like that, it's over?"

Dr. Turabian closed the metal-covered chart with a decisive snap. "Well," he said, "if you want to call twenty-five rounds of radiation, nine months of chemo and two surgeries 'just like that.'" He took off his glasses and slid them into the pocket of his lab coat. "I couldn't be happier with your tests. Everything's where we'd hoped and planned for it to be, right on schedule. Other than taking your immunotoxin every day, there's nothing more you have to do."

Miranda blinked, overwhelmed by the news. "I'm…I don't know what to say." Was there a rule of etiquette in this situation? Thank you, Doctor? I love you?

"You don't have to say anything. I think you'll find getting better is a lot easier than being sick." He grinned. "Go.

Grow your hair. Come back in three months and tell me you feel like a million bucks."

He left her alone, the heavy door of the exam room closing with a sigh. Miranda went through the motions of getting dressed, all the while mulling over her conversation with the doctor.

You're done.

I'm done.

Stick a fork in her, she's done.

After a year of this, Miranda didn't believe you could ever really be *done* with cancer. It could be done with you, though, as you lay on the medical examiner's table like a waxy victim in a crime show.

Snap out of it, she told herself. For once, the doctor's advice didn't make her skin crawl—no precautions about nausea meds and gels and post-op limitations. Nothing like that. His advice was so simple it was scary. Get dressed and get on with your life.

She tore off the crinkly paper smock and wadded it up, crunching it into a small, tight ball between the palms of her hands and then making a rim shot to the wastebasket. Take *that.*

As she reached up to pull her bra off a hook, a familiar, unpleasant twinge shot up her right arm. The post-op sensations never seemed to end, although her doctor and surgeon assured her the tingling and numbness would eventually go away.

Which was—as of a few minutes ago—over.

She told herself she ought to be laughing aloud, singing "I Will Survive" at the top of her lungs, dancing down the corridors of the clinic and kissing everyone she passed. Unfortunately, that was the last thing she felt like doing. Maybe the news hadn't quite sunk in, because at the moment, she simply felt hollow and exhausted, like a shipwreck victim who'd had to swim ashore. She was alive, but the fight for survival had taken everything from her. It had changed her from the inside out, and this new woman, this gritty survivor, didn't quite know what to make of herself.

She turned to face the mirror, studying a body that didn't feel like her own anymore. A year ago, she'd been a reasonably attractive thirty-eight-year-old, comfortable in her size-10 body and—all right, she might as well admit it—downright vain about her long, auburn hair. During the months of treatment, however, she had learned to avoid mirrors. Despite the earnest reassurances of her friends, family, treatment team and support group, she never did learn to love what she saw there.

Some would say she'd lost her right breast and all her hair, but Miranda considered the term *lost* to be a misnomer. She knew exactly where her hair had gone—all over the bed pillows, down the drain of the shower, in the teeth of her comb, all over the car and the sofa. Shedding hair had followed in her wake wherever she went. Her husband, Jacob, had actually woken up one day with strands of her wavy auburn hair in his mouth. Over the course of a few days, her scalp had started to tingle. Then it stung and all her hair had come out and it wasn't lost at all. It had simply become detached from her. She collected it in a Nordstrom's bag and put it in the trash.

As for the other thing she'd "lost"—her breast—well, she knew darn well where that had gone, too. During the surgery, the tissue had been ever so carefully bagged and tagged and sent to the hospital pathology lab for analysis. Her diagnosis was made by someone she'd never met, someone she would never know. Someone who had typed her fate onto a neat form: infiltrating ductal carcinoma, stage one, tumor size 1.5 cm, nodes 15 negative.

She was considered lucky because she was a candidate for TRAM flap breast reconstruction, which took place immediately following her mastectomy. A separate surgical team came in and created a new breast, using tissue from her stomach. She'd struggled to be matter-of-fact about her reconstructed breast, figuring that if she didn't make a big deal of it, then it wouldn't be a big deal. Even though her counselor and support group encouraged her to acknowledge that an important, defining part of her was gone, that her body was permanently altered, she had resisted. She claimed she hadn't been that enamored of her breasts in the first place. They simply...were there. Size 34B. And after surgery, they still were, only the right one had been created with body fat from her stomach, something she didn't exactly mind losing. And the tattooed-on nipple was something of a novelty. How many women could boast about that?

Miranda knew she should be weeping with relief and

gratitude just about now, but she still didn't like looking at herself in the mirror. The reconstructed breast seemed slightly off-kilter, and although the skin tone and temperature were exactly the same as her other breast, she couldn't feel a thing there. Nothing, nada. And her belly button was pulled a bit to one side.

According to the members of her support group, she was supposed to look in the mirror and see a survivor. A phenomenal woman whose beauty shone from within. A woman who was glad to be alive.

Miranda leaned forward, looked carefully. Where was that woman?

Still in hiding, she thought. Her gorgeous self didn't want to come out to play.

After an agony of baldness, she was getting her hair back. Her brows and eyelashes. Unfortunately, the fledgling fuzz of hair on her head was just plain weird. She had a terrible feeling that it was coming in whitish gray. But it was her real actual hair, growing in strangely soft and baby fine, as though she had just hatched from an egg. Her skin was sallow, and new lines fanned outward from the corners of her eyes. The whites of her eyes were yellow. She still hid beneath hats, scarves and wigs. She didn't like looking like a cancer patient even though that was exactly what she was. Correction, she told herself. Cancer survivor, no longer a patient.

She turned away, grabbed her bra and finished dressing, pulling on her khaki twill pants and a front-button shirt. She disliked the twinges she felt whenever she pulled a shirt over her head. It was as though her body kept wanting to remind her that she'd been nipped, tucked and rearranged, and there wasn't a darn thing she could do about it. She slung her butter-yellow sweater around her shoulders and loosely tied it by the sleeves, knowing the morning chill would be gone by now. With a deliberate tug, she put on her hat. Today's accessory was a sun hat made of cotton duck, which she'd chosen for comfort rather than style.

She finished putting herself together—handbag, cell phone, keys—and walked through the now-familiar putty-colored hallway of the clinic. There was soothing Native American–style artwork on the walls and soothing New Age music drifting from speakers in the ceiling. As usual, everyone here was busy, hurrying somewhere with a chart or heading into one of the exam rooms. And as usual, everyone she passed offered a distracted but sincere smile of encouragement.

The waiting room was a different story. There, patients seemed almost furtive as they studied magazines or checked the inboxes of their BlackBerries. It was almost as if they didn't want to make eye contact for fear of seeing something they shouldn't—hope or despair or some combination of both—in the eyes of another patient.

Miranda realized none of the people in the waiting room could know she was leaving the place for good. She wouldn't be back for three whole months, and then only for a checkup. Still, she felt an odd flicker of survivor guilt as she passed through the room, past the burbling tabletop fountain, the aspidistra plant that had doubled in size since she'd been coming here, the magazine rack, for the last time.

She stepped out into the dazzling sunshine of an Indian summer afternoon. For a moment it was so bright Miranda felt disoriented, as if she had lost her bearings. Then she blinked, dug out her sunglasses and put them on. The world came into view. Seattle in September was a place of matchless beauty, a time of warm, golden days, incredibly clear skies and crisp nights that held the snap of autumn in the air. Today had been graced with the kind of weather that made normally industrious people sit out on the patios of urban cafés, sipping granitas and tilting their faces up to the sun.

From the hospital on First Hill—also known as Pill Hill, thanks to the abundance of hospitals and medical centers in the area—she could look toward the waterfront and see the bustle of downtown, with its disorganized tangle of freeways and the distinctive spike of the Space Needle rising above Elliott Bay. Farther in the distance lay Seattle's signature defining view—deep blue Puget Sound lined by evergreen-clad islands and inlets, the horizon edged by mountains that appeared to be topped with blue-white whipped cream. It didn't matter whether you'd been born here—as Miranda had—or if you were a newcomer, Puget Sound dazzled the eye every time you looked at it.

A car horn blasted, causing her to jump back onto the curb. Whoops. She'd been so busy admiring the scenery that she hadn't been paying attention to the signals. She dutifully waited for the little green pedestrian man to tell her when it was safe to move forward. It would be incredibly ironic to survive cancer, only to get squashed by a bakery truck.

She hiked half a block to the bus stop and checked the schedule. The ride that would take her home to Queen Anne, the area where she lived, wouldn't be here for another thirty minutes.

She sat down on a bench and dialed Jacob on her cell phone.

"Hey, gorgeous," her husband said by way of greeting.

"I bet you say that to all the girls."

"Only when I hear your special ring, babe."

"You're using your driving voice," she remarked.

"What's that?"

She smiled a little. "Your driving voice. I can always tell when you're on the road."

He laughed. "What's up?"

"I just came from Dr. Turabian's."

"Are you all right?" This, of course, was his knee-jerk reaction these days. Jacob found the whole cancer business terrifying, and to be fair, most guys his age didn't expect to find themselves helping a young wife through a life-threatening disease. Jacob even seemed afraid of her, scarcely daring to touch her, as if he feared she might break. At first, he had accompanied Miranda to all her appointments—the tests and treatments, the follow-up visits. He was wonderful, trying to mask his near panic, yet Miranda found his efforts so painful to watch that it actually added to her stress. In time, she found it simpler to go on her own or with one of her girlfriends. At first Jacob had fought her—*I'm coming with you, and you can't stop me*—but eventually, he accepted her wishes with a sort of shamefaced relief.

"It was my last visit," she reminded him. "And it went just as we'd hoped. All the counts and markers checked out the way Dr. Turabian wanted them to." She took a deep breath. The air was so sharp and clean, it hurt her lungs. "I'm done."

"What do you mean, done?"

"Like, *done* done." She laughed briefly, and her own laughter sounded strange, like the rusty hinge to a door that rarely opened. "He doesn't want to see me again for three months. And it's unexpectedly weird. I don't know what to do with myself. It's as if I've forgotten what I used to do before I had cancer."

"Well." Jacob sounded as though he was at a loss, too. Afraid to say the wrong thing. "How do you feel?"

She knew what he was really asking: "When can you start back to work?" Her sabbatical from her job had definitely taken a toll on the family finances. Though she felt a pinch of annoyance, she didn't blame him. Throughout this whole ordeal, he had kept the family afloat, juggling work and extra household responsibilities so she could focus on getting on with her treatment, which touched off an exhaustion so crippling she couldn't work. His job, in beverage sales to large grocery chains, kept him constantly on the road. He earned a commission only, no base salary, so every sale mattered. And Lord knew, the bank account needed all the help it could get. They had budgeted for their house on the assumption that they'd be a two-income family.

"I feel all right, I think." Actually she felt as if she had run a marathon and crossed the finish line with no one around to see her do it. The world looked the same. Traffic still flowed up and down the hills, boats and barges still steamed back and forth across the Sound, and pedestrians still strolled past, oblivious to the fact that she'd just completed cancer treatment and had lived to tell the tale.

"Good," said Jacob. "I'm glad."

She watched a pigeon stroll along the sidewalk, poking its beak at crumbs. "Me, too. I'd better let you go. See you tonight?"

"I'll try not to be too late. Love you, babe."

"Love you." She put away her phone and pondered their habit of declaring their love, something they now did without thinking. When she'd first been diagnosed, telling her husband and kids "I love you" every time she parted from them or hung up the phone had seemed mandatory. Facing her own mortality made her painfully cognizant of the fact that every "goodbye" could be the last. Even though her prognosis had been good, she'd been careful to make certain everyone in her family heard her say "I love you" every day. As time went on, however, repetition and habit sucked the meaning from the phrase. Nowadays, signing off with "love you" was not that much different from "see you later."

Rifling through her wallet for her bus pass, she found a note she'd written to herself on a slip of paper. In her support group, other members were big on telling you to write down affirmations and positive thoughts, and keep them tucked in your pockets, your purse, wherever you might come across them. Miranda recognized her handwriting on the note, but she had absolutely no recollection of writing it. The note said, "You can't have today back. So make sure you spend it in the best possible way."

A wise sentiment, to be sure, but it didn't really illuminate what the "best possible way" meant. Did it mean surrounding herself with friends and family? Helping a stranger? Creating an original work of art? She should have been more specific. She folded the note and put it back in her wallet.

The landscaping by the bus stop was uninspired—laurel hedges, asters and mums. The plantings were hardy and dependable, if a bit boring. Miranda adored gardening, but she had become a bit of a snob about it. One of the things she'd promised herself during the treatment was that she was going to get back into gardening.

In the blue distance, the white-and-green ferryboats of Puget Sound glided back and forth between the islands to the west. A tourist was parasailing over Elliott Bay and Miranda felt a smile unfurl on her lips. What a beautiful thing to do, floating high above the blue water, the rainbow-colored chute blooming like a flower in the cloudless sky. From this distance, the tether that bound the rig to the speedboat was invisible, so it really did look as if the person was flying free.

Miranda had never been parasailing. Maybe she should try it one day. She glanced at her watch, and then at the bus schedule. Maybe she should try it now.

Oh, come on, she told herself. You'll miss your bus.

There's always another bus. You can't have today back, a wise woman had once written.

Miranda got up, hoisted the strap of her bag onto her shoulder and started walking. It was an easy walk since it was all downhill. She must have been going at a perfect pace because every single pedestrian light turned green as she approached it. She got the feeling the whole of downtown was urging her on.

As she crossed to the waterfront by way of a pedestrian overpass, she walked through the usual gauntlet of panhandlers. And like the other pedestrians, she averted her gaze, though even without looking, she could picture them perfectly—drowsy castoffs layered in old clothes, all their possessions in a shopping cart or knapsack. Most had battered cups out for change, some with crudely lettered signs that read, Spare Change or simply God Bless.

Miranda kept her eyes trained straight ahead. If you pretend not to see them, they're not really there. She couldn't do it, though, and she experienced the guilt anyone would feel for these people. She reminded herself that there were shelters where panhandlers could go for help, and all they had to do was show up. And of course, everyone knew you shouldn't give them money. They'd only spend it on beer.

Then it struck her. So what if they spent their meager donations on beer? Maybe that was all that stood between them and the urge to walk off the end of a pier and sink to the bottom of the Sound.

She slowed her pace and took out her wallet. There were five panhandlers stationed apart at regular intervals, like sentries sitting guard duty. She didn't have a lot of cash on her but she gave everything away, every cent, trying to divide it evenly among them. A couple of them whispered a thank-you, while the others merely nodded as though too weary to speak. Miranda didn't care. She wasn't doing this for the thanks.

When her wallet was empty of cash, she stuck it in her back pocket and continued to the waterfront. Down on Alaska Way, a busy street that hugged the shoreline and bristled with piers, she encountered another panhandler, this one a woman sitting on an apple crate and holding a sign marked Homeless. Need Help.

Miranda hesitated, then made eye contact with the woman. "I gave all my money to the people up on the Marion Street bridge," she confessed.

"That's okay. You have a good day, now."

Miranda plucked the butter-yellow sweater from her shoulders. "Can you use this?" It was a designer piece from Nordstrom's, made of fine-gauge Sea Isle cotton. The sweater had been a gift from her mother-in-law, who believed that no problem was so huge it couldn't be solved by a great sweater from Nordstrom's.

"Sure, honey, if you don't mind giving it up."

"I don't mind." She handed over the sweater.

"Oh, that's soft. Thank you." The woman's callused hand trembled as she smoothed it over the fabric.

"You're welcome." On impulse, Miranda opened her handbag. She took out the personal items—her cell phone, her keys and a bottle of pills and stuck them in her pockets. What remained were the usual purse things—a pack of Kleenex, a comb and a lipstick, a calculator, a tiny flashlight.

"This might come in handy, too," she said.

This offer made the woman frown. "That's a nice bag," she said, but her voice was dubious.

She had good taste. It was another gift from Miranda's mother-in-law, a Dooney & Burke that had probably retailed for a few hundred dollars.

"I've got another at home."

"You're not from the mission, are you?" the panhandler asked. "I already tried the mission, and it don't work for me."

"I'm not from the mission. Just someone…passing by."

The woman still eyed her skeptically.

Miranda heard the blast of a ferry horn, the cry of a seagull. A breeze tickled across the back of her neck and gently wafted beneath the brim of her sun hat. Out of habit, her hand went up to keep it from blowing away. But then, instead of clamping down on the hat, she took hold of the brim.

Deep breath, she told herself, and then she swept the hat off her head. She was naked to the world now. Everyone who looked at her would know she was a cancer patient. Even after all this time, she felt self-conscious. She wanted to proclaim to anyone who would listen that she was more than a patient. She was a wife, a mother, a coworker, a friend. But when all your hair fell out and your fingernails crumbled and you lost your eyelashes, that was all people saw. A cancer patient.

Survivor, she corrected herself, handing over her hat. Cancer survivor, as of today.

The woman took it, then offered Miranda a brief smile and said, "You have a nice day now."

As Miranda walked away, she felt strangely light, unfettered, as though she were floating already. She hoped like heck the parasailing company took credit cards.

They did, of course. Everybody did. The panhandlers probably did.

Miranda had just given away all her money, but she didn't stop there. Feeling reckless, she paid for a spin over Elliott Bay. The guy helping her into the harness gave her hasty instructions. "There's not much to it. Just relax and let the wind do all the work. You don't even need to change out of your street clothes. You won't get wet, guaranteed."

The old Miranda, the Miranda who had never looked her own mortality square in the eye, would have been terrified. Now, though, she was matter-of-fact about danger and risk. She wondered if the harness would bother her bad arm, but decided she didn't care. She had borne worse than that lately.

"Sounds good to me." She bit her lip as he passed the straps under her breasts. Would he know that one of them was reconstructed? And why the heck should that matter? Don't be silly, she told herself.

He and his partner motored out into the bay, their little

speedboat dwarfed by ferries and cargo barges. Following instructions, Miranda positioned herself on the platform and waited as the chute billowed with the wind and speed. Then they let her go off the back of the boat. For a second, she dipped downward, her bare feet skimming the water. She took in a sharp breath, bracing herself for the bone-chilling cold of Puget Sound. Then the wind scooped up the chute and she went drifting high and fast, like a giant kite on a string.

After her first gasp of wonder, Miranda remained absolutely quiet, just hanging there. She had learned how to be still and stoic during her cancer treatment. She had remained absolutely still while radiologists and oncologists had examined her. Still while the surgeons studied her and made lines on her with a Sharpie marker. Still while she lay on the table of the linear accelerator while a deadly beam of light was aimed at her. Still while the machine burned its invisible rays at her, making her skin blister and crack.

She was good at holding still. And now so ready to leave that behind and let the wind sweep her away.

She saw what the seabirds saw—the dark, mysterious underwater formations, pods of sea lions sunning themselves on navigation buoys, the container ships and sailboats, the blaze of sunlight on the water. She felt the cool rush of wind through her hair—what there was of her hair. The breeze ruffled it like feathers.

She laughed aloud and wished Jacob and the kids could see her now, a human kite tail soaring above the city, with its high-rises and skeletal orange cranes in the shipyards, incongruously set against the backdrop of Mount Rainier in all its glory. Maybe she would buy the ten-dollar photo the guys in the boat had taken of her soaring, because how often did you get a picture of yourself airborne? Yet there was something depressing in the thought of bringing a picture home to Jacob and the kids. She'd done this cool thing alone. She couldn't remember the last time they had done anything as a family.

She gave the parasailing crew a thumbs-up as they expertly reeled her in to the deck of the boat and motored over to the dock. Once on dry land, one of the guys printed up a photo from his digital camera and handed it to her. She reached into her back pocket for her wallet.

"It's on me," he said.

She put her wallet away. "Thank you."

People were extra nice to cancer patients, she had discovered. They looked at the hair loss, the broken nails, the sallow skin and the swollen bodies, and they got scared. *There but for the grace of God go I.* Being nice to victims was a form of self-inoculation, perhaps. She used to think that way herself before she became a member of the cancer club. By now, she had learned to accept kindnesses big and small, from friends and strangers.

Miranda thanked the man again. She would keep the picture as something to take out and study at the odd moment—a shot of herself soaring high and free, alone against the clear blue sky.

She needed to find an ATM. She walked up the hill from the waterfront and took the concrete Harbor Steps, and from there, headed toward Pike Place Market. She made slow progress on the stairs, which was yet another frustration of this disease. Only a year ago, she had been a busy, energetic woman with everything going for her—two great kids, a caring husband, a solid—if boring—job, a spring in her step. She used to pride herself on her ability to cram so much into a single day. In under an hour, she could go from company meeting room to soccer field to fixing dinner without missing a beat.

Now she got winded on a stupid flight of stairs.

That, she decided, was going to end right now.

She squared her shoulders and lifted her chin. This was a big day. She needed to make a big deal of it.

At Pike Place Market, teeming with shoppers, tourists, chefs, performers and deliverymen, she bought the makings of a feast—fresh local asparagus and morel mushrooms, yellow potatoes and wild white salmon fresh off the boat, according to the chatty fishmonger in his slick yellow apron. Spot prawns for the appetizer.

She pictured herself sitting down to a beautifully set table with her family. They had cause to celebrate. This was a red-letter day.

As she exited the market with her parcels, she paused at a row of wholesale flower stalls. Big pails of galvanized steel displayed stalks of dahlias, bells of Ireland, roses in every conceivable shade. Each burst of color was like a small celebration.

Miranda's heart expanded, and she inhaled the green fragrance of the plants. Flowers had long been a passion of hers. She was expert at growing and also arranging flowers. That hobby, like the rest of her life, had fallen by the wayside during her illness. Until she glimpsed the flower stall, she hadn't realized how much she missed it.

She asked the flower seller for a variety—gerbera daisies and rover mums, fragrant yarrow, purple statice, solidaster, hypericum berries and seeded eucalyptus. This, she decided, would be her victory bouquet—a colorful, elegant affirmation that she had survived her treatment and was ready to move on with her life.

On the way to the bus stop, she juggled her parcels and dialed Jacob's number again.

"I went parasailing."

"What?"

He had the driving voice again. Traffic sounds indicated that this was probably not the best time to explain. "I'm making a special dinner tonight," she told him.

"I was going to offer to take you out," he said.

"Thanks, but I was feeling creative, and this probably works out better for the kids, anyway. Andrew has soccer practice until four-thirty, and Valerie goes to work at the theater at eight. So…six-thirty?"

He hesitated. She heard a world of doubt in that hesitation. It was getting so that she could read his silences with more accuracy than she could his words.

"You're going to be late," she said.

"I can move some things—"

"Good idea." Normally, she tried to be accommodating of the demands of his job, but today she wanted him with her. "Call me later and let me know what time works for you."

"I won't be late," he promised.

"Just call me. Bye."

Her husband, she reminded herself, was a wonderful man. He had proven himself over and over again the past year. One of the greatest sacrifices he had made was to increase his work hours when she took her leave of absence from Urban Ice, which supplied bulk ice to commercial operations. Some weeks Jacob put in eighty hours, never complaining, simply doing what had to be done. Despite their health plan, only so many of her medical procedures were covered by insurance, like the mastectomy, but not the reconstruction, which she thought was a cruel irony. Within just hours of diagnosis, they had reached their deductible. Still, health insurance didn't cover the mortgage; that was what her salary was for. Nor did it cover groceries or utilities or taxes, or school clothes for the kids. And it sure didn't cover parasailing or the twenty dollars' worth of flowers she'd just bought.

CHAPTER TWO

Miranda got off the bus at the corner and walked halfway down the block to her house. It was a neighborhood she loved, a place rich with history and an eclectic mix of residents. Queen Anne crowned the highest hill in Seattle and commanded the best views of the city and the Sound. There were modern condo complexes interspersed with historic mansions built by timber and railroad barons long ago. The Sweeneys' street had a cozy, colorful feel to it. Arts and Crafts–era bungalows were brightened by gardens that bloomed on the smallest patches of earth, rockeries and concrete stairs leading up to friendly-looking front porches.

She and Jacob had loved their house the first time they'd seen it six years before. There was even room for both a garden and greenhouse in the back, something she had always dreamed of. She cringed, thinking of her garden now. It had been among the first things to fall by the wayside when she was diagnosed.

She was looking forward to returning to a normal life, getting her house in order, her garden planted, her finances under control. This house was at the absolute top end of what they could afford, and when she'd taken leave from work, she'd told Jacob they should sell the place and live somewhere cheaper. He wouldn't hear of it. She suspected that in his mind, giving up the house was an admission that she wouldn't get better, that she wouldn't be going back to work. There was no way he would concede that.

She'd been grateful for his stubborn insistence on keeping the house she loved, but beginning next year, their mortgage rate would adjust, and the payments were going to balloon. She shuddered, thinking about the size of the check they'd have to write each month.

Not today, she cautioned herself. Today she was not going to worry. As she let herself in, she looked around the house and for some reason saw it with new eyes. Nothing had changed, yet she felt like a stranger here. The silence was marred only by the rhythmic ticking of the hall clock: 4:00 p.m. She had plenty of time to get dinner on the table.

She had learned to keep things simple this past year. When she bothered to fix dinner at all—which was rare—she tended to avoid complicated dishes.

"What did I used to do with myself?" she asked aloud.

Then she grabbed the flowers she'd bought, found a few vases and bowls and grabbed her stem snippers and went to work. She'd almost forgotten how soothing and satisfying it was to arrange flowers, something she'd learned from her grandmother.

In her support group, everyone stressed how important it was to keep doing the things you enjoyed throughout treatment. For Miranda, the problem was that she had a hard time enjoying anything when she was curled into a ball of nausea from chemo, or jumping out of her skin from the discomfort of radiation burns. Some days, it was all she could do to make it from one side of a single moment to the other.

It's over, she reminded herself. You're done.

"Mom?"

Miranda nearly dropped the bowl she was carrying. "Andrew. I didn't hear you come in."

Her eleven-year-old son slung his backpack onto the bench at the back door. "I tried to be quiet."

"You're good at it. A regular superspy."

He sat down and unlaced his soccer cleats. She watched him, experiencing a moment of both helpless love and keen regret. Not so very long ago, he used to come slamming into the house, announcing loudly, "I'm home. And I'm starved."

One of the drugs she'd been given caused headaches and made her hypersensitive to loud noises, and she had to ask him to tiptoe and whisper. It seemed as if the entire family had been tiptoeing and whispering for a year.

"How are you, buddy?" she asked him, using a step stool to take down a salad bowl. Another limitation—postsurgery, she couldn't lift her arm higher than her shoulder. That was months ago, but there was still discomfort. She'd learned to use a stool, ask for help or skip the chore altogether.

"Okay." He set aside his grass-caked cleats and sent her a quick smile as he stood up.

Her heart constricted with love. How tall he'd grown in the past year. How handsome. When she studied his face, she could still see her little boy there. His skin was baby soft, with a dusting of freckles saddling his nose. There was just a hint of roundness in his cheeks but that would be gone soon, as he continued to grow, his face to elongate with maturity.

Come back, she wanted to say to that little boy. I'm not ready to let you go. She hated that she'd missed out on so much while she was sick. She hated missing soccer games and school meetings, just going to the park or weekend rounds of miniature golf or paintball drills.

She wiped her hands on a tea towel and went around the counter, pulling him into a hug. He felt stiff and hesitant in her arms, this boy who used to hurl himself at her in an abandoned tangle of affection. They had taken his mother away one day, and the woman who returned was a bald, puffy-faced stranger with drains sprouting from her chest. She was tender and sore and fragile as an old woman, reeking of Radiacare gel, and for a very long time, that was the end of bear hugs.

She kissed the top of his head. He smelled…golden. Like Indian-summer sunshine, fresh-cut grass and the curiously innocent scent of boyish sweat. "You'll be taller than me soon," she remarked, letting him go. "Next week, probably."

"Uh-huh." He went to the sink for a glass of water.

She saw him looking around the kitchen, everywhere except at her. This was another habit that had developed, and not just in Andrew. Both of her children had stopped looking at her. She didn't blame them. It was alarming to see their mother so ill. She had not been one of those movie-of-the-week cancer patients who grew more delicate and beautiful as the disease progressed. She'd simply turned blotchy and swollen, with circles under her eyes. When her hair fell out, it revealed that her scalp was weirdly ridged rather than smooth. Andrew was barely ten years old at the time of for diagnosis. Seeing her so radically altered had frightened him, and he had learned to avert his eyes.

"We're having dinner together tonight," she said. "All four of us."

"Okay," he said.

"I have good news."

That perked him up. He was apparently so used to bad news that this came as a surprise. His sister, Valerie, had quit asking altogether. "Today, Dr. Turabian told me I'm done. No more treatments."

"Hey, that's good, Mom. You're cured."

She smiled at him. The word *cured* was a dicey term. Her doctors and treatment team tended to say "cancer free" or to cite counts and markers and measures in the lab reports. She wasn't going to split hairs with Andrew, though.

"So guess what I did today," she said.

"What?"

"I went parasailing over Elliott Bay."

Finally he looked at her. Really looked. And his expression seemed to ask if she'd lost her mind. "Nuh-uh."

"Nuh-huh. It was awesome. You should have seen me. It was like being the tail of a kite." She took out the digital print and showed him.

"Jeez, that's you?" he said, studying the little dangling figure in the photo. "Crazy."

He didn't seem thrilled. Impressed, but not thrilled. Miranda was reminded that her son preferred things to be predictable. Traditional. It didn't matter that this was the twenty-first century. Despite all the social advances in the world, boys wanted their moms to be conventional and conservative. They wanted them in the kitchen baking cookies, wearing high heels and a ruffled apron. Where on earth did they get these ideas? she wondered. Andrew had never had a fifties-style stay-at-home mom. She didn't even own an apron. On what planet did women like that exist?

She tousled his hair. "Don't worry, I'm not losing it. After my appointment, I decided to celebrate, and I felt like doing something different."

"Okay."

He headed for the study, and she could hear the sound of the computer booting up. Andrew's new obsession was a very sophisticated simulation game called Adventure Island. His devotion to the game had developed over the past year. Miranda didn't comprehend all the details, but as far as she could tell, the game allowed him to create his own world on the computer and populate it with people of his own imagination.

Miranda clearly saw the motivation behind the act. Andrew had fabricated a world in which he was in total control. His virtual world was an idyllic place where every boy had a pet, where dads came home from work early to play catch in the backyard and where moms didn't sleep all day or puke or cry or get rushed to the emergency room, spiking a fever. In Andrew's perfect world, the moms strapped on colorful aprons over their Barbie-doll figures, sang songs, helped with homework and baked cookies.

Dream on, kiddo, she thought as she turned on the radio to her favorite oldies station. "Ain't No Mountain High Enough" was playing and she joined in, singing loudly and tossing the salad while swaying to the beat. In the past, Andrew might have joined her. He liked oldies, too, and could carry a tune.

Unfortunately, it was too late to draw Andrew away from his virtual utopia, and Miranda felt a squeeze of regret, even as she warbled along with the radio. Prior to discovering the game, her son had spent a lot more time with her, with his friends and especially with his best friend in the world, Gretel, the family dog.

The big, affectionate Bernese mountain dog had been born the same year as Andrew, and they'd been raised together. On Andrew's first day of kindergarten, Gretel had slunk under his bed and refused to move until he got home. When they were together, they played endlessly—chase and

fetch and, Gretel's favorite, rescue. Andrew would pretend
to be lost and injured, and she would drag and nudge him
to safety. It was one of life's most perfect friendships—a
little boy and his loyal dog.

In a twist of stunning cruelty, Gretel had died a few
months ago. Of cancer.

Miranda and Jacob had tried to tell Andrew that it was
just a painful coincidence, that at age ten, Gretel was old for
a Berner, and that having cancer didn't mean you had to die.
Andrew said he understood, but sometimes Miranda
thought he only agreed with her and Jacob just to get them
to stop talking about it. She had said they could get a new
puppy, but that had only made Andrew furious.

"Why would I want to get another dog, just so it'll die
on me?"

"Think of all the love Gretel brought into your life,"
Miranda had said.

"All I can think about is how much I miss her."

Miranda hadn't pressed the issue. Truth be told, she believed
getting a puppy would consume more time and energy than
she could afford. She told herself she'd bring it up with
Andrew again once she was feeling better. Soon, she thought.
Soon, they needed to have a family meeting about the issue.

Before her diagnosis, what did they used to do? It was so
hard to remember. It seemed as though that life had
belonged to a different woman, a woman who had rushed
in a hyped-up blur from family to work, from one over-
planned, overscheduled day to the next.

Never again, Miranda thought, seasoning the salmon and popping it in the oven on a cedar roasting plank. She had lost a lot to cancer, but she'd gained at least one thing. Wisdom enough to realize that, sick or healthy, a woman needed to slow down and pay attention to the things that matter most—her family and friends. Her passions and her dreams. Provided she hadn't forgotten what those were.

An hour later, dinner was ready, but her family was not. The phone rang, and it was Jacob. "I am so sorry," he said. "I got stuck in a sales meeting with West Sound Grocery's company V.P. He kept upping his order, so I couldn't very well duck out of the meeting." Jacob could not keep the smile from his voice as he added, "I made about four times the usual commission thanks to this guy. Turns out he's a fly fisherman, too."

She couldn't remember the last time Jacob had gone fishing. "Well...congrats. Try to get home before dinner gets too cold." What else was she going to say?

She hung up feeling torn. On the one hand, he was coming home late, and she had a right to be irritated with him. On the other, he was late because he was providing for his family while Miranda dealt with being sick.

The sound of the back door slamming caught her attention. "Hello, you," she said to her daughter. "I hope you're hungry."

Valerie, who was fifteen, sullen and gorgeous, shrugged out of her black denim jacket. "Gotta go to work," she said curtly. "I promised I'd go in early tonight."

Miranda's heart sank. "How early?"

"Like, in half an hour."

"Valerie. Give your family a little time."

Her daughter's eyes, which were a lovely blue and almost totally obscured by a deep crust of coal-black makeup, flicked around the room. "I don't see any family."

"Sit down," Miranda said resolutely. "I'll get Andrew."

She found her son frozen like a statue, his rapt face bathed in the blue-gray glow of the computer screen. He appeared not to move at all except for his hand on the mouse, busily manipulating images on the screen.

"Supper, buddy," she said.

No response.

"Your sister's home, supper is on the table and it's time to eat," she said.

"'Kay." He offered a distracted grunt. "Give me a minute."

"Sorry, no can do. Put that all on standby or whatever you have to do, and go wash your hands."

"But if I stop now I'll lose this whole—"

"Andrew. If you don't stop now, I'll lose something and it won't be data."

He heaved a long-suffering sigh, saved his work and headed off to wash his hands.

Miranda manufactured a cheerful mood as she sat down to the dinner table. "Check it out," she said. "A home-cooked meal. When was the last time we had that?"

"Thanks," Valerie said, digging in. She glanced at the clock above the stove.

"I know this past year has been rough on you guys,"

Miranda said. "I'm hoping we're about to hit a smooth patch, Val. The doctor gave me my walking papers today. No more treatments."

Valerie's chewing slowed. Then she swallowed and took a gulp from her water glass. "So that's good, right?"

"It's very good. I'll be taking something to prevent a recurrence of the cancer, and I have to get rechecked every three months, and then every six, and so on. Other than that, I'm a free woman."

"Well. I'm glad." Valerie resumed eating.

Miranda watched her thoughtfully. Valerie's reaction to her mother getting breast cancer had been complicated, a combination of abject horror, betrayal, rage and resentment. And finally, ambivalence. She was old enough to comprehend the stark reality of her mother's mortality, and smart enough to realize how much that put herself at risk for the same disease.

While Andrew had retreated into his virtual world, Valerie had struck out in search of a life apart from her family. Each child was looking for some kind of separation, and Miranda didn't blame them, although it hurt. Valerie found escape and diversion at the Ruby Shoebox, a vintage art-house movie theater in the funky Capital Hill district of Seattle. It was her first real job. She'd started as an usher and then advanced to cashier. Working there every Friday and Saturday night made her supremely happy.

As nearly as Miranda could tell, Valerie had found a whole new set of friends there, too—older kids who smoked cigarettes and wore berets and Doc Martens. In a matter of months, Miranda had watched her sunny, funny daughter transform into a virtual stranger. She'd turned her back on her two best friends, Megan and Lyssa, and completely ignored Pete, the boy next door, whom she'd had a crush on since sixth grade. The old Valerie was inside her somewhere, but Miranda had no idea how to bring her back. She wished she knew how to remind Valerie of the things they used to love to do together, traditions that had once been cherished but were now somehow lost in the shuffle.

For far too long, Miranda had been at a loss, too weakened by the disease to do anything about her kids. Oh, she was angry about that. She resented the disease because it had turned her into a lazy mother.

"I have something else to say," she announced, and her tone captured their attention. "We need to come together as a family. Now that my treatments are over, that's what I want to work on."

"Yeah, tell that to Dad," Valerie said.

"I intend to." Miranda turned her attention to the delicate white salmon, the fresh salad. Finally, finally, food was going to taste good to her again rather than carry that weird metallic tinge caused by her medication. "I was looking at the school calendar," she said, lightening her tone. "Homecoming is just a few weeks away."

Homecoming and all it entailed was a big deal for Valerie's school, and for the Sweeneys in particular. The game was only one component of an entire weekend of celebration, bringing in high-school alumni from all over, wearing their well-preserved letterman jackets and waving pennants proclaiming them state champions more times than any other school in Washington State. Valerie and Andrew had grown up nurtured on stories of how Jacob and Miranda had met at the high school's Homecoming dance back in 1986, when they were both seniors. And the rest, as the story went, was history.

"So I hear." Valerie stabbed at a potato with her fork. "I don't plan on going, so don't get all excited about it."

"What do you mean, you're not going? Everyone goes to Homecoming."

"Not me." She met Miranda's eyes, held her gaze an extra beat.

That was all it took to remind Miranda of last year's Homecoming disaster. As a high-school freshman, it had been Valerie's first time. She'd been soaring with excitement, having been asked by the perfect boy—Pete. She'd picked out the perfect dress and shoes, and was looking forward to the perfect evening. Then she learned Miranda's mastectomy was scheduled for the day of the dance.

Miranda had urged her to go, but Valerie had refused. "How could I?" she asked, and had spent Homecoming weekend at the hospital, sitting with her father throughout the surgery and during the terrible wait afterward. While her friends were all out celebrating, Valerie was watching her mother being transformed from her mom into some sickly stranger. Things had not gone smoothly. There were complications. And for Valerie, there was a horrible association in her mind between Homecoming and illness and worry.

All in all, it had probably been one of the worst weekends of Valerie's life. Here she was a year later, a different person, a dark rebel who rarely smiled, who was secretive and watchful, who held herself aloof from things most girls her age enjoyed—school and sports, hanging out with her friends and looking forward to things like Homecoming season.

"I hope you'll reconsider," Miranda said. "I promise you there won't be any crisis this year."

"Just not into it," Valerie said. "No big deal."

And of course, it was a huge deal, and Miranda knew it, and so did Valerie. Somewhere trapped inside the cynical stranger was a girl who wanted to be on the decorating committee, who wanted Pete to ask her to the dance. She would deny all this, but Miranda knew it was true. Sometimes she wanted to grab this pale-skinned, black-haired stranger, shake her and demand, *What have you done with my daughter?*

She suspected there were moments when Valerie wanted to do the same to her. Because Miranda—the mom she knew—had gone away, too. There were many times this past year when Miranda had looked in the mirror and seen a woman she didn't know. If she didn't recognize herself, how could her kids know her?

"Why do they call it Homecoming?" Andrew asked.

"It's tradition. A long time ago, schools wanted all their alumni to come home for a game against their biggest rival."

A car horn sounded. "That's my ride," Valerie said. "I have to go. I'll be back by eleven." She jumped up, carried her plate to the sink, grabbed her backpack. "I have my cell, I did my homework in study hall and I've got a ride home." She rattled off answers before Miranda could even ask the questions. "Don't wait up."

She was gone in a swirl of black denim and fishnet stockings, leaving a void of silence. Miranda used to be the kind of mom who was proactive, who ran her kids' lives and stayed on top of things. She was determined to regain the strength and stamina to reclaim that role. She only hoped she wasn't too late.

Jacob called again to say he was stuck in traffic on the 520 bridge, a floating bridge that spanned Lake Washington. Miranda set aside his dinner to warm later in the microwave. Andrew loaded the dishwasher without being asked. One of the few aspects of her illness that she welcomed was that her little boy had taken to doing his chores without nagging. There were moments when she almost wished he would need a little nagging, just as a reminder that he needed her.

"Thanks, good buddy," she said as he turned on the dishwasher.

"'Welcome. I'll be in the study."

That was code for, "I'll be on my computer in a virtual world where I'm in control."

The medical family therapist they had been seeing talked with her at length about the many ways the family dynamic changed over the course of a serious illness. It was a natural process that progressed through known stages. There were things Miranda had to let go of in order to focus on getting well. Much of her hands-on mothering had to go. She had not surrendered it overnight. It had been a gradual process of renegotiation. She would not regain it overnight; she realized that. And when she finally did, she knew the whole landscape of her family would be different.

As she was straightening the kitchen, she came across a packet of information the therapist had given her. There were many components to post-treatment: support groups, Web site chat rooms and bulletin boards, opportunities to connect with women who, like Miranda, were facing the sometimes daunting chore of returning to normal life.

The hardest by far was getting to know her family again. Miranda could not imagine where to begin. With Jacob, who sought absolution by doubling his workload? With Valerie, who had morphed into an angry, distant teen? Or with Andrew, who barely had the vocabulary for expressing his deepest fears?

She turned on the radio in time to hear the final chorus of "Girls Just Wanna Have Fun," and the tune lifted her spirits, just a little. She kept telling herself she had cause to celebrate, and not to expect too much too soon.

Oh, but she did. She wanted it all. She wanted her life back. She wanted her daughter to go to Homecoming, her son to race around the block on his bike and practice armpit-farting in the bathtub. She wanted her husband to look at her with more than desperate love in his eyes; she wanted him to look at her with passion. Or, heck, she thought. Right now, she'd just settle for him getting home in time for dinner.

CHAPTER THREE

Jacob walked in the door at sunset, looking weary, worried and heart-stirringly handsome all at once. Miranda's husband had a wonderful face with the features of a cheerful boy who would never grow up. That was what she used to see when she looked at him. Now she saw not just a man who had indeed left every vestige of youth behind, but a man aged by worry.

At present, he had a "sorry I'm late" smile on his face and an enormous and garish bouquet of asters and mums in his arms. Bringing Miranda flowers used to be like bringing coal to Newcastle, but since she'd abandoned her garden, fresh flowers were a rarity around the house.

"Looks like somebody beat me to it," he said, eyeing the flowers she'd bought at the market.

"That would be me," she confessed. "I treated myself."

"I brought some champagne, too." Still holding the flowers, he bent and kissed her briefly. Too briefly. Just enough for her to start to savor the taste of him and the shape of his lips, just enough for her to notice, like a distant flicker of heat lightning, an echo of the passion they used to share. Like so many other things, her cancer had wreaked havoc on the intimate aspects of her marriage. She'd had a long postsurgery recovery period. In the midst of that course of the radiation treatment, she couldn't stand for clothing to touch her, let alone her husband's hands, his lips, his body. Often, even the sensation of the bedsheets rustling when he shifted at night had caused her to cry out in pain. And for several days following each round of chemo, she had been good for nothing, certainly not for reclaiming her husband.

He'd been great through it all. Better than great.

Too great.

She missed the days before the disease had struck, when he would come waltzing in from work, clasp her in his arms, plant a resounding kiss on her mouth. Or if the kids weren't around, he'd come up behind her, nuzzle her neck and whisper a wicked suggestion in her ear. It was frustrating to Miranda that she could remember those moments so vividly, but couldn't figure out how to get back to that place, how to be that sexy, carefree person again.

She warmed his dinner in the microwave and set it down before him. They toasted each other with glasses of chilled champagne, and she savored the bubbly effervescence on her tongue. He ate with an almost comical sense of appreciation, closing his eyes and swooning until she laughed.

"So did you tell the kids?" he asked.

"I did. They seemed a bit underwhelmed. I think they might be suspicious that I'm pulling their leg. They don't really trust me to be well and stay well."

"Oh, come on. They trust you."

"They'll learn to, all over again."

He looked at her, really looked at her, for a long moment. Despite all the changes they'd gone through the past year, Jacob knew her with a depth and intimacy that ran far deeper than any illness could reach. "What's bothering you?"

She poured herself another glass of champagne. "Andrew's obsessed by that cybergame or whatever it is, and Valerie claims she's not going to the Homecoming dance."

"Sounds pretty typical to me."

"Nothing about this family is typical anymore, including us."

"Miranda—"

"I've been too exhausted to really take this up with you, but I'm getting back to normal now. And I mean it. You know I'm right."

"Every family deals with problems. We got through last year. We can get through anything." He pushed back from the table. "And that was the best meal I've had…maybe ever. I mean it."

She smiled. "Don't get too used to meals like this. I was feeling inspired and energetic, and City Fish got in a fresh catch of salmon."

"Well, thanks. It was a treat." He cleared the table, did the dishes. Like Andrew, he seemed to equate obedience with good karma. As if behaving well might help her beat the disease.

With a welling of affection and gratitude, she got up and reached to put her arms around him. He turned abruptly, inadvertently transforming the hug into a brief, awkward collision. "Sorry," he said. "I'd better get busy." He indicated his briefcase, which housed his laptop and the tyrant Black-Berry and his relay module, which gave the whole world access to him 24/7. He was able to put through orders with the touch of a button, insuring that his clients' needs were met on the instant. "I need to turn in some orders and get ready for that big regional meeting tomorrow. Um, that is, if you don't need me anymore."

If you don't need me. Miranda couldn't imagine not needing him, but of course, that wasn't what he meant. As far as he was concerned, he'd had dinner and cleaned up afterward, so he'd done his duty.

"It's fine," she said. Not because it was fine, but because she was in the habit of saying so.

He kissed her lightly and stepped back. "Thanks again for dinner, babe. And congrats on finishing. You are the most amazing woman on the planet."

But apparently not amazing enough to divert his attention from e-mailing an upcoming PowerPoint presentation. The thought made her feel small, resenting the job he did in order to take care of her.

She busied herself with mundane chores, delivering a stack of folded laundry to Andrew's room. There, she sat on the bed, looking around. Her son was at a crossroads between a childhood of Tonka trucks and G.I. Joes and a music-filled, phone-dominated adolescence. Apparently, computer games filled the breach.

She straightened some things in his room, and came across a stack of long-overdue library books—*The Encyclopedia of Dogs. Family Dog. How to Raise a Good Dog. The Book of Puppies.* Every single book had to do with dogs. For a boy who swore he'd never get another dog, he sure seemed interested. Then she went into the study, where as usual, he was absorbed in the computer, busily clicking and tapping as the graphics on the monitor changed and option boxes popped up.

"Hey, buddy."

"Hey, Mom."

"How about you put the game on hold for the night."

"It's not that simple. I need to find a stopping point."

"Not that again," she said in a warning voice. She knew she could make it simple by flipping a switch. That seemed petty, though, and didn't really address the issue. Besides, whether she liked it or not, the computer and games had been Andrew's constant companions when she was too sick to do the usual mom things. "Tell you what," she said, pulling a stool over to the desk. "We can find a stopping point together."

He shot her a look of suspicion.

"I mean it," she said. "I'm interested."

It was a virtual-simulation game. Though he did his best to show her the story and how it all worked, Miranda could tell there wasn't a simple explanation. Vaguely she understood there was a storyline about a family in a dangerous jungle, seeking clues to a lost treasure. Both the parents in the game had superhero qualities and each wore a special badge that had been won in some earlier ordeal. The badge, Andrew explained, gave them immortality.

"Hey," Miranda joked, "where do I sign up for a badge like that?"

"She had to kill a monster and steal a treasure from his nest."

She nodded, studying the mother on the screen, who looked like a weird cross between Angelina Jolie and Aunt Bea. The husband was the Terminator, of course, the role model of all cyberdads. The two boys in the family had special powers of their own. There was a dog, a young, eternally healthy dog.

"They should stop in the cave for the night," she said.

"Nope." He clicked the mouse, instructing them to move on. "Rabid bats."

"What about crossing the strait in that boat?"

"Too risky. Every time I get them on a boat or plane, the weather turns bad." He decided to stop the game with the characters taking shelter in a convenient tree house high above the jungle.

"I love that," she said, watching the characters settle comfortably on the branches, where they immediately fell asleep. "I love it when you're on a trek through an uninhabited jungle and you need a place to stay and suddenly there's a perfectly good tree house right overhead."

"Very funny."

She dropped the teasing. The reason behind his obsession with the simulation game was crystal clear to her, and probably to Andrew, too. In his computer world, he was in control. No one but monsters would ever die.

THAT EVENING, MIRANDA spent a little time in the small backyard, inspecting the old flower beds that were normally so brilliant this time of year. Though the days of summer were growing shorter, the sunny day lingered, throwing long shadows across the patchy grass and weedy beds.

She found a pair of pruning shears that had been left out in the rain. They barely worked, but she took a few desultory snips at the leggy rosebushes. Even the hardiest plants would have to struggle to recover from a year's neglect. Some of the more fragile plants were already gone for good, having succumbed early on to the lack of attention. Maybe it was a good thing that summer was over. Before long, the garden would go dormant, and reemerge in a healthier state in the spring. Last year at this time, she had ignored the garden on purpose, terrified that, come spring, she wouldn't be around to see it bloom again. Now she was able to think of the future and actually feel a glimmer of hope.

Despite her conviction that she would get to work on her garden again, she put aside the rusty shears and went back inside. A constant feeling of fatigue hovered around her, something she had grown used to and was looking forward to leaving behind. By nine-thirty, she was practically asleep, never having made it past the world-news pages of the daily paper.

"I'm going upstairs," she told Jacob.

"I'll wait up for Valerie."

She hesitated at the bottom of the stairs. She knew that if she asked Jacob to come upstairs with her, he would oblige. They had something to celebrate, after all. But she just felt tired, and he was absorbed in his work, frowning at the screen of his computer.

Besides, their intimacy had changed. Neither of them had wanted it to, and they'd worked hard to keep their passion alive. She had not been eager to show her recon- structed breast to Jacob, but knew that putting it off would only make a bigger deal of it. When she finally did show him, soon after her surgery, he had gamely checked it out.

Jacob had said all the right things—you're beautiful to me, you're still the sexiest woman I know, I love everything about you, most of all your courage.

She'd loved him for his sincerity, his loyalty. But at the same time, she had found herself wishing she looked the way she had when they'd married, both of them twenty-two and fresh out of college.

Miranda hovered between inviting him upstairs with her or leaving him engrossed in his work.

She decided to compromise. "Wake me up when you come to bed."

Chapter Four

The next day, she had a meeting with her boss at Urban Ice, where she had worked in the office since Andrew started school. In Seattle, providing bulk ice and cold storage for commercial operations was a little-known but essential business. With the local and Alaska fishing industries, the need for ice was never ending.

She knocked on the door of Marty's office and stepped inside. He was meeting with one of her favorite customers, Danny Arviat, a Native American from Sitka, and their running joke was that she sold ice to Eskimos.

"Hey, it's the ice queen," Danny said, standing up and shaking her hand.

"That's me." She smiled, and Marty gave her a hug. "If this isn't a good time…"

"I was just leaving," Danny said. "It's good to see you, Miranda."

"Same here."

Marty gestured to the chair across his desk. "Congratulations on your good news," he said. "We've missed you." Her boss had shown no sign of impatience when she became too sick to work and requested an open-ended sabbatical. From the start of her ordeal, he had never pressured her. One of the very few gifts of getting sick was that it allowed her to discover how much kindness there was in her life. People stepped up to help, to understand or even just to comfort her.

"I've missed you guys, too." Sort of, Miranda thought. She did enjoy her coworkers, and the company had been supportive through her illness. She was better off than many people. At least she had a job.

Still, it wasn't the sort of job she couldn't wait to get to each day. She worked there because it was safe and predictable, not because she loved it.

"You know I've always said it's not the same here without you…" Marty began.

"Uh-oh." She studied his posture, the strained set to his shoulders. "Why does that sound ominous to me?"

He took off his glasses, rubbed his temples. "Miranda, you probably remember that business has been down. Our balance sheets aren't looking too good."

"Are you saying you don't want me back?" Her stomach constricted.

"Of course we do. But…we've budgeted through to the end of the quarter, and…" He shook his head, his kindly face lined with concern. "What I'm saying is, we can't take you back until next quarter. So if something better comes along, I'll understand."

"Oh." She was surprised to feel a small wave of relief rolling through her. "I see."

"Listen, if you need—"

"I'm okay, Marty. I appreciate your honesty."

She left the downtown office feeling supremely…ambivalent. She didn't relish telling Jacob she wasn't going back to work right away. On the other hand, the prospect of extending her sabbatical didn't exactly depress her.

The good news was, she was meeting her two best friends for coffee. Sophie Bellamy, Lucy Rosetta and Miranda had been roommates as undergrads at the University of Washington and they had stayed close ever since. As she walked along First Avenue, Miranda glimpsed herself in the plate-glass windows she passed. Who was that woman? She still didn't know.

They planned to meet at the Café Lucia, an Italian-style espresso bar that belonged to Lucy. The café was tucked in a cobblestone-paved pedestrian alley near the market. On the way, she stopped at the flower stall and picked up a small bouquet to take to Lucy.

The deep aroma of imported Lavazza coffee greeted her, along with the gurgle and hiss of the espresso machine. Two of the café's six tables, with majolica-tiled tops, were occupied. Miranda went to the counter and stood before a display of sfogliatelle and biscotti.

"You look busy," she said.

"Always." Lucy Rosetta beamed as she stepped out from the work area to give Miranda a hug. "I'll fix us a coffee."

Miranda felt better just being in Lucy's presence. Lucy was an expert at priorities. When a friend dropped in, she dropped everything. She brought a tray with two cappuccinos and biscotti and they had a seat together. Lucy had declared this particular table in the café a worry-free zone. In fact, there was a small sign in the middle, next to the flower vase, with WORRY in block letters and a slash through it.

"Sophie just called," Lucy said. "She's running late."

"That's all right. Let me put these flowers in water." Miranda looked around the café. "I'll divvy them up among the tables."

"You don't have to do that," Lucy said.

"It takes thirty seconds," Miranda told her, creating a small arrangement for each table. "Look at the difference it makes."

"You're right, of course," said Lucy. "I wish I had your touch."

Sophie Bellamy joined them, rushing in with her usual burden of briefcase, purse and tote bag. There was a flurry of hugs and greetings, and Sophie requested her usual—a double espresso.

The three of them were an unlikely trio, but their differences made for a lively friendship. Lucy, the creative bohemian, held fast to her dream of running the café. Sophie had the lucrative, high-powered career. Miranda had taken the traditional route to marriage, kids and house with a white picket fence. They used to joke that if they rolled their lives into one, they'd have a woman with a perfect life, living the dream.

They'd stopped joking about that last year. The year Miranda got sick, Sophie's marriage fell apart and Lucy took out a second mortgage to keep her café afloat. Now when you put them together, they were a *Dr. Phil* show.

Miranda got up and hugged her friend. "I'm so glad you're in town."

"Not for long. I'm flying to New York in a couple of hours." Sophie's international-law firm had assigned her to a case that had her commuting to Seattle every other week. "But please," she said. "Tell me something good. I need it."

"I'm done with my treatments," Miranda announced. "The doc gave me my walking papers yesterday. I get to rejoin the human race."

Lucy's face lit up. "That's fantastic—isn't it?"

"Pretty fantastic. For the foreseeable future, I'm a free woman."

Lucy burst into tears. She buried her face in a paper napkin. "Sorry," she said.

"It's all right," Miranda assured her. "I feel too numb to cry. I might later. The crazy thing is," she confessed, "now that I don't have to fight the cancer anymore, I don't know what to do with myself."

"Anything you want," Lucy said with an airy gesture.

"I appreciate the thought, but it's not that simple. My

treatment has been my life for the past year now. Now that it's over, I have no life."

"Oh, honey," said Sophie. "You're just shell-shocked, but this is wonderful. Your treatment is done. You have your life back."

"Yes and no. I can't just roll back the past year and go on as if it never happened. I've changed. My…marriage has changed. Our family has changed." There. She'd said it. She had given voice to a dark fear, which, in its own way, was more menacing than cancer.

"So change it back," Lucy said simply. "Now's your chance."

"It's not like everything was so perfect before," Miranda confided. "Jacob wasn't home enough, the kids had their ups and downs, I had the usual troubles with work."

"So now you have a chance to turn your life into something even better than you had before," Sophie pointed out.

Lucy nodded. "She's right, Miss Miranda the miracle girl. What will you do with the rest of your life?"

"This is what I love about you." Miranda took a sip of her cappuccino. "You keep things simple. You're living your dream, Lucy. When we were in college, you always said you wanted a café like the Gambrinus in Naples, and here you are."

"Bless you for saying that. I've got a ways to go before people start comparing this place to the Gambrinus."

Miranda felt better just being with her friends. She was grateful that they were here to listen and talk, even when Lucy probably had a zillion things to do in the café and

Sophie had a plane to catch. Sophie was perpetually busy, always on the run. After college, she'd gone to law school, moved to the East Coast, married, had two kids, made partner—the perfect life.

Last summer, she had divorced.

As always, Sophie was beautiful and dressed for success, but Miranda knew her friend was dealing with the pain and loneliness and upheaval of splitting up with her husband. "How are you and the kids doing?" Miranda asked. Sophie's children, Daisy and Max, were close in age to Valerie and Andrew.

"All right, I think. Daisy's busy applying to colleges this fall. Max is actually doing much better in reading. They're sad about the divorce. What kid wouldn't be?" She brightened a little. "We've got a four-day weekend together over Columbus Day. I'm taking them to this incredible place in the Catskills that belongs to my former in-laws." She sipped her cappuccino. "Sometimes I miss the Bellamys more than I miss Greg."

Miranda heard the pinch of hurt in Sophie's voice when she spoke of her ex-husband's family. Having almost no family of her own, Sophie used to be close to the Bellamys. "I'm not surprised you miss them, Soph."

"More than I ever imagined I would. And they're still so good to me." She blinked fast, close to tears.

Lucy passed her a plate of biscotti. "Aw, Sophie. There's only one thing that makes you more unhappy than being divorced from Greg, and that's being married to him."

"True," she said, visibly trying to shake off the mood. She swirled the biscotti in her cup.

"You kept your married name—Bellamy," Lucy observed.

"With a maiden name like Wiener, can you blame me? Besides, I built a successful law practice around that name and made partner. It's on the letterhead. And there's not nothing wrong with the name. The problem was with my marriage."

Miranda felt as if a shadow passed over her heart.

"Sweetie, what is it?" Lucy asked.

Miranda stared at her hands in her lap. These women knew her too well. She took a deep breath and told them what had happened—or, more accurately, what hadn't happened—the previous night. "He said I was sleeping so hard, he didn't want to bother me."

Lucy regarded her thoughtfully. "So how do you feel about that?"

Miranda shook her head. "I feel like a traitor, complaining at all. I mean, Jacob's been great through all of this. But I'm ready to start feeling like a couple again, not patient and nurse."

"Although he makes a very cute male nurse," Lucy pointed out.

"You should tell him," Sophie said. "Sit him down and look him in the eye and explain what you want and need. And while you're at it, ask him what he wants and needs. His answers might surprise you."

"I like that," Lucy said. "How'd you get so smart, Sophie?"

She smiled a bit sadly. "If Greg and I had followed that

advice, we might still be married. I think it's easier to be smart about other people's marriages because you don't have to actually do the work." She patted Lucy's hand. "You're the smart one, staying single."

"How come I don't feel smart, then?" Lucy gestured around the café. "I opened this place ten years ago. I know you guys think I'm living the dream, but the truth is, I'm barely staying afloat. Unfortunately, dreams don't tell you how to take care of details like making the books balance."

"Oh, Lucy." Miranda felt frustrated. Here was another thing the illness had taken from her. Forced to focus on her treatment, she'd lacked the time to be a good friend. "Isn't business picking up?"

"I need to make some changes."

"What sort of changes?"

"I'm going to have to share this retail space, lease out half the shop. The rent is killing me, so that's the solution I've come up with."

"Lease it to whom?" asked Sophie.

"Good question. I've thought of a few possibilities—a book and magazine shop would be a good fit. Cards and stationery. Yarn, maybe, or quilting." She glanced at the flowers Miranda had placed on each table. "Hey, maybe a florist."

When Miranda was young, she used to imagine she had a tuning fork inside her, one that would resonate when just the right note struck. She felt that now, a deep vibration of interest at Lucy's words. Out of habit, she dismissed the feeling. "I wish I could help."

"Oh, I'm not asking for help. What I need is a real partnership here. I'm good until the end of the year. Come January, though, something's got to give. I keep hoping the right person will just walk through that door—poof."

Miranda smiled. "So what are you thinking? A café-newsstand?"

"Those are a dime a dozen."

"A café-music store?"

"There's one less than half a block away."

"A café-legal clinic," Sophie said. "That way, I could quit this dumb job and be bohemian with you."

"Except that it's not a dumb job, it's a great one that you love," Miranda pointed out. "Don't you?"

"True," Sophie admitted. "I complain about the travel and so forth, but honestly, sometimes I think it's the one thing that has kept me from going nuts through the separation and divorce."

"My job," Miranda pointed out. "Now, *there's* something. It's the one thing I didn't miss when I was sick."

In college she had studied retail marketing, but had found her passion in a fluffy-sounding elective area—floral design. She used to picture herself amid buckets of cut flowers and greenery, surrounded by beautiful glassware and pottery, creating bouquets to brighten some woman's home, or lift her spirits when she was sad, congratulate her for a job well done, comfort her when she was sick. She would be renowned for her Homecoming corsages.

Unfortunately, self-employment was a dubious prospect,

especially for someone with a mortgage and two kids, so the idea remained only a daydream, and a private one at that.

Which was why she surprised herself by saying, "I'm tempted to lease the space myself and open the flower shop I've been thinking about since college."

Sophie and Lucy looked at each other and then back at her. "It's a crazy, brilliant idea and I think you should do it," Sophie said.

"I've always said we should be partners," Lucy reminded her.

"You two." Miranda grinned, grateful to have such wonderful friends. "I'm not even sure I'll be able to get my grown-up job back." And then, without warning, she burst into tears.

To their credit, her friends sat patiently by and waited. Miranda finally pulled out a wad of Kleenex and dried her face. "God, sorry. I totally didn't see that coming."

"What's going on?" asked Lucy. "Really."

Miranda tried to pull herself together. She hoped the other customers and the girl behind the counter hadn't noticed her outburst. She told them about the meeting with Marty and her feeling that she didn't belong in her cubicle at Urban Ice anymore. "Lucy. Sophie," she asked urgently. "What if there was some cosmic reason I got cancer? That reason being I'm supposed to change my life in some way?"

"See, that's just what I was saying," Lucy said. "It's a chance to make a big change."

"It's not just the job," Miranda said. "I suppose the one thing that's not fixed is what this disease has done to my family. I feel horrible, like an ingrate, because I shouldn't be thinking about what's wrong. But there's...a sense of loss. I knew this whole experience would change me, but I saw the surgery—the loss of my breast and my hair—coming. I never predicted the loss of my family, though. I mean, we still live under the same roof, but last night it all hit home. We feel like strangers to one another. The kids have retreated, and Jacob's buried himself in work."

Sophie took her hand. "Not good," she said.

"I know. It feels like a hole in my heart."

"And I'm here to tell you, don't ignore that feeling. Because one day you might wake up and realize you've forgotten how to love that great guy you married."

Miranda's blood chilled. Though she realized Sophie was talking about her own situation, she understood the warning.

"I'm afraid," she confessed to her friends. "I've been pretending I'm not, but I am. The thing I fear most is not the disease coming back, but that I'll never be able to reclaim my family."

"Take it easy on yourself," Lucy advised her. "You built that marriage and family over sixteen years. You're not about to let it be taken away in just one."

Miranda nodded resolutely. "Easy enough to say, but you know what my family is like. We're all running in different directions. Getting us together is like herding cats. We're all on fast-forward. What I need is a Pause button."

"I think I can help with that," Sophie said. "I have an idea for you, Miranda. How about taking your family away for a little R & R?"

"I'd love to," Miranda said. "I can't remember the last time we went on vacation." She frowned, feeling a new sort of bleakness unrelated to being ill. Their lives simply weren't organized for a family vacation, even when she was well. Weekends were for catching up on the things she'd failed to finish during the week. School vacations were simply occasions when she and Jacob had to make child-care arrangements for the kids until Valerie was deemed old enough to watch her brother.

"Sometimes Jacob and I talk about piling everyone in the car and taking them to the seashore for a weekend," Miranda said. "But frankly, it's going to take a little more than a weekend. And I know what Jacob will say—we simply can't afford some big family vacation."

"I hear that," Lucy said. "I read somewhere that the average family vacation has shrunk to four days a year."

Sophie placed her briefcase on the table. "So here's my idea." She pulled some brochures from her briefcase and placed them on the tiled tabletop. "I learned about this from a client of mine. It's an organization they have in Canada, called Cottage Dreams. It was created so that cancer survivors could spend some time away with their families after treatment. It gives them a chance to recover and look to the future once again. Anyway, I wanted to tell you about it because even though we don't have anything like this in the

States, I had an inspiration. I started thinking what it would be like to be a host family. And I have a proposal to make you."

Miranda glanced at the information on the table. The glossy pictures of lakeside cottages looked impossibly romantic and remote.

"Remember I mentioned that Greg's family has a summer camp in the Catskills," Sophie continued. "Camp Kioga, on Willow Lake. It's been in the Bellamy family for years, and they renovated it last summer. There's a perfect, perfect cottage that's completely empty this time of year and I've asked the Bellamys if your family could use it for a week. They didn't hesitate for an instant. They would love it if you'd come."

"Oh, good Lord, yes," Lucy added. "It's brilliant."

Sophie was never one to beat around the bush. "I think you and your family should do it as soon as possible. Greg's family was wonderful when I asked them, and they really want you to use the cottage."

"It's a great idea," Lucy said. "Miranda, you finally got off the roller coaster. Just a week at this cottage could change your whole perspective."

Miranda felt a tug of yearning, as though something inside her signaled *yes*. There were a dozen things she could say— probably should say. "It sounds like heaven," was what came out.

Sophie and Lucy beamed at each other. Miranda knew then that this was a planned ambush. Her friends had intended all along to present this idea to her. She didn't mind, though. The idea of a hideaway with her family seemed magical to her. But also…impossible.

"…to JFK, and then you rent a car from there. It's about a three-hour drive through some of the prettiest countryside you've ever seen," Sophie was saying, and Miranda realized she had drifted off to the realm of fantasy. The mention of travel arrangements brought her crashing back to the real world.

"Unfortunately that's probably going to be a deal killer," she confessed. She told herself that these were her two best friends; she could tell them anything. But still it pained her to admit that she and Jacob weren't in such great shape financially. "Airfare for four makes it a bit too rich for my blood," she confessed.

"Hello?" Sophie gave a dry laugh of disbelief. "In case you haven't noticed, I've been commuting between New York and Seattle for months. I've got enough frequent-flier miles to fly a small army there and back."

"I couldn't take —"

"Maybe not," Sophie interrupted. "But I can give."

"I don't get it. Why would you do this?"

"Because you're my friend and I love you, and I know you'd do the same for me."

"But the Bellamys—they don't even know me."

"That doesn't matter," Sophie said, her expression softening. "It's…um…I suppose they realize that it's a fragile time for a family. Ours as well as yours."

Miranda nodded. What an enchanting, impossible idea. There was no way Jacob would ever go for it.

CHAPTER FIVE

A week away in the wilderness seemed like the most remote of possibilities for Miranda and her family. Yet the more she thought about her conversation with Sophie, the more she was convinced that this was what her family needed. Healing time away.

It was so very simple, yet so vital. Miranda was already aware that recovering from this devastating illness was much more than just a physical process. There were emotional and spiritual components that were just as important. She also knew that being in a natural environment, far from everyday distractions, played a crucial role in healing, too.

When she got home, she changed into dungarees and gum boots, and headed out into the garden. There was something that happened to her out here, digging in the dirt, working with her plants. She gained a sense of her own worth, felt a connection to the earth and to nature. Just being outside, breathing the air and contemplating the gardening chores ahead felt right.

She didn't make much headway before fatigue set in, but she refused to get discouraged. She had cleaned up a patch of earth, planted some cosmos seeds that would bloom in the spring, thrown a barrowful of clippings into the compost bin. It was enough. She felt satisfied. But…lonely.

She welcomed the shush of the school-bus brakes at the corner bus stop. Valerie would be home in a few minutes. Miranda shook out her gloves and removed her boots, then went inside to fix their favorite snack—chips and salsa, and limeade to drink.

"Hey, thanks," Valerie said, putting down her backpack. "I'm starved."

They sat together at the counter, nibbling the chips. Miranda told Valerie about Sophie's offer. "So what do you think?" she asked. "Can you see our family doing something like this?"

Valerie laughed without humor. "Come on, Mom. You think the whole world is going to stop for a week while we go commune with nature?"

"Maybe we're the ones who need to stop, not the world."

"Dad'll never go for it."

"I'm asking *you*. Would you go for it?"

Valerie shrugged, putting on her I-don't-care attitude, the one she'd worn for the past year. Then, keeping the blasé mask in place, she said, "Pete asked me to Homecoming."

A year ago, those exact words had elicited delight from

both mother and daughter, because a year ago, cancer was a remote concept, not a real threat. Then came Miranda's diagnosis, a bomb dropped on the unsuspecting family. Being sick had brought all Miranda's deepest, fiercest mothering instincts to the surface. She'd wanted to protect her children at all costs. She'd even tried to reschedule her surgery so it wouldn't coincide with her daughter's first formal dance. The two surgical teams wouldn't hear of it, though, and cancer had scored its first victory against her.

Over the past year, everything they did and said to one another took on a special significance. Faced with the possibility of not seeing her children into adulthood, Miranda worked hard—too hard—to impart lessons or extract meaning from every possible situation. She caught herself working so hard at mothering that she forgot to enjoy her children.

So now, when Valerie made her casual announcement, Miranda had to tamp down the urge to jump on the opportunity, insist that her daughter go this year. She restrained herself from marching Valerie to Pete's house to accept the invitation.

One of the things she had to avoid with her kids during the year of her illness was doing all the emotional work for them. Part of growing up was figuring out how to navigate their way through life on their own. And there, beneath the surface of that excellent parenting advice, was the unspoken terror: She had better teach them independence from her now, because she could be gone this time next year.

With great care, she took a drink of her limeade and set down the glass. "Oh?" she asked. Just that. Nothing more.

"I'm going to tell him no," Valerie said.

"So you haven't given him an answer yet."

"I was just so…so shocked when he asked that I blurted out that I'd let him know. God. I should have told him no right then and there."

"But you didn't."

"I will," Valerie said softly. "I wanted to…think about it a little bit." The expression on her daughter's face said it all. She wanted to go to Homecoming, just like any girl her age.

BEFORE BED THAT NIGHT, Miranda felt inexplicably nervous with Jacob. Only tonight, it wasn't about making love. It was a terrible feeling in her stomach—the sense that she had drifted so far from him that he was now a stranger. He lay in bed, the pillows propped behind him as he tallied the last of the day's sales.

"Always working," she said, leaning down to place a kiss on his head.

He offered a distracted smile. "I don't mind. You know that. How did your meeting with Marty go today?"

She took a deep breath. "He was really nice, as always. Really understanding."

"So, did the two of you…" Jacob hesitated. It broke her heart, the way he resisted pressuring her.

"Marty would be just as glad if I waited until next quarter. For budget reasons, he says." She watched his face. Impulsively, she reached out, grazed the back of her hand along his cheek. "If you think that's okay."

"Sure, honey." There was not a single beat of hesitation in his reply, and she loved him for that. Then the worry moved in like clouds across the sun. "Are you all right?"

She smiled. In the past year, she had learned that "all right" was a relative phrase. Sometimes "all right" meant her postsurgery drainage tubes were working properly. Other times it meant she had lost the last of her hair, or that the gel for her radiation burns was having a soothing effect.

Taking a deep breath, she said, "Better than all right after yesterday's visit with Dr. Turabian."

He waited. "Yes?" he prompted, somehow knowing there was more.

She got it out, all in a rush. "I want us to go away together, the four of us."

The worry darkened his face even more, but he quickly shook it off. "I guess we could drive down to the shore for a weekend—"

"That's not what I'm talking about." She told him about Sophie's idea. "The Bellamy family has made an incredibly generous offer. They've got a cabin at a place called Willow Lake—"

"Offer? God, Miranda. What are we, a charity case now?"

She ached for him. Her proud husband. Sometimes, though, his pride blinded him to the bigger picture. "That's not what this is about," she said. "It's not a handout."

"We don't even know these people—"

"We know Sophie. Jacob, there's still so much we need to do. This past year has fractured our family. It's devastated our finances and wrung out our emotions. All the pain of the surgery and treatment was nothing. I could deal with it. But I can't deal with losing my family. Sometimes I think if I hurt any more, I'll break into pieces."

He set aside his paperwork. "Honey, you're not losing us."

"But everything's changed. The kids, you and me, *us*. We need to do this," she insisted. "It hit home yesterday, when I got back from my appointment. Just because I've finished treatment doesn't mean all is well. This family's been damaged, Jacob. It's had its heart ripped out, and all four of us are suffering. We're in a post-traumatic state."

"You just finished," he pointed out. "We'll adjust, but we need time. I feel better already, knowing the worst is behind us."

"We need more than time. We're strangers, Jacob. Andrew spends all his time creating a virtual family with some computer game. Valerie is never home, and she's completely changed the kids she hangs out with. You're always working. And we—" She didn't want to go there, not right away. "I miss you, Jacob. I miss us, together. I miss the way we used to be."

"A week in somebody's lakeside cottage is not going to be a cure-all," he said.

"It's not," she agreed. "And it isn't supposed to be. What it could be, I think, is a start to the healing this whole family needs. We can't go on the way we have been. We're strangers under the same roof that used to house a happy family. We need this time away—from work and school and stress. I know it's only temporary, but we'll have a chance to focus on each other, with no distractions or interruptions."

"Honey, I do see your point," he said, "but unfortunately, we can't swing it right now. The kids have school, and I've got some major surveys coming up at work—"

"Jacob, we're always going to be busy. It's the nature of our family. I accept that. What I hope you'll accept is making time for what's important to you, even if it doesn't seem like the most responsible course of action. I already talked to Andrew's teacher and Valerie's adviser. They both agreed to put the kids on independent study for the days we're away."

"When I'm not working, I'm not earning anything," he reminded her, as if she could ever forget. She could tell he was struggling to be patient.

"I'm aware of that. We'll just have to deal with it."

"Miranda, sweetheart, maybe we can plan something for the holidays or next summer." He took her by the shoulders and kissed her forehead. "Right now, we can't afford to go."

She blinked back tears. "We can't afford not to."

CHAPTER SIX

"Okay, this is not what I generally think of when someone says New York." Miranda gazed in wonder out the window of the rental car. For miles around, she could see nothing but rolling hills draped in a patchwork of glorious fall color, each gentle rise cleft by a narrow country road or rocky stream. Occasionally they passed through quaint towns with white-painted houses and picket fences, funky resale and outdoor shops, colonial-style village greens and church spires.

"Me neither," said Jacob, behind the wheel of the rented Ford Escape. "Pretty up here."

The kids were asleep in the backseat. The red-eye flight from Seattle to JFK had made for a very short night, and the drive up into the Catskills had taken its toll on Andrew and Valerie.

Miranda reached over and patted Jacob's leg. Given his worries about their financial situation, his agreeing to take time out from work was a big step for him. He had been good-natured and positive throughout the whirlwind preparations that kicked in once they decided to go for it. Miranda knew him well, though. She knew he lay awake at night, worrying and crunching numbers in his head.

A familiar twinge of anger pinched her heart. Not at him. In the very worst moments of her illness, she certainly had been angry at Jacob. Ridiculously, insanely furious at him. How could he stand by her bed looking so young and healthy and handsome while she lay on rubber sheets, bald and gray-faced, her body misshapen by surgery and swelling, and dripping drains sprouting from her body? It wasn't fair.

Yet her anger at Jacob was always fleeting, an irrational flash of emotion. This man was the love of her life. More than once, he had broken down and vowed that he would willingly trade places with her, take her pain away if he could. And he meant it. She knew that. He made her ashamed that she got angry at him.

They drove through Kingston, designated by an historic marker as the first capital of the state of New York. They stopped to fill up the gas tank and drive past the regional hospital. Miranda had spoken at length with her doctor, and she didn't anticipate any problems, but he advised her to make sure there was a hospital nearby.

Just in case.

In contrast to the charm of the river-fed hills that surrounded the region, the hospital was sleek and modern, its glass-and-brick edifice sharp against the blue autumn sky.

"Want to stop in?" Jacob suggested. "Familiarize yourself with the place?"

"No, thanks. I've seen enough of the inside of hospitals to last a lifetime." She had a love-hate relationship with them. On the one hand, the hospital was the place that had saved her life; it was filled with caring, dedicated people. On the other, it was a repository of sickness and grief, and represented the terrible threat and stark consequences of her disease.

Valerie woke up as they drove westward along a scenic state road. She blinked at the dazzling golden autumn light. "Are we there yet?"

Miranda twisted around on the seat to look back at her. "Just about. Take a look outside. The scenery is absolutely beautiful here."

"I'm not into scenery."

Miranda ignored her daughter's sour attitude. "Check this out—a covered bridge."

"Cute."

"Wake up your brother and tell him to look at the bridge."

Valerie nudged Andrew with her foot. "Hey, geek-boy. Mom says wake up and check out the bridge."

"Back off," he groaned, wiping his face with his sleeve. Then he looked outside gamely enough. "Cool."

Jacob slowed down as they crossed the bridge. Briefly, they plunged into shadow, and the wooden bridge deck creaked beneath the tires of the car. When they emerged on the other side, they were greeted by a painted sign that said, Welcome to Avalon. Population 1347.

"Looks like a happening place," Valerie said.

"Come on, now," Jacob cajoled her. "At least try to act as if you're enjoying this."

"Oh. Okay. It's charming, like something out of a Washington Irving story. And the turning leaves are beautiful. And, gee, did you know that according to legend, Avalon is the name of the place King Arthur went to die? There. Is that cheerful enough for you?"

"Nice," Jacob murmured, gritting his teeth.

"At least we got you out of a week of school," Miranda pointed out.

"I didn't ask to get out of school," Valerie said. "And I've got that big honkin' assignment due when I get back, so it's not like I'm actually getting a break."

Valerie's teachers and adviser had been very supportive all through Miranda's illness, and this week was no exception. "You'll be back just in time for Homecoming," Mrs. Pratt had pointed out, handing Miranda the paperwork for independent study.

Valerie hadn't met her adviser's eyes. She'd simply mumbled her thanks and ducked out of the school office. This week she had just four things to do. She had to read "The Specter Bridegroom" by Washington Irving. She had to write an essay, do a math assignment and a biology project on the structure of mosses and lichens.

They made a stop at a grocery store, where they bought

a week's worth of provisions, including things for the barbecue and for s'mores, since they were planning to build a campfire by the lake. Driving through the beautiful small town, they made one final stop at a family-owned place called the Sky River Bakery, where they treated themselves to jam kolaches, homemade bread and freshly squeezed cider from a local farm. With Miranda reading from the printed directions they'd been sent, they drove along the river road, resplendent now with fall color. A few miles outside town, they were plunged into wilderness along a narrow road that followed the curve of the Schuyler River.

The colors of the turning leaves ranged from pale buttery yellow to deep fiery pink, so vivid that, coupled with the blue of the sky, they hurt the eyes. Miranda found herself blinking back tears. I'm so glad I'm getting to see this, she thought.

She reached over and switched on the radio. The tail end of "I'm Gonna Be (500 Miles)" by the Proclaimers was playing and she glanced across at Jacob. She could tell by the funny little smile on his face that he remembered the song the way she did. He used to belt it out to her, complete with phony Scottish accent, in the mornings when they were younger. Much, much younger. Young enough to risk being late for work because they needed to stay in bed just a little longer.

She hadn't thought about those days in quite a while. She hadn't thought about much of anything in quite a while. She'd been too consumed by her illness—first, learning all she could about it, then choosing a course of treatment, then following that course even if it killed her.

That was chemo, she recalled. It was designed to kill things off. In destroying the cancer cells, it tended to take other things with it—hair, eyelashes, energy, appetite. Dignity. You couldn't very well hold on to your dignity when you had nine different doctors feeling you up.

"We're supposed to be watching for a wooden sign on a tree," she said. "That's where we turn."

"Spotted it," Andrew said. Wonder of wonders, he even sounded slightly excited. "There, on the left."

The rustic sign pointed out an even narrower gravel road that led them uphill. They passed a No Trespassing—Private Property sign, and the last of civilization fell away. Here, it was hard to believe they were not all that far from town. It felt as if they were the first pioneers, blazing a trail into unknown territory.

"Looks like we've found it," Jacob announced.

Miranda sat forward, peering out the window at the rustic timber archway with Camp Kioga Established 1932 spelled out in wrought-iron twigs. Past the gateway, the camp opened up before them, a breathtaking compound with rustic buildings, broad meadows and sports courts. Cabins and bungalows bordered a placid, pristine lake—Willow Lake, glittering like a sapphire and crowned by a tiny island with a gazebo.

Jacob parked in front of the main pavilion, a huge timber structure marked by flags flying from three poles in front.

There was a railed deck projecting out over Willow Lake. According to Sophie, the pavilion, with its huge dining hall, used to be the main social center back when the camp was in operation.

They got out of the car, and everyone was quiet for a few minutes, trying to take it all in. Miranda pictured the camp in its heyday, when families from the city flocked to the mountains. The air smelled impossibly sweet, of fresh wind and water and the dry, crisp aroma of turning leaves. The reflection of the colorful trees in the water gleamed. Miranda nearly flinched at all the beauty.

All but one of the buildings had been closed and shuttered for the season. Jacob pointed out a large, well-kept cottage set off by itself at the edge of the lake. There were fresh flowers on the front porch and a Welcome banner hanging under the eaves. "I guess that's where we're staying," Jacob said.

The digital photos Sophie had sent them didn't do the place justice. It was a beautiful timbered lodge, solid with the passage of years. The porch had a swing, two rocking chairs and a hanging bed suspended from chains. A pier jutted out over the lake; tied to it were a kayak and a catboat with its colorful sail furled like a barber's pole.

Inside, the cottage was intimate, with cozy reading nooks, an upstairs loft under slanting ceilings and dormer windows, a river-stone fireplace. The main bedroom featured a bed with a birch-twig headboard and a bathroom with a deep, claw-foot tub. Everywhere, Miranda found small touches that helped her understand why it was so hard for Sophie to say goodbye to the Bellamy family—a collection of postcards dating back fifty years and more, framed photos from the era when Camp Kioga was a bungalow colony, pictures in hand-crafted frames, vintage posters of the Adirondack Great Camps. Each bed was covered in a handmade quilt, and there was a cedar chest filled with colorful striped Hudson's Bay blankets.

The cottage had been readied for them with thoughtful care. Kindling and firewood were stacked by the fireplace and woodstove. There was a crockery vase of dried flowers on the table and jars of colored leaves on the windowsills. They found a collection of art supplies and a guest book on the coffee table, opened to a blank page. On the scrubbed pine dining table, they found a handwritten note of welcome, signed by Jane and Charles Bellamy. There was also a collection of literature about the camp, an area nature guide and trail map.

"Wow," said Miranda, taking it all in. "This is paradise."

"Can I go look around outside?" Andrew asked.

"Sure. Don't get lost in the woods."

"Mo-om." Andrew ran out of the house and pounded up and down the dock, then raced into the woods behind the lodge. His small, compact body expressed exuberance with every move he made and it was a joy watching him. For the first time since this ordeal had started, Miranda looked at her son and had the sense that everything was going to be all right.

She felt both gratitude and nervousness as they brought in their things. She was grateful for the opportunity they had been given but suddenly and unexpectedly anxious about the unbroken string of days stretching out before them.

"Well?" asked Jacob. "Is this what you had in mind?"

She smiled at him, still nervous, then looked at Valerie. "Even nicer. And you know what's crazy?"

Valerie nodded. "No TV. No phone. No computer. That's crazy."

Miranda tried to shrug off her daughter's glum sentiment. "To me, what's crazy is that I'm having trouble remembering who I used to be...what I used to be like before I got sick. I got so used to running from one appointment to the next, and waiting around for tests and monitoring myself that I lost myself. I lost who I really am. So this week, my job is to find that person again."

Valerie raised her eyebrows. "Are you sure you quit the anxiety medication, Mom?"

"Very funny." Miranda had stopped taking it, and a part of her missed the way the prescription pill softened the harsh edges of her worry. Another part of her felt triumphant. That bit by bit she was reclaiming control of her life. Relearning how to manage her emotions on her own was a huge part of that.

They spent the day settling in and exploring the camp. Miranda took pictures of everything, capturing a loon in flight, the sun filtering through the forest, her children's faces, her husband turning to grin at her while leaves fell all around him. Dinner that night was a simple affair—spaghetti, salad and bread, ice cream for dessert. Afterward, she and Jacob took their glasses of wine outside to sit on the porch and watch the sun go down across the lake. In the yard in front of the cottage, the kids played badminton, their voices echoing brightly off the water. They played until it was too dark to see the birdie and the first stars of twilight appeared. A chorus of peepers rose from the reeds down by the lakeshore.

Swaying slightly on the porch swing, Miranda felt a rare sense of contentment as she looked around at each of their faces. "Just let me savor this for a minute. I have all my favorites right here with me, right in this moment."

"Not Gretel." Andrew swatted the ground with his badminton racket.

"Nice," Valerie muttered. "Way to go, moron."

"Well, it's true," he grumbled.

"I miss Gretel, too," Miranda said, wishing the mood could have lasted a few more minutes. "Come on. We'd better go inside before the mosquitoes find us."

Jacob did a surprisingly good job making a fire in the wood-burning stove. Once that chore was over, though, everyone seemed to be at a loss.

"So what, exactly, are we supposed to do?" Valerie asked.

Andrew rummaged through his backpack. "Good question," he said.

"We sit around and talk, or draw and paint, play cards and board games, or read, or…just be together as a family," Miranda said. "Listen, this is not going to work at all if we don't make it work." She looked at Jacob for support, but he didn't seem to be listening. He was standing at the big picture window, staring out at the darkening lake. Tension seemed to hover around him.

The kids decided on their own to get going on the assignments they'd brought from home. It was amazing, Miranda thought, how interesting they found schoolwork now that they didn't have a TV or computer.

Jacob found a flashlight by the front door. "I think I'll hike over to the main lodge and check messages," he said, heading outside again. Camp Kioga had one phone, they'd been told, and there wasn't a cell-phone signal in a five-mile radius.

"Jacob," said Miranda, following him out. She bit her tongue to keep from saying more.

He clearly knew what she was thinking. "It's our livelihood, Miranda. It would be irresponsible of me to lose an account because I was playing *Last of the Mohicans.*"

"Is that what you think this is?" she asked. "Some drama we're playing? God, Jacob. We haven't done anything as a family in over a year. This has nothing to do with drama or role-playing or fulfilling some kind of fantasy."

He held up both hands, palms out, in a gesture of surrender.

"Okay, sorry. You're right. We need to be here, and from here on out, I'll try to park my worries at the door."

She knew he was sincere as he spoke the words, but she also knew he'd continue to worry about work. He would just do so quietly, not sharing his concerns with her. She sighed. "Is this what the whole week is going to be like?" She picked up an embroidered pillow and tossed it at him. "I miss the way we used to fight."

"Come again?"

"You heard me. Before I got sick, we'd fight like equals instead of you backing down as soon as you see me getting upset."

"I don't—"

"And then we'd get furious with each other, and then the fight would end and we would forgive each other and then we would make love and—"

"Could we maybe just skip the fighting part?" He slipped his arms around her from behind. "Maybe just cut to the chase?"

She laughed and turned to face him. "You can chase me anytime."

He switched off the flashlight and kissed her, and finally, she had the sense that they were making progress.

CHAPTER SEVEN

"I'm bored," said Andrew the next day, coming down from the sleeping loft.

Miranda was sitting in a window seat, idly drawing in a sketchbook. She looked over at her son and smiled. "Good morning to you, too. Is your sister still sleeping?"

"Of course. She'll probably sleep the whole time we're here."

"You and I are the early birds of the family," Miranda said. "We always have been." To her surprise, Jacob, too, was still sound asleep. Back home, he was up before the sun every day. In fact, when she'd awakened this morning and seen him lying next to her, she'd been startled. She couldn't remember the last time she'd awakened to a warm, sleeping husband.

"So we've got art supplies, blank journals, board games, decks of cards, sports equipment," she pointed out. "Not to mention that." Her gesture indicated Willow Lake, which looked mystical and gorgeous, with a light mist swirling across the surface and the sun breaking through the trees. "I don't think being bored is an option."

"I can't help it," he said. "I don't feel like doing anything."

"Draw something," she suggested. She turned the sketchbook so he could see. Using colored pencils, she had done a passable sketch of the view from the window. It was no work of art, but when she'd looked out the window at the misty lake and the fall color, she'd been possessed by a desire to draw it.

"That's really good," Andrew said.

"It's really not, but you're nice to say so. I took a lot of art classes when I was in college."

"Why?"

"Because I loved it." The words were out before Miranda had a chance to think about what she was saying. Her degree was in marketing, which she didn't love. She'd chosen that because it was practical. Something that would help her get a job after college. All her adult life, she had made choices based on expedience rather than passion.

She tore the drawing out of the sketchbook and wrote her name with a flourish in the bottom right-hand corner of the page. "I'm going to take this home. It'll remind me of this trip every time I look at it. Here, your turn."

Andrew looked dubious as he took the sketchbook from her. "I don't know what to draw."

"Draw something from your imagination."

"Like what?"

Her son, she reminded herself, was the most concrete thinker she knew. "Draw the first thing you thought of when you woke up this morning."

"Taking a leak?"

"Okay, the second thing."

He looked out the window, his face solemn. "That would be the same thing I think of every time I wake up."

"What's that?"

"Gretel."

Her heart lurched. "Maybe you should draw her, then."

He picked out a brown pencil and stared at the blank page. "That'll just make me sad."

"You look kind of sad now," Miranda pointed out. "Do you think it'll make you sadder?"

He thought about that for a moment. "I don't think I could get any sadder than I already am."

Miranda nodded. "I'm sad about Gretel, too. I miss her so much."

"You do?"

"Of course I do. I adored Gretel. It was sad to see her get old and sick, but when I think about her, I think about what a happy dog she was, and how happy she made us while she was here, and all the happy memories I have of her time with us. Tell you what. You sit here and draw a picture of anything you want, and I'll fix breakfast for us. Sound good?"

He nodded, and she moved to the kitchen to fix his favorite—cornflakes with a banana, and honey drizzled on top. She glanced at Andrew, who had quickly become absorbed in his drawing. Good, she thought. Creative expression was beneficial in ways that couldn't be measured. She just knew it was true. When she drew or arranged flowers or even hummed a song out of tune, just the act of doing it was soothing.

She took her time making breakfast, wanting to give him plenty of space for drawing. After a while, she brought two bowls of cereal to the table with a bottle of milk.

"Hungry now?" she asked.

"Starving," he said without looking up. He added a few more flourishes to his drawing, then angled the sketchbook to show her. "This," he said with a chuckle, "was kind of fun to draw, but it's really bad."

"How can it be bad if you had fun drawing it?" Miranda looked at the picture. "And how can it be bad if it's Gretel?"

"It doesn't even look like her," he complained.

"Sure it does. It looks like a smiling, cartoon Gretel. Now, come and get your breakfast."

He wrote his name in the bottom right-hand corner of the picture, just as Miranda had. Then he came to the table. "You're having the same thing I am."

"Yep."

"I didn't know you liked cornflakes with banana and honey."

"I didn't used to. I've decided I need to try something new every day, even if it's just something minor, like cereal."

"Why?"

She took a bite of cereal and chewed it thoughtfully

before answering. "Trying new things is good. It means you're moving forward."

He shrugged. "I guess."

They finished their cereal and put the dishes in the sink. Glancing at Andrew, she could see the "I'm bored" cloud creeping across his face. "Tell you what," she suggested. "How about we go for a hike?"

"A hike to where?"

Miranda paused. Not too long ago, she got tired just going up the Harbor Steps in Seattle. How would she manage this?

Steeling her will, she indicated the array of trail maps the Bellamys had left for them. "We can just pick something. There's a mountain we could climb—Saddle Mountain. On the way down, we'll pass a waterfall called Meerskill Falls. Sound okay?"

Another shrug. "I guess."

"Don't wet yourself with enthusiasm, kiddo."

THEY LEFT A NOTE—illustrated with Andrew's silly drawings—and put some bottles of water and PowerBars into a day pack. The trail up Saddle Mountain was well marked, winding through the breathtakingly beautiful forest. Miranda took it all in, the crisp scent of the air, the rustle of fallen leaves on the forest floor, the fecund aroma of plant life. It didn't take long to climb the mountain. The Catskills were old, gentle rises in the earth, and the trail curving up its side an easy walk. Even so, she had to stop and catch her breath; Andrew was heartbreakingly patient.

"I love this," she said as they reached the summit and headed down the other side. "I love being out in the woods. I love it even more because you're with me."

"Uh-huh." Andrew looked pleased. "I guess it's okay."

"Okay." She imitated his tone. "Here you are, playing hooky from school for a week to come to this incredible place, and it's just okay?"

He didn't seem to be listening. He was looking past her at something on the trail. "Whoa," he said.

She heard the rush of the falls below and moved ahead, eager to have a look. It was just beautiful, a small pool formed by the waterfall. The rocks had been smoothed by the water constantly pouring down on them. Miranda felt drawn to the place, mesmerized by the beauty. The water was perfectly clear, its motion throwing rainbows against the backdrop of rock. Thick mosses and ferns fringed the edges, lush from the microclimate created by the ever-present falling water. Taking out her camera, she veered off the path to get some pictures. She hoped the rainbows would show up in the pictures.

"Come check this out," she called to Andrew. He probably couldn't hear her, though, over the sound of the water.

She took some pictures and then put the camera in the backpack, because a fine mist sprayed everything in the immediate area. There was something almost magical about standing here, on this rock, with a cloud of mist rising up around her. She felt strong and hopeful, and the fine spray on her face felt impossibly soft and gentle.

I'm so glad to be alive, she thought. So glad to be standing here in this place.

"…are you?" Andrew's voice, all but drowned by the roar of the falls, stirred her from the moment.

"Over here," she called, heading back toward the main path. "I wanted to get some pictures of—Andrew?"

He was standing alone in the middle of the trail, his eyes wide with panic as he looked around, yelling, "Mom! Where are you!"

"Hey!" she called back, hurrying over to him. "Hey, buddy, I'm right here."

"Mom!" And then he was hugging her hard, burying his face against her shoulder. "Mom, where did you go? I couldn't find you."

He was crying. Andrew almost never cried; he'd left that behind like the toys of his childhood, but he was crying now, hard.

"I'm right here," she said, closing her eyes and holding him.

"You just…disappeared. Why didn't you say something?"

"I'm sorry, Andrew. I thought you were right behind me."

"I wasn't. I left the trail to get some pictures, and then I looked up and you were gone. I thought you'd fallen or that you were lost."

"I'm truly sorry," she repeated. "I'll be more careful from now on. I promise."

He seemed a little embarrassed by his outburst as he stepped back and scrubbed at his face with his sleeves. "Yeah, okay," he said.

"Andrew, I know this whole year has been terrible for you—"

"Mom."

"No, listen. I know you hate talking about this, but that's one of the reason's we came here." This was perfect, she realized. Here they were in the middle of nowhere. He couldn't retreat into his computer world. He had to listen.

"I don't see why we have to talk about anything." His chin jutted out, stoic resentment banishing his tears.

"Because we have lots to talk about," she said. "This family has spent a whole year being worried and scared and I don't know about you, but I'm ready to get over it." She knew the real reason he was so upset had nothing to do with hiking in the woods. "Andrew, I made a mistake just now," she said. "I should have made absolutely certain you saw where I went. I'm sorry."

"Oh, boy. Now you sound like Barbara," he said. Barbara Mills was the medical family therapist they'd been seeing.

"I'm trying to sound like your mom, but I'm out of practice. Anyway," she went on, "here's the deal. I used to wish I could be exactly like the mom in your story game. The mom with the perfect health and the strength of Hercules and the superpowers. The mom who will never die. That's who I wanted to be for you."

She smiled, took out the water bottles. "I don't really want that anymore," she continued. "Not at all. I want to be myself, and I am *so* not perfect. But I am what I am—your mom, warts and all."

"You have warts, too?"

Laughing, she ruffled his hair. "It's just an expression. What I mean is, I'll never be that perfect video mom, and that's actually a good thing. Sometimes I think it's the things that aren't perfect that make a person so easy to love."

"So, like, when I bring home a really bad report card, you'll be okay with that?" There was a teasing note in his voice.

"I'll be okay with you no matter what," she clarified. "That's the point I'm trying to make. I really would like to guarantee that you'll never lose me, ever, but that would be wrong of me. What I can guarantee is that I'll always love you, and I'll never be perfect, but I'll never stop trying. How's that?"

He was quiet for a while. He leaned down, picked up one of the rounded white quartz pebbles that lined the gorge. He put the rock in his pocket. "Sounds good to me."

She studied him for a long moment, seeing a boy who was growing up, a boy who still needed his mother. "I love you, you know," she reminded him.

"Yeah," he said, then flashed her a smile. "Me, too."

They started walking slowly down the trail together.

CHAPTER EIGHT

———————————————————

Miranda was on the porch swing, intermittently dozing and reading a book, enjoying the warmth of the Indian summer sun. Jacob had taken Andrew fishing, and though she couldn't see them, she could hear the sounds of their laughter carrying across the water. Down by the dock, Valerie was checking the rigging of the catboat, singing along with the tunes coming from her iPod.

It was a moment of supreme contentment for Miranda, something she'd rarely felt this past year, but a feeling that crept up on her frequently here at Willow Lake. She loved the slow, dreamy rhythm of their days, the delicious simplicity of having nothing to do.

It was their fourth day at Camp Kioga, and things were going better than she'd expected. The shock of being deprived of phone, TV and computers had worn off. In fact, they'd amazed themselves with their own inventiveness.

None of them could deny the charm of sitting around the fire in the evening, playing Parcheesi or Scrabble. Yesterday, Andrew had found a book of ghost stories, and Jacob had treated them to a spooky reading of a tale by Edgar Allan Poe. With each passing hour, it seemed, they were acclimating to the place and to each other. It was a magical time, remarkably undisturbed.

Miranda wasn't idle, though. Whether she carried it out or not, she had made a plan for herself when she got back to Seattle. She wanted to pursue the partnership with Lucy. The prospect of doing something so risky and entrepreneurial was frightening. But after surviving the past year, she was intimately familiar with risk and fright, and nothing could daunt her anymore. Nothing, she thought, except presenting her idea to Jacob.

"Ready," Valerie called out from the dock. "I think I've got all the rigging done."

Miranda set aside her book and headed down to join her daughter. "I have a confession to make," she said as they pushed the catboat away from the dock. The little wooden sailboat thumped against the pilings and listed in the water while Miranda pushed at the tiller.

"What's that?" Valerie asked. She leaned back to study the single gaff-rigged sail. The boat inched forward, the sail hanging slack.

"I have no idea what I'm doing," Miranda said.

Valerie twisted around to look at her, clumsy in the bulky

life jacket. "Now you tell me. You mean you don't know how to sail this thing?"

"In theory, I do. I was on the high-school sailing team, but we used Lasers. This is just a bit different. We'll figure it out, though." Miranda injected a cheerful note into her voice. "There's a nice breeze. It should be enough."

The catboat was beamy, with a shallow draft and centerboard. The wind was adequate for a sail this size. How hard could it be?

"Hey, Mom." Valerie swiveled back around. "It's working."

She was right. The wind took the sail, and Miranda showed her how to control it with the main sheet. "You watch the sail," she said. "Stay as close to the wind as possible."

"Does it matter?"

"It does if we want to get anywhere and back before dark."

They were a good team, considering their lack of experience. They got the little boat up into the wind, and Valerie gave a little shriek of delight as they heeled. "Now what?" she cried. "We're going to go over."

"No, we're not," Miranda assured her. "Just sit up on the side, there, to counterbalance the weight."

"Sit where?" Valerie asked.

"Wherever the boat sails best."

She leaned out over the edge, whooping excitedly as the boat scudded along on a gust. It was thrilling to Miranda to see her daughter so carefree for a change. Caught up in the moment, Valerie dropped her surly persona and yelled with delight. "This is awesome," she said. "I had no idea you knew how to do this."

"I know how to do lots of things," Miranda pointed out. "Are your arms getting tired?"

"Totally. I'm about to lose it."

"Hang on, and we'll jibe."

They executed the maneuver and practiced some others, scudding back and forth on the lake. Miranda loved the feel of the wind ruffling through her short hair, the golden warmth of the sun on her face, the sound of her daughter's laughter on the wind. "This," Miranda declared, "is as close to a perfect afternoon as I've ever had." She grinned at Valerie. "I need more days like this, days when I can forget I was ever sick."

"I'm glad, Mom. Really."

"So how about you? How are you liking our vacation?" Miranda asked. It was a daring move, she knew. She was giving Valerie an opening to list a whole litany of complaints.

"It's all right," Valerie said, surprising her. "I had no idea Dad was so cutthroat at horseshoes."

"Or that Andrew knows words like *shirk* and that you can add an *S* to *naked* and get something totally different," Miranda added, referring to last night's game of Scrabble.

"The important thing is, Dad lost," Valerie reminded her. "That means he has to fix dinner tonight, start to finish."

It wasn't such a hardship. This past year, Jacob had done more than his share of the cooking, and so had the kids. "We should head back," Miranda said. "Give ourselves time to clean up."

It took some maneuvering, but they managed to bring the boat around to the dock. The afternoon had turned hot, a reminder that it was the height of Indian summer. Once they got the boat tied up, Miranda took off her sandals. "You know what I feel like doing?"

"What?"

"Jumping in the water."

"But it's—"

Miranda didn't wait to be talked out of it. She peeled off her life jacket and jumped off the end of the dock into the crystal-clear water. It was so cold, it felt as if her body was going into shock. She bobbed to the surface, her legs working like eggbeaters. Because of the cording in her arm, she couldn't swim, but managed to stay afloat by kicking. "Feels great," she lied.

"You're insane," Valerie said.

"Come on in. You know you want to."

"Insane," Valerie repeated, falling forward into the lake, as if she'd been shot. Seconds later, she came straight up out of the water, her mouth working like a fish's. "Omigod," she gasped. "This is the coldest water I've ever felt."

"Swim around a little," Miranda suggested through chattering teeth. "You'll get used to it."

"Your lips are turning blue," Valerie pointed out after a while.

"Your makeup's all washed off," Miranda said. Without the thick mascara, blood-colored lipstick and gel-spiked hair, Valerie looked like herself again.

They lasted maybe five more minutes, then raced for shore. Gasping and shivering, they lay side by side on the dock and waited for the sun to warm them up. Miranda looked up at the sky, seeing pictures in the clouds. "This is what I call a gift moment," she told Valerie.

"What's that?"

"A really great moment you don't go looking for but it happens anyway. I just like being here with you, feeling the sun on my face."

Valerie was quiet for a minute. Then she said, "I like it too, Mom."

"Andrew and I had a good talk the other day, when we hiked up to Meerskill Falls," Miranda said. "I thought maybe you and I could do the same."

"We talk all the time, Mom."

"I know, but—"

"Look, you got sick and now you're better and I'm good with that, okay? Do we really need to analyze it to death?"

"That's why we came here."

"Great. Go ahead, then. Analyze me."

Miranda hesitated. "You know what? You're right. We can just enjoy being together."

Valerie gave a soft, knowing laugh. "You want to talk about it. You know you do."

Miranda chuckled. "Busted."

Valerie was quiet for several moments. Finally, she started to speak. "Okay. I never told you this before, but you getting cancer—Mom, I'm sorry, but it made me feel like a freak, okay? And breast cancer. The same thing Grandma died of. God, do you know how many 'helpful' people came up to me to say they're sorry for me, they're praying for me, because my risk for getting the same disease is now, like, ten times higher than normal?"

Miranda turned on her side to look at Valerie. "Who said that?"

"People who called themselves my friends. So I figured, who needs friends, anyway?"

Oh, God. Miranda's heart sank as she pictured Valerie suffering at school, turning her back on her friends and hiding her pain. "Baby, I wish you'd told me—"

"I'm sorry, okay?" Valerie's anger bubbled up quickly. She sat upright, drew her knees to her chest and glowered out at the lake. "I'm sorry I'm not the kind of daughter you want."

"You know the only kind of daughter I want is one who's happy being who she is. And I'm sorry, too. I'm sorry that it's true—you are at a higher risk. But that doesn't mean you have to be miserable, worrying about something that is probably never going to happen. All it means is that you and I both need to take extra care of ourselves. Why do you think I started getting mammograms at thirty-five?"

"It's scary, Mom. I can't be brave like you."

Miranda sat up, propped her hands behind her. "Oh, baby. You have been so incredibly brave this whole year. So have Andrew and your dad. I wish you'd think about something, Valerie. This girl, the one you've been for the past year—is this who you really are?"

Valerie pushed a hand through her damp, artificially black hair. "I have no idea. All I know is that, after you got sick, it felt stupid to go to pep rallies and football games."

"But having friends isn't stupid. Your friends are the ones you lean on when the going gets tough. Hey, if it wasn't for my friend Sophie, we never would have had the chance to come here." She paused, studying her daughter's profile, so innocent-looking without the makeup. "Don't you miss them, Val?"

Her daughter nodded slowly. "I was horrible to them. To Megan and Lyssa, and especially to Pete. I just didn't want them around. I hated everyone, hated the world, because they were all normal while my life was falling apart."

Miranda winced. "I blame my cancer for a lot of things, and you're allowed to do that, too. Up to a point. Sweetie, it was your first year of high school. I wanted to be there for you so badly. But this happened, and I wasn't there for you, and we both have to forgive ourselves and each other and move on."

"I have moved on."

Miranda brushed a damp lock of hair off Valerie's forehead. "I think you ran away."

Valerie surprised her by nodding in agreement. "I think you're right."

Miranda chuckled. "All right, now I'm speechless. You're agreeing with me?"

Valerie dropped her head down into her folded arms. "I miss them," she said. "I wish we could go back to being friends. But how do I just start over with them?"

Miranda slid her arms around her daughter. "Ah, honey. You'd be amazed to see how forgiving people can be. That part is easy."

"Sure."

"Have you given Pete an answer about the Homecoming dance yet?"

"I, um, I couldn't really figure out how to tell him no."

"Because you didn't really want to tell him no," Miranda said.

Valerie looked over at her, grinned. "You think you're so smart."

CHAPTER NINE

"I can't believe we have to go home tomorrow," Andrew said, following Jacob out onto the sunny front porch of the cottage. "I bet no one would notice if we stayed an extra week."

Miranda and Valerie were sitting on the porch steps, painting a little scene on an oar to commemorate their stay at Willow Lake. It was a long-standing tradition at Camp Kioga to paint an oar, and there was a display of them in the main lodge, some of them dating back to the 1930s. Miranda and Valerie had created a rustic lake scene, depicting themselves in the catboat. Under it, they made a banner that read Thank You from the Sweeney Family.

Miranda put aside her paintbrush. She sensed that the moment had arrived to tell her family what she'd been thinking about. "All week long," she said, "I've been asking myself who I was before I got cancer. And you know, I was okay, because I have a family I adore. But one thing being that sick taught me was the importance of time. I spent every single weekday at a job I didn't like. And you know, the way you spend your day is the way you spend your life. I don't want to do that anymore. Now I wake up each morning, and I tell myself, 'Don't waste this day.' It's really changed my perspective."

"We thought you liked your job, Mom," Valerie pointed out.

"It wasn't like I was being tortured," Miranda said. "I worked with good people. The job was predictable, secure. Then I got cancer and I figured out that you can surround yourself with all the security in the world, and crazy things still happen to you. Like cancer. When we get home, I want to make a change. Because in all the shuffle and planning, I forgot to do something very crucial. I forgot to follow my dream." She looked at Jacob. "I sometimes wonder if you did that, too."

"Nope," he said immediately. "I never think that."

"Come on, I know you. Your dream was never commissioned sales."

"Maybe so, but you asked about my dream. And that's always been you, Miranda. You and the kids. This family. *Us.* And that's why I'm so happy to have our life on any terms. All the rest—the work, the traffic, the bills—it's nothing but details. That's what being at this cottage has reminded me. I'm going back to the same old thing but I'm different. I'm glad I had a chance to remember the things that are important to me."

By the time he finished speaking, Miranda was staring at him with tears of joy running down her face. "I love you, Jacob. When you talk like that, it reminds me just how much."

"Whoa," said Valerie. "Way to go, Dad." They high-fived each other.

"Now, wait a minute." Miranda dabbed at her cheeks. "I hope this isn't your very charming way of saying I should be thankful for what I have and go back to the same old thing. I meant what I said," she insisted. "I want to make a change."

Jacob regarded her with apprehension. "Can you be more specific?"

"I can be very specific." She felt her heart speed up as she told them about Lucy's café and her idea of joining her friend. It was the kind of excitement she'd felt when she was on the verge of realizing a longed-for goal—going to college, marrying Jacob, having her children. This was something she hadn't felt in a very long time. "I know what I'm asking," she said to Jacob. "I know it might not be the best thing for us right now, financially. But—"

"But nothing," he said. "I can't believe you never told us this before."

"I thought you'd tell me it was a terrible idea, financial suicide."

"Maybe you should check with me before you decide what I think."

LATER ON, JACOB INVITED Miranda to come with him on a sunset paddle on the lake in the two-person kayak. The evening promised to be absolutely beautiful. There were only a few high, torn clouds in the sky, and the lowering sun turned the lake to a vast sheet of gold.

The hush of nature surrounded them—a light breeze in the high branches of the maples and willows, the lonely cry of a loon, the quiet dipping of their paddles into the still water. The lake gave all the colors and sounds a special clarity. Nature had its own special healing power, Miranda reflected. Each day they spent here she felt stronger, closer to her family.

"I'm so glad we made this trip," she said over her shoulder to Jacob.

"So am I. It's been good for all of us. I've finally stopped dreaming work dreams at night."

"I didn't know you had work dreams."

"Nightmares. Workmares, I guess you'd call them. Classic stuff—I'm late for a meeting, or I show up without my pants on, or I get lost."

"You never told me that. We used to tell each other all our dreams, good or bad. When did we stop?"

"When mine got boring because they were all about work," he said.

"Maybe we ought to start telling each other again."

They rowed toward the windward side of a small island in the middle of the lake. According to the hand-drawn map in the cottage, it was called Spruce Island.

"The people who own this camp—the Bellamys—were married on this island more than fifty years ago," Miranda told her husband. "Last summer, they came back to reenact the wedding for their fiftieth anniversary."

"Let's go check it out," he said. They paddled to the shallows and brought the kayak ashore on the sloping beach. Everything on the island was tiny and intriguing, a whole world in miniature. There was a path leading to a garden gazebo, now overgrown with roses and dahlias gone to seed. It was marked with a commemorative plaque that read, Charles Bellamy and Jane Gordon were married here August 26, 1956. Renewed their vows here August 26, 2006.

"They've been married fifty years," Miranda said. "Imagine that." To her surprise, she saw a dark flash of anger in his eyes. "Jacob?"

He made a visible effort to smile. "I just want you to get old, Miranda. That's all I want. I try to be happy for people like the Bellamys, but it's damn hard sometimes."

"I know," she said, slipping her arms around him. "I know."

"I wish I'd been better for you when you were sick," he said, his voice low with emotion.

"Jacob—"

"No, let me finish. I wish we'd spent more days like this. But I was just so scared. The cancer took over our lives, and no matter how hard I tried, I couldn't fight it. So instead, I focused on something simple—my work. I shouldn't have done that. I should have been there for you more, instead of burying myself in work. It's no excuse, but the truth is, I was freaking terrified, Miranda, at the idea of facing life without you, and at how much that would hurt. And so I…I stepped back, bracing for a blow. As if, by pulling away before you were even gone, maybe I wouldn't miss you so much." He shoved a hand through his hair. "I'm a freaking idiot. I should be shot."

Miranda took hold of his hand and brought it to her mouth. "I've got an idea. Let's do this. Instead of worrying about being married for fifty years, let's just work on being married right now."

He held her gently, yet she sensed a desperation in his embrace. "Good plan," he whispered.

They waited for sunset, then paddled back to the dock. Miranda frowned, seeing an unfamiliar car parked in the cottage driveway. "I wasn't expecting anyone," she said to Jacob. "Were you?"

He didn't answer, but his telltale grin gave him away. "Help me tie up the kayak, will you?"

"What's going on?" she asked.

Just then, Sophie and her two kids, Daisy and Max, came out of the cottage. "Surprise," yelled Sophie. "We were just in the neighborhood…"

Miranda laughed with joy and went to give her friend a hug. "It's fantastic here. I can't thank you enough."

"We have a little something planned for your last night at the lake," Sophie said, leading the way into the cottage.

Miranda gasped. The table was set for a candlelit dinner for two, with a linen tablecloth, a bottle of wine and a beautiful meal set out. "I'm taking the kids to the drive-in movie in Coxsackie for the last show of the season. We probably won't be back until late…if that's okay with you."

"We already said it would be okay," Valerie said, coming down from the loft. She looked a lot more like her old self, in cropped jeans and a Camp Kioga sweatshirt.

"Fine by me," Miranda said, feeling a little thrill of anticipation.

They left in a swirl of laughter, and Miranda found herself alone with Jacob. He held out a chair for her. "Dinner is served."

It felt exactly like a date, with a lovely meal, a glass of wine and the knowledge that they would make love afterward. She looked at her husband's face in the glow of the candlelight and felt such an intense wave of love that it brought tears to her eyes.

Though she hadn't said a word, he must have felt something from her. He set down his wineglass, and said, "Let's go to bed."

SHE TOOK HER TIME getting ready, putting on a spritz of perfume the way she'd done when she was younger, and taking out a nightgown she'd bought just for this trip. It was cream-colored and floor length, gathered softly at the waist.

She stepped out into the bedroom. Jacob was standing by the night table in boxers and a T-shirt. He'd turned down the bed and was flipping through some photographs.

When he saw her, his face lit with a smile. "You look good, Miranda."

"I feel good." She crossed the room to him. "What's that?"

"These are the pictures I took of you the night before the surgery," he said.

Miranda felt as though she'd been punched in the stomach. She remembered that night well. She had wanted him to photograph her, naked and whole for the last time. The pictures had a quality of searing intimacy, the camera somehow revealing more than a mirror ever did. She remembered how they had talked that night, and cried together, and made love with a fierce intensity they'd never recaptured.

"I had no idea you carried these around," she said. "My God, Jacob. No wonder you can't get used to me the way I am now."

"Miranda, no." He grabbed her hands. "You don't understand. These are pictures of my wife, my best friend, my college sweetheart, the love of my life. You were getting ready to face unbelievable pain, and you still had the strength to look at me like that. I don't keep these around to remind me of what you used to look like, Miranda. I keep them to remind me of how brave you are."

It struck her then that they hadn't made love in the daylight since before her surgery. And whenever they did make love, Jacob was careful and considerate, straining to hold her gently—too gently. "Then treat me like I'm that woman, Jacob," she said. "That brave woman. Not like someone who'll break. That's what I've missed this past year. You've been too careful with me."

"I don't want to hurt you, Miranda."

"I swear I won't break." She moved forward and kissed him—not a good-night kiss but a frank, sexy, openmouthed, how-about-it kiss.

He pulled back and smiled at her. "You sure?" he whispered.

"Of course. I'm ready to quit acting like a patient, you know?"

"I know."

There was something shining in his face, a love so strong that she felt warm all over, as though she were standing in the light of the sun. And she realized something then, something she'd always known but had managed to forget in all the busy chaos of their lives. Their love was a force so strong that it would never end, no matter what happened to her.

"Oh, Jacob," she whispered. "I feel like I've come back from a long trip. And I've missed you so."

He pressed her down on the bed and unbuttoned her nightgown. "Ah, honey. I've missed you, too."

SUSAN WIGGS

EPILOGUE

"Smile, just one more time." Miranda knew she was probably trying Valerie's patience, but she couldn't help herself. "You look incredible in that dress. How about right here, on the front porch?"

"Okay, Mom." Valerie seemed happy enough to pose but cast a worried look at her date, Pete. In a crisp, rented tux, his hair newly cut and his shoes polished to a sheen, he appeared both nervous and elated. "Just a few more minutes, okay, Pete?"

"I don't mind." He blushed, looking so boy-next-door cute that Miranda herself wanted to hug him.

"I lied," she confessed. "I don't want just one more picture."

"Miranda," Jacob said. "You've probably got enough."

But she didn't, and in the end, she got her way. She took pictures of every possible combination—Valerie with her date, with her dad, with her brother. And then a shot of Valerie and Andrew and the puppy, Kioga. When they returned home from their week at the cottage, they had adopted the pup from a local shelter. At about twelve weeks old, he looked like a shepherd mix, with one ear up and one flopped down, and he had become the center of Andrew's universe. Andrew was raising the dog, training him, and it was hard work. So hard, in fact, that he almost never had time to get on the computer anymore. And he didn't seem to miss it one bit.

"Good night, Mom and Dad," Valerie said. She gave them each a hug before getting into the car with Pete. As she hugged Miranda, she gave her an extra squeeze. "Thanks, Mom," she whispered.

Jacob stood behind Miranda and put his arms around her as they watched the car drive away. The last of the evening sunshine lingered, painting the front garden with a deep sheen of gold. She leaned against Jacob, grateful for his solid presence, grateful for…everything. This past year, she'd learned not to fear death but to accept its presence—a reminder that you can do anything with this day except waste it.

Dear Reader,

Thank you for spending some time with Miranda and her family. I hope you were as moved as I was by the great work done by Cottage Dreams. Marie S., a cancer survivor who corresponded with me about Cottage Dreams, writes, "Even though I feel a part of my spirit was taken from me during my cancer journey, I can't help but look at the importance of people who continue to reach out to others in trying times…"

Now you have an opportunity to reach out. In the fictional story, Sophie took inspiration from Cottage Dreams to offer a haven to a family that desperately needed to heal and reconnect. In reality, this organization is only able to carry on its work through the charitable contributions of caring people. If possible, please open your heart and your purse strings and make a contribution to Cottage Dreams. There is also a need for items to go into "Welcome Baskets" for arriving families. To find out how you can reach out, please visit their Web site at www.cottagedreams.org or send a check to Cottage Dreams, The Heritage Building, 33A Pine Avenue, P.O. Box 1300, Haliburton, ON K0M 1S0.

Thank you for caring,

Susan Wiggs

Rollingbay, WA

Gloria Gilbert Stoga

Puppies Behind Bars

What can be said about Gloria Gilbert Stoga, who routinely sells hardened convicts on raising puppies in their prison cells? Not only that, the tiny hundred-and-ten-pound marathon runner has the inmates rolling on the ground, crowing like a rooster and dancing—all to train the pups.

Gloria is president and founder of Puppies Behind Bars, a nonprofit organization that uses prison inmates to train puppies to become guide dogs for the visually impaired or Explosive Detection Canines for law enforcement. Through her dreams and efforts, Gloria has been able to provide a new "leash" on life for both the inmates participating in the program and the eventual recipients of the working dogs.

For the blind who receive the specially trained dogs, Puppies Behind Bars gives them the confidence and freedom to travel independently with safety and dignity. For the law enforcement officer who receives a trained Explosive Detection Canine, it provides a partner that helps keep society safe. For the inmates who nurture and train these special animals, Gloria's program provides a sense of purpose, accomplishment and responsibility by allowing them to care for a small, dependent—not to mention wriggly—life; prison inmates contribute to society rather than take from it.

"The knowledge that we're doing something to help is a sense of great pride," says Gloria.

The story begins back in 1990 when Gloria and her husband adopted a Labrador retriever from one of North America's most prestigious guide-dog schools, Guiding Eyes for the Blind. Arrow had been on his way to becoming a guide dog, but was released from the program for medical reasons. Gloria started reading about Arrow's training and was amazed to discover how much time, effort, love and money—twenty-five thousand dollars—goes into each guide dog. She also learned there was a shortage of guide dogs in the United States.

Gloria wanted to find some way to help the cause. But how?

An idea turns real

It wasn't until Gloria's sister cut an article out of a magazine telling the story of Dr. Thomas Lane, a vet in Florida who started the first guide-dog prison program, that Gloria found her answer. But starting a similar program in New York, New Jersey and Connecticut meant leaving her job on New York mayor Giuliani's Youth Empowerment Services Commission and heading out into a great unknown. Would anyone give her the dogs to train? Could inmates really be responsible enough to work with these dogs full-time? How would the puppies learn to be guide dogs if they were never exposed to a normal, nonprison environment? Was Gloria crazy to even launch the project?

It was finally Gloria's husband who gave her a not-so-gentle nudge.

"I talked about it for two years, and after two years my husband finally said, 'Gloria, you either have to shut up or do something about it,'" she says with a laugh.

She quit her job and got down to work.

Today sixty-two women and eighty-one men in seven different prisons in three different states are currently raising eighty-five dogs to be either potential guide dogs or Explosive Detection Canines. Close to 85 percent of these pups pass their tests to go on to get further training.

The program works. Puppies Behind Bars now has ninety-six working dogs helping people every day. Fifty-one are guide dogs throughout the United States and forty-five are Explosive Detection Canines in the U.S. and abroad. Seven others function as companion and therapy dogs for blind children. They're a well-traveled bunch. One former prison puppy now works to keep the president of Egypt safe. Another was at Pope John Paul's funeral. Other dogs are used at Kennedy and La Guardia airports. There are also Puppies Behind Bars dogs at the United Nations.

Lucie, one of the first guide dogs to come out of the program, gave a retired registered nurse, who was imprisoned in her home after losing her vision following a stroke, the gift of independence and mobility.

No wonder one of the inmate dog trainers currently in the program calls Gloria "an unsung national treasure, the poet laureate of puppies."

A dog's life

Certainly inmates at the maximum-security prisons who take part in the Puppies Behind Bars programs must be screened carefully. The inmate has to have a clean prison disciplinary record for at least a year, must participate in facility programs and be considered reliable by prison officials. He or she must also have at least two years left to serve before potential parole, since dogs are with the inmates for a year and a half.

Once chosen for the program, puppies live in their cell and the trainers attend weekly puppy classes, and complete homework and exams. The trainers also swap the puppies so the dogs will be accustomed to different people and environments.

But dogs in training need to get out of the prison system, too. A weekend puppy-sitting program means the puppies stay with volunteer host families in the suburbs surrounding the prisons and in New York City at least six times a month. Some of these visits are for several hours, while others are overnight "furloughs."

While the dog's recipients and inmates obviously benefit from the program, inmates' families also gain plenty, says Gloria. After the puppies find their way into their lives, inmates finally have something positive to talk about. They share their puppy's reaction to the first snowfall or how cute they are when they dream. Family and friends see that the person behind bars is giving back to the community.

"It strengthens family bonds, because there is a common positive thing to talk about.

"Families can feel proud of their incarcerated loved ones instead of just feeling embarrassed," she says.

Even dogs that do not make it all the way through the training program after they are released from the inmates' care go on to help people. These dogs are given to families with blind children. One boy, a quadriplegic blind child who received "Jack" as a pet, is now able to move his arms to pet him.

"We do effect change. I don't mean to say that with either arrogance or levity, but we really do affect a lot of people's lives," Gloria says.

For more information visit www.puppiesbehindbars.com or write to Puppies Behind Bars, 10 East 40th Street, 19th Floor, New York, NY 10016.

KAREN HARPER

Find the Way

Karen Harper

New York Times bestselling author Karen Harper has written over thirty novels, which range from historical romances to contemporary suspense to historical mysteries and a historical novel set in Tudor England. Karen, a former high-school and college English teacher, has been nominated for a RITA Award from Romance Writers of America and won the Mary Higgins Clark Award in 2006. Though she is now a full-time writer, Karen still loves to teach by conducting writing workshops and giving talks about how to get published. Karen and her husband divide their time between Columbus, Ohio, and Naples, Florida.

CHAPTER ONE

"You mean you're going to get a Seeing Eye dog?" her mother demanded, her voice rising. "But you don't even like dogs, Alexis. You've always been a cat person!"

"I'm not looking for another pet. It isn't like that at all. And they're called guide dogs, not Seeing Eye dogs."

Alexis heard her mother flop into the beanbag chair. She had been expecting surprise at best, scolding at worst when she'd made her announcement. She knew her mother wasn't going to accept this bolt from the blue so easily. No, that would not be like Jillian Michaels at all, so there was surely more protest coming.

Her mother had been visiting for two days, and it had taken Alexis this long to mention her big decision. Before she was permanently blinded by a head injury when she fell down a flight of stairs while fleeing a stalker, Alexis Anne Michaels had been an independent twenty-six-year-old on her own in the big city of Elizabeth, New Jersey, just a short hop to both Newark and Manhattan. But these last two years, everything had been sadly different.

She fought to keep calm, to explain things well. "Guide dogs are raised and trained to be gentle and would never jump up on anyone or hurt them. It's like a partnership." She stared at the spot where she judged her mother's eyes to be. The memory of that pert, pretty face suddenly illumined the darkness like a TV being turned on.

Before her mother could say more, Alexis plunged on. "These dogs are only part-time pets because they're working dogs when in harness. They're intelligent and well behaved, so much so, I hear, that I can keep Chaucer, too." She bent over to pet the gray-and-white longhair Persian rubbing against her ankles.

It had taken the poor cat only one day to learn she could no longer put herself in her mistress's path without getting kicked or causing a tumble. Only when Alexis was sitting, standing or lying down did Chaucer approach her now.

"I know you haven't liked using your white cane," Jillian said, "but I thought you were considering my suggestion that you move back home with me for good. I can see why you can't cope with a busy, crowded neighborhood in a huge city. You need to be home with me where it's much more quiet—and safe. Since your father's no longer with us, I can devote myself to taking care of you, to getting you here and there, just like old times before you could drive. You know, my old soccer-mom days."

"We have to accept that my blindness means there are no more old times, only new ones," Alexis reminded her mother. "You have your friends at home, your bridge and reading clubs. Now that Daddy's gone, you're still finding your way into a new life, too."

Alexis opened the crystal of her braille watch and felt the hands and numbers. Nearly five o'clock; she wanted to fix soup and a sandwich before her mother set out on her two-hour train ride home. Besides, if Alexis had something to do with her hands, she wouldn't wring them. Her mother didn't want to admit that anything in their lives had changed. Not that her husband had dropped dead from a heart attack two years ago at the age of sixty-two, or that four months later, a sick stalker's obsession had resulted in an accident that had ruined her daughter's sight.

At first, after two tragedies so close together, Alexis had been very willing to let her mother take care of her in her small New Jersey hometown. But she'd felt like a child, and despite fears that her stalker might turn up again, she had returned to E-town, as the locals called it. After all, Blair Ryan, the detective investigating her case, had eventually concluded that "the perp" had fled the area.

Still, Alexis had changed apartments—with the help Detective Ryan and another officer had insisted on giving her. She knew they were still trying to trace Len Dortman, the man who had stalked and assaulted her. Dortman wouldn't find her at the high school where she'd taught either, because she'd had to take a leave of absence, which she was afraid would be permanent unless a guide dog could work miracles.

Previously Alexis had shared a renovated town house with a friend, another high-school teacher, who'd been married last summer. The place was too expensive for Alexis to afford on her own, had a loft, a basement and a curving staircase. Her new apartment was smaller and cheaper and all on one floor, though she'd had to learn its layout since she'd never seen it.

She'd been here over a year now, and the fact that nothing had happened surely meant that Len Dortman had fled with no clue where she was. Otherwise, his disturbing phone calls, the bizarre letters and the all-night vigils he'd made outside her old place would have started up again by now. Alexis had had a lot of time to memorize her new place. She supported herself with disability checks and income from tutoring students in her apartment. Despite her visual impairment, she helped them with reading comprehension and composition skills to prepare for college entrance exams. She also graded essays for two other teachers by having her talking scanner read the works aloud, then she dictated her corrections and suggestions.

During her days of deepest depression, it had boosted her spirits that her former students had taken up a collection and bought her software that read e-mail to her. Alexis was getting more proficient with braille, but only as an aid, so she relied on talking books a lot. For ten weeks, a special bus had picked her up and taken her to a center for courses that taught her to trust her senses of touch, smell and hearing. But, even with all that and her white cane, her sense of independence eluded her. After barely escaping being hit by a truck that cut a corner too close, Alexis feared going out on her own.

"Come on into the kitchen while I fix us a light early supper," she said, gently moving Chaucer aside with one leg.

"Here, let me take care of that," Jillian said, popping up so quickly she created a draft.

"Mother, what have you been buying me all these fancy talking devices for if you don't let me open my own cans?" Alexis felt along the familiar cupboard shelf for the can she wanted. She'd had them placed in a specific order, but her mother must have scrambled them.

"Well, it's one thing to tell a tuna can from a soup can," Jillian said, following Alexis to the door of the narrow galley kitchen. "But those little things I bought online will tell you exactly what kind of soup and play a helpful little message, too. How did you ever do it on your own, or do you just eat potluck?"

"Didn't you see these braille markers I attach to the tops with rubber bands? I can label them that way, just as I do my clothes, to know what's what. I just remember which marking is which," she explained, then realized her mother must have removed her braille markers from the cans and replaced them with these new doodads. Alexis jumped when she touched the tiny button on the magnetic cap and it spoke.

"Hi, darling, your mother here," the recorded message

said. "This is a can of cream of mushroom soup, which goes well with almost any sandwich. You can pick out veggies by touch to make a salad, but be careful cutting things up. You might want to doctor this soup up a bit by add—"

Though Jillian had spoken quickly, the message ended in midword. *You might want to doctor this up*...echoed in Alexis's mind as her mother came over and reached past her to play the messages on the other cans, joking lamely that living at home with a *doggedly* helpful mother would be better than getting a dog. But Alexis was hardly listening.

Doctored up, she thought. The best ophthalmology specialists and surgeons had not been able to doctor her up to restore her sight. Her fall had caused a stroke, which had affected her optic nerve but nothing else.

Her relationship with her stalker had started normally enough. Len Dortman was the assistant custodian at the school where Alexis taught. He hung around a bit too much, always trying to help her, but that was all. At first she'd tried to be nice, then to put him off, then to avoid him. When she'd told him to leave her alone, Dortman had stalked her for weeks, though she hadn't realized it at first. Eventually Alexis had phoned the police; an officer ordered Dortman to completely avoid her. When he didn't, she'd obtained a restraining order. The fallout from that got him fired; evidently he'd tried to assault her as she jogged. She still had memory loss from the day of the attack, but she must have fought him off and run. Either he'd pushed her or she'd fallen down a flight of steps at the old amphitheater in the park. Two teenagers looking for some privacy had found her and called 911. But the police had not located Dortman, who had left his apartment and not returned. Alexis prayed he never would.

Though she dreaded recalling that final confrontation with Dortman, Alexis had tried to get the memory back. Detective Ryan surmised what happened when a witness later came forward to say he'd seen both the victim and her stalker running but thought they were having some sort of race. The last thing Alexis could recall of that dreadful day was opening her mail at home after school and finding the videotape she'd ordered of Kenneth Branagh's *Hamlet* to use in class. Branagh was in a photo on the front, all in black, holding poor Yorick's skull. Two days later, she'd wakened in the hospital to voices and sounds, because her eyes were bandaged. The first voice she'd heard was her mother's, followed by the deep, sure tones of Detective Ryan. Alexis realized her world had gone dark, and ever since, she'd seen only sliding, shifting black-gray shapes.

How she longed to stride outside these narrow walls with confidence. To be her graceful, athletic self again, not to walk fearfully and bump into things and look like a drunk or a klutz. To get back some semblance of her once-independent life, and that included figuring out if the attention Blair Ryan still paid her was professional or personal. The nightmare of the stalker had damaged more than her vision; she had terrible issues with trusting men now.

Yet just thinking about Blair made her stomach cartwheel. Kenneth Branagh and even Sean Connery couldn't compete with Blair's rich, resonant voice. Alexis had never seen his face and had no intention of asking him if she could touch it, so she always pictured him as Kenneth Branagh, all in black. She did know that Blair was about six inches taller than her five foot six, with a compact, strong build. She'd leaned on his arm more than once, and he'd hugged her the day she'd been released from the hospital. Her heart pounding, she'd hugged him in return, but she had to wonder now, why did he keep coming back?

She figured that if it wasn't pity, it must be guilt that he hadn't found Dortman, that the case wasn't closed. And that's why she'd turned down Blair's invitation for dinner and dancing—dancing, no less!

"How much does a guide dog cost anyway?" her mother asked, startling Alexis from her thoughts.

"Twenty-five thousand dollars to raise and train, but," she added hastily when she heard her mother gasp, "absolutely free to those who qualify and need them. I need one, Mother. I really do. And I've agreed to accept one raised in a prison, Eastern Correctional Facility. It's not far from here."

"What? That's a maximum-security prison!" Jillian stepped forward to grasp her by both arms. "You won't know who's handled that dog, or what's happened to it that might make it—well, snap."

"I've been told these dogs are beautifully trained and gentle." With the hand not holding the soup can, Alexis grasped her mother's wrist. She hoped she was looking her straight in the eye. "The dogs are raised under a strictly supervised program called Puppies Behind Bars. The whole thing was the inspiration of a woman who's had great success with it since she founded it in 1997."

"But a murderer could have raised that dog," her mother whispered, as if that very felon might be eavesdropping.

"The program's founder used to think we should just lock inmates up and throw away the key. But she's proved that having them raise these puppies and give them basic obedience training before they go on to guide dog school has helped the inmates too. The program is not only assisting the blind, but showing that inmates are people who can make a contribution and change their ways."

"Alexis Anne Michaels, don't you realize that the person who raised your dog could be just like that horrible man who did *this* to you?"

"This particular prison has only women, and this is not up for a vote. I've applied and had a phone interview already, so that's that. I hope you'll support me in this and—"

Her mother's grip on her upper arms loosened. But to Alexis's relief, she didn't back away or protest further. Instead, Jillian hugged her hard, and Alexis clasped her mother in return. They stood, holding tight, one in relief—the other, probably, with regret. But they both laughed when the talking can of soup Alexis still held was jostled and sang out, *"Hi, darling, your mother here…"*

TINA CLAWSON, inmate #81A1268 at the Eastern Correctional Facility for Women, aged thirty-two, was serving a ten-year sentence for cocaine possession with intent to distribute. She knelt on the hard concrete, cuddled her ten-month-old black Labrador retriever and cooed, "Puppy, puppy, puppy. I love my good girl Corky!"

Tina picked up Corky's sopping-wet duck squeaky toy and heaved it again. The retriever's paws skidded on the concrete before she got enough traction to scamper after it, yipping in delight.

"Get it, Corky!" Tina shouted over the encouraging cries of the other puppy raisers to their dogs. "Get that big bad toy and bring it back to Mama!"

She did think of herself as Corky's mom, and cherished every minute with her just as she had with her first dog, Sterling, a chocolate Labrador retriever. That was the only downer with this Puppies Behind Bars program. After bonding with the puppies, loving and training them for sixteen months, the inmates gave them up so they could attend guide dog school or get training to become Explosive Detection Canines, called EDCs. The few dogs that didn't fit either program became release dogs given to families with kids who were blind.

The first dog Tina had raised went to a person who was blind, but this time the prison had puppies that would become bomb sniffers. After the 9/11 tragedy, a lot more canines were needed for domestic- and even foreign-security assignments.

Five other female inmates exercised their dogs in the puppy rec area they visited three times a day. *Jollying,* the program's founder had called this playtime when she'd gotten Puppies Behind Bars under way here. Now the once-a-week training classes—training for raisers and dogs—was taught by someone else. Still, the founder herself had interviewed the inmates and made certain they understood and accepted their responsibilities before they'd signed a contract with PBB.

Corky scampered back again, proudly dropping her toy at Tina's feet. She looked up for approval, then lowered her head and continued to stare at the stuffed cloth duck as if she had just brought in a real bird for a hunter. That desire to please a handler as well as the search-and-retrieve instincts would help to make Corky a successful EDC.

Overwhelmed with love for the little mite, Tina gently wrestled with the bundle of energy. They even butted heads, Tina's spiky blond hair against Corky's silky, ebony coat.

"Corky, sit," Tina said.

The dog obeyed. Corky understood all the basic commands like *sit, stay* and *heel,* Tina thought proudly. Tina had felt like a failure herself, but through her puppies, she was gaining confidence that at last she was doing something right.

"Only ten more minutes, ladies and canine companions," Ellen, the officer with them, announced with a grin. Ellen liked watching the cavorting puppies as much as anyone else, but puppy rec was the only time Tina had ever seen her laugh.

How Tina wished her two kids could have a puppy, but her widowed mama was barely making ends meet keeping them in food and clothes. Tina's husband had died when he'd

OD'd on crack, so when Tina got sent here, their grandma was the only person that little Larry, age eight, and Sandy, seven, had in this world. Tina had a sister, Vanessa, who could have taken the kids, but she'd argued with their mama years ago and moved who knew where.

And though Tina was totally off drugs and would never use again, it would be nearly four more years till she got out of here. *Four more years...four more years,* a chanting voice repeated in her head. She was so scared something would happen to her kids while she was stuck in here.

The puppy raisers had been told that very first day, "Never set up a dog for failure, because we build on success." Tina had tried, God knows she'd tried, but when you were just a big bundle of failures and regrets yourself, it sure was a tough thing to learn confidence and then teach it to a dog. Being told about "Sterling's sterling success" in guide dog school had helped bolster her fragile confidence.

"Tina!" Ellen called to her when she'd put Corky back on her leash and was ready to head to the prison laundry room to work. Corky loved to watch the clothes and water in the big, front-loading washers swish around. "Warden Campbell wants a word with you."

Now, *that,* Tina thought, was never good news. "Corky, come," she commanded.

As Tina preceded Ellen down the long corridor toward the warden's office, other officers and inmates said hello to her and Corky. Though Tina didn't break stride, several stooped to give the puppy a quick pat. Having these animals around made everyone happier and calmer, but not Tina right now. She felt so uptight she could throw up.

Tina had heard that Warden Marian Campbell had been against the PBB program at first, but she was gung ho for it now, especially since it made the prison atmosphere better. Sometimes the warden even let the dogs visit women who were ready to walk into their parole hearings because it calmed them down. Sterling had visited the domestic-violence training classes more than once, since having a dog there seemed to help the women open up and share their feelings. One of those inmates had told her that Sterling, who was usually calm, used to get a little upset if the women became distraught. It was like the dog could feel someone's pain, Tina thought.

Right now, her own feelings were on hold—iced up, just the way she used to feel all the time before she became a puppy raiser. To help herself face the warden as she entered the office, she scooped Corky up in her arms and held her tight.

"Have a seat, Tina," Warden Campbell said. Tina obeyed, scooting back into the hard, wooden chair, with Corky on the floor at her side. The warden came around her big, cluttered desk and perched on the edge of it, looming over Tina. The woman had striking, high cheekbones and smooth skin the color of milk chocolate. Though she could be really stern, the puppies had always made the warden smile. But not now.

The warden frowned. "I'm afraid I have some sad news, Tina."

"Not one of my kids?" Tina cried. She knew she shouldn't interrupt, but she couldn't help it. "They're hurt? Worse?"

"You're an honor inmate making great strides here, Tina, so I've decided to tell you this myself. I'm sorry, but your mother had a massive heart attack last night and did not survive. Your children—" she glanced down at a folder open on her desk behind her "—a girl and a boy, both minors, were taken in by the neighbors for the night. But because there is no known next of kin, they have been remanded into the custody of children's services, which will try to place them in foster homes. There is no other next of kin, is there?"

"My sister Vanessa, but she's—moved somewhere 'fore I got in here. She'd take them though. She loves kids, loved my kids…" Her voice choked on a sob.

It seemed to Tina as if another woman had said that to the warden. She should have been there with Mama and the kids. *She should be there now!* Fury poured through her. Anger and hatred at herself, at the world. Mama had been so good to take the kids when their parents had let them down. It had been a real burden at her age. A heart attack—it was Tina's fault, and now the kids would be with someone who was not kin.

"Tina, I'm so sorry for your loss," the warden said, and leaned forward to squeeze her shaking shoulder before briefly touching Corky's head. "I've arranged for someone else to take your place in the laundry room today if you need time alone."

Alone. When would she ever see Larry and Sandy again? They'd forget about her by the time she got out. The prison wasn't that far from her mama's home, but children's services or new foster parents wouldn't bring Larry and Sandy here for a visit like Mama had. And was there money to bury Mama proper, and was there money for stuff the kids needed?

Tina had never felt more of a failure—again. *Don't set the puppies up for failure but for success…* She sat in the chair in the warden's office, silently sobbing, while the puppy licked her hand.

CHAPTER TWO

It was a great spring day, so Detective Blair Ryan sat at a sidewalk table and ate his tortilla. The taverna made it just the way he liked it, with Spanish onions, red peppers, guacamole and lots of meat. He swiped some salsa off his chin, then took a swig of his soft drink.

He kept his back against the wall—instinct from officers' training and also his year in Afghanistan. This wasn't Kabul, though these could be mean streets, too. With the large influx of Latinos, the area was making a transition from traditional blue-collar to ethnic-hip. It was also popular because of affordable rents, despite its proximity to Manhattan.

A hometown boy from nearby Newark, Blair liked E-town and chose to live here. This neighborhood especially was a great mix of Latino, Polish and Indian cultures.

Blair tossed the last of his crust to a watchful seagull, one of many that flew in from Newark Bay, where container ships were being loaded and unloaded. It seemed like just yesterday that his mom had brought him and his sister, Kate, down here on Saturdays when their dad was working—almost all the Ryan men had been cops—to eat in a restaurant overlooking the loading docks and harbor. But cancer had claimed Kate when she was only nine, and he'd never gone near that restaurant again.

He tossed his trash in a KEEP OUR CITY CLEAN can and strolled down the street toward the renovated apartment block where Alexis Michaels lived now. She'd pretty much given him the brush-off the last time he'd seen her. Funny, he mused, how people used the word *see* all the time, like "Nice to see you...you see what I mean."

At first Alexis had been distraught over losing her sight. She'd fought her way back to health and sanity, helping him as best she could to find the bastard who'd attacked her, only to have him slip through their fingers.

Somehow, Alexis really got to him—really moved him. He'd once feared he'd left the soft side of himself back in the service, where he'd seen innocents maimed and killed. But Alexis had made him feel things again.

Blair realized he was half a block from the apartment he and his buddy Jace had helped Alexis move into last year. He popped a breath mint in his mouth in case he had dragon's breath after that sandwich. He'd just stop by for a sec to see how she was doing. Twice she'd turned him down for dinner, but he still couldn't get her out of his head.

As far as Blair could tell, Alexis had the smallest apartment in the rehabbed building. At least it was on the first floor, so she had only three stairs to deal with.

He went into the dim, narrow hall that led to the three first-floor apartments. Good, her mailbox and door did not bear her name. Voices sounded within. It would be great if she'd made new friends, since she'd distanced herself from her former acquaintances so that sicko Dortman couldn't trace her.

Squaring his shoulders, Blair knocked. The voices stopped; maybe she'd had the radio on.

"Who is it?" she asked through the door.

"Blair Ryan, Alexis. I was just in the area and thought I'd see how you're doing."

He heard her unlock the dead bolt, fumble with a safety chain, then turn the lock in the door handle. He'd installed the dead bolt for her the day he and Jace had moved her in here. He was relieved she used the safety measures even during the day, but then light and dark were the same to her. To his surprise, when the door opened, she stood bathed in sunlight from her front windows. With a little smile, she stuck out her hand.

He took it and shook it, then covered it with his other one for a second until she pulled gently away. She looked really good. Her jet-black hair was shorter, but it framed her lively face with gentle curls. He was glad she didn't have on the dark sunglasses she'd insisted on wearing after she was released from the hospital. Ironically, the appearance of her snappy, brown eyes had not been damaged, and she still turned them in the direction of speakers or noise. The cuts and bruises on her forehead that had taken so long to turn to pale scars were hidden beneath wispy bangs. She was a natural beauty who didn't need makeup, with her dark, arched brows and thick eyelashes. She'd always looked pale, but now color suffused her cheeks and throat above the aqua, peasant-type blouse she wore with jeans. She was barefoot, and damn if she didn't have her toenails painted. He felt a bit guilty looking her over so thoroughly, something he would not have done if she could see him.

"Can you come in for a minute?" she asked. "I have something to tell you."

"Sure—not about Dortman?"

"No, thank heavens. I'm glad the coward's long gone, except that he might be harming someone else. Do you want to sit down?" she asked, gesturing toward the couch under the windows. "I can get you some iced tea if you'd like—or I can make coffee. I remember you like it with no cream but two packets of sweetener."

That little detail touched him. He cleared his throat. "Iced tea would be fine. It's warm out for April."

"I know. I've been enjoying the sun pouring in the windows."

He sat and she walked gracefully toward the kitchen. If he hadn't known better, he'd think she could see.

"I thought I heard voices in here when I knocked," he called to her, looking around the room. Everything was neat and uncluttered. Orchid plants and African violets bloomed on the window ledge.

"One of my talking books," she said from the kitchen. "Actually, it was a travel book about walking tours in London. I'd love to go visit again someday, maybe make a tour of famous literary places. Do you get that feeling—wanderlust?"

Man, she was in a good mood compared with other times he'd seen her. He bit his lip, smiling at the way she'd phrased that question. It wasn't wanderlust that called to him when he was around Alexis Michaels.

"After my stint in the marines, I'm pretty content at the old age of thirty-one to settle down, and this part of New Jersey's still home."

She came back into the living room with two glasses of iced tea and handed him one—right where he could easily take it from her.

Though he knew she couldn't see him, her gaze met his, and she nodded. She searched for her beanbag chair with her foot, then curled into it, cradling her glass on her knees. With this woman, even when she was laid out in a hospital bed, newly blinded with that beautiful face all bandaged up, he'd felt she could see inside him. As badly hurt as she'd been, she'd always shown great concern for his feelings, and she'd never blamed him for not finding and arresting Dortman— though he'd sure blamed himself.

"What I wanted to tell you," she said, "is that I'm getting a guide dog in two days. I'll be gone for a month's training and then—hopefully—have much more freedom when I return. Sometimes, though I still have students in to teach, it's like—like being in prison. Which reminds me, the dog I will get was raised in prison before it was trained."

"I've heard of that program. Puppies in Prison?"

"Puppies Behind Bars—prison bars, not the kind you Irish cops like to check out when you're off duty."

He chuckled. "Alexis, that's great. It will give you a lot more confidence to come and go."

"I thought you might give me a lecture that I'll get out more where someone who knows Dortman—you know—someone might see me."

"All life's a risk," he said, taking a big swig from his glass, then putting it down on the slate-top coffee table beside the sofa. He leaned toward her, elbows on his knees. "I've seen security soldiers and explosives experts work with dogs in the middle of minefields, and the department here uses bomb- and drug-sniffing dogs. I'm pretty sure some of our bomb sniffers are from the PBB program."

"I feel it's a big step, but I'm ready for it. And I just want you to know that I appreciate all you've done for me since my acci— Well, I know you always call it an attack."

"That it was. Listen, how about we do something to celebrate this big step you're taking?" He could have bitten his tongue once he blurted that out. Each time he'd tried to get personal with her, she'd backed off, but it was too late now. "And I want to meet your new partner when you get back, okay?"

"Sure—about meeting my dog. You know, when I told my old roommate about the dog on the phone, she said, 'You mean a blind dog?' Of course, she meant a dog for the blind, but I told her, 'I hope he's not blind because he's going to have to take the lead,' and we laughed and laughed."

He was thrilled to see a smile light her face, and had to blink back tears. Lucky she couldn't see them, because she always seemed to think he pitied her when that wasn't the case. Not at all, and he hoped to hell she'd let him prove it.

"About the celebration, Blair, I've got a student coming here in about an hour—she's preparing for college entrance exams she has to retake to get her scores up."

"Then how about a walk right now, even if it's just once around the block? Like you said, the sun's great today, spring has sprung and all that. I'm not as good as a guide dog, but we'll be just a couple of friends out for a short stroll, okay?"

He watched her grip her glass. She was going to turn him down again, and if she did, then that was that. He'd just phone her someday to ask how she was doing with her canine partner.

"I know it's always bothered you that Dortman took off before you could nail him," she said, "but I owe you so much, including letting me get iced tea for you without asking if you can help or doing it for me, like my mother and my friends always do."

"I'm not here because I feel guilty about Dortman, Alexis, and I'm not here to make sure you're keeping your door chain on or your new phone number unlisted. But if you don't have the time…"

"But I do," she said, getting up. "A walk outside sounds

great. I've never had a dog, Blair. Can you tell me more about the ones you've seen people working with?"

He was so excited he felt like a kid again. She got her shoes and jacket, and though he wanted to help her into it, he let her do it alone. But he did take her hand and put it in the crook of his arm as they stepped outside together.

ON HER THIRD DAY at the Independence Guide Dog School, Alexis was more keyed up than ever. After three days of general orientation and basic instruction about working with a guide dog, the students would meet their dogs today.

"Now, just let me review a few things," their instructor, Andy Curtis, told them in their classroom. "You've all come a long way since you arrived, but today you need to begin to bond with your partners before we can go on to make the two of you a great working pair. But keep in mind, even after this month of intensive training, you have not arrived. Training's an ongoing, lifelong thing with these dogs. It can take up to six months or more to become a good team. And, remember, the dogs are not only going to be your work companions when in harness, but your pets when they are out of harness. Today, you begin to build on that lifetime relationship with these dogs—their working lifetime, at least."

It sounded like a marriage, Alexis thought, a good one. But she was still nervous about making a commitment to a dog. Sure, she was ready to meet her partner, and she trusted the great job the staff at the school had done to prepare her, yet she was still scared.

So far this week, she had been surprised to learn how much work was required to exercise and groom a dog. Why, cats pretty much groomed themselves. And the dog would need periodic awards and praise for things well done, unlike cats, who were quite independent. But this had to work; she just had to bond with this dog. She knew her dog would be female—they all were—and she'd asked Andy if the partnerships sometimes didn't work out. He'd shaken his head and said, "It rarely happens." That worried her, too.

In the coming weeks, one trainer would work with six students. Quickly, Alexis reviewed the commands the dogs would already know: *sit, stand, stay, heel, forward, backward, steady* and *hup up,* meaning to speed up. Other commands would be optional, depending on the needs of the dog owner.

When Andy dismissed them, the students went to their private rooms down a long hall to await delivery of their dogs, which had been carefully matched with their new owners for size, strength and speed. Alexis had held on to a metal and leather harness connected to her instructor, then to a "demo-dog," so she could get the feel of it, all the while being observed for her pace and stride. She had also answered numerous questions about the area where she lived, her activities and lifestyle. She'd admitted she had felt like a recluse but was hoping the dog would help her get her freedom back. All she'd been told was that her dog was a twenty-two-inch-high, sixty-pound chocolate Labrador retriever named Sterling.

Alexis now sat on the floor with her back against her small

bed in the room where so many other blind people must have waited to meet their dogs. Andy had suggested sitting on the floor because the dogs had learned not to leap up on furniture, and their initial exuberance could knock someone over. Her heart was pounding as hard as it did whenever Blair Ryan showed up in her life.

Alexis thought about all the help and support Blair had given her, even during the short walk they'd taken just five days ago. "Tree growing in the sidewalk at ten o'clock," he'd said as he'd steered her around the block. "Rough concrete coming, we're going to turn right in about four more steps." In a way, she thought, she would use the same sort of verbal commands and the dog's physical moves to help her maneuver.

She jumped at a knock on the door—no, it must be the one next door. The dogs were here.

Alexis felt bad that some of the people in her class had been blind from birth and would never really know what a Labrador retriever looked like. She felt blessed she'd seen Labs—yellow, black and chocolate—and knew how regal, how alert they were with those big, kind eyes. Chocolate for a color sounded warm and safe. Chocolate was also her favorite comfort food, and surely this dog would be a comfort.

Another knock, louder. She gripped her hands together in her lap. Yes, it was her door. She heard it open and felt the cooler breeze from the hall, then heard the dog's toenails on the tile floor.

"Alexis, here's your new partner, Sterling," Andy said. "And she's very excited to meet you."

That was all. She heard Andy drop the leash, then close the door. A solid, warm body covered in sleek fur pressed against her and a wet tongue licked her chin. Two big paws rested on her shoulders. Sterling's collar jingled; she was panting, and her tail *thump-thumped* against Alexis's knees.

Alexis patted her head and stroked her strong back and her muscular neck. She scratched Sterling behind her ears and, finally, found her voice.

"Sterling, Sterling, good girl, good girl! We're going to be best friends, work together, walk outside together…"

That was all she could manage before she hugged Sterling hard.

WITH THEIR PUPPIES under the table at their feet in the noisy, crowded prison cafeteria, the Puppies Behind Bars trainers sat down to eat lunch at the same table. Corky nestled tight against her legs, which Tina liked, though it was best that the puppies eventually learned to lie quietly and patiently, not touching legs or feet while their human partners sat at the table.

At first there was little chatter but the usual complaints about the food, which was downed fast enough. Tina kept her eyes on her plate because they were still red and swollen. She'd been a real wreck since the day of Mama's funeral. It was probably harder *not* being there than if she could have gone. The prison rules allowed her to go, but the expense for a guard would have come from Tina's family, and she was too worried there wasn't even enough money for a proper funeral. Besides, if she'd seen her kids, she could never have left them again. She was scared she'd have done something screwy and gotten herself even more time in here. Thinking about her little Larry and Sandy staying with strangers was even worse. Showing emotions in here was a sign of weakness, but since she'd started in the PBB program, she felt she could at least let loose a little with this bunch of inmates without being ridiculed or preyed upon. The puppies kind of softened everybody up.

"Man, that's really something, us teaching these dogs foreign phrases," Shawanna said. Like Tina, she was a veteran of the previous PBB program. She too had trained a guide dog last time. "Only foreign language I ever spoke was lotsa cursing and street slang. It's really neat to feel trusted. One year you're on the level with pond scum and the next you're helping out blind folks or preparing dogs to find explosives to save lives."

"I'd hate to think about Corky leaving the country, though," Tina put in. "But there's so much need here for EDCs that odds are our dogs will probably be somewhere nearby."

"I heard dogs have over a hundred million sniffing cells while people only have about five million," Lou Ann put in from farther down the table. She was new to the program, but it seemed to be helping her a lot already. She was pretty smart but had got in trouble for her big mouth at first. Still, being part of a team effort had made other people more tolerant of her.

"But I have to tell you, Tina," she went on, "some of the dogs so far have ended up working with cops in South Africa, Italy and the Far East. Hell, that's places I'll never see. PBB dogs worked at the pope's funeral and the Democratic and Republican national conventions. And one screens the mayor of New York's jet, as well as planes at the big airports."

"Wow, talk about that old telephone company ad, 'Reach out and touch someone,'" Karla mumbled, her mouth full. Karla had been over two hundred pounds when she first got here, but she'd been dropping some weight since she'd started exercising with her puppy, Brady.

Tina moved her foot closer to Corky's warmth. Even if she could get past mourning Mama and worrying about her kids, she'd still be worried about giving up Corky to a world of danger.

"Pretty funny, huh?" Shawanna said. "Here I was doing my best a coupla years ago to outsmart the cops, and now we're helping them outsmart the bad guys."

PANICKED, his heart thudding, Blair Ryan sat straight up in bed. His sheet and blanket were wrapped like tight bandages around him. It was pitch-black. For a minute he couldn't recall where he was. He'd been falling, tumbling into blackness… Kabul? Hiding from the Taliban in the mountains? No, no, he was in his apartment at home.

Sweating, he strained to listen. Maybe a car had backfired to wake him. Or else he'd been dreaming about tank or gunfire.

Blair put his head in his hands. Please, dear God, not memories of those days. He'd never get back to sleep tonight. Jagged pieces of those nightmares floated through his sleep-sodden brain.

Or was he dreaming about Alexis, about what happened to her? He'd reached her right after the emergency squad did—seeing her crumpled like a doll at the bottom of the steps. Had Dortman been hiding there in the dark somewhere, watching, enjoying what he'd done?

Bits of the dream he'd just awakened from came back to him. Alexis had died. She was holding his hand, telling him that she needed a dog to be able to run away from cancer, but now it was too late. When he'd held her hand, her hair had turned lighter, and her face became Kate's.

He muttered an oath, ripped off the cocoon of covers and got out of bed. He hadn't dreamed of losing his sister for the longest time. She'd been eight years younger than him, and he'd felt he was her protector as well as her big brother. Although he knew you couldn't fight cancer with fists or even guns, he sometimes felt he'd failed her. How he'd love it if Kate were around. He could teach her things, show her things. He'd like her to meet Alexis.

He padded to the window and peered through the vertical blinds. His bedroom overlooked carports and more apartments. The late-April moon was half-full, throwing gray shadows. Was Len Dortman out there somewhere, harming other women, as Alexis feared? Did he know what he'd done to the woman he'd been obsessed with, or did he think he'd killed her and fled a murder charge? It wasn't the M.O. of an obsessive-compulsive like that to just move on.

Blair shook his head to clear it. Though he was still sweating, he felt chilled. Standing at the window, legs spread, his fists thrust under his armpits, he wished he could hold Alexis in the moonlight, in the sunlight, anytime or place—protect her and yet help her regain her independence. He hoped Dortman was gone for good, although a part of him couldn't help but wish he could get his hands on the guy—just once.

CHAPTER THREE

W ith Sterling guiding her, Alexis walked with grace and confidence again, not afraid to stride out, not fearful that she'd take a tumble over some object she couldn't see. The dog had even pulled her back from a pothole in the street—at least that's what Andy had called out to her to explain Sterling's sudden detour.

She held the leash between the index and middle fingers of her right hand and the harness handle with her left. At first it had felt strange to trust her movements to an animal, but after a week of practice she felt as if she had wings—or at least steady feet again.

"Don't let her set the pace, Alexis!" Andy called from behind her. "Remember, you're the alpha dog here, not her."

Alexis nodded and smiled. In one of the classes, they'd discussed dog psychology. Dogs were inherently pack animals and needed to know where they came in the pecking order of power, so to speak. She'd been surprised to learn that a dog as beautifully mannered and trained as Sterling would test whoever was in charge, but the two of them struck a better balance every day. And, though dealing with a dog for the first time in her life had taken getting used to, she already appreciated and admired Sterling.

The Lab led her into the obstacle course that was the adventure of the day, as the students called these excursions. Yesterday they had walked down a busy street and tomorrow would begin practice in crossing streets. The students and their dogs had worked this course, which was set up in part of a parking lot, earlier in the week, but the obstacles had been rearranged.

And that made Alexis realize that trying to fix the pattern of the barriers in her mind had been foolish. That, and banging her shins into what felt like a tall, plastic garbage can.

"Ow!" she cried, inadvertently jerking on Sterling's leash. "It's okay, good dog," she added quickly. After all, the dog had tried to lead her around the obstacle.

"Alexis," Andy called out, "the point is to trust your seeing partner. Did you feel Sterling try to take you farther left to avoid that garbage can?"

"Yes," she admitted. "Mea culpa. I guess I was trying to guide her."

"Trust, trust and more trust," he said, his voice coming closer as he approached. "Let Sterling make those key decisions. It's what she's been trained to do—wants to do."

"Right. Sorry." Alexis knew she needed Andy's help, but

it was making her nervous that he kept following them, watching them. It reminded her of the way she'd felt those weeks Len Dortman trailed her—both the times she knew he was watching her and the times she only feared he was. But she was not going to let that get to her, absolutely not.

"Go ahead, Alexis," Andy encouraged her. "As my high-school football coach used to tell us, the most important play is the next play, not the one where you just fumbled. These dogs have been taught 'intelligent disobedience,' remember?"

She did remember. Guide dogs were taught to obey commands unless they saw a problem or danger, such as an approaching car that their partner did not hear. Even if the dog had been told "forward," the animal would disobey if she sensed or saw a threat.

"Forward, Sterling. Good girl, forward."

Alexis allowed the dog more leeway now, walking with her, not fighting her, trying to feel her moves through the harness. Ha, like dancing with a partner who knew how to lead, she thought, then thrust from her mind the memory of Blair asking her to dinner and dancing. She had to focus on this and not let her thoughts wander. Sterling was concentrating, and she must, too.

But the dog seemed to have led her into a dead end. Sterling stopped and turned them both one hundred eighty degrees around in a small space.

"Is this a maze?" Alexis called to Andy.

"Only if you don't follow your partner's lead. And this

might be a good time to decide if you want to teach Sterling the additional command of 'find the way,'" he suggested, coming closer again. "It's different from 'forward.' When you're in a tight or crowded place without a straight-ahead path or exit, it's a useful command—up to you."

Alexis nodded. "I have a very smart partner here. Yes, I'll teach her that. Especially because I believe that I—we—are in another dead end," she announced as the stalwart dog pivoted them again.

"Find the way, Sterling," Alexis commanded in the calm, clear voice she was learning to use with the Lab when she was working. She used softer tones when Sterling was out of harness, when she played with her or groomed her, or when they just relaxed together. "Find the way."

And Sterling did.

TINA LIFTED an armful of soiled prison uniforms into the big washer, set the controls and turned it on. Nothing happened. But it had just been working a minute ago.

Then she saw she had not completely closed the door. She slammed it, automatically glancing down to where Corky should be. But this was the weekend the puppies were gone to host families on the outside, a part of the program that happened as often as twice a week. All of the prisons raising dogs for the blind offered "Puppies by the Hour" to outsiders who wished to puppy-sit and play with the dogs. This helped to socialize the dogs, letting them ride in a car, live in a house, be around kids.

Kids…

Tina sniffed and blew her nose before she went back to sorting piles of dirty towels. Besides missing her kids so bad, she was still mourning Mama. Whether she wanted the memories or not, scenes from her childhood had been rotating through her mind like the clothes going around in the washer…

Happy times, mostly. There'd been a bad fallout when she'd married Hank. Mama had seen he was rotten to the core even then, but Tina had had to find out the hard way. "You oughta be more like your sister Vanessa, trying to make something of herself!" Mama had scolded. But Vanessa took off and didn't look back. Still, Tina was sure Vanessa would be heartbroken if she knew Mama had passed on and her sister's kids were more or less orphans.

Tina had also been real antsy waiting to hear whether her kids were going to be placed in foster homes or stay with children's services in the city. She was torn about that. She'd like them to have a family, but what if they then realized what losers their own parents were? What if Larry and Sandy decided they hated her when each day she knew just how much she loved them and how badly she'd hurt—damaged them.

She threw a ripped-up towel in the recycle bin, then leaned her elbows on the counter and propped up her head with her hands. But she looked up as a new inmate, Lupe, noisily rolled another huge hamper of soiled uniforms into the steamy room.

"You miss-eeng that leetle dog again, *sí?*"

Tina nodded and went back to sorting. Lupe's English had been pretty bad when she'd come in here, but she'd been trying to improve. She said she might as well learn something worthwhile in here.

That's the way Tina looked at the PBB program—learning something useful while she was in prison. The fact she took such pride in caring for her dogs made her think she might try to open a dog-sitting or grooming business when she got out. Not that people would trust an ex-con to dog-sit in their homes, not that she'd ever be able to afford a shop of her own, but surely someone would hire her. Her dream was to own a van and go house to house, working right in the van—dog groomer on call.

Tina sighed. Could she make enough doing that to support her kids, make things up to them? Could—

She looked up and saw Ellen enter the laundry-room door and head straight for her. Tina twisted the towel she held, feeling as edgy as if she'd been caught shoplifting.

"Tina, some good news," the officer told her, glancing down at the notebook she carried. "The warden would have told you herself, she said, but she's in a parole board hearing and thought you should know this right away. Your little girl's been taken by a foster family, people who live in the country and have two other kids and a dog for her to play with. Bet that cheers you up!"

"But—not my boy? Larry's not with her?"

Ellen frowned down at her notebook. "No—I—nothing about him, just your girl."

"I was hoping, praying they wouldn't be pulled apart. They need each other—that's all they have left right now."

Oh, damn, Tina thought, she was going to cry again. And Corky wasn't here to help.

BLAIR RYAN WAITED until two days after Alexis said she'd be home before calling her. He didn't want her to think he was overanxious to see her—which he was. Then too, he'd been working a tough domestic-violence case where the husband, despite a restraining order, had returned to the home and assaulted his estranged wife really badly. They'd caught and arrested the guy. The situation wasn't that close to Alexis's, and yet her case returned to haunt him again.

He leaned back in his desk chair and reached over piles of files and reports for the phone. The buzz of business could be heard outside his cubicle.

He punched in redial. Again, Alexis's home phone rang. For the second time today—and it was only midmorning—his own voice came on with, "If you wish to leave a message…" The day she'd moved into her new place, he'd suggested that he record the answering machine message for her so that a caller who didn't know her—or was looking for her—would think a man was on the premises. It had gone unspoken between them that, even though the number would be unlisted, someone as devious as Dortman could find it.

Not wanting her to worry about a call where the person just hung up—that had been one of Dortman's tricks before things escalated—Blair said, "Alexis, Blair again. I'll bet you're out with your new guide dog. Call me if you get a chance, because I'd like to meet him or her. I'm at my work number, but I told you that you can always phone me at home, and my cell number's the same. Hope to see you—hear from you."

He hung up, wishing he hadn't sounded so forlorn. But he missed her. Man, get a life, he told himself as he hunched back over his desk and fingered through the folder he kept on Len Dortman. Blair was overburdened with work and should have filed it by now. In a way, he was hoping it would turn into a cold case that would never be needed again. But the guy's psychological workup indicated his single-mindedness, and that scared Blair.

He skimmed Dortman's psychological profile. The perp's mother had deserted him as a child, and he'd evidently had violent reactions to rejection or separation from women because of major self-esteem issues. The guy wasn't that bad-looking, and came off as Mr. Nice-and-Helpful at first, so it could be possible he'd find a victim who needed him—though she'd be in real danger if she acted even slightly independent, let alone tried to get rid of him.

AS SHE AND STERLING walked from the apartment to a small, neighborhood grocery store, Alexis was thrilled to realize what a difference this dog had made in her life already. Holding on to the harness and trusting the dog, she was no longer afraid of taking a walk or going on an errand.

Besides, a guide dog was a real attraction. People she

didn't know talked to her and Sterling, though if they edged too close and she thought they might pet Sterling, she explained that it was best not to touch a guide dog when she was working. "She's gentle as can be," she'd tell people, "but when she's in the harness, she leaves her pet status behind to become my guide and protector."

Even strangers said things like, "Wow, I can tell your dog's real smart!"

"She sure is," Alexis would tell them. "Sterling is smart and well trained—she totally impresses me!"

But when they were walking, Alexis had to concentrate. No strolling along just daydreaming. She had her cell phone with her in case she needed to make a call, but she didn't turn it on because she didn't want that distraction either. Alexis had to make key decisions about where they were going and when they'd arrived. It was indeed a working partnership, and she cherished Sterling for giving her some semblance of the independence she'd had before disaster struck.

When Sterling was out of harness, she became a lively, loving pet, and Alexis knew the dog's big, warm body well now from playing and hugging: the distinctive tail, thick at the base and tapering toward the tip; the short, dense coat and powerful jaws, which were so gentle. She lavished affection on Sterling—even scratching the dog's belly when she rolled on her back.

Alexis knew she'd never responded to an independent, sometimes aloof cat this way. It didn't even startle her now when Sterling licked her face, and she talked to her so much more than she did to Chaucer. The cat got along with the dog quite well, since Sterling stuck to the floor and stayed off the sofa and window ledges where Chaucer perched among the potted plants.

The only thing that still bothered Alexis was crossing busy streets, and there were plenty of those around here. Not being able to tell if the traffic light was in their favor or not, the dog stopped at the curb. It was up to Alexis to listen for vehicular and pedestrian traffic before giving Sterling the forward command. But the dog then looked to be sure it was safe. If Sterling saw something Alexis hadn't discerned, she might refuse to cross or even pull her firmly back from danger. If only she'd had a protector like this when her life had turned into such a nightmare.

This time Sterling didn't budge when Alexis gave the forward command. "Good girl, Sterling," Alexis told her as a cyclist turned a corner so close she could hear the pedals moving the chain and feel the push of wind as the rider sped by. "Forward, Sterling." When it was all clear, the dog took her across the street.

Some observers were certain Sterling was reading the traffic lights. A man had said to them yesterday, "Hey, lady, I thought dogs were color-blind. Do they teach them that the one on top is the green light?"

Alexis had to bite her lip not to laugh at that one. Yes, both she and Sterling had to make decisions, but they got around, farther and better each of the days she was back home. She couldn't wait to show her mother what a change this had made in her life. And she wanted Blair to see. That way if he still kept coming around, she'd be sure it wasn't out of guilt or pity.

THE NEXT DAY, Blair sat at a table outside the Tapitias, a café-restaurant about six blocks from Alexis's place, waiting for her. "I'll be the one with a dog," she'd told him with a little laugh when she'd returned his call. She'd sounded lighthearted and confident. No tremor in her voice, no hesitation. His hopes soared.

And now, here she came, striding along at a good clip, her hair blowing, her lips moving. Evidently she was talking to the dog. Sterling was a brown beauty, and Blair's eyes stung with unshed tears. He and Kate had owned a Labrador like that, only black instead of this chocolate color.

He stood at the table he'd taken for them. He wasn't sure whether to call to her or approach her. There was a low, plastic barrier around these tables, but she'd chosen the place, so she must know it well. As she came closer, he saw the dog hesitate a moment at the barrier, which reached its nose.

"Forward," he heard Alexis say. Then she must have felt the barrier, because she added, "Find the way, Sterling, find the way." At that, the dog took her around to the entry.

ALEXIS COULD FEEL Blair's presence before she heard him say, "Alexis! I'm over here, coming your way."

She smiled in the direction of his voice. He must have been watching for her. Strange how she was developing a sort of sixth sense when someone was studying her, not just passing by. She wasn't sure if it was because she'd spent three weeks being watched by her instructor, or whether she just knew that more people were watching her now, the blind woman and her smart dog. Despite the warm day, she shivered. If someone stalked her now, would she sense his presence, separate from those who had no intention of harming her?

She prayed she wasn't slipping back into the paranoia and trauma of the days when Dortman stalked her. No, it couldn't be that. She'd been so oblivious to him at first, but once she'd spotted him, he seemed to be everywhere, following her on the street, in his car, watching her front door, skulking behind every darn tree!

"Blair!" she said, recognizing his familiar quick stride. She heard him stop right in front of her. "As you can see I've got my hands full or I'd shake your hand," she added with a smile. "Let's sit down."

"Sure, I have a table—right over here. This way," he added.

But she just said, "Forward, Sterling," and moved in his direction with the dog.

The minute she dropped the leash and harness, the Lab lay down under their table, quiet and patient, while Blair helped to seat her. "That's one beautiful animal," he said. "I'll bet she enjoys roughhousing."

"She's beautifully behaved indoors and out, but yes, she loves to play."

A moment's silence hung between them while life bustled all around—voices, car horns, even the song of a robin as the city edged from winter into spring.

"It's working out great, isn't it?" he asked.

"Better than I could have hoped. She's given me back my legs and my life, at least this version of it. It's taken some getting used to, being so responsible for her well-being, too, but I owe her so much."

Their server came. They ordered fajitas and sangria. The dog didn't budge.

"Nothing for Sterling while she's working, right?" Blair asked.

"If it's a hot day, I take water along, but that's it. Would you believe it—a dog that doesn't stop to sniff at things or beg for food when she's out? You could put a piece of prime rib in front of her, and she wouldn't take it when she's in harness. She's my gentle giant."

"That reminds me—I checked and learned that the same program Sterling came from has supplied several of our police department's bomb-sniffing dogs. Those EDC dogs need to be calm and obedient and want to please their owners—handlers, in this case. The love and care they're given as puppies also prepares them to handle the later extensive scent-association training. They're far different from the attack-on-command police dogs, though people sometimes get that confused."

After they ate, they walked together toward a small park behind the local elementary school. A jumble of kids' voices filled the air. Blair told her that Latino kids were playing soccer in a field next to a baseball diamond where Indian students were enjoying a game of cricket. This park was an arm of the big city park where Alexis had been jogging the night Dortman attacked her, the night she fell—or was thrown—down the concrete steps by the old amphitheater.

She took Sterling's harness off and let her run a bit. She and Blair took turns throwing a small, foam football, which the dog retrieved, faithfully dropping it at Alexis's feet, even when Blair had heaved it.

Blair didn't want to talk about his latest case, and all she wanted to talk about was Sterling, but their conversation eventually spun off to everyday topics like the weather and local politics, their favorite CDs and TV shows. He was amazed she was familiar with a popular new dance competition on TV.

"What?" she said, taking a little swipe at his shoulder and landing the blow. "There's a police department rule that blind people have to stick to radio or CDs instead of TV? I just listen to the music on the show and imagine what they're doing, then listen to the judges' evaluations. Sometimes I dance around myself, just for fun," she admitted. "Sterling watched every move I made the other night and thought I did really well. I believe she gave me a ten."

Alexis hadn't meant to say all that. It sounded like a come-on to get him to ask her to go dancing again.

She was about to change the subject when Blair blurted, "How about just for fun, I take you dancing? You said no before, but things are different now that you've cleared a big hurdle. Of course, Sterling would come, too, and sit like a guardian angel under the table."

Blair sounded breathless—just the way Alexis felt. He'd asked her to go to some retro place called Casablanca before, which played 1940s music and was really popular. She'd wondered if the place was decorated with blowup photos of Ingrid Bergman and Humphrey Bogart from the old black-and-white movie. What was that famous line the two endangered lovers said? Oh, yeah, "We'll always have Paris." But if she didn't at least accept his invitation this time, she'd never have memories of dancing—even in the dark.

"All right," she said, and thought she heard him exhale in relief. "If you and Sterling are game, so am I."

CHAPTER FOUR

It turned out that the Club Casablanca was just on the other side of the big park from Alexis's neighborhood. The evening was so lovely and mild that she and Blair decided to walk. Alexis had to smile, and not just from happiness: it had been years since she'd had a chaperone when she went out on a date, and never one so welcome as Sterling.

And she'd never cared for anyone she'd been with as much as she cared for Blair Ryan. She'd admitted it to herself now, though the possibility of being more than friends still seemed as distant as sight and light.

"I know it's dark, but here I am picturing this walk as if it were daytime," she told Blair. He walked easily along on Sterling's other side, content to let the dog lead, satisfied not to talk too much so she could concentrate. Of course, with Blair, she could have left Sterling home, but after all, he'd invited the dog, too, and being in an atmosphere of music and movement would be good practice for her canine companion as well as for herself.

"The streetlights are on and, better yet, there's a moon," Blair told her. "It's almost full."

When they stopped at an intersection with a light, she asked, "Can you see the mountains and plains on the moon clearly tonight?"

"Pretty clear," he said.

"Remember Neil Armstrong's words when he first set foot on the moon? Something like 'One small step for man, one giant leap for mankind'? Well, working with Sterling has been one small step for this woman and yet one giant leap, too. Thank God for Puppies Behind Bars and that great guide dog school—and you, Blair."

"I hope you'll whisper something like that in my ear when we're dancing and not when we have Sterling walking between us—and the light just turned green."

"Sterling, forward."

The club was noisy with chatter and music. A live band—Blair said six men—accompanied a male and a female singer and played golden oldies, great dance tunes from the 1930s and '40s. While Sterling lay quiet and content under their table, they danced to a tune made famous by Fred Astaire and Ginger Rogers, "I Won't Dance." But they were dancing, cheek to cheek, their arms around each other, moving closer together with each spin around the dance floor.

"I agonized about whether to keep calling you," he whispered as the live band switched to "In the Mood." "I didn't want to seem unprofessional, and I didn't want you to think that I was just upset I hadn't found Dortman."

"Don't say that name," she said, touching her forehead to his strong, square jaw. "I just want to forget about him."

He sighed so hard that his chest shifted up, then down, against her breasts. She felt that little touch clear down to the pit of her belly.

"I know, Alexis, but I've tried that with a personal tragedy, and it doesn't work. We lost my younger sister, Kate, to cancer when she was nine. When I try to forget about it, bury it, it comes out in nightmares and depression. I've hated hospitals ever since and tried to keep from really caring deeply for someone so I wouldn't be hurt again—that's nuts, I know."

"But I understand," she reassured him. "I didn't know about that—and you were so good to keep visiting me when I was in the hospital. Blair, I know it's far too late, and I didn't even know Kate, but I'm so sorry. When I was in the hospital, I got to know some people who've been blind since birth. I had so many sighted years and I'm still healthy—and alive, no thanks to Dortman. That makes me realize how blessed I am, especially now that I have Sterling. But I'll take your advice about not trying to shut the bad things out."

"That doesn't mean you let the bad past get in the way of the good future," he murmured and gave her waist a little squeeze as he spun her again.

"Blair, forward," she said with a little laugh. "Find the way."

"Yes, ma'am. But just remember, cops are very—well, dogged—about following commands. I would like for us to find the way."

She smiled and clasped his neck and hand just a bit harder as they slowed again, standing almost in place, swaying with the music. Dancing with Blair, she could just close her eyes and move, feeling his lead, his strength—even his deep concern. And if that was love, could she trust it would be enough? Earlier, he'd said all good things were worth the risk.

She inhaled the clean, tart scent of his aftershave. He emanated warmth and security. Yet as safe as she felt with him, in his arms like this, she was also afraid of how much she wanted him. She wondered if she had spoken the thought out loud, because he tipped her chin up and covered her lips with his.

Instantly, she stopped moving, her mouth responding to his. They stumbled slightly, but he held her up, which broke the kiss. They laughed, and clasping his hand tightly, she let him lead her back to their table. She reached down to stroke Sterling's head as she sat.

"Let's get back," he said, his voice a rough whisper.

No, that wasn't Kenneth Branagh's voice, she thought, and not his face either, only Blair's. She wanted to see him with her fingertips and her lips. She wanted to know everything about him.

"All right. I'm ready."

He paid the server, and they downed the rest of their wine. The male singer began to croon a tune called "Begin the Beguine" as they made their way out of the club.

"Let's cut through the park," she said, surprised at her own request. "I do want to move beyond the past, and besides, there are some nice benches by the lake. The area still has lots of streetlights, doesn't it?"

"Sure, and people are walking there. Fine by me."

"Besides, Sterling deserves a little romp."

"Sterling? How about me?"

She laughed again, and they crossed the street, walking along the soft park grass to the gravel path, the one she'd been jogging on the night she was attacked. It hadn't been in this part of the park, though. Still, the amphitheater loomed between here and the area where she'd been running when Dortman must have appeared. She wished she could recall what had happened, but then again, maybe she didn't. She took off Sterling's harness, and Blair threw sticks for the dog to chase while they sat on a stone bench. The leaves were budding on the trees, and the wet soil of spring smelled fresh and fertile.

They held hands, then kissed. They made plans to go to the beach this summer, to have a picnic in the country—just the three of them. She said she'd like him to see her small hometown, and he even volunteered to meet her mother. It seemed, Alexis thought as she bent to put Sterling back into harness, her nightmares had turned to dreams.

IN HER CELL that evening, after dinner, Tina reread the fax from her son Larry's caseworker for the fourth time. Even though she was incarcerated, children's services was trying to keep her informed, no matter how bad the news. The fax read:

> We are endeavoring to place Lawrence Clawson in a stable, welcoming foster home. But most of our place-ments are currently of younger children or girls. So for the foreseeable future, until someone suitable is lo-cated and approved, Lawrence will remain in the cus-tody of children's services. We regret that your children are not together, but circumstances dictate that—"

Tina threw the paper down and hit the mattress with her fist so hard that Corky jumped and looked up from her padded bed on the floor of the cell.

"Sorry, girl. It's all my fault. But, you know, I think if I'd had you and Sterling before I'd had my own two babies, I'd have been a better mom, and then this wouldn't all be happening."

"Hi, Tina," came a voice through the barred window of the steel door. Tina jerked her head around. It was Brenda, a floor officer, with Jeannie, their silver-haired Puppies Behind Bars instructor. Tina and Corky were due at a rare evening meeting in a little while, so she had to pull herself together. But why was Jeannie coming here?

This must mean more bad news. Tina felt her insides freeze over with fear.

"Ms. Lancer would like to have a little chat," Brenda said, unlocking the cell door.

Tina stood. Corky did, too, staring at the two intruders as if she was on guard. Then she evidently scented or recognized Jeannie and padded over to be petted. Everyone in the PBB program liked this woman, who was formerly a breeder of Labradors. Tina tried not to frown, but she felt herself stiffen.

"I'm just wondering how you and Corky are getting along," Jeannie said, bending to pat the puppy. "Since you had such success with Sterling, I thought maybe you could give me an honest appraisal. The thing is, I know you've been through some really tough times lately, and I just want to be sure you don't think your…depression…is affecting Corky's well-being."

Tina's stomach twisted. Were they going to take Corky away?

"I know Corky relies on me, but I rely on her, too," Tina blurted, then could have kicked herself. She didn't want to give Jeannie or anyone an opening to reassign her puppy. What if they thought she was too unstable to help raise Corky?

"Do you think that your needs sometimes get in the way of her concentrating on the task at hand—that is, what you're trying to teach her?" Jeannie asked.

"No, she can concentrate real good. I think the love I give her and the way we need each other—maybe even more right now than most inmates need their puppies—is good for her. After all, think how much her handler is going to have to rely on her to be strong to sniff out all kinds of explosives. The way I love Corky is a two-way street, and that's what a dog like this will need in the future—love and feedback for the good job she does."

"Tina, I just want the best for both of you," Jeannie said. "You proved what a fine job you can do with Sterling last time, so—"

"I'm working through my problems, and I can still change more. I changed a lot since I been serving my sentence here."

"What about your family situation right now?" Brenda asked.

"Yeah, my daughter's been placed in a foster home, and I just got a letter about trying to place my son, too…" Her voice trailed off. She retrieved the letter from her bed and held it up to them before she realized that in her frustration she'd twisted it like a licorice stick.

"I heard about your family, and I'm so sorry," Jeannie said.

"I appreciate that." Tina struggled to show these women she could keep calm. Were they putting her through this questioning to see if she would break? "I'm handling my tough times. Just like these puppies, I'm learning patience. I've learned teamwork and self-control in this program, and I can teach that to Corky. I've seen how much having a routine and plans and responsibilities have helped the dogs and me. Give me more time with her—all the time she should have, and you'll see a dog as perfect as Sterling was."

As she spoke, Corky moved forward to stand beside her. Damn, but it was like the dog understood what was going on and was trying to help out. Didn't that count for something?

"Tina," Jeannie said, holding her hands up, palms out, "no dog—just like no person—is perfect. As gentle as Sterling was, you remember how she would sometimes growl when voices were raised. The guide dog instructor told me she was steady as a rock when walking by jackhammers blasting apart a sidewalk, yet when those women in the domestic-violence class cried or shouted, she reacted."

"But Sterling came through with flying colors, and Corky—and I—will, too," Tina insisted.

"Good enough." Jeannie gave a quick nod. "Then I'll see you and Corky in about—" she glanced at a large watch on her left wrist "—half an hour."

"For sure. We'll be there, ready to go."

Once she heard them walk away, Tina collapsed on the edge of her bed and leaned over to hug Corky. "Thanks for the help, girl," she whispered. "See how smart you are? You just sniffed out how bad I needed you to stand up with me."

"DO YOU WANT to come in for a few minutes?" Alexis asked Blair as he and Sterling brought her to her door after walking the rest of the way through the park, even past the amphitheater. Alexis had said it was like exorcising some demon, but she'd admitted she still could not recall exactly how she'd fallen down those steps.

"Sure," he said. "And I'll try to abide by your few minutes' curfew."

As she dug her keys out of her purse, Blair was tempted to take them from her to open the door, but he let her feel for the keyhole and put the key in herself.

"Home, Sterling," she said as she opened the door. "We're home."

"Is *home* one of the regular commands?" Blair asked as he followed her in and closed and locked the door behind them. She snapped on the light over her small dining area, then removed Sterling's leash. The Lab shook herself once as if to say, "That's a good night's work done," then plopped on her padded dog bed along the far wall.

"No, but I've been slowly adding commands like that and f-i-n-d t-h-e w-a-y," Alexis said, spelling the words as if Sterling were a kid. "Make yourself at home. Can I get you anything?"

"Just get yourself over here so we can continue what we started in the park."

It thrilled him that she simply dropped her purse on the table and strode to the couch. It was a deep, soft sofa with bolsters along the back, which made it hard to sit erect. He reached for her hand and tugged her down beside him. Their weight rolled them into the pillows so they were half sitting, half lying back.

"Blair, could I feel your face? To—to see you as best I can?"

In answer, he guided her right hand upward so her palm

and fingers touched his left cheek. She'd known how smooth his skin was from dancing so close, though now she felt the slightest hint of stubble. No mustache; very short sideburns. She felt the angular line of his jaw and high cheekbones, too. Gently, she ran her fingertips along his temple, through the crisp, short hair on both sides of his broad forehead, then back where it became thicker and longer. She had wondered if his haircut would be marine-short or artsy long, but it was in between.

"I grew it out from the jarhead look I used to have," he whispered as if he'd read her mind.

"Shh!"

She ran her fingers along his thick, sleek eyebrows and down the strong bridge of his nose. It was just slightly crooked with a bump. "A broken nose from when you were a kid?" she asked.

"An arrest gone wrong. But I thought I was supposed to keep quiet."

Ignoring his teasing, Alexis felt where his nostrils flared, felt his warm breath coming quickly. She touched his thick eyelashes and then his lips. Straight, taut lips, but the bottom one slightly pouted—poised for another kiss perhaps? He did kiss her fingertips, then nibbled at them.

"If you don't know how my lips feel by now," he said, "we have a lot of work to do."

He pulled her to him so she was sprawled across his lap and kissed her once, twice. They breathed in unison, their breath coming more quickly with each kiss. Perhaps, now, Alexis thought, she had really found the way.

BLAIR LEFT shortly after—and it was a good thing, because he was showing more self-control than she was. Alexis was so excited she couldn't sleep. Was the impact of kissing magnified when someone was blind? If so, making love with Blair would send her off the charts.

And, she thought, trying to make herself settle down to earth, she and Blair Ryan seemed meant for each other. After all, he'd kept coming back even after the way she'd treated him at first. And she knew she could trust him. A man who was willing to drive to a tiny town two hours away on his day off to meet her mother had to be sincere. She'd been so wrong to let what had happened to her make her fear men.

"Sterling, my girl," she told the dog, "we are going to celebrate. I'm getting you an extra treat and a bath."

Sterling knew what *treat* meant. The word seemed to be branded on her canine heart. In the kitchen, she gobbled up the milk-bone snack, then marched right into the bathroom with Alexis while she filled the tub and got the doggie shampoo and three big towels. She made sure the water was the right temperature, because Sterling was anxious, bumping and nuzzling her.

"All right, in you go," Alexis said, and the dog got in as if she knew all those words, too. The running water made a lot of noise, but she thought she heard—or sensed—a knock on the front door. "Sterling, stay. Sit."

Could Blair have come back and be knocking? In the hall, at the door to the bathroom, she strained to listen.

No, nothing. But there did seem to be a cool draft from the back of the apartment.

Behind her, Sterling started to whine and slosh around in the water.

"Blair?" Alexis called.

A hall floorboard creaked in the direction of her bedroom.

"Lover boy's gone," said a voice she knew all too well. She gasped and stepped back against the bathroom door frame. "But don't be sad, 'cause you got me, babe—this time for good."

CHAPTER FIVE

This was a nightmare! Alexis thought. She had to be dreaming. But she knew she wasn't.

Len Dortman's voice was just as she'd remembered. The apartment felt heavy with his presence.

Her first instinct was to scream—to run for the front door, but she'd take too long with the locks. She could try to get to her purse on the table and her cell phone so she could call Blair, call 911. Or turn off the lights so Dortman couldn't see, then run to the front window, break the glass and scream. He must have come in the back. Did he jimmy open a window, one she could use to escape?

Her brain processed all her options in a split second of disbelief and horror. His footsteps came closer. He slammed the bathroom door, evidently to keep Sterling in, and grabbed her arm, then half heaved, half spun her into the living room and onto the couch. She felt her robe split open; she wore only a sleep shirt under it.

She righted herself fast, but he slammed down beside her, pulling her to him. His fist clenched her hair to hold her still, inches from his face; she smelled him and his clothes—sweat, liquor, tobacco.

And then she knew she'd have to find much more courage than she'd ever had in her life. More than she'd needed to face blindness or risk trusting—and loving—Blair. *Blair!* she tried to send him a mental message. *He's back, he's here. Come save me!*

But she knew she'd have to save herself. One of her neighbors was away this weekend, and the other was a hard-of-hearing old lady, so screaming might not work.

She chose not to fight—not yet at least. *Stay! Sit!* She gave herself Sterling's commands and willed herself to be as steady as her dog.

"Long time no see, Alexis," Dortman held her upper arms in a brutal grip. She almost gagged as she inhaled his breath.

Did he know that she was blind? She wasn't sure, but she could think of no way to fool him on that. She braced herself to remember all that she and Blair had discussed about this monster. Don't anger him, she told herself. Don't let him think you're rejecting him.

"You do know I can't see anymore?" Her voice was quavering. She spoke up to make herself sound less afraid. "That night you left me hurt at the bottom of the steps, I lost my sight."

"I read it online from the *Star Ledger.*"

She had to keep him talking.

"You're the one who ran," he said, his voice accusing. "I

only meant to grab you—hold you—at the top of the steps, but you fell down backward. It wasn't my fault."

"I realize that now. I'm not blaming you. Actually, I could hardly recall what happened that night—head injury."

"What happened is that I stopped you on the path and told you how things had to be between us—what a mistake you'd made to get me fired."

"I didn't intend that. It's just that I expect someone who cares for me to give me some space if I ask for it."

"Space!" he roared, shaking her. "You wanted me out of your way, out of your life!"

"No, your—your intensity just scared me, that's all."

"If you want a wimp, you're not the woman I thought. I could tell you wanted me, too, so why did you have to play hard to get?"

"I just wasn't ready for such a commitment then. But now that I've had a lot of time to think things over, I'm not so sure."

"Blindness taught you that—or missing me?"

"It's hard to say. I'm still working it all through, and I just need a little more time from you."

He snorted. "*Away* from me, you mean."

But she was grateful to feel him ease his grip on her arms a bit. She heard Sterling pacing in the bathroom. Guide dogs were bred to calmly, gently accept new people, so what good would it do her to have Sterling in here? Whatever happened to her, she couldn't bear to have that beautiful dog hurt, too.

"The thing I want to know," he said, giving her another little shake, "is that if you agree it wasn't my fault, then why were the cops on my back?"

"Of course it wasn't your fault, especially since you say I just fell. I guess the police have to investigate everything, that's all. I had weeks in the hospital to think things over—and then to be blind and need someone to help me." The words almost burned her mouth to say them. "I remember how much you wanted to be with me… Well, that's one reason I had to get a guide dog. I need someone with me all the time to lead me around. And I realized too late how loyal you were to me, how much you tried to care for me."

"You're lying. I seen Mr. Twinkle Toes dancing with you tonight—and you invited him in."

He'd been watching her and Blair. And if he knew Blair was the one who'd been hunting him…

"How long have you been back in town?" she asked, stalling for time, praying she could reach something to hit him with.

"Long enough to see you necking in the park with that guy, and who knows what else. I mighta been content to just keep watching you and the dog for a while, but what I saw tonight made me realize I got to get you away from him, one way or the other."

BLAIR COULDN'T SLEEP. He kept pacing back and forth from his kitchenette to his front door in the dark. Everything seemed to be going his way, but he still couldn't sleep. His mind was going a mile a minute, and he was on his third peanut-butter-and-jelly sandwich and glass of milk, even though he and Alexis had enjoyed dinner earlier. Talk about women being stress eaters!

He was certain that he wanted to marry Alexis Michaels. Sure, there would be risks and challenges, but that was true of many marriages. Yeah, there would be things they'd never be able to do together because she was visually impaired. It would mean always having a guide dog with them, though he'd rather be in the company of Sterling than many humans he'd known. Rearing kids someday would be a huge challenge for Alexis.

He knew he was rushing things—probably rushing her—but he couldn't help it. Not that he was going to show up on her doorstep tomorrow morning on bended knee, holding out a diamond engagement ring, but he wanted to level with her soon. He wanted to build on the trust they'd started to share. He didn't like or want any surprises when he told her he loved her and wanted to spend his life with her—and Sterling—and live happily ever after.

"So, HAVE YOU moved back to town?" Alexis asked, desperate to keep Dortman talking.

"Can't trust you not to be recording this," he told her with a harsh laugh. "I took a look at some of the electronic equipment you got in here."

"That's only stuff I use for tutoring students. I just wondered if we'd be staying in town or not. This apartment is pretty small, but you can probably find one nearby."

"You think I'm falling for all this—this sudden change-of-heart crap?"

She had to match his fervor, his anger. He could not think her weak, though she hoped he saw her as being compliant—until she could escape or knock him out.

"Look, Len. You don't think I'm the same person I was after going blind—after living in the dark, where I've done a lot of soul-searching, do you?"

He seemed to have no answer to that. But the fact she'd raised her voice evidently upset Sterling. Instead of just pacing, Alexis could hear her scratching at the bathroom door, something a guide dog would never do. Could she have sensed that her partner was in danger?

"It sounds like my dog needs to go outside—you know, just for a second," she said.

"Oh, right." His voice was mocking as he scooted to the edge of the couch and yanked her to stand beside him. "You think I'm gonna fall for that?"

"Guide dogs are not watchdogs or attack dogs, Len. They're bred to be gentle and calm and to obey orders. If you've been watching me, you've seen that. I hope you'll grow to admire Sterling as much as I do."

For the first time, she could sense Dortman waver. She could almost hear his mind working behind those thick glasses he always wore. And if he still wore them, would it even the playing field if she could get them off his face?

"One thing that's changed for me," she said, fighting back the nausea that began to make her feel even more shaky, "is that I see in many different ways now. With my ears, my hands. Can I just touch your face?"

"So you can try to scratch my eyes out? I'm not really buying any of this, not after the things you done, like getting the cops on my tail. And don't try anything funny, 'cause I got a weapon this time."

A gun or a knife? But he'd had both hands on her. If he was telling the truth, could a weapon be stuck in the waistband of his pants or had he put it down somewhere? But so what? Even if she got her hands on it, she had no clue how to use a gun or a knife without being able to see.

"At least let me feed my dog to quiet her down. She'll get louder and louder if I don't, and that will upset my neighbors." She prayed that he really didn't have a gun—or that he'd be afraid to discharge it.

But she still wanted to let Sterling out of the bathroom. At the very least, the dog seemed to have a calming effect on people. At best, Alexis realized that if she could just make her way into the kitchen, she could get her hands on some sort of weapon.

And the electrical breaker box was there.

THOUGH THE LIGHTS were out on her floor and in her cell—the officers always turned them out at ten—Tina sat on the floor next to Corky's bed, petting the dog.

Puppies Behind Bars—People Behind Bars. Only the dogs flourished with the care and love they were given. That's the way it should have been with her kids, Tina thought. She should have been there for them, held them, played with them, raised them up right, not been out at all hours screwing up her life, thinking only of herself. But raising Sterling and Corky showed others and herself that she was capable of more. And despite the mess she'd made of her and her kids' lives, she would cling to that, be proud of that.

Corky was so black that Tina almost couldn't pick her out in the cell, though wan light filtered in through the grate in the door. The dog flopped over, closer, putting her jaw on Tina's knee.

"Sure would like to have you with me for a demo-dog when I start my grooming business in four years, Corky."

How she wished the dog could grasp what she was saying, Tina thought. Sterling and Corky had given her something precious. She wanted to help herself live a better life, and others, too. She'd found hope and purpose working for and with Puppies Behind Bars.

Corky seemed to nod, and put her paw up on Tina's knee as if to say, "That's doggone right."

ALEXIS'S SKIN crawled each time Dortman touched her. Now, with his hands so hard on her wrists, she went numb clear down to her fingertips. He shoved her into the hall and banged her into the closed bathroom door.

"You shut that dog up, or I will."

"If you won't let her out to relieve herself, just let me give her one of her treats to calm her down. She's been trained not to bark."

"Oh, yeah? Give her something then, but I'm right behind you, babe, just like the old days, huh? And either of you gets out of line 'fore I get the treat I came for, you'll be real sorry. I'm gonna open that door now, but that dog so much as growls at me, she's a goner."

He did have a gun. He must have a gun.

"I told you, Len, guide dogs are gentle and kind and accepting of strangers. Just let me take her into the kitchen."

When he loosed her left arm, the blood rushed back into her hand, making it prickle. She felt for the knob and opened the door.

"Good girl, Sterling," she crooned, and stooped as far as Dortman would let her to pat the dog's head. "Everything's all right. Want a treat?"

The Lab, soaking wet, followed Alexis toward the kitchen. Although Dortman let go of her other hand at last, he stayed close to her. Alexis reached in the cupboard for the milk bone, then decided to grab several. She dropped the first one to the floor and heard Sterling devour it. For the first time, she wished the dog were a security dog who would respond to an attack command.

"Can I fix something for you, Len?" she asked, edging past him. "Excuse me, but I just want to get some dog food out of the first cupboard."

"Oh, yeah, bet you'd like to put poison in something for

me. And I don't like the way the dog keeps looking at you and then me."

Yes, Alexis thought, this had to work. Because it was going to be her only chance. If she turned off the lights and tried to grab his glasses, she'd have the upper hand. She knew this place in the dark, and he didn't. If he had a gun, it would take him a minute to get it out. She'd call Sterling and flee—if he fired the gun, the sound might summon someone.

"Would you believe my mother got me some talking cans?" she said, desperate to have him believe she was calm, ready to obey him, when she was prepared to risk her own life to be rid of this man once and for all. Whatever his plans for her, she had to fight back. Having Sterling, trusting Blair—she'd made so many key decisions lately that she suddenly wasn't afraid to make this one.

She hit the button on one of the cans, hoping it would distract him. "Hello, darling," the recording device spoke. "This is applesauce, though you should buy the kind in jars since it tastes much bet—"

Alexis seized the can and heaved it at the spot where she was certain Dortman's face would be. He grunted. Had it hit him? She threw another can, another, then flung herself past him, reaching for the metal cover of the electrical-control box on the wall at the end of the galley kitchen. She slammed it open, yanked down every breaker switch, even as she heard Dortman curse and come after her.

He grabbed her hair and dragged her back. They both

went down to their knees. She had to get away from him before he righted himself.

She reached out with both hands to claw at his face and ripped his glasses off. Then he swung a fist at her, hitting her shoulder, and she did what she had been trying so hard not to.

She screamed.

Sterling growled and bumped into her legs. In the scuffle, she felt, then heard Dortman go down on all fours. Was he scrambling for his glasses, or had Sterling tripped him? Alexis vaulted out of the narrow kitchen, but she heard him cursing behind her.

What if he did have a gun? What if he shot Sterling? Was the dog still in the kitchen?

"Sterling, forward! Heel!" she shouted, but she wasn't sure what a dog out of harness would do.

The moment she felt the Lab beside her, she ran for the door, fumbling with the safety chain with one hand, trying to turn the bolt with the other.

She heard Dortman coming. It sounded as if he was bumping into things. He was going to reach her before she got out.

She threw herself back from the door and heard him crash into it. His eyes would adjust to the light seeping in from the street outside. Even without his glasses, he might see her form against the window.

Despite the fact that it would give her position away, she seized a lamp and threw it at him. It shattered against the door. Trying to keep low so her silhouette wouldn't be outlined by light from the window, she began to heave potted plant after plant at him. Some pots shattered against the wall, others onto the floor, but she was certain more than one hit him. And then she hefted the largest of her plants, the painted stoneware pot, and threw it through the front window, screaming, "Help me. Help me! Help!"

Sterling growled; her big, wet body stuck to her legs like glue. Perhaps the dog was trying to push her back from Dortman. Could he be on the floor?

She knew there could be jagged glass, but she was going through that window!

Yet as she clambered over the couch and got on her knees to lunge toward the opening where cool night air poured in, Sterling placed her solid body against Alexis's knees again, shoving her back onto the couch.

Frenzied, almost hysterical now, Alexis held to the dog's neck, then realized the room had gone silent except for Sterling's panting and her rapid breathing. Had Dortman gone out the back window where he'd come in? Was he hurt but furious, ready to leap on her? Was he just hiding so she'd think he was gone?

Alexis scrambled for the door. The chain was unhooked, so she must have gotten that loose earlier. She turned the safety lock and bolted out into the hall, yelling, "Sterling, heel!"

She heard the dog behind her. From out on the street came male voices, no one she knew.

"Call the police!" she shouted as she made her way outside. "There's a man after me—in my apartment. Tell the police to get Detective Blair Ryan, please—Blair Ryan!"

She heard one of the men make a hurried call as she stumbled down the sidewalk. His voice carried to her as she huddled behind a tree, her arms around Sterling's neck.

"Yeah, 911? There's a woman with her pet dog here and some guy tried to attack her…"

She heard him report the address and ask that they send Detective Blair Ryan. But her Good Samaritan didn't mention that she was blind. All that she'd been through, yet for now, Alexis was just a woman with her dog. A wonderful dog helping her find her way to a wonderful life, she vowed, wiping tears away.

It began to spit rain. Someone draped a raincoat around her. Sterling kept close to her. A car screeched up, and she heard Blair's voice.

"Alexis!" he cried. She heard him run toward her, but she pointed to her apartment.

"I think Dortman's still inside!"

He almost skidded to a stop, then vaulted past her up the steps.

CHAPTER SIX

"Blind Woman Battles Attacker—And Wins." Blair read the newspaper headline to her.

"My mother's paper said, Dog Proves To Be Local Woman's Best Friend."

"Or did they mean *loco* woman?" he teased, and she managed to find his shoulder with her fist.

"At least he lied about being armed," she whispered as if to herself.

She'd just gotten off the phone with her mother. Alexis had urged her not to come right now, and no, she wasn't moving home. Nor was she changing apartments again. For now, this was home and Dortman was going to prison. Her comatose attacker, under police guard, had been hauled off to the hospital with a skull fracture—either from a can of applesauce or a potted plant—and from there would be going straight to jail until his indictment and trial.

Blair had offered his apartment for her and Sterling, since hers was both a crime scene and a war zone. But when she had decided to stay here, he'd boarded up her broken window and helped her sweep up shards and strewn potting soil.

"Don't read me the rest of that article," Alexis told Blair, who was leaning in the doorway to the kitchen as she fixed them a tossed salad. "I'm in too good of a mood right now."

"It does mention that you had help from your canine companion. It's good publicity for how well dogs like Sterling are trained. I hope the inmate who raised her gets to read it. You know—'Prison-reared Dog Helps Send Attacker to Jail.' That's the headline I would have used."

"That's it," Alexis said.

"What's it?"

"Let's inquire if we can take Sterling to visit the woman who raised her to thank her and the program for what they do. Sterling helped me by tripping Dortman and she kept me from throwing myself out a broken window, but the fact she remained calm helped me to stay calm—for a while, at least."

Alexis heard the newspaper crinkle, and Blair's arms came warm and strong around her. She stopped washing the broccoli and turned into the circle of his embrace.

"The prison visit's a great idea," he said. "Let's see if we can get permission—if you'll let me go, too."

"I think Sterling would miss you if you didn't."

"And Sterling's partner?" he said, lowering his head to nuzzle her throat.

"Could always use another partner—a human one who has been as faithful as Sterling. All this has made me see— yes, *see*—how much you mean to me. So, of course—" was all she got out before his mouth silenced hers.

As ALEXIS WALKED deeper into the prison, the clanging doors behind her seemed to reverberate in her soul. She had not realized what the security would be like here, layers of it. But she was not afraid, and not only because Blair walked by her side. It was the utter lack of fear she sensed in Sterling. In a way, Sterling was coming home.

It had been arranged that they would meet with the entire Puppies Behind Bars class of inmates and their dogs, but first they would have some private time with Tina Clawson, the woman who had raised Sterling. Afterward, Alexis would thank the inmates for rearing dogs for the blind, and Blair had permission from his police department to express their appreciation for the EDCs that served as their bomb-sniffing dogs—and in advance for others they hoped to obtain from the same program.

"Tina has a dog, too," Jeannie Lancer, the PBB instructor, was telling them as they waited for Tina in the classroom. "Not only has she helped the dog, but the dog's helped her. Oh, here they are. Alexis Michaels and Blair Ryan, I would like you to meet Tina Clawson."

Alexis felt Sterling quiver. The dog stood steady because there had been no command, but she obviously was moved to see her raiser. Alexis thrust out her hand to shake Tina's and realized Tina was trembling, too. The moment Tina's palm touched hers, Alexis put Sterling's leash in it, then bent to quickly release the dog from her harness.

"It's okay, Sterling," Alexis said.

She heard the dog's toenails on the concrete floor as she stood on her hind legs to reach up toward Tina. She heard Tina's sobs and "Puppy, puppy, my Sterling, I'm so proud of you. And here's Corky—Blair and Alexis, this is my Corky."

Blair, his voice raspy, too, said, "My sister and I had a beautiful black Lab just like Corky when we were growing up—not as well trained though."

"Corky's going to end up as a great bomb sniffer," Tina said, still evidently choking back tears.

"Those dogs are amazing and make a huge contribution," Blair told her.

Jeannie's voice cut in. "Now I'm going to get out of your way so you three can talk. I'll be right over in the corner catching up on some desk work if you need me."

Alexis squatted down since she could tell Tina was still at Sterling's level. "I guess you heard how Sterling helped me fight off an attacker."

"I hear a lot of bad stuff in here," Tina said, "but I don't get how someone can be so screwed up to stalk and try to harm an innocent person."

"It's no excuse for him," Alexis explained, "but he was deserted as a child by his mother and—Tina, are you okay?" she asked when the woman burst into tears.

"Sorry," she said, stifling her sobs. "It's just that my

daughter's been sent to a foster home, and no one wants my boy, and I'm scared he'll think I've deserted him. If only I could find my sister Vanessa, she'd take them both, but I'm afraid I'm just going to lose them."

"You need to locate your sister?" Blair asked. "She's run off or what?"

"She had a sort of falling-out with my mama before she died, and Vanessa just took off. She had a good enough job as a nurse's aide, so she's prob'ly back working in a hospital somewhere around."

"Listen, Tina," Blair told her, "I may not have been able to trace the guy who stalked Alexis, but I'd like to take a shot at finding Vanessa, if you can give me a couple of leads. It would be the least I could do for the contribution PBB has made to this nation's security."

"You mean you could try to trace Vanessa online or something like that?"

Alexis reached out and found Tina's shoulder, then gave it a squeeze. "Blair's a police detective. We just didn't want to mention it right away."

"That's okay," Tina cried. "I feel we're on the same team, now that we're raising puppies for bomb sniffers as well as guide dogs. And I couldn't ever thank you enough if you'd try to help me! So—I have a feeling you two are not just together 'cause you caught that guy Sterling helped you nab. It's more than that, right?"

"A lot more," Blair said.

"That makes me happy, just like seeing how good Sterling's doing. You know," Tina said, her voice calmer now, "I'll just bet you could get Sterling to walk Alexis right down the aisle at a wedding."

EPILOGUE

As far as Alexis knew, their wedding today was a first for the PBB program: Sterling actually walked her down the aisle, even though her mother was on the other side to give her away. Alexis sensed Blair's nervousness and happiness as he squeezed her hand, and her mother took Sterling's harness, leaving them standing at the front of the church to face the minister and a new life together.

During the service, Alexis heard the occasional click of cameras. A friend of Blair's was taking wedding pictures for them, and Tina's two kids both had cameras and promised to take the photos to their mother next week when their aunt Vanessa took them to visit her again. Blair had traced Tina's sister through her career as a nurse's aide and found her not far away, working at a seniors' health center. She'd been more than willing to raise both of Tina's kids until Tina was paroled.

The wedding reception was going to be a great reunion.

The guest list included some of Alexis's students; Andy Curtis, Sterling's guide dog instructor; and even the police officer, a close friend of Blair's, who was going to train Tina's dog, Corky, to be a bomb sniffer.

Wanting to cherish every moment, Alexis inhaled deeply. She smelled Blair's pine-scented aftershave as he bent close to kiss her, the sweet roses in her bouquet—and everyone's joy. She might be blind, but she could clearly see a lovely, blessed future.

Dear Reader,

I am so impressed with Puppies Behind Bars. Not only does the program benefit the visually impaired and provide bomb-sniffing dogs to help keep us all safe, but it gives purpose to prisoners' lives. PBB is also wonderful for the canine companions it trains: the loving care and work ethic poured into dogs' lives is returned tenfold to humans.

PBB is a charity that makes a difference where the rubber meets the road—or, in this case, where the paws meet the pavement. Take a look at the great Web site for Gloria Gilbert Stoga's PBB at www.puppiesbehindbars.com. There you can learn about supporting this outreach through deeds and dollars as it breaks down the barriers of blindness, low self-worth and fear.

And, despite demands on your time, I would encourage

you to get a new "leash" on life by working with charities
in your own neighborhood.
Karen Harper
Columbus, Ohio

Deb Fruend

Team Activities for Special Kids

Few would deny that Deb Fruend is busy. When she's not putting in eight-hour days as an adaptive physical education instructor for the Special School District of Saint Louis County, she's spending evenings on the basketball court, soccer field and even the bowling alley running TASK, or Team Activities for Special Kids.

But ask Deb what drives her to burn the midnight oil and she barely misses a beat.

"The kids," she says simply. "It's the look in kids' eyes when they accomplish something they haven't been able to do before. It's the look in their eyes when they know someone believes in them."

Yet when Deb first launched TASK back in 1996, she was also thinking of the parents. Sitting in on education meetings with parents of special-needs kids, she kept hearing the same refrain. "My child doesn't have anywhere to play a sport," the clearly frustrated parents would say.

Finally Deb decided to do something about it. She formed an instructional T-ball league specifically for special-needs kids who were itching to be athletes like their brothers, sisters and friends.

"When we started we had one little sport. It was just a bunch of kids on a church field. We've come a long way," she says.

That's no exaggeration. Today TASK offers twelve sports to special-needs kids in the Saint Louis area—basketball, bowling, coach pitch softball, dance, floor hockey, golf, soccer, softball, swimming, T-ball, tennis and volleyball. Over two hundred volunteers, from teachers to physical therapists and speech and language pathologists, work with more than eight hundred kids to help them with anything from how to do the butterfly stroke to learning how to play as a team. Each sport focuses on learning and practicing athletic and interpersonal skills, with an emphasis on teamwork and good sportsman-ship.

Sports are often tailored to match the abilities of players. For instance, in modified softball, batters are allowed five strikes instead of three. Swimming classes include one called "terrified of water" for children who have an extreme reaction to water and do not like to swim.

The kids' needs run the gamut from visual impairment to learning disabilities, mental disabilities, Down syndrome, behavioral concerns and autism. No child is ever turned away. With such a wide range of abilities, not to mention ages, it's no wonder Deb has her work cut out for her, matching the right kids with each team. But, says Deb, playing a sport is more about developing self-worth and accepting others than it is about playing to win.

"I wanted to create a league atmosphere so the kids could feel good about themselves," she says. "I wanted them to say, 'My sister has a game this weekend. Well, I've got a game this Saturday, too.'"

Building esteem

TASK is about helping kids feel they belong. Before Deb's work with the organization, parents often complained that their children were struggling out on the field or on the court. Other parents were yelling at the child because he didn't seem to be listening to the coach. The other kids yelled at him because he wasn't running fast enough.

At TASK the motto is: We build self-esteem, self-esteem builds confidence, confidence builds skill.

And that is exactly what seems to happen, says Deb, a firm believer in the benefits gained from team activities, including the development of self-esteem, physical coordination, cooperation skills and other critical life skills.

"If the kids feel good about themselves they're going to try harder. If they try harder they're going to do better," she maintains.

Kids who are part of TASK also build esteem by developing relationship skills. Many become close friends away from the league, sometimes driving an hour to visit each other at home or watch a movie together. These children probably never would have met if it had not been for TASK.

To help these relationships grow, TASK has branched out to create a Kids' Club and Social Club so the children can find new buddies and socialize. Then there's also TASK Summer Camp, a weeklong program offered to kids with special physical and mental concerns. The campers enjoy what other camp kids have always taken for granted: assembling crafts, taking a dip, riding bikes and making new friends.

"It's amazing to me how excited kids can get whenever they've accomplished something and they feel they are part of a team. What does belonging mean to a special needs child?" Deb asks. "Everything. Absolutely everything."

The parents also become good friends while watching their kids score goals or learn to bowl.

Off the field

While TASK athletes certainly learn skills that come in handy while dribbling a ball or passing the puck to their teammate, Deb says many of the more important skills are transferred to everyday life.

One of her favorite stories revolves around a boy who is adamant that he call her "Miss Fruend" while in school and "Deb" during TASK events. One afternoon he ran up to her in the school's hallway. He was beaming.

"Miss Fruend! I just came in from recess and I scored three soccer goals," he said.

"You did?" Deb asked.

"Yes, and I was picked fourth," the boy answered. "Last year they didn't pick me at all."

Then her student turned, looked up to Deb and simply said, "Thanks."

Deb says she's lucky to be a teacher to some of her TASK kids. She can see the benefits of the program spilling out into recess, during phys ed classes and even at home. Some parents claim that since joining TASK, their kids have become more responsible, doing their chores more often because they know they can accomplish a goal if they try. When kids believe in themselves, their confidence blooms and Deb couldn't be happier.

"That's what we stand to do—help these kids be the best that they can be. They get knocked down a lot, but this is a way for them to shine. That's what keeps me going," says Deb.

Not surprisingly, it all comes back to the kids.

For more information visit www.tasksports.org or write to Team Activities for Special Kids, 11139 South Towne Square, Suite D, Saint Louis, MO 63123.

KASEY MICHAELS

Here Come the Heroes

Kasey Michaels

USA Today best-selling author Kasey Michaels is the author
of nearly a hundred books. She has earned three starred
reviews from *Publishers Weekly,* and has been awarded the
RITA Award from Romance Writers of America, the
Romantic Times Career Achievement Award, the Walden-
books and BookRak Awards and several other commenda-
tions for her writing excellence in both contemporary and
historical novels. During her impressive literary career, Kasey
has coped with time travel, ghosts, the dark side, the very
light side and just about everything in between. Kasey resides
in Pennsylvania with her family.

CHAPTER ONE

The fourth house down from the corner and on the east side of Redbud Lane looked very much like the other houses in the small, rural Pennsylvania development, except that maybe the cars in the driveway were a few years older than those of the neighbors, and the trim around the windows could probably use a fresh coat of paint. Otherwise, there were no real outward signs that for the past several years life had been a financial struggle for the Finnegans.

Inside the three-bedroom ranch house, the television set might be older, the couches in the family room more broken than broken-in, the second mortgage a little larger, but the Finnegans didn't care. They'd been in a battle—a rough one and a long one—and they'd come out winners. Charlie was still with them.

Unfortunately, tension was also in residence in the white brick house on Redbud Lane; it had moved in when

Charlie got sick, seemed to like the place, and now was reluctant to leave.

"Charlie, please slow down," Laura Finnegan said as her son shoved another forkful of roast beef into his mouth. The family was sitting around the kitchen table, the afternoon sun streaming in through the large window overlooking a fenced backyard that sported its own home plate and makeshift baseball diamond. "We've still got plenty of time."

"Do I have to go, Mom? I don't understand why I have to go." Nine-year-old Sarah Finnegan, with her father's sandy hair and his stubborn streak, too, had strong opinions on the subject of being dragged along to baseball practice every night for the past two weeks, none of them good. "I'll bet I could stay at Brenda's house. Her mom won't mind. She almost never minds."

"Oh, honey, I know. But not tonight." Laura tried to pretend she wasn't planning to use her own daughter as a buffer if things got too bad—Jake was always careful not to go ballistic around the kids. Then again, she also was less likely to let her emotions control her mouth and, yes, her tears, if she knew the kids were within earshot. After all, in the past couple of years she and Jake had both had a lot of practice in hiding their emotions, their fears, their anger when the terror had threatened to devour them.

To some, they'd survived their ordeal and should just be grateful and move on. But the Finnegan family couldn't do that. Nothing was the same now, and they had changed, too. They could only move on, carrying all the baggage that had been heaped on them, do their best to learn to live with that baggage. Memories. Fears. Uncertainty. And, yes, tension. Always, always that tension that hung around, refusing to leave, that feeling of waiting for the other shoe to drop.

Like tonight. Tonight wasn't going to be pretty. Tonight both she and Jake knew what was coming, even if one didn't want to admit it and the other didn't want to have to watch it. When was enough enough? When did it become too much? And, damn it all anyway, why wouldn't it just, please, *stop?*

"Ah, come on, Mom. *Please?*"

"Sarah, honey, I said no. We're all going to be there tonight to root Charlie on, right?"

"Can't I root now, and stay home and play video games with Brenda?" Sarah pulled a face, looking very much like her father, which was usually a good thing for her. That look tended to wrap Laura around her little finger. But not tonight.

"We're all going, Sarah. For moral support." As she spoke, Laura looked across the dinner table at her husband, trying to signal him with her raised eyebrows: *This isn't going to be good. You know it, I know it. Say something!*

Jake didn't seem to be getting the message or, if he had gotten it, was ignoring it. "You've got second base cold, Charlie, don't sweat it. If not first team, then second. I know the bat's been a bit of a problem, but we'll work on that."

Laura shut her eyes. Why did she always have to be the bad guy? When did Dad and Mom turn into Good Cop, Bad Cop? "Charlie, you do realize that the coach is going to cut at least six players tonight, right? I want you to be prepared…just in case everything doesn't go the way we hope." *Life isn't always fair, my sweet baby boy. Sometimes you win and sometimes you lose. The luck of the draw is just that and, oh yeah, Coach Billig is a card-carrying jerk.* She didn't say any of that as she looked at her earnest fourteen-year-old son. But she thought it.

Charlie lived for baseball. He also lived because he'd had a kidney transplant six months ago. He was healthy now, after years of not being so healthy, but a kidney transplant wasn't a magic bullet. It didn't make everything all right again, turn back the clock so Charlie could start over and be on an equal footing with the world.

He was small because children without kidney function don't grow, and Charlie had a lot of catching up to do. He was fourteen, but he looked ten. He'd begun to grow now, sure, but he was already fourteen, and he was running out of "growing time." Soon Sarah would be taller than her older brother. He was smart, eager, and had more guts than almost anyone else on the planet…but he could not stand toe to toe, physically, with other boys his age, especially other boys his age trying out for the local summer baseball team.

But that was the way the deal worked; teams were divided into age groups. Not ability groups. Not common-sense groups. Age groups. So what if two of the kids already topped six feet and her kid still hadn't hit five feet? So what if Charlie could stand behind the wide-body catcher and disappear?

What had Coach Billig said the first time he saw Charlie?

As if Laura would ever forget: "Second base, huh? Does the kid want to play second base, or *be* it?"

And then he'd laughed at his own joke. The bastard.

No, Laura wasn't holding out much hope that Charlie would make the team.

But not Jake. Not the optimist. He thought it was great that Charlie walked nearly every time he was up at bat during practices because the pitchers couldn't locate his small strike zone. He thought Billig would see the advantage there, put Charlie in when the bases were loaded and assure the team of a run. Jake would take any crumb, cling to any hope, so that his boy could be on the team. Good old Jake, always the cheerleader, the optimist who never saw the blow coming until he was flat on his back with another disappointment.

It was enough to make Laura hide out in the shower so nobody would hear her when she cried. Or cursed. Why could she watch, dry-eyed and resolute, as Charlie was put through painful tests, then fall apart now, when he was healthy again, just because some thoughtless moron decided it would be fun to get a laugh at her son's expense?

The world was upside down...she was upside down...

"Laura, are you going to finish that, or what?" Jake asked, and Laura realized she'd been holding a forkful of salad halfway between her plate and her mouth, probably for a full minute or more.

"Oh, sorry," she said, putting down the fork, her appetite gone. "Just let me rinse the dishes and put them in the dishwasher, and I'll be ready to go. Sarah, finish your broccoli. What time is practice? Six?"

"I'll take care of the dishes, hon." Jake was already on his way to the sink with his plate, pausing only to rub Charlie's mop of dark red curls. "And it's five-thirty, Laura, not six, so we've really got to move. *Women,*" he added in that special husband voice men acquire the moment they say *I do.* "Right, Slugger?"

"Right, Dad," Charlie said, shoveling one last bite of mashed potatoes into his mouth, then following his father to the sink. "I have to be early, maybe get in a little more batting practice before the last tryout. I think you're right, Dad. If I just step up a little in the box, I can..."

Laura tuned them both out and left them to rinse the dishes as she ran upstairs to change her sneakers. Maybe, if she was extremely lucky, she'd trip on the stairs, sprain her ankle and not have to go to the ball field at all. But that would be chickening out, and Charlie never chickened out, so neither could she.

In ten minutes they were in Jake's car, heading for the Harley Memorial Playground, named after a young boy who had lost his battle with leukemia twenty years earlier, a young boy who had loved baseball. *You'd think people would take a hint and remember that,* Laura always thought when she sat on the grassy hill during practice, watching Charlie do his best to impress Coach Billig.

"I don't need this, Mom," Charlie complained once they arrived at the field. He was dancing in place as Laura strapped the homemade protector around his waist and let the Velcro secure it. Charlie's new kidney was in the front of his body, not shielded by his skeletal structure, and a fastball to the gut could be real trouble. Laura tried to be upbeat, but there was a part of her that still wanted Charlie protected at all times…even if he did look as if he was hiding a pillow under his T-shirt.

"Humor me," Laura said, as she always did, then resisted the urge to grab her son close, beg him to duck if he saw a ball coming his way.

Once Charlie had his bat and glove and was running down the grassy slope to the ball field, and Sarah had found a playmate to run up and down the hill with her, Laura turned on Jake. She'd planned to be tactful, but plans like that rarely worked out. Not when they'd been left to simmer too long. "You have to stop building him up for a fall, Jake. Billig doesn't want him. He wants to win. That's all he cares about, winning. Not the kids. Not our kid."

Jake smiled at her, that dumb, melting smile that still had the power to weaken her knees. "I pulled Billig aside and talked to him, Laura, after last night's practice, after you and Sarah left for the mall. I explained to him about Charlie, why he's shorter than the other kids, and maybe not quite as fast. But I told him what Charlie lacks in size, he makes up for in heart, in determination, and he'll get better as the season moves on. Billig understood, he really did."

"Oh, Jake." Laura rolled her eyes. "I don't know who's going to be more disappointed tonight, Charlie, or you."

Jake wasn't smiling now. "Why do you always have to be such a damn pessimist, Laura?"

"I don't know, Jake. Why do you always have to be such a damn optimist? Charlie's different. He's ours, we love him, but he can't compete with other kids his age, not on the ball field. It's just not possible." She lowered her eyes for a moment, and then said what she didn't want to say. "He could get hurt."

"Ah! And now we have it, don't we? Charlie could get hurt. Laura, we can't wrap the kid in cotton wool. We didn't work this hard to get him well and then only allow him to live half a life. It's not fair, damn it!"

Quick tears stung behind Laura's eyes, and she just as quickly blinked them away. "I wish it had never happened, too, Jake. I wish he were still our perfect little boy. But he's not. He's special. That doesn't mean we can't be proud of him."

"I *am* proud of him, Laura. He's my son. I couldn't have done what he did, fight the way he fought. And I'm not going to let him down now, you understand? He's going to play baseball, and if this is the only team in town, *this* is damn well where he's going to play baseball." He shoved his fists into his pants pockets. "I'm going to go get a soda. You want one?"

Laura shook her head and watched as Jake walked away, putting a little space between them, which was probably a good thing. It was all so hard for Jake, and always had been. His own son, and Jake couldn't help him, couldn't stop bad things from happening to him. Laura couldn't either, but at least she was the one who'd stayed with Charlie at the hospital, had performed dialysis on him three times a week. Jake hadn't had that hands-on involvement in his care, so he'd stepped into the role of cheerleader, always doing something to take Charlie's mind off the pain, the problems, the fears.

And all the while screaming silently inside, angry with the world and God and himself, because he couldn't do more to help his son. Jake just wanted them to be a normal family again. He wanted to forget the scary years, and she didn't blame him. But if every family taking care of a chronically ill or disabled child needed an optimist, it probably also needed a pessimist, someone who worried, someone who planned ahead, someone who kept them all grounded.

Or at least that's what she'd read in one of those ridiculous self-help books that are so great in theory but not always so terrific in practice.

She'd read so many books, tried so many things, and couldn't beat out of her head the worst thing she'd read…that the majority of parents who have a seriously ill or impaired child are divorced; the deck is stacked against them.

Laura and Jake had, she believed, pretty much avoided the more obvious pitfalls while Charlie was so sick. They'd been too busy fighting the problem, solving the problem. But now? Now that Charlie was okay? Now they had to learn to live with something that was so much better—so very much better—but was still not the life or the dreams they'd had before Charlie got sick.

And it wasn't easy.

"I figured you really did want one," Jake said, holding out a soda for her, and then bending to kiss her cheek. "Sorry, I was being a jerk."

"I love you, too," Laura said, going up on tiptoe to return his kiss. "And I will think positive on this. I promise."

"No, you won't," Jake teased, ruffling her dark copper curls just as he'd done earlier to Charlie. "You worry better than anyone I know, and you're really good at it. But just ease off this one time, okay? Charlie's going to get some bumps and bruises, but he'll be fine. He'll prove himself."

"Does that mean I have your permission to close my eyes when he comes up to bat and Richie the Giant Killer tries to,—what did you call it last night?—back him up with his curveball?" Laura asked, smiling.

"Permission granted…you wuss." Jake hugged her close against his side. "Uh-oh, here comes Billig, and he's carrying a piece of paper." He dropped his arm to his side. "What the hell? He's going to make the cuts *before* practice? How can he do that? He has to give Charlie another chance to—damn it!"

Laura felt as old as time as she watched Charlie and five other boys walk away from the group gathered around Billig, pick up their bats and gloves from the bench and slowly head back up the hill. *Oh, God.* She hadn't wished this on him, had she? She was heartbroken for Charlie, but was she also relieved that he wouldn't have to compete physically with boys twice his size? Would that make her an unnatural mother?

Charlie reached them, dragging the barrel of his aluminum bat along the ground. He didn't stop, he just kept walking, his steps plodding, his head down. "Let's go. I'm done."

Jake grabbed his son's arm. "Whoa, wait a second, son. What happened? What did he say?"

"Later, Jake, please," Laura pleaded. Charlie wasn't crying. He wouldn't cry, not in front of the other kids, but he was on the brink. The best thing to do would be to get him out of here before the dam broke. "Let's go get some ice cream. Take Charlie to the car. I'll round up Sarah and be right behind you."

Charlie looked up at his mother. "Mom? Coach said I should come back when I grow some more." Then he dropped the bat he was so proud of and the mitt he'd worked a good pocket into with linseed oil every night for the past month, and ran for the parking lot.

"Why, that no good son of a—"

"Jake. Jake—*stop*. It won't change anything if you hit him."

"Oh yeah? It would make me feel a whole hell of a lot better."

"I know," Laura said in sympathy, because she'd like to pop the tactless guy herself. "But that won't help Charlie, will it? Just let it go."

"Let it go. That's your answer for everything, isn't it? You know what, Laura? I'm tired of letting it go. Here," he said, taking the car keys from his pocket and tossing them at her. "Take the kids for ice cream. I'm going to walk home."

Laura couldn't keep her own anger and hurt out of her voice. "And just how does that help Charlie?"

"I don't know, Laura, I honestly don't. But I can't face that kid right now."

"Because he's disappointed? Or because you are? Because you helped set him up for this fall?" She quickly put a hand on his arm. "Oh, Jake, I'm sorry. I didn't mean that…"

"Don't wait up," Jake said, glaring at her for a moment before he turned and walked away.

Laura looked toward the parking lot and could see that Charlie was already in the backseat of the car, watching as his father strode off. So now she'd have to go to Charlie, tell him how sorry she was that he didn't make the team, that maybe next year would be better, even though she knew that wasn't true…and then explain to her son how much his father loved him.

Because that was how it had to be, how she and Jake had learned to operate. They tried their best to present a strong, united front, but when one couldn't do it anymore and fell down, the other had to pick up the ball. They'd been taking turns like this for years. Tonight was her turn to pick up the ball.

She signaled to Sarah to follow her and began the slow walk to the car, hoping her daughter didn't climb into the backseat beside Charlie and say something typically nine-year-old, like, "Hooray! Now I can go play with Brenda!"

Yeah. Life was just one long carnival…

"Excuse me! You forgot these."

Laura stopped and turned around to see a petite, blond woman she'd noticed at a few of the other practices. She was holding up Charlie's bat and glove. "Thank you," Laura said, taking the equipment. "I don't know where my head is tonight."

"If it's anywhere near where mine is, you're plotting to go home and stick pins in a Billig doll. I'm thinking a bad knee first, then on to his gallbladder, maybe a migraine."

Laura smiled at the woman. "Only if I get to stick in the pin that gives him a raging case of hemorrhoids." She tucked Charlie's mitt under her arm and held out her hand. "Hi, I'm Laura Finnegan. You're Bobby's mother, right?"

"When he acknowledges me, yeah, I am. I have this tendency to cheer a little too loud, you understand, and fourteen-year-old boys don't like that." She extended her own hand. "Jayne Ann Maitz. Bobby also got cut, but I'm guessing you know that."

"Oh, I'm sorry, I didn't realize—" Laura stopped, shook her head. "I was so wrapped up in watching Charlie that I didn't even notice who else was cut. How's Bobby taking it?"

Jayne Ann shrugged. "He's used to it. This is his third year in a row. I think Billig figures he's going to give up, not come back, but he doesn't know my Bobby. He's afraid of him, but he doesn't know him."

"Afraid of him? I don't understand."

"Bobby has a seizure disorder," Jayne Ann told her as both mothers proceeded toward the parking lot. Bobby had run ahead, and Laura saw that Charlie had rolled down the window in the backseat and the two boys were talking. "We've got the seizures pretty well under control, but we still have our…well, we still have our moments. Unfortunately, two years ago Billig witnessed one of those moments. Bobby hasn't had a chance since then."

Laura rested the bat on her shoulder as she and Bobby's mother stopped just at the edge of the parking lot. "Did you ever hear the monologue where Bill Cosby goes on and on about the problems with having kids, raising kids, and says he doesn't know what happened—all he and his wife wanted was to have some kids to send to college? And that was years before his only son was murdered. Life doesn't always work out the way we think it's supposed to, does it?"

"No. Not even close. And definitely not the way my ex thought it was supposed to. He took a hike a year after Bobby had his first seizure. Just couldn't take it that his son wasn't perfect, so whatever was wrong with Bobby had to have come from my side of the family. He's got a new wife and three perfect kids now. Maybe, while you're at it, you could give him a dose of hemorrhoids, too? I'd even pay you."

"You saw my husband stomp off, right?" Laura asked, smiling weakly as she came to Jake's defense. "He's not ashamed of Charlie. He just remembered that when we married I promised to love and honor him—possibly even obey him from time to time if I'm in the mood—but did not agree to bail him out of jail after an assault-and-battery charge."

"Well, damn, you should think about putting that in the marriage contract," Jayne Ann said, grinning. "I would have loved to see Billig go down on his skinny, sanctimonious backside. I mean, I don't know what's going to happen in your house tonight, but there's going to be a lot of crying and throwing things and feeling sorry for ourselves going on in ours. And that's just me. Bobby will be worse."

"Yeah, sounds like we'll be running the same program at our house. Look, Jayne Ann, if we can't change what's going to happen, maybe we can at least delay the inevitable. How about we all go for ice cream?"

"Sounds like a plan to me. Ripley's? I'll follow you in my van."

"Okay, good," Laura said, looking back toward the ball field one last time as the kids who'd made the team began their practice session. "Jayne Ann? How about the other kids who were cut? Why did he cut them?"

"Well, let's see. There were six, and we're two of those six. The other four kids? Marvin Bailey couldn't hit a barn door with a cannon. Someday his father is going to figure out that the poor kid plays a mean game of chess, but that's it. As for the other three, two of them are about as good in the field as Marvin is with the bat—which leaves Bruce Lee Pak."

"Bruce Lee was cut? I thought he was fairly good, not that I know much about baseball. Why him?"

"Bruce Lee's just a little slow, God love him. Not a lot, but just enough that his reactions are not always as fast as they should be. Billig could have cut him a little slack—let kids like Charlie and Bobby and Bruce Lee warm the bench and come in when the score is already out of reach, or something. That's all they want, to be part of the team. Marvin Bailey was relieved to be cut, and the other two are only thirteen, and can try again next year. But our kids? Next year they'd have to move up again, to the fifteen- and sixteen-year-old bracket, and we already know that's not going to work. Sorry, I got on my soapbox there for a minute. Why do you ask?"

"Nothing. No reason." Laura hefted the bat a time or two. "But...don't you think a kid should be able to play baseball if a kid wants to play baseball?"

"Well, it is America's pastime," Jayne Ann said. "But America likes winners, remember?"

Laura knew she was close to tears, which she hated, because that meant a loss of control, and she needed to be in control, Charlie needed her to be in control. "Charlie *is* a winner. Your Bobby is a winner. The fact that they're still both *here* makes them winners, damn it! So is Bruce, because he won't stop trying. This is wrong, Jayne Ann, just plain wrong."

"Hey, hand me the petition and I'll sign it. Baseball for all kids! Then what? We work on that world peace thing?"

"I don't know," Laura said, feeling her blood pump through her veins. She was making sense, she knew she was—baseball is for *all* kids. "But there has to be something, doesn't there? Something we can do? I mean, hell, these are our *kids*. We've climbed other mountains for them. They've climbed a lot of mountains. Are we really going to just...just take our bats and mitts and go home?"

"I think I really like you, Laura Finnegan." Jayne Ann flipped a fistful of keys in her palm. "Let's talk about this some more over butter brickle, okay?"

CHAPTER TWO

Once upon a time, Laura and Jake Finnegan refused to go to bed angry. Once upon a time, their arguments didn't go much deeper than who forgot to record a check in the checkbook. But somewhere along the way the arguments stopped, because the problems they'd had back then didn't mean a whole hell of a lot when compared with the possibility of losing their son.

Also along the way, they'd lost the power to communicate on one very important emotional level. Maybe Laura was trying to hide her fears from Jake so as not to worry him; maybe Jake was trying to keep a positive attitude. Or maybe they were both so afraid that if they let themselves go, let themselves feel too much, the resulting explosion would flatten them all.

So when Jake came wandering home just before ten o'clock that night, Laura greeted him from the couch with a quick whisper as she pointed to the television set. "Two minutes left, and I'm still not sure why he killed her."

Jake wearily sank down into the worn-out cushions beside her. "Probably because she forgot she had his keys and locked the front door so he had to come in through the garage, which she did forget to lock. But that's just a wild guess."

"Uh-huh," Laura said, only vaguely listening. Moments later she slapped a hand down hard on his leg. "I *knew* it! She didn't know he was the one—he only *thought* she knew. If he had just let it alone, not killed her, he would have gotten away with the whole thing." She hit the mute button and looked at Jake. "Do you want something to eat? There's still plenty of roast beef. I could make you a cold sandwich?"

"Would you mind?" Jake asked as she handed the remote to him, because she knew she only ever had the thing on loan—remotes were the property of men. Women couldn't be trusted not to turn on some shopping network or, worse, Martha Stewart, and then, next thing the poor guy knew, he was sitting on flowered slipcovers.

Laura got to her feet and smiled down at him. "So you built up an appetite on your walk?" She'd keep it light, because otherwise she'd have to ask him where he'd been for the past three hours.

"I stopped down the street to talk to Gary about the transmission of that old car he bought, and he's set up a TV in his garage, so I stayed to have a friendly beer and watch the game with him. The Phillies won, by the way, and if Gary puts one more dime into that transmission, Julia has threatened to have him committed. And I'm sorry, Laura, sorry I left you to deal with all the fallout. I just…I don't know. I just couldn't take it tonight."

She sat down once more and laid her head on his shoulder. "I know. And Charlie's fine, honest. He cried a little, and I'm afraid his Jim Thome bobblehead doll bit the big one, but he'll be all right."

"His Thome bobblehead? Damn. That thing could be worth something some day." Jake dropped a kiss on the top of her head. "Might have put Charlie through one full day of college. Okay, come on. Let's make the sandwiches together. You're hungry, too, aren't you?"

And so they paved over another bump in the road, all mention of the way Jake had left her at the ball field shelved, supposedly forgotten. But both knew it was just a temporary fix, and the pothole would open up again some other time, and be even bigger, large enough to fall in and trap them both.

"I met someone tonight," Laura said as she watched Jake slice the beef.

Jake grinned at her. "Really? Is he going to sweep you up and take you away from all this? Don't believe him, Laura. Men are animals. We all make the same empty promises, but we're really only trying to get in your pants."

"Funny," Laura said, leaning against the kitchen counter. "And it was a woman…is a woman. Jayne Ann Maitz. Her son is Bobby, one of the kids Billig cut."

The knife hovered over the hunk of rump roast. "He cut Bobby Maitz? That kid's got a good arm. Damn. Why'd he cut him?"

"Epilepsy," Laura said, her jaw tight. "I guess he didn't want to take the chance Bobby might have a seizure on the field. Jayne Ann said he cuts him every year."

Jake finished slathering slices of bread with mayonnaise, nodding his head. "Laura, Gary made a good point tonight. As a lawyer, he says he can understand why kids like Charlie and Bobby can't make the team. You know. Insurance. Liability. Whatever." He handed one sandwich to Laura, waggling his eyebrows at her with pure devilishness. "But he's still willing to toilet-paper Billig's house with me if I'm game."

Laura tried not to laugh. "Really? Tell me, just how many friendly beers did you two boys have?"

"Two each, and they were small bottles. Come on, you want to watch the early news?"

"Not especially, no," Laura said, following him back to the family room. "But I would like to talk to you about something."

"You backed my beautiful seven-year-old four-door into a telephone pole?"

"Jake, be serious," Laura said as she sat down on the couch, bending one leg beneath her and balancing the paper plate in her lap. "You said something just now—about insurance. And what else? Liability? What did you mean?"

He spoke around his first bite of sandwich. "Oh, this is good. I love cold roast beef sandwiches. Why would you want to know that?"

"I don't know. Why not? I'm...I'm interested, that's all.

And it's easier than finding a pagan priestess to put a curse on Billig, I guess."

"There's a story there that I don't want to know, right?" Jake asked, taking a drink straight from the soda can he'd popped in the kitchen. "Okay, this is what Gary told me. The township owns the ball field, and if anyone's hurt, coaches, players, spectators—bam! The township could get hit with a lawsuit. Same for the Summer League, of which Coach Billig has been president for the past two thousand years, give or take a century. So, having a kid like Charlie—and, yeah, a kid like Bobby—on one of the teams just ups the ante for them, I suppose."

"But when we signed up Charlie—and there's thirty-five bucks we'll never see again, I suppose—we had to show proof of health insurance or else he couldn't even go on the field. You're saying that's not enough?"

"Apparently not, at least not according to Gary. Both the league and the township are taking a risk every time those kids are on the field. Add a Charlie or a Bobby to the mix, and I guess it could all get pretty dicey. I still want to take the guy apart, but that's because of what he said to Charlie. I mean, why didn't he just tell him the truth up front? Tell us the truth? Why'd he have to make that crack about going home and growing, then come back and try again?"

"Maybe he didn't want to give the boys a final no vote. Maybe he didn't want to completely dash their hopes." Laura shook her head. "Naw, never mind. It's Billig. If he could say what he said, make jokes at Charlie's expense, then he could have told the truth."

Jake nodded his agreement as he concentrated on his sandwich and Laura weighed the pros and cons of telling him what she and Jayne Ann had discussed over hot-fudge sundaes at Ripley's—butter brickle didn't have enough calories for their "weighty" discussion.

"Um, Jake, honey?"

He pushed back a thick lock of sandy hair and grinned at her. "No, you can't have my body. I'm in training."

"In training for what?" God, how she loved this man. He tried so hard...even if tonight he was trying too hard in his attempt to skate over what had happened at the ball field.

"Olympic pogo-sticking," he said, finishing off his sandwich in one large bite. "Oh, hell, go ahead. Ask your question. I can see you're dying to ask me something. You're wearing that earnest expression I've learned to fear."

Laura adjusted her leg beneath her and leaned closer to her husband. "Are you and Gary saying that Charlie, or Bobby—kids with special circumstances, I guess I'm saying—that they'll never be able to play ball on any township fields? Because of insurance and liability, I mean?"

Jake sat back, frowning. "I don't know. I guess so, but even Gary couldn't be sure. I remember seeing some news stories on towns putting a stop to sports teams because they didn't want to get sued someday. Maybe Gary's wrong. Maybe he was just throwing a possibility out there. You know, trying to make me feel better. Damn, it didn't work." Then he looked at her, and Laura attempted to put an "I'm only asking this in a clinical, objective way" look on her face. "Why did you ask?"

Okay. It was now or never. "Well, because Jayne Ann and I were talking tonight, and we were saying that every kid should be able to play baseball if he or she wants to play baseball and—"

"Bobby can come over here anytime, play in the backyard with us. I hope you told her that."

Laura nodded, biting her lip for a moment. Maybe that was enough for tonight. Maybe she needed to think this thing through, before she dumped it all in Jake's lap, even got his hopes up in time for another fall.

Then again, he *was* listening, wasn't he?

"That's nice," she said. "Of course he can. And Bruce Lee Pak, too, and anyone else who wants to play. But that's not the point. Put aside the possible insurance problem for a minute, and let's just think about the kids. Why shouldn't the kids get to play on a real team, on a real field? Why can't they play on the Harley Field?"

"Because Billig is more interested in filling the trophy case at the recreation hall than letting more kids play the game?" Jake sat up straighter. "What's going on, hon? You've got that gleam in your eyes."

Laura lowered her eyelids. "What gleam? There's no gleam. You didn't see a gleam."

"Oh, brother," Jake said, raking his fingers through his hair. "I should have been good. I should have gone for ice cream with everyone and just come home. Laura—there's nothing we can do. I wish there were, but there isn't."

"And that's it? You have a couple of beers with Gary the Attorney and it's all over? We're not going to fight this?"

"Laura, I don't get it. You should be doing flips here. No more pipe dreams for me—or disappointments for Charlie. You were right, I was wrong. Baseball just isn't in the cards for him, not since he got sick. And you know what? I'm tired of beating my head against stone walls. I'm tired of watching the legs kicked out from under our son. No matter what, Charlie's different now. We're different now, and we've all got the scars to prove it. We just can't beat the system. I get that now—finally, I get it."

She got to her feet. "Oh yeah? Well, you know what? If you can't beat the system, Jake Finnegan, then maybe it's time for a new system. Charlie is going to play baseball. This year. On a real field. I mean it, he will."

Jake also stood up. "Terrific—just as I see reason, you take a lap around the bend. Okay. Fine. Go swirl your cape and perform a miracle. But I have to go upstairs to apologize to Charlie. He's still awake, right?"

Laura rubbed at the back of her neck, where the muscles had gone all tight. "I'm sure he's been waiting up for you. Like I said, he had a rough time for a while, threw his bat and mitt in the garbage, but he's over it now. Oh, and remind him that even though there's no school—some teacher in-service thing—we still have his checkup and blood work at the hospital tomorrow. I want to leave by nine o'clock for the blood work so they have it back by the time we see the doctor."

"Another long day at the zoo, huh?" Jake put his arms around her. "I'm sorry I can't go along, hon. But this is just routine, right?"

Laura snuggled against his chest, wrapped her arms around him. "Just routine. His tests will be fine, everything will be fine. And some fine day we might even be able to think of it that way, without our stomachs being tied in knots until we hear the results."

"I know," Jake said, giving her a squeeze, then gently pushing her away from him as he looked down into her face. "How do you think Charlie feels about it? About the tests, waiting for the results?"

"I never really asked him," Laura said as she picked up the paper plates and handed Jake his empty soda can. "Isn't that strange? I've never asked. He just *does,* doesn't he? But he's got to be tired of it all. He just wants to be fourteen, you know?" She blinked rapidly as tears once more stung behind her eyes. "Oh, damn it, Jake, we do so well, we've *been* doing so well. Why does the world think it has to keep raining on our parade?"

"The world rains on everybody, Laura. We just have to figure out a way to get a bigger umbrella than a lot of other people need, that's all. Look, I'm sure you and Jayne what's-her-face had a great time tonight, trashing Billig and dreaming up some scheme to get the kids onto the team, but—"

"It's Jayne Ann," Laura told him, wiping away her tears, "and we weren't just dreaming. We're going to do it, Jake.

We're going to find a way. You weren't here tonight when Charlie finally had his meltdown, but I was."

She watched as Jake's face seemed to close in on itself, his features shuttered. "So it's my fault? Is that it, Laura? I couldn't take it, so I took a hike, left you to do all the dirty work?"

"No, I...*yes*. Yes, Jake, you did. What was Charlie supposed to think when he saw that, huh? I can tell you what he did think. He thought you were disappointed in him because he didn't make the team. While you were off having your pity party, your son was here thinking he's not good enough for you."

Jake pressed his palms against his head as if he was in real physical pain. "Oh, Christ. That's not—it wasn't like that. I just—what did you tell him?"

Laura shrugged, wishing she hadn't said anything, wishing she'd kept her mouth shut. "I...I told him you were really angry with Coach Billig and needed to take a walk to cool off, which is what grown-ups should do rather than yell or hit or—I told him you love him."

He scrubbed at his eyes. "I shouldn't have taken off like that, and you shouldn't have had to deal with Charlie on your own."

"It's okay, Jake. We pick up the slack for each other all the time. But I know how you can make it up to me. Maybe speak to Gary about ways around this liability thing he talked about."

Jake shook his head. "No, Laura, I can't do that. That's one decision I came to tonight on my walk home. I'm through fighting this. Charlie has his physical limits now, that's just the way it is, and we all have to acknowledge that, face it and move on—all that touchy-feely crap. I never want that kid to think I'm not proud of him, but I'm done helping set him up, giving him hope, when I know in my heart he's just going to get shot down. I'm hurting now, I admit it, but I can't be hurting half as bad as Charlie is. Now I'm going upstairs to talk to him. You haven't told him about this idea of yours, have you?"

She shook her head, unable to speak.

"Good. Don't, please, Laura. Charlie's been slammed to the floor enough, and a couple of hours ago you'd have been the first one to point that out, remember? Now I finally see the light, understand where you were coming from, and you do a one-eighty on me? I don't get it."

Laura tried to smile. "Maybe this pessimist is just coming late to the party?"

"Maybe. Shame this particular party is already over," Jake said, leaning down to kiss her.

Laura watched as her husband left the family room. She couldn't have been more surprised if Jake had set his own hair on fire. Jake, turning into the pessimist? No! That wasn't the division of labor they'd decided on. Sure, they'd never discussed it, but that's how it had shaken out—Jake the cheerleader, Laura the worrier. How dare he try to change the ground rules now?

"Except it's just what he said—*I'm* changing the ground rules, too," she muttered to herself. "Man, talk about lousy timing." She headed back to the family room with another can of soda, hoping Jake would be in bed and asleep by the time she went upstairs, because she was too chicken to see him right now. "Cluck," she said quietly as she collapsed onto the couch and picked up the TV remote. "Cluck, cluck, cluck..."

Oh yeah. Life was just one big carnival....

CHAPTER THREE

By ten o'clock the next morning Laura, Charlie and Sarah were munching junk food in the cafeteria of the local hospital. It was too late for breakfast, too early for lunch, but Charlie hadn't been allowed to eat before his blood was drawn, so they all took what they could find. Laura had a slice of lemon meringue pie that had probably been on the shelf since the Kennedy administration. She'd never had to chew meringue before…

Laura was the proverbial bundle of nerves, which upset her because she liked to think she had gotten beyond that. And she had to stay cool, look relaxed, because the kids took their emotional cues from her, and she couldn't let them know she was nervous.

But waiting for Charlie's blood test results was pretty much like waiting for that last thread to snap and the two-ton safe hanging three stories above your head to fall. Your chances of moving, getting out of the way, were pretty good. But there was always the possibility you'd get your foot caught in a crack in the sidewalk and couldn't jump fast enough or far enough.

She stabbed at the slice of pie one more time and the entire wedge of lemon pulled away from the crust and hung on her fork. She'd always said that the best diet aid would be eating all your meals in a hospital cafeteria.

She wished Jake could have been here with them. He'd be laughing and telling jokes with the kids, making the time pass quickly instead of the way every second, every minute was dragging now. And he was going out of town on business again, leaving her to deal with everything on her own. She'd like to go out of town. Hell, she'd like to go to the supermarket alone. When was their last vacation? Too long ago, if she couldn't even remember it.

"I could have stayed home with Brenda, but she has an orthodontist appointment," Sarah whined, not for the first time.

"I know, honey," Laura said with all the sympathy she could muster as she leaned over and kissed her daughter's curls. "And I would have left you with any number of total strangers if I wasn't afraid they'd bring you back, so let's just make the best of it, okay? We'll be home by two."

"Here, Sarah," Charlie said, handing over his Game Boy. "You can play with this if you promise to do it over there where I don't have to watch. Oh, and don't erase my scores."

"Thanks, Charlie," Sarah said, grabbing the toy before her

brother could change his mind and retreating to an empty table some distance away.

Laura looked at her son, amazed. "I thought you said you'd never let her play with that."

Charlie shrugged. "She was being a pain in the neck so I figured I'd shut her up," he told her with the infinite wisdom of a fourteen-year-old. "Dad says life is full of compromises."

Laura smiled across the table at her son. "Oh, he did, did he? And when was that?"

Charlie slid his arms forward on the tabletop, resting his chin on the worn Formica. He'd learned, over the years, how to make himself comfortable anywhere, especially during long waits in hospitals. "Last night. Compromises and trade-offs, he said. I can't play on a team with kids my own age and I can't play with younger kids who are more my size because those are the rules, so maybe I should think about writing about baseball, being the team statistician or maybe taking photographs of baseball. Whatever."

"But you still want to play?"

"Yeah, well, sure." Charlie made a face. "But it's not going to happen, Mom. I'm not good enough. It's not just the kidney. I'm just not good enough. Not tall enough, not fast enough, not strong enough. It's like Coach said—if I tried to block second base on a double play, I'd be buried alive under the guy sliding into the bag."

"Then nobody should be allowed to slide," Laura said,

sifting through this information and mentally purchasing a baseball rule book online. A rule book and a highlighting pen.

Charlie sat back in the chair, sliding down on the base of his spine, and grinned rather condescendingly at his mother. "Mom, baseball players *slide*. It's part of the game, for crying out loud. I can't ask the other kids not to play the game the way it's supposed to be played."

"No, you can't," Laura agreed, the wheels turning in her head again. "But maybe there's a way for a team to play by different rules, rules that make more sense for the kids…"

With inimitable eloquence, Charlie said, "Huh?"

Laura mentally slapped herself. Jake had warned her not to say anything, not to do anything that got Charlie all excited, just so he could be knocked down again. "Oh, nothing, honey, I was just thinking out loud. Women do that, you know. Hey, there's Duane. You remember him, don't you? Duane Johnson. He was your roommate here for a few days last year."

Charlie swiveled around as Duane and his mother entered the cafeteria. "Oh, yeah, sure. Duane. Wow, he's walking a lot better, isn't he?"

As the boy came closer, Laura could see the braces sticking out from beneath the cuffs of his slacks. "He is. No more crutches. Isn't that wonderful? Why don't you go say hi?"

As Charlie got to his feet, Laura waved to Cherise Johnson, motioning for her to come sit at the table with her.

"Hi," she said as the other woman sat down. "We haven't seen you guys in a while. Duane looks great."

Cherise smiled widely. "He does, doesn't he? This last surgery really has worked a miracle. Charlie looks good."

For a few minutes, the two women caught up on their children's' medical histories, because that was what the mothers of kids like Charlie and Duane did. Sometimes, when things were really bad, that became their only topic of conversation, something that had always scared Laura.

So she did her usual "he's been fine since the transplant, knock wood," then actually did knock wood by tapping the seat of her chair, and Cherise did a little bragging about twelve-year-old Duane's progress with his guitar lessons and his expertise at model plane construction.

"Does Charlie have any hobbies?" Cherise asked.

"If you can count computer games, I guess so," Laura said, smiling. "Oh, and he loves baseball. My husband actually carved out some bases in the backyard. We like to make sure Charlie gets exercise, gets outside in the fresh air, you know?"

"Yeah, I hear you, girl. That's always been the tough part with Duane. You know, that old thing—an object at rest tends to stay at rest? He's starting to put on a few too many pounds, and that has to stop."

Laura spoke before she thought, or before she could think to keep her mouth shut. "Does Duane like baseball?"

Cherise frowned. "Baseball? Duane? I don't know. To tell you the truth, I think he tries to stay away from things that might make him upset because he can't do them very well. When did Charlie start playing?"

"He started on a rubber-ball team back before he got sick, but now he can't seem to make the hardball team. While the other kids were growing bigger and stronger and playing ball, Charlie was stuck attached to a machine three days a week and too sick to do much of anything for most of the rest of them."

"I'm still hearing you. For a lot of years, Duane was either waiting for an operation or recovering from an operation. We've had several minor miracles, but not without a fight. Baseball, you said? Tell me more."

Laura felt the excitement she'd experienced at Riley's with Jayne Ann coming back to her. "Another mom and I started thinking last night—why shouldn't kids who want to play on a team be allowed to play, you know? We could make up our own teams—oh, and our own rules, as my son just pointed out to me. All we need are the kids. And a field. And some coaches." Laura wrinkled her nose. "And some uniform shirts and caps from a sponsor, and some bats and balls and mitts, and—well, we were just brainstorming."

Cherise looked over at her son, and then back at Laura. "Brainstorming, huh? But you're really serious, aren't you? Who all could be on the team? I mean, Duane's two or three years younger than Charlie. Could he be on the team?"

Laura's enthusiasm ratcheted up another notch and she leaned her elbows on the table. She hadn't been this excited, this hopeful, in a long, long time. "Sure, why not? Everyone's welcome. I mean, that's the whole idea, Cherise—getting the kids to play baseball. Giving them a team, making them feel part of a larger whole, allowing them to recognize their abilities and not just dwell on what they can't do. And the moms and dads, too. Getting them together, giving them something hopeful, you know? Something to cheer about. Not like a support group where we all sit around and dwell on what's wrong in our lives and try to comfort each other, but a reason to feel *happy* and *hopeful*. A reason to *cheer*..." She swiped at her stinging eyes. "Sorry, Cherise. It seems I care more about this than I realized."

Cherise grinned. "I thought you were coming over the table for me for a minute there, sweetie. But you know what? I like it. I like it a lot, and I know my husband will like it, too. Bert's always trying to get Duane up and off his butt. Now, tell me again what we need, because I think I can help on one thing at least."

"Really? Because I have to be honest, a friend and I just started talking about this last night. I mean, it's mostly a dream right now."

"If you can't dream, what's left?" Cherise said, spreading her arms, and suddenly Laura did want to "come over the table" and hug the woman. "So, if you can figure out a way to get enough people together to do it, we can loan you a couple of acres Bert's dad owns about five miles out of town. You know, our own field of dreams?"

"A field of dreams," Laura repeated, looking over at the kids in time to see Charlie helping Duane to steady himself on his feet before they headed toward their mothers. Sarah was bringing up the rear, still madly pushing buttons on the Game Boy. "And a team of heroes."

"Right. All we're missing is Kevin Costner, and while I have to tell you that's a damn pity, I think we can manage without him." Cherise hugged her son against her side and planted an embarrassing kiss on his chubby cheek. "Hey, hero, how'd you like to play baseball with Charlie?"

Laura bit her lip and looked at her son. It was too late to back down now, wasn't it? She'd opened her big mouth and stuck her foot right in it.

"You mean in our backyard, Mom?"

"Well, sure, to start," Laura said, trying to keep the excitement out of her voice. "But maybe, if we can get enough kids together to make up a team, we could play on a real field."

"What kind of kids?" Charlie asked, looking at his mother as if she'd suddenly grown another head. "Kids like me, you mean? Kids like Bobby, and Bruce Lee, and Duane here? That kind of kids?"

Oh no. Was Charlie going to reject the idea out of hand? They'd tried so hard to impress on him that he was as normal as the next kid, that his problems were over and he could go on with his life, and now here she was, classing him with kids with different problems from his, but problems that clearly weren't ever going to go completely away.

"A bad idea, Charlie?" she asked him as he sat down beside her.

"Heck no, Mom, it's a great idea. I could play *and* coach, don't you think? I mean, I know the game, right? But we'd need more than one team. You need two teams to play baseball, or else it's just practice. I bet Jacob Cohen would want to play. You remember him, Mom, right? He used to ride the special bus with me when nobody wanted me riding the regular bus that year."

"No, I'm sorry. I don't think I remember Jacob."

"Sure you do, Mom," Sarah piped up. "He's the kid with, like, only one and a half arms. How could you forget that?"

Laura closed her eyes in embarrassment. Children were so unfailingly blunt. "Thank you, Sarah," she said, hoping Cherise didn't think she was raising rude, insensitive children. "I do think I remember Jacob now."

"He'd be fine, Mom," Charlie said. "There was this guy, Jim Abbott, who was a lot like Jacob. He only had one hand, but he pitched in the big leagues for the Angels and the Yankees, even pitched a no-hitter one year. That's *big,* Mom. He only batted twenty-three times because he mostly played in the American League and didn't have to bat, but he got *two* hits. That's better than a lot of pitchers with two hands. Oh, and he got a gold medal in the Olympics. Not that Coach Billig ever would have let Jim Abbott play on one of *his* teams."

"How do you know all of this?" Laura asked. Her son's ability to remember baseball statistics still amazed her.

Especially when he couldn't seem to remember where they kept the clothes hamper.

"Grandpa got me his rookie card for Christmas last year. Hey, Duane, do you collect baseball cards?"

Duane shook his head. "Hockey cards. Me and Dad love the Flyers."

"Dad and I," Cherise said singsong, rolling her eyes. "Duane loves the idea of being on ice skates," she explained to Laura.

"They move so fast, up and down the ice. It looks like they're flying." Duane's huge brown eyes were filled with dreams. "Hey, maybe if we can play baseball in the summer, we can play ice hockey in the winter."

"Oh, Mrs. Finnegan, just look what you have started," Cherise said, laughing. She turned to her son. "One bite of the apple at a time, hotshot, all right? Why don't you and Charlie take my notebook and pen and go over there and write down some names. You know, kids you think might want to play baseball."

"Do we have to have girls on the team?" Duane asked warily.

"Do we have to have boys with braces on their legs on the team?" his mother shot back just as quickly, raising her eyebrows at her son.

Duane rolled his eyes. "Okay, okay. Everybody plays. Even *girls.*"

Laura watched, her chin in her hand, as the three children returned to the table across the room, and then she looked at Cherise. "What have we started here? We don't have a clue what we're doing, but those kids think we do. Plus, my husband is going to *kill* me because he made me promise I wouldn't get Charlie's hopes up about this until and unless I knew we could do it."

"Sweetie, that horse left the barn awhile ago," Cherise said, pulling a second small notebook from her enormous purse, then extracting a second pen and pushing both pen and notebook across the table to Laura. "Now, let's make a list. Oh, and how many kids are on a baseball team? We should know that, right?"

Laura looked at the empty page of the notebook for a few moments, and then sat back, grinning from ear to ear. "Cherise, I haven't the faintest idea how many kids are on a baseball team. There's nine on the field at one time, but there's also a bunch more on the bench. Tell you what. I'll call Jayne Ann Maitz—her son will be on the team—and maybe the three of us can get together tonight and talk about all of this some more. In the meantime, now that he knows what we're planning, I'll raid Charlie's room for a book on baseball. Oh, and I think I'll take a look around on the Internet. Somebody must have had this idea already, right? I mean, we're good, but I doubt we're original. Maybe I can pick up a few pointers for us somewhere. Does that sound like a plan?"

Cherise nodded, reaching into her purse yet again, this time coming out with her computerized planner. Laura got the feeling that if she'd asked for a kitchen sink, Cherise would have promptly pulled one from her purse. "How about after dinner? Seven o'clock? Oh, and where?"

"You like ice cream?"

"Riley's," Cherise said, rubbing her palms together. "I am a glutton for Riley's. What about this Cohen kid?"

"I think Charlie knows where he lives. We'll stop off there on our way home, ask his mom if she wants to join us. Because you know what, Cherise? No men. Not right now at least. They'll go all logical on us and point out all the problems, and I think we're safer going into this like wide-eyed optimists, not worrying about pitfalls because we don't know where to look for them. Plus, I think Jayne Ann is pretty good at baseball—she'll be our expert for now. And you can bring anyone you think of who might want to become eligible for a good mental health plan—because we're nuts, you know, Cherise. Certifiably crazy, if we think we can pull this off."

"I'll have to tell Bert, since it's his dad's land. He'll be fine with it. Bert learned a long time ago that, with me, it's easier to just go with the flow, because that way there's less chance of getting run over. But you don't want to tell your husband yet?"

"I should. I know I should. Jake's a wonderful husband, and a wonderful dad. Please don't think he's an ogre or something. But he's kind of tired of being knocked down, and watching Charlie get knocked down. It's a phase and he'll get over it. I'd just like to come to him with something already accomplished, something positive." She tried to smile. "We've been taking a few hits lately, you know?"

"Yeah, we all know that story, chapter and verse," Cherise said, reaching across the table to squeeze Laura's hand. "We'll get some good news for him, and then you can hit him with the uppercut."

The two women giggled like children, until their own children told them to stop.

IT WASN'T UNTIL she was driving home from Jacob Cohen's house after speaking with his grandmother that Laura realized she'd sailed—positively sailed—through Charlie's appointment with the nephrologist, happily accepting his good lab numbers as something to be expected and then forgetting them because she was in a hurry to get home and think more about the baseball team. When was the last time she'd done that? Never. That was the last time. Lab test days were hell, always had been. The waiting, the worrying. But not today. Not since she and Cherise had put their heads together with Charlie and Duane in the cafeteria and started making plans.

It was only when she saw Jake's car in the driveway that her smile finally left her, because she had just done what he'd warned her not to do, and now she had to tell him.

Did she have to tell him? Cherise thought so, and she was probably right. "Nothing good ever comes from secrets," she had warned, and then grinned. "Besides, girlfriend, it's too late for you to back out. We're already in this up to our necks now that the kids know."

Laura tried bargaining with herself. She could wait to tell Jake until after the meeting tonight, because maybe their dream would come to nothing, and then there'd be nothing to report.

But Charlie would tell him. She couldn't ask Charlie, or Sarah, to keep secrets from their father.

So she'd tell him.

After dinner. No, before dinner. Before Charlie got to him.

"Stop it," she told herself out loud when she realized she was dreading seeing her own husband.

"What, Mom?" Charlie asked from the front passenger seat as he undid his seat belt. "Stop what?"

"Nothing, Charlie. I was just talking to myself. Dad's home. Why don't you go tell him about your great lab results?"

"Yeah," Charlie said, opening the car door. "He'll like that."

"And that's probably just about all he's going to like tonight," Laura mumbled as she struggled with her own seat belt, then walked into the house, her feet dragging, all her enthusiasm gone.

Maybe if she went on the Internet, as she'd discussed with Cherise, she could find something she could use with Jake as a good argument on how to turn this dream into a reality....

CHAPTER FOUR

"Is that it?"

"That's it."

The silence, except for a few snatches of birdsong and the sound of an eighteen-wheeler roaring down the highway to their left, was pretty deafening.

"Wow."

Laura tried to keep her expression neutral, even after Jayne Ann's rather awed *wow*. "Well, it's flat," she said, looking over the weed-choked ground that spread out in front of the three women and Jacob Cohen's father. Jacob's mother had died when Jacob was two. And Laura thought *she* had problems. "I mean, there is that, right?"

"Right! There is that," Jayne Ann said brightly, probably to make up for the less than enthusiastic *wow*. "And it's not as if anyone is going to run off a cliff into a quarry way out here, not with the highway bordering us on two sides and the—what is that over there?"

"The sewage-treatment plant," Laura said quietly. "It could be worse."

"How?" Jayne Ann whispered back. "Granted, I don't see any warning signs about this being a toxic-waste dump, but it's pretty terrible, Laura. It will take us years to get this place ready for a baseball court—diamond—whatever. I'm always getting them mixed up, which drives Bobby crazy."

"Diamond," Laura said as Cherise and Larry Cohen walked deeper into the weeds. "And, for your information, it's home plate, not home *base,* and baseball has umpires, not referees. So much for me thinking you'd be our resident baseball expert. Charlie gave me a crash course this morning, and my head is still reeling. I always went to Charlie's games before he got sick, but I was usually too busy chasing after Sarah to pay much attention to what was going on."

"You're lucky," Jayne Ann said. "Bobby doesn't share much, although, after I told him about our idea, I did notice that his mitt is back on his desk, not on the floor of the closet underneath his dirty clothes. The dirty clothes are still there, unfortunately. We're having a serious mental struggle to see who lasts longer, me, the neatnik—or him, the slob. I think he's winning. One more day, and I know I'm going to gather up his laundry—before the Health Department steps in and his *room* is declared a toxic-waste dump. So, how's Jake?"

Jayne Ann had slid in her question just as Laura was smiling at the battle of the dirty clothes, which sounded very familiar. Charlie's room had been the scene of more than one skirmish over the same problem. Her smile faded slowly. "Good, he's good," she said, nodding her head. "We're good."

"That bad, huh?" Jayne Ann said, wincing. "I guess you were right to keep him out of this for a while. Or am I wrong, and he would have taken one look at this field and said, 'Yippee, perfect, just what we need'?"

Laura sighed, remembering something she'd thought yesterday at the hospital. "I'm turning my own husband into an ogre. And he's not, Jayne Ann. He's just had enough. He doesn't want to see Charlie hurt again."

"Or himself," Jayne Ann said. "It's hard, this acceptance thing. And I think it's harder for men with their sons."

"Jake played baseball in college," Laura told her, sighing yet again. "Second base, just like Charlie. He brought a tiny glove to the hospital with us the day Charlie was born." She raised her hands in a helpless gesture, then let them drop to her sides once more. "He never wanted to live through Charlie, recapture old glory or anything like that. He just wanted Charlie to enjoy what he'd enjoyed, you know? Oh, and he did. Charlie, that is. Jake made up that little field out back, and I'd watch them every night after dinner, as I washed the dishes. Charlie and his daddy. I wanted rosebushes, a real garden, you know? But I wouldn't give back one moment of watching the two of them out there for the most beautiful garden in the world."

She turned away from Jayne Ann, swiped at a tear that had

escaped, then turned back with a smile. "Sorry. Jake was pretty good when I told him last night, he really was."

"But he's not going to have anything to do with this, is he?"

Laura shook her head. "Not yet, no. But he can't seem to really give me a reason, and I didn't push. He just needs some time, Jayne Ann. It's only been six months. He thought when Charlie was better that everything else would be better, too, that everything would just sort of morph back to the way it was before Charlie got sick. I tried to tell him, more than once, that it wouldn't be like that, but he's always been the optimist. Somebody had to be, Charlie needed that. So now it's my turn to be the cheerleader, I guess, and Jake's turn to take a little time off, get his head back in gear. It only seems fair, since he's propped me up plenty over the years. He leaves for Boston tomorrow, on business, and won't be back for a week. That's probably a good thing."

Jayne Ann nodded. "If it keeps him from looking at this field? Yeah, I'd say it's a good thing. Okay, here come Cherise and Larry. Put on your cheerleader uniform, because sounding optimistic right now is going to take pom-poms and high kicks to pull off."

Cherise was busy pulling her electronic notebook and cell phone from her purse as Larry Cohen approached, rubbing his hands together in front of him. Larry was a small man, rather thin, and had a bald spot that actually made him look rather endearing, Laura thought.

"He's cute, isn't he?" Jayne Ann whispered, fluffing her

hair. "I mean, I gave up on Hugh Grant years ago, after he was caught with that hooker."

"Down, girl," Laura said, trying to regain her good humor. "But, yes, he's cute. In a sort of 'take him home and feed him dinner' sort of way."

"Thanks, Laura. I'll have to dig out my lasagna recipe."

Larry had his endearing smile firmly in place as he stopped in front of Laura and Jayne Ann. "Wrong sports analogy, ladies, but I think we're going to have to go back ten and punt. There's just too much work to do here to have a baseball field ready before the first snowfall."

"That's what I was afraid of," Laura said, her shoulders sagging. "And, you know, it's not just the field. Charlie said we need—wait, I've got a list." She dug into her own purse and came out with a folded sheet of pink paper with kittens stamped all over it that she'd commandeered from Sarah.

"You really should get one of these, Laura," Cherise said, holding up her electronic organizer. "Not that the kittens don't look professional, or anything," she added, winking at Jayne Ann.

"Hey, in my house, you get what you find, even if that means ripping off a nine-year-old," Laura said, grinning. Cherise was good for her, she really was. "Okay, here we go. Benches—the team has to sit somewhere. No bleachers, because parents can bring their own blankets and lawn chairs. Bases, home *plate,* some sort of backstop." She looked at Cherise. "You know what that is?"

Cherise nodded. "I have a vague idea. Go on. I'm typing this all into my organizer. What else?"

Larry started counting out items on his fingers. "A line-marking machine to put down the baselines and batting box every game. Bats, mitts, balls. A pitching rubber. Protective gear for the catcher. Shirts and caps, because we don't need actual uniforms if we get everyone matching T-shirts and caps."

"A hot dog, soda and candy stand," Jayne Ann said, then shrugged her shoulders. "Hey, a girl can dream."

"So," Cherise said, closing the organizer, "what we're actually saying here is money. We need money. Who's up for robbing a bank? I'm in for driving the getaway car. I just got a tune-up and a new muffler."

Larry was wearing the rather stunned expression common in men who suddenly realized they were badly outnumbered by females and couldn't begin to understand their language. "We, um, we need a sponsor. Maybe more than one. Probably more than one."

"A sponsor? Oh, wait," Jayne Ann said. "You mean like we used to have for my bowling league? Although I have to tell you, I think the real reason we disbanded is because nobody could face another year of hot-pink shirts with Sam's Exotic Delights stamped on the back."

"You're making that up," Laura said, turning around as she heard a pickup truck pulling onto the edge of the field.

"Oh, come on, Laura, who could make that up?" Jayne Ann placed her hands on her hips. "And, far be it from me to be a wet blanket here, but we have only five kids for this team—these teams. Charlie, Jacob, Duane, Bruce Lee Pak and my Bobby. Until and unless we get a field, get *something,* how are we going to attract more players? Who's that?"

Cherise was waving at the tall man walking toward them. Tall, and fairly close to immense, actually. "That, my friends, is my baby brother. Did I happen to mention that he owns a construction company? You know, a *construction company?* One of those companies that owns bulldozers and backhoes and all those good things? So you can stop worrying about the field. I called him a few minutes ago and he said he'd be right over. He's so obedient, but that's probably because I used to babysit him and he's still afraid of me."

Laura looked at her new friend in amazement. "Cherise Johnson, have I told you lately that I love you? Now," she said, rubbing her palms together, "who else has a friend or relative we can use—that is, ask to volunteer?"

An hour later, after a quick lunch at a fast-food restaurant, the four split up, each with their own assignment except for Jayne Ann, who had just gotten her Realtor's license and had a showing for a customer on the other side of town. Cherise went off to see her sister, who worked for the township (bless the woman, she had eight siblings!), to find out what the chances were that the recreation department had some old baseball equipment lying around that nobody was using anymore. Larry had to go back to work at the bank, but he'd promised to print up some flyers they could deliver to the pediatric departments in all three of the area's hospitals and to several pediatricians' offices.

Once those flyers were out, there'd be no turning back!

And that left Laura the job she hated most but felt she had to tackle since it had been her idea—finding sponsors for the teams. When it came to being a salesperson, she'd always thought of herself as the kind who would knock on a stranger's door, then say, "You don't want to buy a set of encyclopedias, do you?" Jake could sell sand in a desert, but she'd rather eat that sand than try to do the same thing.

But this time she had a mission, and it wasn't calendars for the high-school band, or candy bars for their church group, or even Girl Scout cookies (one of the worst failures of her youth). This time she was raising money for the Heroes. That was the one thing they'd all agreed upon at lunch, the name for their league. The Heroes. Jayne Ann had thought the letters could stand for something and had even come up with Helping Everyone Rise Over…but then they'd all drawn a blank on the ES, so they gave up that idea as a bad job and just stuck with Heroes.

Larry's "Egregious Stuff" hadn't been all that bad, really. And definitely much better than Jayne Ann's pithy suggestion for the S-word.

Laura also had what she believed to be two aces in her pocket—Charlie and Sarah—and she wasn't above using them, either. Charlie was so damn cute with his shock of red hair and his big smile, and if that didn't work, Sarah, who had begged to stay home with Brenda, would wear any prospective donor down with her "my dog just died" expression.

Yes, Laura knew, she was shameless. But it was for a good cause, and that's what she'd keep telling herself.

"So, how much do we need?" Charlie asked as Laura drove along what was known locally as the Golden Strip, home of the two large and four smaller shopping malls in the township. This street had it all—clothing stores, restaurants, automobile dealerships, movie theaters, mattress stores, tanning salons. Laura looked at all the signs, considering which places she could hit up for money. *Hit up.* Yes, she was feeling rather ruthless.

"I don't know," Laura said as she eased up to a red light. "Do you?"

Charlie rolled his eyes. "Mom, I'm fourteen. But a good mitt is over a hundred bucks, easy, and aluminum bats aren't much cheaper, although we'll only need about five or six of those and everyone can share. I've got my own mitt and bat, and so does Bobby, but most of the kids won't, right? And the moms and dads might not be able to afford them, either."

Laura had a quick mental flash of the parking lot at the dialysis center, the one filled with run-down cars. You could pick out the patients' cars by their age and condition. It was the first rule of having a chronically ill or disabled child, or adult, for that matter—go quietly broke, no matter how well cushioned you might have been when the Egregious Stuff first hit the fan. She tapped her fingertips against the steering wheel. "Right. Okay, first stop, a sporting-goods store. We'll price things, and then we'll go asking for money."

Their investigation at the sporting-goods store took another hour and added more items to their "we have to have this" list. Laura was beginning to feel the butterflies back in her stomach when she totaled up the figures in her head and decided they needed over a thousand dollars—and that was if everyone on the team chipped in a sign-up fee, which she didn't want to ask for. She'd been at the bottom of the well herself and knew that even twenty-five or thirty dollars could sometimes seem like a million. The Heroes were supposed to be an opportunity, not yet another problem, so they'd all decided that the fee would be happily accepted but not mandatory.

With Jake leaving in the morning (and her nervousness threatening to get the better of her), Laura decided they'd had enough for one day, so they stopped at the local grocery store for three freshly cut T-bone steaks for dinner—Jake's favorite. After all, once he was off to Boston they could eat more hamburgers and pizza, which the kids liked better anyway.

Laura stood in front of the glassed-in meat counter while Sarah scoped out the homemade cupcakes and Charlie opened a bottle of a sports drink and chugged down half of it. For over two years the amount of fluid he could drink a day was severely restricted, so now he was always drinking something.

"Jerry?" she asked as the butcher loaded three steaks onto

a piece of brown paper and tossed them on the scale. "Have you ever thought about sponsoring a baseball team?"

Then she smiled, because she hadn't realized she was going to ask the question until she heard it coming out of her mouth. And, hey, it hadn't been so bad. All Jerry could do was say no, right?

"Sure," Jerry said, eyeballing the scale. "I already do. You know, the township youth league?"

"Oh," Laura said, her shoulders sagging in spite of her best efforts to keep smiling. "Then you wouldn't want to help sponsor another one, would you?"

You don't want to buy a set of encyclopedias, do you...?

"Sure, why not? For Sarah, right?"

"Uh, no. Not Sarah. Charlie."

Jerry hesitated as he reached for the steaks. "Charlie? But Jake was in here last night, and he said Charlie just got cut. I'm sorry about that, Laura. That really stinks."

"I know." Laura stepped to the end of the meat cooler and Jerry joined her there. "We're putting together a new team, actually. One where anyone can play. We..." Suddenly she was speaking quickly, her enthusiasm overcoming her nervousness. "We're gathering up kids who normally couldn't play on a regular team and giving them the chance to learn about baseball. Teamwork. And anything else good about team sports. Charlie's friend Bobby has a seizure disorder, and Duane Johnson has spina bifida, so he wears leg braces— but he's doing great, he really is. Jacob Cohen—"

"I know Jacob," Jerry said. "He and his grandmother come in here a lot." He leaned a hip against the meat case. "How about Toni D'Amato? Antoinette, I mean. She's ten, I think. Cute kid. She comes in here for sour balls all the time. But deaf, you know?" He shook his head. "No, she couldn't play. What if she had her back turned and the ball was coming at her? Nobody could warn her and she could get hurt."

"Then…then she'd have her mom or dad or somebody else in the field with her to make sure she pays attention. That would work, wouldn't it? We're making up our own rules, Jerry. If Toni wants to play, she plays. That's what the Heroes is all about."

"The Heroes, huh?" Jerry walked back behind the counter and pulled out a long pack of solid American cheese, then sheared off a few slices and laid them on a small square of waxed paper. "Here you go—Sarah likes cheese."

"Thank you, Jerry," Laura said, handing the cheese to Sarah, and then picking up the wrapped steaks.

"Put me down for two hundred, okay? Oh, and let me look up Toni's mom's number in the phone book for you before you go. Name's Lucie. Lucie D'Amato. And I'll ask around, see if anyone else wants to chip in. The Heroes, huh? I like that."

"Yeah, I do, too," Laura said, grinning. "Thanks, Jerry."

"Hey, for Charlie? For Jacob and Toni? How could I say no? You're doing a good thing here, Laura. A good thing."

"WE'RE DOING A GOOD THING, Jake," Laura told her husband five hours later, once Charlie and Sarah had gone to bed and she was watching Jake pack his suitcase.

He stopped halfway to the bed, where Laura was refolding each piece immediately after he tossed it in the suitcase. "I know that, Laura. You mean well. But Gary—"

"I talked to Gary. He says there's a way around all that liability mumbo jumbo, and he's offered to do any legal work, gratis. Besides, we're not going to use a township field. What else is bothering you?"

Jake's jaw tightened. "You talked to Gary? On your own?"

Laura rolled her eyes even as she rolled up a pair of Jake's black socks. "Yes, *on my own*. They do let me out of the Helpless Females Club once in a while, you know. Why shouldn't I have talked to Gary?"

"Because…" Jake let his arms fall to his sides. "I don't know why, sweetheart. Of course you could talk to Gary. But this is all happening pretty fast, don't you think? And Charlie's all charged up, talking about how he wants to help coach the team, and Sarah was on the phone with one of her friends earlier, rounding up a cheerleading squad, for crying out loud. It's just moving too fast. I don't think you and your friends have really thought this thing out."

"It's already the end of May, Jake. If we're going to float a team, we have to move quickly."

"*Field* a team, Laura, not *float* a team," Jake said, grinning over his shoulder at her even while searching in a drawer for his toiletries bag, the one she'd given him when they were newlyweds. He unzipped it and headed into the bathroom, calling back over his shoulder, "Tell me more about this field you found."

Laura punched her palm with her fist. She wasn't going to get away with it, she would have to tell him about the field. "I thought you didn't care," she said as he came back into the bedroom, trying to zip the stuffed bag shut again.

Jake stopped in front of her, his shoulders sagging. "Charlie cares, Laura. You care. Sarah cares, bless her heart. I'm sort of stuck with having to care. Now, tell me about the field."

Maybe she could sell sand in the desert. Or at least she could give it the old college try. "Well, the land belongs to Cherise Johnson's father-in-law, and he's delighted to let us use part of it for the kids. It's about five miles north of town—plenty of room for parking right in the field. When I was out there today the birds were singing and the sun was shining, and I could just close my eyes and imagine how it's all going to look once we do a little work. Just what these kids need, you know? Fresh air, sunshine, exercise. The cama-raderie…"

"Yeah, I get that part. Now maybe you'd like to enlarge on what you mean by a *little work?*"

"Well, you know, Jake. It's a field. But it's flat, and once the weeds are gone there should be no problems. And Cherise's brother is going to use some of his big machin-ery, so that will get rid of the weeds." *And the rocks. And the beer bottles. And the dog poop…at least, let's hope it's dog poop and there aren't any wild animals out there...* "So, can I sign you up?"

"To rake the field? Sure, why not. You've got to get all the stones out of the infield, Laura, and with these kids, the infield and a little bit of outfield is all you're probably going to need. So you don't have to worry about planting grass— just putting down a layer of good rolled clay. And that's expensive, by the way."

Laura mentally added *good rolled clay* to her list. "Where do we get that?"

Jake closed the suitcase and zipped it shut. "I have absolutely no idea, sorry. But, then, it's not my project, is it?"

"You're still angry," Laura said, following him downstairs as he put the suitcase in the foyer, then headed for the kitchen and a bottle of soda from the refrigerator. "You still think we're going to fall flat on our faces and Charlie and the other kids are the ones who will be hurt."

Jake closed the refrigerator door and turned on her, so that she involuntarily stepped back. "Look, Laura, don't make me into the bad guy here. I'm thinking about our son."

"Then *do* that, Jake, think about Charlie. He's over the moon with this idea."

"Idea? More like a pipe dream. I guess we have different names for it. I said I'd help, Laura, and I will, when I get home from Boston. But I'm not going to pretend to be happy about any of this. Charlie isn't going to enjoy himself, and you know why?"

"No, Jake, but why don't you tell me why."

"Oh, *that* tone. Don't patronize me, Laura, because I'm not being unreasonable here. All right, I'll tell you anyway. Charlie's not going to like it because it isn't going to be *real* baseball. It can't be."

"Half a loaf is better than none," Laura said, and then winced at the old saying.

Jake pushed his fingers through his hair. "Half a loaf? Is that what Charlie fought for all these years? Half a loaf? Is that all he gets? All he deserves? It's not fair, Laura. It's just not *fair*."

"We have to accept that, honey. Sooner or later, we have to accept that. Life isn't fair. If it were, kids like Charlie and Bobby and the rest would be just like all the other healthy kids on the planet. And, by the way, our idea isn't all that far out. I was looking around on the Internet, and—"

"Oh, boy, this ought to be good."

"Well, it is, Jake. I found this great site for an organization in Saint Louis. They call themselves TASK—that stands for Team Activities for Special Kids. We tried that with the Heroes, but we couldn't come up with words that fit—well, that's another story. Anyway, this group started about ten years ago, pretty much the way we're starting, with just a little over two dozen kids and a T-ball baseball team. Now, ten years later? Jake, they've got over eight hundred kids involved, and not just in baseball. It's big—a year-round deal."

"And parents started this TASK deal?"

"It wasn't their idea originally, no, but that of a woman who worked with special kids. I talked to her by the way, when I called down there. She was a *huge* help. Parents are a big, big part of everything, along with community volunteers. These kids play tennis, golf, softball. Twelve different sports in all, I think. They have their own social club and hold three dances a year."

"And you think that's what you're going to do here?"

"Of course not! Well, not at first. But others have done it for their kids. Why shouldn't we try it for our kids? Face it, honey, if anyone can find a way to make this work around all the possible pitfalls, it's parents like us, who've had to learn how to fight for their kids."

"Golf, huh? I've been thinking about golf for Charlie. He wouldn't have to make a team, you know? It would be just Charlie against the golf course, with nobody saying he's too small." He shook his head. "I don't know, Laura. You're biting off an awful lot, don't you think? We've barely got our own lives back on track without trying to fix the world."

"Just our part of it, Jake. I think we need to fix just our small part of it—you and me and our kids. I hate to say this as much as I know you hate to hear it, but we've been handed some lemons. Maybe it's time to make some lemonade. We can't get back what we lost, Jake, that's impossible. But we can't stay like this, either, in this limbo we're living in now. We have to accept that we can't get our old lives back just because Charlie finally has his new kidney. We have to find a way to move on, and this idea might just be what we need. Please, Jake."

Laura reached out a hand to him but he waved her away, heading into the family room. "I need to think about this some more. I don't know that I'm ready to give up yet,

Laura, throw in the towel on what we had, what we thought we were fighting so hard to get back. I…I'm going to try to catch the travel forecast on cable, then watch the sports report for the line scores. Don't wait up."

Laura threw up her hands, both literally and figuratively, and went back upstairs, because a long bubble bath was the most polite way she could think of to keep a closed door between herself and her husband. "*Another* closed door," she muttered. "We've already got one."

CHAPTER FIVE

"Mom?"

Laura had been staring out the kitchen window at nothing in particular, her chin in her hand. Jake had been up and gone before the alarm went off at six, but he'd left her a note on his pillow: *Kissed you goodbye, Sleeping Beauty. I'm sorry—again—and I love you.* So she guessed they were all right, which was what most marriages were most of the time—all right, or not all right.

Without looking around, she said, "Yes, Charlie? What's up? Your math homework is on the dining-room table."

"Yeah, I've got it, Mom, thanks," Charlie said, slipping into a chair on the other side of the table. "I've been thinking about something we should do."

Laura sat back against the chair and gave an exaggerated sigh. "That's usually dangerous. How much will it cost?"

"Not a lot," Charlie said, his expression serious. "But that's not why we should do this."

Laura watched as Sarah reached into the pantry closet and came out with an icing-covered cherry toaster tart. "Ahem, *madam,*" she said, and smiled as Sarah returned the box to the shelf in exchange for a box of cereal. "You're learning," she told her daughter. Laura got up and headed to the refrigerator for a carton of milk. "Why we should do what, Charlie?"

"Not play hardball."

The milk carton almost hit the floor, but Laura recovered in time. "What? You don't want to play?"

"Relax, Mom, I said hardball, not baseball." Charlie opened his social studies textbook and pulled out a sheet of paper, which he laid on the tabletop. "I've been thinking about this. Aluminum bats, regulation balls? I don't think the Heroes are going to be up to that. I think we need to play rubber ball, like I used to play. And maybe even use Ts for some of the kids. You know, like I did when I was a kid?"

Laura closed her eyes against the pain. *When he was a kid. Before the kidney disease. Before he had to grow up years before his time. God bless the boy.*

"I remember, Charlie. That tall black rubber stand, or whatever it was, with the baseball perched on top so you could hit it. But…aren't you a little beyond that?"

"Well, yeah," he said, taking the cereal box Sarah had just put down and pouring a liberal amount into the bowl in front of him. He still ate his cereal dry because he hadn't been allowed enough liquid to have milk on it. Now he liked it dry. "But I'm not going to play much, you know. If it's all right with everybody, I'm going to coach."

His words skittered through Laura's brain and she pretty much had to totter back to her chair and sit down. "Coach," she repeated. "Not play? I know you said that, but I didn't really think—Charlie, you love baseball."

"I still love baseball, Mom, but what I like best is being on a team. Practicing. I can still do that. I'm not good enough for the township team, but I'm probably a little too good for the Heroes. What Dad said the other night? He was right. You don't have to play baseball on a team to be a part of the game. I think I'll be a pretty decent coach, too." He grinned. "All I have to do is remember not to do anything Coach Billig does."

Laura rested her chin on her hand once more as she grinned back at her son. "I love you to pieces, Charlie Finnegan."

"Oh, gross!" Sarah said, picking up her empty cereal bowl and heading for the sink. "I can still be a cheerleader, can't I? Brenda says we can get matching outfits and her mom will buy us pom-poms when you choose the team colors."

"How about red and blue, like my favorite superhero?" Charlie suggested, peeking up at the wall clock. "Come on, Sarah, or we'll miss the bus."

"Okay," his younger sister said, grabbing her lunch bucket from the counter. "Oh, Mom? Do we have any Popsicle sticks anywhere? I have a diorama of an African hut to do for geography class."

Laura narrowed her eyes, remembering a scene very much like this a few years ago, except that Charlie had waited until the night before the project was due to tell her about it. She'd ended up using toothpicks for the hut and nearly a full jar of oregano for the landscape around it. Charlie had only gotten a C+, but his project had smelled good. "Due when, little girl?" she asked, dreading the answer.

"Tomorrow," Sarah said, already halfway out the door so that her mother's groan barely reached her.

The phone rang just as Laura had her hand deep in the freezer in search of Popsicles, then decided it would be better to make a run to the local hobby store than to have the three of them go on a marathon Popsicle-eating binge.

"Hello?"

"Back at you. I'll be by to pick you up in twenty minutes. No, make that a half hour. I still have to walk the dog, and he's looking faintly constipated."

"Jayne Ann?"

"Who else do you know who'd admit to a constipated beagle? Cherise just called, and we're all meeting for breakfast at that little place at the other end of the strip mall from Riley's. She says Larry has all kinds of good news for us. I knew I liked that man."

Laura looked down at her pajamas, which consisted of a pair of pink, pull-on knit shorts and one of Jake's old navy blue Penn State T-shirts. "How about I meet you there?"

When Laura found the others at a large round table at

the back of the small restaurant, the first thing she noticed was that there were three people she hadn't met yet.

Larry Cohen did the honors. "Laura, I'd like to introduce you to my boss, Harry Walters, who is going to hand over a check for five hundred dollars as well as help us to set up a free checking account and anything else we need. And this is my son's pediatrician, John Ryan, who's agreed to act as official team doctor. His son Johnny hopes to play with the Heroes. And last but certainly not least is Arthur Brightstone, who has generously offered to provide us with all the hats and shirts and whatever other gear we need. Gentlemen, genius and founder of the Heroes—Laura Finnegan."

Laura looked at her friends, who were grinning from ear to ear, and then numbly held out her hand to each of the three men.

She simply let the conversation wash over her for a few minutes. She thought it was nice of Larry to call her the founder of the Heroes, but everything would still be just one big daydream, wishful thinking, if it weren't for Jayne Ann, and Cherise, and Larry, and… "Volunteers!"

"What, Laura?" Jayne Ann asked around a bite of toast.

"Oh, I'm sorry. I said, 'Volunteers.' We're going to need a bunch of them." She smiled at Harry Walters. "Please forgive me. I have this tendency to think out loud, and usually at inappropriate times."

"Geniuses do that, Mrs. Finnegan," he told her. "You know, Larry here was rather vague—not that I wasn't immediately intrigued and knew the Heroes is something the bank very much wants to be involved in. Perhaps you'd like to tell me more about the program?"

The program. Well, that was terrifyingly formal, wasn't it? It seemed that the moaning about the lack of a team for Charlie and Bobby to play on had turned into a program. A program with a team physician and free checking, no less.

Laura didn't know if it was her lost expression that brought Cherise to the rescue, but she was soon sipping her coffee and making polite comments while her friend talked about the "field of dreams" that was even now taking shape five miles out of town.

By the time the check came and Mr. Brightstone graciously picked it up, no one could have been faulted for thinking the Heroes was all but a done deal, with their first practice only days away.

Once the men, including Larry Cohen, had gone, the women pulled their chairs closer together and looked at each other. Just looked at each other.

And then Jayne Ann began to giggle, rapidly joined by Cherise and Laura, until all of them were in gales of laughter. Their waitress, a woman who looked as if she'd been born harried, plunked down a fresh coffeepot and commented that she wouldn't mind a sip of whatever "hard stuff" they were slipping into their cups.

"It's not that funny!" Jayne Ann gasped as she held on to Laura and tried to catch her breath.

"Yes, it is," Cherise told her sternly, then laughed and snorted at the same time…and set all three of them off again.

"We're really doing this," Laura said. "We may not know *what* we're doing, but we're definitely doing it." She wiped her streaming eyes. "God, I haven't laughed this hard in...I don't even remember, to tell you the truth."

"Well, maybe we all needed a good laugh," Cherise said, pulling out her electronic organizer yet again. "Beats crying all to hell, girlfriends, doesn't it?"

CHAPTER SIX

Laura dug into her shorts pocket for her cell phone, then collapsed onto her backside in the dirt, hoping whoever was calling wanted to recite the entirety of the Declaration of Independence in her ear, because then she'd have a good excuse to rest for at least ten minutes.

She had muscles today she hadn't known she owned three days ago, and all of them ached. She'd broken three fingernails and finally given in and cut the rest of them down last night after soaking in the bathtub until both her fingers and toes were pruney. She had a bandage on her left knee, a blister at the base of her right thumb, and she was pretty sure that she'd be tasting dirt in her mouth whenever she chewed for at least the next year.

"Hello—*ouch,*" she said into the phone, reaching beneath herself to pull out a fairly sharp rock and toss it into the basket beside her. "Hello?"

"Laura, honey?"

She covered her other ear with her hand because several eighteen-wheelers were passing by on the highway. "Jake? Is that you?"

"You keep a list of men who call you *Laura, honey?*" she heard him ask, and she smiled in the general direction of the entire world.

"I do, I do. But it's a short list, with only one name on it. Where are you?"

"Back in Boston after a four-day tour of the suburbs. But that's the thing, honey. I'm going to have to stay a couple of extra days."

"What's a couple of extra days? You won't be home until Sunday?"

"Try next Wednesday. But there's a good chance we'll see a nice bonus out of this, so I said yes to the plan—think how happy all our creditors will be. I found a Laundromat a few blocks from the hotel, and I'm going to head there now, so you don't have to worry that I'll get hit by a truck and the doctors and nurses will find me in dirty underwear."

"Ha-ha," Laura said, wincing at Jake's joke. "Not until next Wednesday?" she asked, trying to keep a Sarah-whine out of her voice. "But the Heroes start practice on Monday night. Their first *game* is that Saturday."

"I know, and I want to be there. I *will* be there, Laura, I promise. What's that noise in the background? Where are you?"

"I'm at the ball field," Laura said, looking around at the bald, scraped earth that stretched out around her. "I think I'm pretty close to third base, as a matter of fact. It's really coming along, Jake. There are only three parents who haven't been able to volunteer, and that's because they've got new babies at home, or they already work three jobs. But everyone else has been out here as much as possible. We've got twenty-six kids now—can you believe that? All it took was those flyers, and the phones started ringing off the hook. Maybe next year we'll—"

"I miss you, Laura."

She sighed, her muscles relaxing as she crossed her legs and put her other hand on the small phone—physically drawing herself away from the noise and dust of the ball field and into that small, cozy cocoon that was Jake and Laura's World. "I miss you, too, sweetheart. Are you eating enough? Sleeping enough?"

"I'm on an expense account in a four-star hotel, and I feel guilty as hell about that lobster I enjoyed last night while you guys were probably eating macaroni and cheese, but I'll get over it."

"Hot dogs and hamburgers."

"What? Hon, you'll have to talk louder. You've got a lot of noise around you."

"I said, we had hot dogs and hamburgers—and lots of other great picnic food. Sharon Baxter, one of the moms, had us all over to her backyard for dinner after we got done here. I wish you could have been there, Jake, to meet some of the other parents, some of the other kids. Did I tell you we've got twenty-six kids now?"

She could hear Jake's frustrated sigh all the way from Boston even as she winced, realizing her mistake. God, she was nervous. Nervous, speaking to her own husband! "Yes, Laura, you already told me. You have quite the social life all of a sudden, don't you? I thought you didn't like being around other mothers of sick kids. I thought all the depressing *sick talk* upset you."

Laura stood up, began walking into the outfield, away from anyone who might overhear her. "But, Jake, this isn't sick talk. This is something *positive* we're all doing for our kids. Nobody's having a pity party here. We're having fun! The kids are having fun. We're climbing mountains, Jake. And if those mountains are things like making sure the baselines are wide enough for a wheelchair or walker, or making up flash cards so that Johnny Ryan can, hopefully, memorize the bases and where to run to first after he hits the ball—well, we're climbing them. One by one. Even Kenny Baxter is going to play, and that's fantastic."

Jake's voice sounded more resigned now than angry as he asked, "What's so special about Kenny Baxter?"

"He's blind, that's what's so special about him."

"Blind? You're kidding, right? What the hell position do you have him playing?"

Laura took the phone from her ear and looked at it for a moment—glared at it—before putting it to her ear once more. "That should be obvious, Jake... he *pitches,*" she all but growled.

And then she snapped the phone shut and waited to see if it would ring again, which it did, five seconds later.

"What?"

"You hung up on me."

"I know that."

"And you should have yelled at me more before you hung up on me. You should have called me a few choice names, too."

Laura smiled as she gripped the phone, one of Sarah's expressions coming to mind. "All right. You're a dumb bunny. Oh, and your mother wears combat boots, whatever that means."

"I never did figure that one out, either," Jake said, and even though the connection was good, he had never sounded so far away, or quite so tired. "Oh, cripes, hon, I'm sorry. I just wanted Charlie away from all that. I wanted him to get his transplant and get back into *life*. I thought we both wanted that, Laura—that we all just wanted to be normal again. I mean, I *heard* you the other night, and I think I understand. Hell, I know I understand. I just have to get from understanding to *accepting*. And it isn't easy, Laura. It just isn't."

Laura looked back toward home plate to see Charlie standing behind young Toni D'Amato, positioning her hands on a bat and helping her swing at the ball on the rubber T. He'd been working with the girl for over an hour, his expression one of almost angelic patience. "Charlie's doing what he wants to do. If you were here, you'd see that."

"I'm trying, Laura. I'm really trying. But this is all happening so fast."

"It's all right—we'll all be all right," Laura said, heading into the outfield once more. "And I'm as guilty as you are. We spent so much time in the hospital, watched so many kids suffer, so many kids die—there were times I thought we'd never recognize normal again when we saw it. I agree, we need to remember what normal life is, what it's like to just be two people trying to raise our kids. But there's a *need* here, Jake. I didn't really see it, I just wanted Charlie to play ball because he wanted to play ball. But Charlie saw the need, and he's really happy. Please be happy for him."

There was another long pause before Jake said, "What would I do without you? I want to be home with you. I want to hold you, just hold on to you."

Laura blinked back tears. For a woman who had willed herself not to cry for more than two years, she certainly was making up for lost time lately. "I want to hold you, too. We're going to be all right, Jake. It's only been six months since the transplant. We're still learning how to live again, that's all. And I think Charlie's showing us how."

CHAPTER SEVEN

Clay was a great thing. And it was even greater when it came free, courtesy of three separate landscaping companies in the area. Clay wasn't full of sharp stones that could prove to be a problem for the kids. Clay looked really terrific when neat white chalk lines were drawn on its reddish surface. Clay, in short, made Hero Field appear, if not professional, then at least pretty damn good.

Clay did not, however, look good on people, clothing or bathtubs, all of which Laura and the other volunteers found out as thirty extremely filthy adults and several children, armed with rakes, spread, rolled and variously stamped down the clay over the course of three long, hot, sweaty days.

But the worst was over, another mountain had been climbed—and if anyone knew how to climb or even move mountains, it was the parents of very special kids—and now it was time to play ball.

"I think I'm developing some definition in my biceps," Jayne Ann said, flexing her muscle in Laura's face as the two of them loaded canvas bags full of used baseball equipment into the back of Jayne Ann's van. Cherise's sister who worked at the township had come through with bats, mitts and even a dozen batting helmets. "Larry says he can already feel the difference."

"Larry does, does he?" Laura teased, grinning. "And how was the lasagna last night? And no, that's not a euphemism for anything else."

"Bobby was home, and Larry brought Jacob with him," Jayne Ann said, slamming the van door. "Believe me, it was strictly a G-rated evening. We're doing it again tomorrow night, after our first real game. So, do you think Sarah would want to be a flower girl or a junior bridesmaid? I'm open to either."

The two women slid onto the cracked-leather front seat and Laura shook her head at her friend. "One plate of lasagna, and you're hearing wedding bells?"

Jayne Ann turned the key in the ignition and Laura winced as the gears made a grinding sound before the engine reluctantly came to life. Jayne Ann had told Laura that her ex had a BMW and his new wife had a minivan that did everything except steer itself, but that was all right, because "Old Bessie still has a couple thousand miles left in her."

Jayne Ann winked at her. "Never underestimate the power of my lasagna, Mrs. Finnegan. Besides, Larry's lonely, Laura.

I'm lonely. His mom is getting older and is making noises about moving to Florida to live with her sister. Shared loads are easier to carry. He can't be put off about Bobby's problems and I can't moan about Jacob's problems. We understand problems, and we know how to deal with them. Besides," she said, grinning rather lasciviously, "he's hot."

"He's short, skinny, and when he gives up on those few long strands he combs over the top of his head, he's going to be bald. Cute maybe, but not hot."

"Eye of the beholder, Laura, eye of the beholder. And relax, I didn't mean it about the flower-girl thing. We're friends, Larry and me, that's all. If there's one thing I've learned, it's not to immediately fall for the first guy I think is cute—I mean, look what I ended up with the first time. Where to now?"

"Home, please," Laura told her, quickly buckling her seat belt as Jayne Ann threw the van in Reverse and all but did a wheelie out of the township parking lot…and directly past the police station. "Jake will be home in about an hour and I want to have dinner ready for him before I leave again to pick up Charlie at the field."

"Jake won't come along?"

Laura shrugged. "I don't know. I don't want to push him."

"Have you considered simply bopping him over the head with a heavy object?"

"Funny. He's promised to come to our first game tomorrow, and maybe that's when he should see the Heroes for the first time. You know, with their shirts and caps and everything. Hey, do you think Toni D'Amato is going to be there? She really took a hit yesterday when Johnny Ryan ran over her."

"Yeah. Poor kid. We forgot she couldn't hear us yelling *get out of the way*—she was too busy watching Sarah and Brenda practice their cheers. And Johnny was so happy to get a chance to show he knows where third base is that he plowed right through our shortstop. Lucie sure picked a heck of a time to visit the Porta Potti, didn't she? But Toni's fine, I'm sure she is. She was laughing when she got up, wasn't she?"

"We need another rule." Laura had said that a lot lately as their dream rapidly evolved into a reality. Only two weeks ago, Hero Field had been nothing but a dream. "One volunteer on the field at all times for each two players on the field, not three players. How does that sound?"

"Crowded," Jayne Ann said with a grin. "Relax, Laura. They're kids. They bounce." She pulled up in front of the Finnegan household. "Uh-oh, look who beat you home."

"Jake," Laura said, struggling with the door handle of the van. "Not until eight o'clock, right?"

"Right. Now go—and wipe that goofy smile off your face. Some of us are still at the lasagna stage."

Laura ran into the house, stopping in the foyer to call Jake's name, then racing upstairs when she heard his voice. She trotted into the bedroom and barreled into Jake's open arms with at least as much happy abandon as Johnny Ryan had shown rounding second, and the two of them fell back onto the bed.

"I've got to go away more often," Jake said into her hair as he held her close after they'd kissed. He ran his palms up and down her back. "Have you lost a little weight?"

"You try pushing fifty wheelbarrows full of clay, Jake Finnegan. I may even be developing biceps," she added, stealing a line from Jayne Ann. "Are you impressed?"

"That's one thing I am," he teased, cupping her bottom with both hands. "Where are the kids?"

Laura propped herself up on her elbows and grinned down at her husband. "Charlie stayed at the field—I'm picking him up at eight o'clock—and Sarah is at a sleepover at Brenda's, so we're alone. Why? Did you have something particular in mind?"

"I'll assume that was a rhetorical question," Jake said, rolling her over onto her back as she laughed and held on tight.

NINETY MINUTES LATER, freshly showered and munching on the last of the cold chicken sandwiches Laura had thrown together in lieu of the supper she'd planned, they were on their way to Hero Field, and Laura's nervousness was back.

"It's not perfect," she told him as he drove along what, to her, had become very familiar country roads. "The backstop is in pretty bad shape, and Cherise's brother still has to level more weeds for a parking area. Oh, and Miranda Gilbert's father still hasn't quite mastered the line-marking machine, so the third-base line is a little crooked today."

"Miranda? Which one is she?"

"She plays right field for Heroes Two. Oh, you mean

what's her problem? We really don't think about that much, except when we're planning how to help the kids play better, but Miranda has cerebral palsy. Duane says he's jealous because she only has a brace on one leg, so Cherise told him she could arrange for a brace on his *head*. You're going to love Cherise. To her, kids are kids, and she doesn't tiptoe around their problems, not one bit. Everyone adores her."

"Just one big happy family, huh?"

Laura snuggled deeper into the leather seat of Jake's sedan. "Yes, we are. John Ryan—the pediatrician, remember? Anyway, John got serious the other night and talked about what we're doing. How we're building confidence and self-esteem, instilling sportsmanship, improving social skills, teaching the kids how to work together, cooperate with each other the way you have to do in team sports. He talked about helping to increase their physical coordination, showing them how to interact with their peers—all those really good things."

"And?" Jake asked, turning onto the road that led to the ball field.

"And Cherise told him, heck, don't scare us with all this technical talk—we just thought we were showing the kids a good time."

"You're right, I'm going to like Cherise. The last thing those kids need is to be told this is *good* for them. Keep the technical jargon out of it, and play ball."

"I knew you'd be okay with this."

"It took me awhile, and I'm sorry for that. But yeah, I finally get it. What's in the bag?"

Laura reached down to pick up the plastic bag she'd brought with her at the last moment, and pulled out a blue shirt with white lettering on the back.

Jake nearly ran the car into a ditch. "Brightstone's Funeral Home?"

"These are for Heroes Two. Heroes One wears red. Look." She shoved the shirt back into the bag and pulled out a red baseball cap with the same logo sewn on the front and stuck it on her head. "Mr. Brightstone's our main sponsor. Bless him, his grandson died last year. Brain tumor. He told us Stevie loved baseball."

"Poor guy, and that's a damn nice gesture. But, Laura, don't you see anything a little strange about plastering the name of a funeral home on shirts for these particular kids?"

"We talked about that, but when Charlie and Bobby told us they thought it was sort of funny, we realized we were overreacting. Kind of. Sort of." Laura smiled. "I guess it is sort of funny, if you just don't think about it too hard. There's the field—on your left."

There were at least twenty other cars pulled into the mowed weeds, and Laura saw that Jayne Ann and Cherise had made it there ahead of her. With her hand on the door handle, Laura turned to Jake. "Now remember. This is not your ordinary baseball team. Some of them hit from the T-stand, some of them swing on their own. One of the volunteers pitches, not one of the kids, because that's sort of difficult for a lot of them, although Jayne Ann's Bobby pitches for Heroes One. Patty Gerbach runs the bases in her wheelchair, and that takes awhile because she has to blow in a straw to get the thing to move—it's a pretty neat chair, actually—so she gets more time to reach first base. Oh, and Nick O'Brien still uses his walker, but his hip replacement was only last month, so he's really coming along, and—"

"Laura, honey, stop trying to convince me, okay? It's going to be fine. You said Charlie's okay with all this, and if he's okay with it, I'm going to learn to be okay with it. I had a lot of time in Boston to think about everything, and the Heroes aren't a half loaf. They're just a different loaf." He grinned at her as he took her hand. "I'm thinking maybe pumpernickel."

"Are we pumpernickel, too? Not a half loaf, just a new loaf."

"Yeah, I guess so. We're still here, we're still whole. We're just a little different now."

"Okay," Laura said as they walked toward the ball field. "But I want to be raisin bread. With white icing."

Jake squeezed her hand. "It's a deal," he said, then sighed. "We almost lost it, didn't we, hon?"

Laura pretended not to understand, hoping to find time to come to grips with what her husband had just said. "It? What it?"

"Us. That it. It's funny, really. We made it through the bad times, only to start to self-destruct once Charlie got better. But we're going to make it now, right? We're going to talk, and not be afraid to yell when we feel the need. We're allowed to fight. Married people fight sometimes. We've just got to realize that not everything is a life-and-death decision anymore, thank God, and that sometimes that other shoe just isn't going to drop. We're a team, and we'll always be a team. We're going to be…we're going to be—"

"New-loaf normal," Laura said, squeezing his hand. "I love you, Jake Finnegan. Even when I don't."

He grinned at her, then looked out over the field. "Hey, there's Charlie. What's he—oh, God…"

Laura watched as Charlie stood behind Kenny Baxter, who was taller than Charlie by at least eight inches. Kenny Baxter, who had been blind since birth. Charlie had his arms wrapped around Kenny, his hands gripping the bat over Kenny's hands. "Come on, Mr. Johnson, give us your best stuff," he called out to Cherise's "little" brother. "You ready to run, Kenny? We're gonna nail this one."

Walter Johnson leaned forward and tossed the ball in a soft underhand.

"Now!" Charlie yelled, and he and Kenny swung the bat.

"He hit it!" Jake said as he stood behind Laura, his hands on her shoulders.

They both watched as the bat fell to the ground and Charlie grabbed Kenny's hand and ran with him to first base, talking to him, encouraging him all the way.

When they reached the bag it was hard to tell whose smile was the widest, Kenny, who had run through the darkness, his trust in Charlie complete, his excitement overcoming his natural fear of the unknown, or Charlie, who had helped make it all happen.

Laura turned to see Jake's reaction, only to watch him rub at the tears running down his cheeks. "Look at him. That's our son, Laura." His voice broke as he pulled her into his arms. "Thank you," he said, holding her tight. "Thank you…"

"Dad! *Dad!*"

"Charlie's calling you, honey," Laura said, disengaging herself and wiping at her own eyes.

"Hey, Dad! Mr. Johnson has to leave. You wanna pitch for a while?"

Laura took the cap from her head and reached up to put it on Jake's. "Go get 'em, slugger. And remember, the object of this game is to *let* them hit the ball."

Then she watched, hugging herself, as Jake trotted onto the field.

"Everything okay?" Jayne Ann asked, stepping up beside her.

"Everything is fine, better than fine," Laura answered, watching her two boys on the field. "Jayne Ann, you know what I've finally figured out? Life *is* a carnival—you just have to learn how to hang on and do your best to enjoy the ride."

Dear Reader,

The story you just read is fiction, but sometimes authors take bits and pieces from their own experiences and weave them into their stories. At age nine, our son had his first kidney transplant; at fourteen, his second. The "Come back when you grow" line was said to our son when he so desperately wanted to play for the local baseball team. And yes, his heart was broken.

There was no Deb Fruend in our area, no organization like TASK. And we, I'm sorry to say, didn't think to start an organization like TASK. For our son, for other children who had to fight so hard, who just wanted to be children.

Now you've read this story…this fiction. Now you know that when people care, when people get involved, a child's world can be changed for the better. That's *not* fiction.

Please go to www.tasksports.org and read the story of TASK. And when you do, remember, there are children out there, parents out there, who would give anything to have an organization like TASK in their own community.

Maybe you can do something. Maybe you can help. Because children need more than words…

Thank you.

Kasey Michaels

Debra Bonde

Seedlings Braille Books for Children

Who could have imagined back in 1984 that a small seed of an idea would eventually grow to become one of the world's foremost supportive organizations of literacy for visually impaired children and their families? Debra Bonde, founder and executive director of Seedlings Braille Books for Children, in Livonia, Michigan, can scarcely believe it herself—and it was her brainchild.

It was 1978 when Debra began wondering what she could do to make a difference in the world.

"Our job on earth is to help other people, but I was so incredibly shy that it made it very difficult. I needed to come up with a vocation where I could help other people—without talking to other people," she says with a laugh.

She stumbled into Braille transcription almost by accident

after speaking with a transcriber. She soon signed up for a community-based class and immediately fell in love with the detailed work. But it wasn't until she spoke to another student in the class—a mother with a visually impaired daughter—that she realized how few books for children were ever produced in Braille. The young girl owned only two books, despite the fact that she lived in an affluent suburb.

"It tugged at my heartstrings because it's appalling that there were so few Braille books available, and those that existed were generally very expensive—like a hundred dollars for a Hardy Boys book," Debra says.

Joy and wonder

After volunteering as a transcriber and giving birth to her daughters, Anna and Megan, Debra turned her attention to transcribing books for children exclusively. She cherished the time spent reading to her daughters, who had perfect sight, as they shared the gift of literacy through their growing collection of books. Why couldn't blind and visually impaired children experience the same joy and wonderment as her own kids? Debra vowed to find a way to erase the inexcusable disparity between blind and sighted children, to make children's books in Braille more accessible and affordable.

In 1983 Debra acquired one of the first computer Braille transcribing programs. Her father, Ray Stewart, stepped in and modified her antiquated Perkins Brailler from manual to electric and Debra began printing the books from her basement. In the first year Seedlings developed twelve books for the catalog. The project was on its way.

Despite her extreme shyness, Debra mustered the courage to solicit donations to subsidize book production. Between running her house and taking care of her kids, she also burned the midnight oil, arranging for grants.

And the hard work paid off. In 1985 Debra produced 221 books in her basement office. By 1990 Seedlings was producing five thousand books per year. At last count Seedlings, which employs nine people and uses dozens of volunteers, has produced a total of over two hundred thousand Braille books for blind children all over the U.S., Canada and over fifty countries around the world.

A vision grows

Although Seedlings created only straight Braille books in the beginning, parents and teachers approached Debra with requests for other options. Now Seedlings also offers Print-Braille-and-Picture-Books for toddlers and preschoolers, board books with Braille superimposed over the pictures using clear plastic strips with an adhesive backing. The organization also moved into fiction and nonfiction for older children. Then there are the Seedlings books that run printed text above the Braille so sighted children can read along with a blind parent or vice versa. *Goodnight Moon* remains Seedlings's all-time bestseller.

Not surprisingly, Seedlings has moved out of Debra's basement and into an office not far away. But despite the increased cost in keeping Seedlings afloat, Debra does everything she can—from using volunteer labor to recycling—to ensure the books sell for an average of only ten dollars.

"Most companies will make something for ten dollars and sell it for twenty. We make these books for twenty dollars and sell them for ten. I would lower the prices even more if I could," she says.

Despite the long hours and low pay, Debra stays driven because she knows her books have a huge impact on young children who might not ever have become literate in Braille without access to books they love at the beginning of their reading career.

Take a young woman, Heather, for example, once one of Debra's most voracious readers and supporters. When Heather was ten, she asked friends coming to her birthday party to give donations to Seedlings in lieu of presents. Today Heather is a university graduate now going to law school in Ottawa, Ontario.

"Just knowing that we've had a positive influence on lives like hers makes it all worthwhile," says Debra.

The freedom to learn

In the past years Seedlings has expanded its scope to offer programs to encourage children to love the written word. The thriving nonprofit organization offers the Rose Project, which provides free encyclopedia articles in Braille. Children working on projects contact Seedlings by phone, fax, e-mail or via its Web site and request the information. Seedlings staff pull the articles from the World Book CD into their computers, translate them into Braille, print them and send them out by courier or mail—usually the same day. For the first time blind students have access to the same research materials as their sighted friends.

Seedlings also offers a "Keep Kids in Touch" summer reading program, which ships out two free Braille books to kids in Michigan, Illinois, Indiana and Wisconsin so they can keep reading over the summer. "Hooray for Braille" kits introduce Michigan families of blind babies and preschoolers to Braille literacy. Debra hopes to open the programs to other states if funding increases.

But the project closest to Debra's heart is "Anna's Book Angel Project." Five years ago a drunk driver killed Debra's nineteen-year-old daughter, Anna, as she was on her way to New Orleans to tutor disadvantaged children. Memorial donations immediately flooded in. Today that money is used to send at least ten free books out to children in Anna's name each week.

Despite her grief over Anna's death, Debra never swayed from her dream to give visually impaired kids a chance to foster a love of reading. But even with the incredible successes Seedlings gains every day, Debra says they still have a long way to go.

"Even with all our effort, less than five percent of all books out there in print are transcribed into Braille," she maintains. "We still have a ton of work to do."

For more information visit www.seedlings.org or write to Seedlings Braille Books for Children, 14151 Farmington Road, Livonia, MI 48154.

CATHERINE MANN

Touched by Love

Catherine Mann

Five-time RITA Award nominee Catherine Mann blasted
onto the romantic suspense/adventure scene in June 2002.
Already her books have garnered bestseller status, critical
praise and numerous awards, including a Bookseller's Best
and a RITA Award. Prior to publication, Catherine graduated with a B.A. in Fine Arts: Theater from the College of
Charleston, and received her M.A. degree in theater from
UNC Greensboro. She finds that following her military-
flyboy husband around the world with four children, a
beagle and a tabby in tow offers endless inspiration for new
plots.

CHAPTER ONE

Librarian Anna Bonneau was well on her way to landing in the pokey. And that's exactly where she wanted to be.

She'd handcuffed herself to a park bench in protest all afternoon, and though she'd spent the time reading—hardly a hardship since books were her life—she was beginning to suffer a real case of fanny fatigue while waiting for the police to take notice.

Finally, a cop cruiser squealed to a stop by the curb.

She should have realized the small-town police wouldn't have a problem with her sit-down protest until closing time—5:00 p.m. The recreation area was empty except for autumn trees awash with colors and swings twisting in the breeze off Lake Huron.

Anna's mother used to bring her to the park for tea parties, but she had died in a car accident when Anna was only twelve. That had been the most difficult time in Anna's life. Her father—a local retired judge—had tried to continue the picnic tradition, but their differences of opinion during her teenage years made things difficult.

All in the past. Right now Anna did her best to focus on her book while making a peripheral check of the police officer stretching out of his cruiser. Finally, progress for her cause.

She'd always wanted to be a librarian, and landing a job in her sleepy hometown of Oscoda, Michigan, was a dream come true. She'd worked for three years in a library in the Detroit area, waiting for this position to come open.

Two weeks from now, she would start her job. And there was no way she was going to let the shortsighted members of the town planning commission rip up this park to plop a "gentlemen's club" restaurant and bar right beside *her* library.

She shifted her numb backside off the metal bench, which was growing cooler by the second in the autumn temperature, all the while keeping her eyes firmly focused on re-reading a Suzanne Brockmann reissue. Yes, Anna adored her romance novels as much as the long-ago classics.

A child's scream pierced the air.

Anna jolted up from her seat, only to be yanked back down by the handcuff—*ouch*. Her book fell to the ground as she caught sight of a man with a kid in his arms rapidly gaining ground on the approaching police officer. Howling shrieks echoed in the silence of the park, tugging at her heart until she recognized the man with the child—someone she'd hoped never to lay eyes on again after he'd broken her heart in high school.

Forest Jameson.

As he crossed the lawn toward her, Anna's stomach backflipped—just as it had when she'd first seen him bat one over the fence at the baseball field. He was a hunk, but too uptight during their teenage years. She'd heard he'd come home about four months ago to set up a legal practice in her father's former office, but she hadn't seen him since her return a week ago.

Why was he at the park, and why was he hauling a child? They could have come here to play—not that the kid sounded happy. Forest was likely here because her father, his long-ago mentor, had called and asked him to save Anne from spending a night in jail.

The cop, old Officer Smitty, stopped short of her bench. Closely following, Forest juggled the boy, a briefcase and a tote bag stuffed with toys.

"Anna." He nodded a greeting. "You still look the same."

She wasn't sure how to take that, but before she could answer, he'd turned back to the child.

Forest jostled the wailing, magenta-faced kid. Tears streamed down his cheeks behind the small sunglasses the boy wore. "Hang on, Joey. Just a few minutes and we'll be through here. I promise, son."

His son? Anna quickly checked out Forest's ring finger. Bare. She didn't want to think about the little zing of relief she felt.

Forest met her gaze. "Divorced and the nanny quit."

His tight-lipped answer engendered sympathy, along with embarrassment at her obvious interest.

Forest strode over to the cop. "I'm here to represent the interests of Ms. Bonneau."

Well, sheesh. Wasn't that convenient? "Uh, hello? Miss Bonneau has something to say about that."

The child—around four, maybe?—arched his back, pumping his feet. "I want to go home!"

"Well, you're not going anywhere if you don't settle down." The calmly stated parental threat was betrayed by Forest's harried expression.

Officer Smitty jumped in with a universal key and unlocked the handcuffs confining her to the bench. "H'lo, Miss Bonneau. How about you take care of this little stinker and I'll have a conversation with the lawyer?"

Click. The handcuffs fell away, ending her latest protest, and there wasn't a thing she could do about it. Maybe she would ride this one out and see what Forest had to say—in the interest of being entertained. Right?

She snagged her book from the ground, placed it on the bench and reached for little Joey. He didn't even loosen his lock hold on his dad's neck. Single-parent Forest was clearly overwhelmed.

Hmm. It seemed he needed her to bail him out more than she did him. She might have wanted her standard quick stop in jail, but her father said Forest never lost his cases, so she would simply stay near enough to listen until she came up with plan B.

And the kid surely was a heart-tugger. "Could I take him for you while you work your attorney magic?"

Forest hesitated, which irked her to no end. Finally, he nodded and eased the boy's arms from around his neck, speaking the whole time. "It's okay, son. This is Miss Anna. She's going to play with you while I talk business. Okay?"

Joey hiccuped. "'Kay." His chocolate-colored curls stuck to his head with tantrum-induced sweat. "Can I go swing?"

"Of course." Forest passed Joey to her. "Anna? You're sure you don't mind?"

If he was surprised that she'd guessed his reason for being here, he sure didn't show it.

"Not at all."

She took the child, a solid weight. The scent of baby shampoo and sweat soothed her with its sweet innocence. The little guy was a cutie in his striped overalls, conductor's cap and Thomas the Train sunglasses.

Forest opened his mouth as if to speak further, but Anna turned away. Her nerves were on edge, and she was having trouble resisting the temptation to stare at the grown-up Forest. She used to watch him volunteering with Little Leaguers back in high school, and his gentleness with his son could well draw her in the same way.

She headed toward the swings, offering soothing words both for herself and Joey.

"Can you sit in the swing and hold me, please?" Joey asked.

"Of course, sweetie."

This was easier than she thought. She could hold the child, keep him happy *and* listen to the two men decide her fate as if she weren't even there. *Grrr.* She tickled Joey's chin with the tail of her braid until he chortled. His sunglasses were the cutest things she'd ever seen.

Unable to resist gloating at her success in calming the little guy, Anna glanced past Joey to his father. Bummer. Forest hadn't even noticed. He was too busy unloading kid gear. As he placed the toy bag and briefcase on the bench, his suit coat gaped open to reveal a broad chest covered by his crisp white shirt. She swallowed hard.

He whipped off his steel-rimmed glasses and snatched a tissue from the briefcase to clean away the evening mist. Anna's breath hitched. Even as she swung with Joey, she could see Forest's blue eyes glittering like a shaken bottle of soda water.

Darn it, she wouldn't let herself forget that he had left town without so much as a farewell.

"Miss Anna, higher!" Joey squealed, yanking her braid. "Miss Anna, let's go higher."

Joey had the strength of a fifth-grader, and Anna welcomed the wake-up call.

Why couldn't her father understand she believed in justice as strongly as he did? She merely approached it from a different angle, organizing protests since her first petition in the second grade for new monkey bars in the playground.

The men finished their discussion and the older cop

ambled off to his patrol car. Forest strode toward her with determined steps and held his arms out for his son, tapping the boy on the shoulder. "Time to go, Joey."

The little fella pivoted in her lap and launched himself at his dad with obvious affection. This time, however, he squirmed down to walk, holding his dad's hand.

Anna eased herself up from the swing. "What's the verdict?"

"Since we made it out of here before closing, you got off with a simple ticket, but no jail time."

"I guess that will have to do, but I was hoping we could squeeze in some news coverage."

A tight smile crooked his perfectly sculpted mouth as he mimicked her voice. "Why, thank you, Forest, for keeping me from paying an expensive fine. And heaven forbid I might have actually had to go to jail and eat their fine cuisine. It's great to see you again."

She slumped back in the swing. He had gone to a lot of trouble for her and she was being ungrateful. "Thank you for your time and help. It's, uh, good to see you, too."

Even if it had cost her the short stint in jail and a much-coveted feature in the weekly local newspaper.

Forest shrugged through the kink in his neck and picked up the pace as he made his way back to his truck in the now-dark park, carefully leading his son around trees and over jutting roots.

Anna had seriously snagged his attention in high school, even if she was more than a little quirky. And yeah, spunky.

He'd admired those qualities, even though he'd craved normalcy after a lifetime spent with parents who hip-hopped from one outrageous commune to another. But she sure was pretty and he knew her beauty owed nothing to the pricey spa treatments his ex craved.

His newest client wore her corn-silk blond hair in a single thick braid down her back. Her hair had a bit of spring to it in the curl at the end of the braid and the stray wisps teasing cheeks pink from the cool lake breeze.

Her fresh-scrubbed face glowed with health, even the freckles dotting her nose. The flowing green dress she wore, with its sunflower pattern, and her cheery yellow sweater brightened the drab overcast evening.

But despite her uncomplicated beauty, understanding Anna required more study than the bar exam. Forest had given up second-guessing her when she'd staged a protest outside his high-school baseball game. She and a group of her friends had handcuffed themselves to bike racks in a protest against budget cuts that cost the chorus teacher his job, while leaving the sports budget intact.

"Where's your car?" he asked.

She strolled past him to the bicycle stand. "I rode my mountain bike."

Anna worked the lock that secured her bike to the metal rack while Officer Smitty fired up his cruiser over by the curb. Forest sighed at the inevitable.

"Let me give you a ride. We can store your bike in the back of my truck."

Still she didn't face him, just stowed her lock and wheeled her bike backward. Was that a yes or no?

He couldn't let her pedal off in the dark. Even in this sleepy little town, with Officer Smitty readying to cruise the streets, it wasn't all that safe for an attractive woman to be out alone on the backwoods roads that ran along the lake. Shoot, he was here in the first place to watch over her because of the debt he owed Judge Bonneau for mentoring him during the year his parents spent in Oscoda—their longest stint anywhere in his entire life.

The cop rolled down his car window and nodded to Forest. "Good evening, Counselor. Quite a change from your regular stuff, with, uh—"

"Insurance litigation." Forest smiled tightly as the wind wafted the scent of vanilla. He was mighty sure that didn't come from Smitty or Joey. "Every client's important."

Anna waved to the cop. "Hi, Officer Smitty. Hope to see you at the recycling drive this coming weekend. Make it a family day. There'll be treats for the kids."

"Thanks for the tip. I'm always looking for things to occupy the girls on my weekend with them." He nodded sympathetically to Forest, another single father.

Anna pulled a flyer from her oversize backpack and passed it to the cop. "Always happy to help out. About my handcuffs—"

Smitty had begun to roll his window up again. "Oh, right. Here ya go."

Forest waited while Anna chatted with Smitty about his

kids. Joey ran circles around him, trailing his hand around his father's knees as he wore himself out. Anna flung her braid over her shoulder, her face animated and her eyes sparkling as she spoke to the police officer.

Beautiful eyes.

Forest almost dropped the tote bag full of toys.

Maybe he should start dating again. He'd been celibate since his divorce three years ago, but he didn't trust his judgment in women. He and Paula had seemed a perfect match with shared dreams, but it hadn't worked. He definitely wasn't ready for a relationship, especially not with a woman who was trouble incarnate.

Besides, his son needed him as he grew up without the love and care of a mother to help him through the tough times ahead.

Forest snagged Anna's helmet from her handlebars to impede any thoughts of escape. Her tantalizing vanilla fragrance teased his nose. "Anna, can we speed this along? I need to get Joey fed and tucked into bed."

He could almost feel the wind whipping over him. Countless summers, he'd tooled around the country in his parents' motorcycle sidecar. Other children, kids blessed with family trips in the comfort of a station wagon, had giggled and pointed. Forest's grip tightened on the helmet buckle.

He would take her home to her little cottage on the water and then his debt to the judge would be canceled.

So why did that vanilla scent seem to taunt him, making him believe that Anna was back in his life for a reason?

ANNA KNEW when to fight and when to surrender with grace.

Insisting on biking home in the dark would sound petty. And while she considered herself independent, that didn't give her the right to be rude. Inside the extended-cab truck, she reached into the backseat to stroke Joey's chocolate-brown curls and savor the feeling of peace that stole over her as the child tipped his face into the chilly night breeze drifting through the open windows.

Forest leaned toward her as Anna grappled with her own seat belt. Her arm brushed his chest.

"Uh, Anna—"

"I don't know what's wrong with this seat belt." She wrestled with the buckle. "I can't seem to get it clicked."

Forest shifted in his seat. "Do you, uh, need some help?"

Heavens, she hoped not. She straightened, her palm extended. "Gummi Worm!"

"What?"

"There was a Gummi Worm stuck in it."

"Joey's snack. A token of single fatherhood. Bribes." He passed the half-full bag of Gummies to Joey. "Here ya go, son."

"Well, I didn't think it was yours." She flicked the biodegradable candy out the window. "Actually, I'm starving. I ran out of snacks around three."

She'd sneaked off for bathroom breaks when the place

looked deserted, but there weren't any vending machines, and going into a restaurant to grab a hamburger seemed like cheating.

Oaks and pines whizzed past as they drove along the deserted roads. Forest was quiet, and so was Joey, happy with his treat. But Anna was still geared up.

Five minutes passed before she finally exploded, "They want to build a—" she glanced back at Joey then over at Forest "—S-T-R-I-P club there. Oh sure, they're calling it a 'gentleman's club,' but we all know what that really means. It's bad enough to have an establishment like that in our town, but especially awful right next to the library." She shook her head. "I can't stand silently by."

"I'm frustrated, too, Anna, but it sounds like a done deal." The dashboard light illuminated his strong square jaw.

"It's not over until they roll in the bulldozers. I couldn't stay quiet while there's time to make a difference."

"I hear you and I understand. But there are better ways." Forest turned into Anna's driveway, gravel crunching as he drove toward the brick cottage she'd rented last week.

Headlights swept across the dormant garden and high-lighted the man rocking on the front porch. Judge Edward Bonneau sat bathed in the hazy glow. Her father.

No doubt he'd received his courtesy call from the police station on how things had shaken down. Politics and protocol were more than a little loose in small-town Oscoda. Of course. Why else would Forest have shown up in the first place?

Could the night get any worse?

Anna eased her achy body out of the vehicle, stiff from sitting so long. She really could have benefited from a bike ride home. Her father pushed to his feet, short and wiry, but imposing nonetheless. The porch light cast a friendly glow over the paver stones she'd crafted with inset marbles. She'd carted those hefty steppers from home to home—treasures she'd made with her mother as a child.

Her father snapped his suspenders over his seersucker pajama top. "Sugar, you've come to the end of the line. I hear my old rival Judge Randall's gonna crack down next time you get a ticket, and throw the book at you. We're talking serious jail time, daughter dear."

Sugar? Daughter dear? She was twenty-five years old, for Pete's sake. Why couldn't they communicate as adults?

Uh, wait. Her feet stalled. *Serious* jail time? She was cool with being booked for a few hours or even a night, as had happened in the past. But nothing more, especially if it interfered with her new job. "I'll be working at the library before he can make a big stink."

Her father ambled down three of the five steps, stopping eye level with Forest. "Well, boy, what's your plan?"

"Pop, calm down." She breezed over and kissed his leathery cheek. She missed the simpler days of their attempted picnics and homework review. "Forest will take care of everything. You can go home."

"Not a chance. I need to hear his plan of action."

Of course he would. She knew this battle wasn't worth fighting. Her father showed his love through trying to micromanage her life. She'd learned to basically keep her silence and go her own way.

She might as well play with Joey, who was squirming to get out of his booster seat. Anna turned to the two men on the porch.

The sooner Forest could talk to her dad, the sooner both men would head home. "Fine. I'll just let Joey out to play."

"Anna," Forest called out. "About Joey—"

She waved over her shoulder. "Don't worry. I may not be a parent, but I can handle one little boy."

The dome light illuminated Joey's frustration as he strained against the confines of his booster seat. He continued to thrash until his precious little sunglasses flew off to one side—

Revealing wide, unseeing blue eyes.

CHAPTER TWO

"Forest?" She turned to look at him for affirmation of what she couldn't deny but didn't want to voice out loud in case she upset the child.

Little Joey was blind. Only now did she see the white stick at his feet on the floorboard. Forest had been carrying him earlier or holding his hand. She thought of all his sentences, which she'd interrupted, and now—

Forest simply nodded his head, his expression fiercely protective. Of course. Any normal parent would be, because she'd learned long ago that people could be cruelly imperceptive at times.

Her heart ached for the little guy and the extra challenges he would face. As if life wasn't already tough enough. But she refused to make Joey feel self-conscious. He was an active young boy, just like the students she'd worked with in her reading groups—special needs or not—during her previous library position.

The minute they cleared up things with her father, she would go online to the Seedlings Braille Books for Children Web site to place her order for some preschool books with Braille added.

"Hi, Joey. It's Miss Anna." She announced herself so he wouldn't be surprised. "I'll let you out now so you can play while we talk. If you're hungry, how about graham crackers?"

"I'm full of Gummies now. I just wanna play."

"Fair enough, big guy."

She unstrapped him and helped him out of the seat, then slipped her hand into his. She leaned into the truck for his white cane and passed it to him. In her work at the library, she'd learned that small children needed a cane that reached shoulder level rather than sternum level. The smaller canes caused too many injuries if a child stumbled forward. At four, Joey would still be acclimating to the cane, so she called out potential hazards and kept hold of his hand.

"Big tree root ahead," she announced, lifting him over it with a squeal of "Whee!"

His giggle swept away all the frustrations of a long day. She glanced up to the porch. The gratitude on Forest's face stirred an entirely different sort of excitement in her.

Swallowing hard, she returned her attention to Joey. She needed to think of something to keep him occupied in this unfamiliar environment while the adults spoke. Her eyes lit on the wheelbarrow. "Would you like a ride in my magic wagon?"

"Magic?" His face tipped up to hers, his sightless gaze slightly left of her.

"Magic and super speedy." Most little boys enjoyed fast-moving toys, and bottom line, he was like any other child.

She slid her hands under his armpits, plopped him in the wheelbarrow and started steering him along the bumpy yard. He clutched the sides and squealed, apparently content with the magic chariot for the moment at least.

Her father made his way down the steps of her two-bedroom cottage so they could converse while she jostled around the yard with Joey.

"Anna," Pop said, "word around the courthouse has it Judge Randall wants to get back at me for all the years I beat him out for a position on the bench. We all know he's a vindictive old cuss. You're playing right into his hands with your protesting." His expression of concern mirrored Forest's for his child a few minutes earlier. "I'm worried about you."

That small show of affection from her father almost crumbled her defenses. *Almost.* But she'd stopped looking for his approval long ago. They just didn't connect. "Pop, I'm an adult. What I do doesn't reflect on you. Disown me. I officially absolve you of responsibility."

Gasping for breath, she turned and jabbed her finger toward Forest, quickly grabbing the wheelbarrow handle again. "And you—there won't be any need for you to defend me, because I will simply lie low as Dad suggests."

Her father fished out a handkerchief from his pocket. "Now, sugar, don't get all fired up. You look just like your mama when you do that. You're gonna make me get all maudlin, and that's not good for the old ticker."

Sometimes, Anna thought, listening to her father, it was hard to believe he was a respected judge. She steered a cheering Joey toward her father. "Pop, you have the heart of a sixteen-year-old."

"Please, Anna." He raked a hand through his rusty-red hair. "Listen and pretend to care about my opinion."

Anna reminded herself that her father didn't pay her bills, hadn't since she'd graduated from high school and landed her first scholarship. So why should she care about his opinion?

Because he was still her father and she was a natural-born caregiver. She sighed. "Five minutes, tops."

"Five it is then. Come on over here and have a seat, you two. Pass that little fella to me."

A possessive feeling stirred within her. "I've got Joey."

"Joey," her father called. "Wanna come sit with me?"

"Papa Bonneau! You have any candy?" The boy turned his head, a huge smile creasing his precious chubby cheeks.

He scrambled out of the wheelbarrow, but Anna caught him a split second before he hit the ground. She took his hand and led him to her father, which was apparently where he wanted to be.

Her father scooped up the little guy and pulled out a roll of Lifesavers. "Forest?"

Anna wilted onto the porch swing. "We might as well

hear Pop out," she said to Forest. "He'll only track us down later."

"Fine." Forest scrubbed a hand over his face, shaking his head as if to clear his thoughts.

He climbed the steps slowly, like a man marching toward the gallows. His eyes narrowed as he joined Anna on the swing, the only seat left on the porch. Had the swing shrunk with the last rain?

She breathed in the calming, earthy scents from the vegetable garden. "Okay, Pop. I'm listening."

Her father thumbed another piece of candy for Joey, tapping his shoes as he rocked. "You've done well for Anna today, Forest. I always knew you'd make a levelheaded attorney. But daughter dear, I'm afraid even Forest can't save your hide if you land in Randall's court."

Anna drummed her fingers along the armrest and studied a water bug scuttling across the planked porch. Forest shifted, crossing his long legs at the ankles as he set the swing into motion. How much had he grown since high school?

"I appreciate your, uh, concern, Pop, but I'm not giving up my protests for anyone." She'd seen in college how effective a simple sit-in could be to protest a book banning at the library. "If Judge Randall wants to turn tough next time, I'll be the one stuck with the consequences."

Her father shot a pleading look at Forest. "Got any thoughts on this in your bag of summation tricks?"

Forest hooked his arm along the back of the porch swing and faced Anna. "Do you realize how lucky you are to have grown up in a town like this? An established good name isn't something to throw away."

She hesitated. Of course she had considered that aspect, not that she would acknowledge it to the pair of controlling males on her porch. The answer flowered in her mind like the blossoming buds on her tomato plants in season.

"You're both right."

Their slack jaws could have trapped a healthy supply of flies.

She continued while she had them off balance. "I know the best way to keep me out of Judge Randall's radar. Poor Forest is in a real pickle with no nanny. How can he work with his son underfoot all day?"

Forest stared at her with a deep intensity until she couldn't resist the gravitational pull. He had such beautiful eyes, baby blues, now filled with a concern that caressed her like a refreshing spring shower.

"Okay, Anna, what's your idea?"

She inhaled deeply, afraid if she actually considered this scheme any longer than a few seconds, she'd back out before telling them. "While you're looking for a permanent nanny, I'll be Joey's sitter for the next two weeks. It's a way to help you and at the same time will keep me out of the judge's radar."

And quite frankly, it was something she *wanted* to do, to help that precious little boy.

She looked up for their reaction.

Forest jerked and attempted to stand up, launching the swing forward. Anna grabbed his arm just as the chain closest to the edge of the porch snapped, tipping the swing seat sideways.

They slid off the swing and the porch, tumbling into the tomato and cucumber patch. And the only thing that surprised Anna was why she was still holding on to Forest's arm.

"Forest? Forest? Are you okay?"

Soft hands patted his cheeks. His head throbbed. The aroma of mashed vegetation hovered around him. How many veggies could be left in the garden this late in the season?

He struggled to pull himself out of this dazed fog. He couldn't move yet, so he just lay sprawled on his back.

"Wake up. Come on, Forest. You're scaring Joey."

At the mention of his son, Forest forced his eyes open. He had to be okay for his son. There was no one else to take care of Joey with his mother in the Riviera and the nanny out the door. But there was something soft pressing down on him, preventing him from moving.

Anna. She lay atop Forest without room for a summons to slide between them.

"Forest? Forest!"

Forest. He cringed at the constant repetition of his name. What had possessed his parents to name him for the place where they'd conceived him? He should probably be grateful they hadn't opted to name him after the stars or something. Betelgeuse would have been beyond bearing.

He winced, and it wasn't from the lump on the back of his head or the lovely woman on top of him. Hadn't he suffered enough from his unconventional family life? His biker parents turned commune teachers had served up plenty of embarrassment.

"Forest?" Anna rested her elbows on his chest, her face less than an inch away. "Are you awake?"

"Barely."

"Thank goodness."

Forest could feel her relax against him. "Anna? It's time for me to—"

"Why didn't you tell me about Joey?" she whispered.

"I tried. There wasn't a chance."

She nodded and stayed politely quiet while he formed his explanation.

Forest stared up at her, a fierce protectiveness surging through him. "Joey was a preemie, two and a half months early. He has retinopathy of prematurity—ROP. He can see light and dark, but that's it."

He didn't want pity for his son, simply acceptance, and thank heavens, that's exactly what he saw in Anna's beautiful green eyes…

The porch floor creaked. Judge Bonneau peered over the broken swing. Joey was cradled to his chest, drooling a green Lifesaver. "Are you two all right?"

"I think so." Anna's breath puffed over Forest. "And you?"

"Just fi—"

"Daughter dear," the judge said, grinning, "you'll make a wonderful nanny for little Joey."

Nanny? Nanny! Forest's hands fell away from Anna as if he were scalded. How could he have forgotten her proposition? He jackknifed up, and Anna rolled to the side in a flurry of arms and legs.

"It's perfect." Her father nodded in agreement. "You could use the money to tide you over, and you have the time free before you start to work at the library. Forest needs the help since his ex is away."

Forest scrambled for words in his definitely scrambled brain. "I've had some women in town offer to help out."

The judge shook his head, jowls jiggling. "Those aren't the kind of women to look out for Joey. They're not interested in the child, just the father. Not like you, daughter dear."

Forest wasn't sure whether to be relieved or insulted.

Anna shoved to her feet. "So, Forest? What's your verdict on me as a sitter? Yes or no?"

As if on cue, Joey started to cry. Before Forest could even think to move, Anna had rushed to her father's side and scooped up the child from his lap.

"Would you like some chocolate milk?" she whispered. "Hmm?"

The judge tapped Forest on the arm. "Watch."

Anna swayed gently, running her hand over Joey's curls until he sagged against her and buried his face in her neck. With his fingers, he traced her features, learning her face.

He wanted to know her.

"I like chocolate milk." His soft voice carried on the wind.

Forest didn't consider himself a man stirred by strong emotions, but his heart gave an extra *ka-thump,* like an engine turning over. He wanted a normal life for himself, and the same for his son. Yet, he couldn't even manage to keep a nanny for Joey, much less a mother.

"Sir, no disrespect meant, but I'm fairly certain your daughter and I would find it hard to get along even for that short a time."

"It's only a couple of weeks, until her job starts and your ex is back in the country to pitch in. You'll be at work during the day." The older man leaned in for the kill. "Forest, my boy, think of your son. We fathers have to put our children's interests first."

Joey snuggled closer to Anna. A hiccuping sigh shuddered through his solid body as she headed inside for the promised treat. Forest had always prided himself on his control, but Anna had a way of breaking down barriers.

It was only for a couple of weeks.

He could feel himself caving. He had to do the right thing for Joey. The kid rarely had his mother around. How could Forest deny him the closest thing to maternal affection in town?

He couldn't, no matter what the cost to his personal sanity.

CHAPTER THREE

"Are you sure you'll be all right?" Forest stood in the middle of the kitchen in his newly constructed track home, shuffling his briefcase from one hand to the other.

"Stop worrying. I have a bachelor's degree in early childhood education as well as library studies. I had reading groups for special-needs children at my old library job. I can care for one small boy."

Anna settled into the breakfast nook, planting herself in a seat beside Joey's booster chair to keep from shaking the kid's overprotective father. If he gave her one more list of ways to pacify a four-year-old...

"We're going to have a great time. Aren't we, sweetie?"

Joey slapped his spoon against the bowl of oatmeal and grinned. "I don't wanna eat this. Bleck!"

Forest slammed his briefcase on the oak table. "That's it. I'll cancel—"

"Don't even think about it. He's only testing me." Geez, no wonder the other nanny had quit. Somebody needed to lighten up. "I'll keep him so busy he won't have time to act out. Go."

"If you're sure." He still didn't leave, but let his hand rest on the baseball mitt hanging on the post of his kitchen chair, rubbing the leather like a talisman.

"I'm positive. You've left a pageful of phone numbers."

Anna tucked aside her resentment. Forest was only displaying textbook signs of an overanxious parent and yes, there were special concerns for Joey, but the best thing Forest could do for his son was treat him as normally as possible.

Still, his concern was rather sweet. She gentled her scowl into a smile. "He'll be okay once you leave. If I have a question, I'll call. I promise."

He glanced at his watch. "You're right, and court starts in less than an hour." He ruffled his son's hair. "Be good for Anna."

"Scoot." Anna waved her hand to shoo him away.

"All right, I'll get out of your hair, braid, whatever. Don't worry about supper. I'll grill something for us all when I get home since you'll probably be worn out from the full day."

She froze. Was that a dinner-date invitation?

Forest grabbed his briefcase from the table and scooped his jacket from the chair, slinging it over one deliciously broad shoulder. "Anna?"

She was startled out of her daze. "Yes?"

"Thanks." The screen door swooshed closed behind him.

She twisted her braid through her fingers as she stared out the bay window. Elbow on the table, she watched him saunter along the walk toward his truck. Such a bold, confident stride.

Pivoting away, Anna focused on the son instead of the father. "Well, sweetie, how about we clean up the breakfast dishes. You can help."

He scrunched his nose but didn't argue.

"After lunch, we'll walk to the park and feed the ducks."

"Ducks? Yay!" Joey catapulted out of his seat and into her arms with such trust her heart twisted.

"That's right. We'll take some bread along."

Anna passed him a damp cloth while grabbing one for herself, and the two of them cleared the dishes and wiped the table.

"Good job, Joey," she said when they'd finished.

She tossed their cloths into the overflowing laundry basket on top of the washer. She would show her father *and* Forest Jameson. She'd aced her way through a degree in early childhood education as well as library studies, unable to tell which she enjoyed more, until a wise college counselor advised her to apply that love of children to her library positions.

She was a well-educated, seasoned pro now.

How much trouble could one kid be?

ONE WELL-BEHAVED, chipper child would have been simple.

The tiny tyrant looking too cute in his overalls and train-conductor cap wasn't chipper, sweet or even remotely well behaved. Why was he so cranky?

Anna had tried everything to keep him entertained at home for the morning. They'd hung out in his amazing backyard, full of playground equipment specifically designed for Joey. But he hadn't wanted any part of it today. She'd moved on to story time, singing and dancing.

After lunch, they'd walked to the duck pond as promised. The edge of the pond had a brick border where they could sit and let the ducks come right up to them without getting their feet wet.

"Yuckie!" Joey flung the bag of bread into the pond. "The bread smells gross."

"Oh, sweetie." Anna sighed as the bag floated away. She couldn't leave it behind and risk a duck choking on the plastic, but she couldn't leave Joey unattended either.

"Come on, Joey. We're going in." She hitched him onto her hip and waded into the pond. Her muslin dress soaked up the cold water as she grabbed the bag.

Joey smacked the water, cheerful for the first time in an hour. "This is fun!"

"Yes, it is, sugar." And *sooo* chilly.

Still, she considered hanging out in the muddy pond all afternoon. She would gladly sacrifice her favorite dress, patterned with Shakespearean verses and flowers, if it would keep Joey from fussing and testing her further.

Anna glanced down at her wet dress and read, *What fools these mortals be…* No kidding. She'd topped that list of foolish mortals by wading into a duck pond to scoop out a bag of bloated bread.

"The fishes are tickling my ankles!" Joey squealed.

"Cool, kiddo!" Maybe she could work in a quick science lesson. The plan seemed sound and the kid definitely needed to be kept active, but he also needed a nap, and she did *not* want Forest to hear about their impromptu swim.

His next instruction list would rival the Magna Carta.

Anna scanned the clusters of mothers and children scattered around the playground, having picnics and making memories under leafy bowers.

She recognized some of the families, but no one seemed to have noticed her and Joey. She should be able to make a clean getaway.

Her gaze snagged on Mrs. LaRoche. Joey's ex-nanny had brought her granddaughter to the park. The blue-haired bat waved to Anna. She stifled a groan and waved back. The know-it-all would probably turn cartwheels at Anna's lack of success with Joey and report it to Forest.

Anna hugged him closer. "We need to go home now—"

His face scrunched. "I don't wanna—"

"To get a treat!"

"A treat? Graham crackers?"

"Two of them." She reminded herself it wasn't a bribe, merely positive reinforcement.

A rose by any other name… Shakespeare's words mocked her.

Anna trudged forward, her clothes sponging up the water. Joey hadn't fared much better.

By the time Anna rounded the last corner on their way home, she was truly worried about Joey. Something wasn't right. She pressed her wrist to his forehead, then against his warm stomach. He wasn't just irritable. He was sick.

Guilt chugged through her. He must have been coming down with something, and dragging him through a chilly pond hadn't helped. "Do you feel bad, sweetie?"

Joey wriggled against her. "I'm sleepy. I wanna nap."

The kid *wanted* to go to sleep? It must be serious.

"Poor fella. No wonder you've been grumpy." She cuddled him closer, his damp body shivering against her. Anna walked faster up the driveway toward the one-story ranch-style house. "We're almost there. You can curl up in your own bed."

"Thank you, Anna." His chubby arms clutched tighter.

An odd ache squeezed her chest. He *needed* her. Her world consisted of books, think tanks and causes. No one had ever needed her before. That hug meant more to her than a dean's list semester.

She pressed a kiss to Joey's forehead. He really was feverish. Logic told her it probably wasn't anything more serious than a common virus. That didn't make her feel one darned bit better.

Joey opened his mouth. She tensed, preparing herself for more whining or worse yet, an ear-popping tantrum.

He spewed his lunch all over her.

Joey crinkled up his nose. "Yuckie!"

"Yeah, sweetie," Anna agreed. "Defintely yuckie."

Several hours and countless loads of laundry later, she surrendered to fate. She'd tried to call Forest, but he was in court, and then when he'd called to check in, she'd told him she'd finally gotten things under control. Sort of. The pediatrician's nurse had thought that as long as Joey was keeping down liquids, there was no need to worry. Even so, Anna felt out of her league.

She cradled Joey, who was now asleep, wrapped in a blanket with just his tiny boxer shorts on. There wasn't a clean T-shirt or a pair of jeans left in the house, since he'd thrown up on everything in sight. She'd had such great plans for starting their reading tomorrow with the Seedlings print-and-Braille books she'd ordered express mail off the Internet last night. With luck Joey would be feeling better then. Funny how plans for this child were already filling her life.

She pushed back a hank of sweaty hair from her brow, picked up the kitchen phone and dialed from memory. "Dad, could you bring me a change of clothes, please?"

FOREST WHIPPED into the driveway with uncharacteristic haste just as a car pulled away from the curb. He slid the truck into Park and looked at his house, his haven.

It was still standing. Anna and Joey must have survived their first day together.

Working without the stress of worrying about his son had lightened his mood. A call home during a court recess had reassured him that Anna seemed to have everything under control, even though Joey was not feeling well.

She'd been right. Hiring her as a temporary sitter was the perfect solution for everyone. Meanwhile, Forest told himself, he'd exaggerated his response to Anna the night before.

He stepped into the spotless kitchen. The humming washer and dryer greeted him in the otherwise silent house. The nursery monitor was on the table, light glowing, but no grumbling from his son filtered through.

Peace? Or the calm before the storm?

"Anna? Joey?" Forest called over his shoulder while reaching into the refrigerator. He dodged the pitcher of tea with mint leaves, Anna's no doubt, and grabbed a soda. "Hello?"

"Hold on a second! Joey's asleep." Her voice wafted from behind the laundry-closet doors. "I'll be right out."

"No need to hurry. I'm going to check on Joey." He tossed his briefcase on the table, kicking the refrigerator shut as he guzzled his cola on his way down the hall. After brushing a hand over his son's cool forehead and tucking the baseball mitt back under the covers, Forest breathed a sigh of relief and returned to the kitchen.

Anna shoved the louvered doors closed. She brushed aside a stray lock of hair with a harried sweep of her hand. "You're home early."

Wow, she looked good. Her face was flushed and her eyes wide, and that green dress hugged her curves like a wet leaf. "I brought paperwork with me so I could check on Joey. How's he feeling?"

"Better," she told him. "I called his pediatrician's office again. Joey's keeping liquids and Tylenol down, so there's no need to worry for now. He wanted to take your mitt to bed with him. He seems to take comfort from the smell of the oils."

Her insightfulness caught him square in the midsection and squeezed hard.

Being around Anna so much wasn't going to work. He needed to feed her the grilled steak as promised, then take her home.

"I guess there's nothing left for me to do but crank up the grill."

"Good idea." She lounged against the doors, arms behind her.

There was something very different about her. Her hair had been braided when he'd left, and now it was in a ponytail. And she'd been wearing some kind of sack dress with weeds and quotations all over it, but now was in a formfitting silk dress.

The door behind her moved. Her eyes widened. "Maybe you should check on Joey again?"

Her high-pitched voice grated along Forest's heightened nerve endings. A first-year law student could note the body language red flags. She was concealing something.

Why would a woman shower and change into a slinky little number in the middle of the day? And what was she hiding in the laundry closet?

Or rather, *who?*

Forest saw red, and it wasn't a flag. Could Anna have put his son down for a nap while she "entertained" a guy?

He told himself that the pounding in his ears was merely

the thumping of the off-balance washing machine. If not that, then it stemmed from anger because she'd abused his trust. It was *not* jealousy. She was simply an old high-school girlfriend. That relationship had no bearing on their present.

He mustered a cool voice. "Joey was fine when I looked in on him."

"Oh, all right then."

The door bucked behind her. She flattened both hands against it and smiled, a tight, overbright grimace that told Forest too much. She had some boy toy hidden behind that door.

Time's up. Forest pinned her with his best witness-breaking stare. "Anna, please, step away."

"I, uh, I can't."

"Why?"

Her full bottom lip quivered. "It's too embarrassing."

"Embarrassing?" He hadn't considered there might be a *half-dressed* sap in the closet.

The washer clicked, then hit the spin cycle. *Ker-thunk. Ker-thunk.*

Forest almost felt sorry for the guy. He knew what a wallop Anna delivered to an unsuspecting male. He'd wanted a reason to get over his absurd attraction to her, and now he had it. Why wasn't he happy?

He closed the last three steps between them. Anger and disappointment warred within him. He stuffed his hands in his pockets so he wouldn't shake her by the shoulders. "Anna, step aside so we can get this over with."

Ker-thunk. The washer spun and rattled. *Ker-thunk.*
Ker-thunk.

Anna sniffled. "Do you ever get tired of being right?"

"No more procrastinating."

She eased forward. The louvered doors inched open as if
nudged, then burst free. Anna stumbled into Forest's arms.

Baskets tipped. Loose laundry overflowed around them.
Forest clutched Anna's soft body while clothes tangled
around their ankles.

Not a cowering male in sight: "Anna?"

"I'm just so mortified!" She sniffled. "Only one day
alone with Joey and I took him into the chilly pond. Now
he's sick. The laundry is out of control. I've been through
three outfits of my own—although why my dad would
send *this* for me to wear while watching a kid is beyond
me. And you so don't want to see where Joey upchucked
on the comforter in your bedroom."

She collapsed against Forest's chest, bursting into shud-
dering sobs. He didn't want to feel the incredible relief that
surged through him as she leaned into him.

In a flash, he lost his battle with suppressing the desire to
kiss the freckles on the bridge of her nose. He tried to
remind himself that he wanted a peaceful, normal life—
something a woman like Anna was incapable of.

Forest looked into her mossy green, heartbroken eyes, and
knew he'd not only forsaken peace, but plunged headfirst
into a hurricane.

Chapter Four

Anna stood wrapped in Forest's arms and blinked back tears. She'd never failed at anything. She'd studied her way into A-plus achievements. Why then couldn't she manage one tiny child? And why couldn't she stop this attraction to that same boy's totally uptight father?

Forest's arms locked around her waist, anchoring her to him. His solid muscles beneath her palms turned her legs to half-set Jell-O. His head dipped toward her and she couldn't resist the temptation to stretch up on her toes. His pupils widened, darkening his blue eyes to a murky sea.

Anna plunged in headfirst.

She slid her hands up his chest and around his neck. Shouldn't she be pulling away? She'd barely formed the thought when his mouth skimmed along hers. How could she have forgotten the lovely sensation of Forest Jameson's kiss?

He inched away. "Anna? What are we doing?"

"I don't know. But I want to do it again."

A low growl rumbled in his chest.

He nuzzled her neck, inhaling. "Why do you have to be so appealing?"

Anna resisted the urge to laugh. She'd never considered herself much of a femme fatale. Heaven knew, Forest could have his pick of the multitude of big-haired women with perfect makeup who strutted themselves through her father's office begging for advice on their overdue parking tickets in hopes of snagging a lawyer husband. Were those same sorts of women trailing through Forest's office? A chill settled over her.

"Forest." She stepped back. "I think I hear Joey."

"Joey. Right." Exhaling long and hard, Forest glanced over at the silent nursery monitor.

She wrapped her arms around herself. "One of us really should check on him."

The quiet house mocked her.

"Uh-huh." Forest stuffed his hands in his pockets, his breathing ragged. "Give me five seconds to remember how to breathe and I'll apologize."

"I don't want an apology."

"I owe you one anyway."

"Don't be silly. We're both adults. It was only a kiss." A kiss guaranteed to peel the paint off the walls. "It's not as if either of us is interested in a relationship. Right?"

Forest looked up fast. "No!"

"You don't have to be quite so emphatic."

"Sorry." He gripped her wrist, sliding his hand along the length of her hair. "No offense meant."

"None taken. Not much anyway." Did he have to look so nice, so genuinely concerned that he might have hurt her feelings? "You were only being honest. We're too different."

Anna felt as if she'd swallowed a dryer sheet. Forest all moody and brooding was easier to resist. This man with twinkling eyes, mussed hair and a five o'clock shadow was dangerous. She canted toward him anyway. "Forest—"

"Of course you're right, though. It didn't work in high school. There's no reason to believe it will be any different now." The sparkle faded from his baby blues.

Anna hugged herself again, a poor shield against the emotions chugging through her. She should be long over the sting of insecurity caused by years of censure from her dad, but for some reason, hearing Forest question her judgment really stung. "It's okay. I know we have to think of Joey. He and I formed a bond today. Besides, those big-haired bimbos would toss me into Lake Huron if they saw me as competition."

Forest leaned back against the counter. "Big-haired bimbos?"

"You mean you haven't noticed an increase in unpaid parking tickets lately? My dad always rolled his eyes over the phenomenon. It seemed as if every single female in town landed herself in trouble to garner his attention."

He cocked his head to the side. "Is that what you're doing with me?"

"No!" She blinked fast, banishing memories of the times

she'd peeked through the stadium fence as a teen to watch him practice baseball. "I was talking about those spike-heeled jaywalkers who apply their makeup with a spatula before wobbling into your office."

"Oh, them. Yes, I've noticed one or two. Only an idiot would be attracted to women like that. They don't really want me, just a husband. Any guy would do."

"Whatever." Didn't he ever look in the mirror?

"I doubt I'll get married again, anyway. I can't afford another mistake. Joey doesn't need more upheaval in his life."

Anna got the message. He might as well have shouted it over a megaphone. She was fine as a temp sitter, maybe even a candidate for a tumble in the towels, but that was it.

She should have been mad. Instead, she was hurt. "I really should check on Joey. And don't worry, Forest. I won't throw myself at you again."

Anna raced into the hall, wondering, wanting. *Why not?* Too bad she didn't have a textbook answer.

FOREST STUFFED laundry into the baskets, cursing with each fistful of socks and towels. Kissing Anna had been beyond stupid. She'd spent only one day in his house and already he'd stepped over the line. If he'd kept his hands off her, he could have deluded himself that the attraction was all in his imagination.

Now he knew better. He wanted her, and nothing he could do would change that fact. All his life he'd tried to exert a strong control over his actions to overcome what he'd learned to think of as his irresponsible genes. But one simple, relatively tame kiss from Anna had made him want to do something really crazy. He had to consider his son and rely on willpower to get himself in control of his life once more.

Silence echoed from down the hall, broken only by the creak of an opening door. Forest couldn't stop himself from listening, absorbing Anna's husky voice.

"Joey?" she whispered softly. "Still sleepy? Enjoy your nap, precious boy. You can play ball with your daddy later."

One of those Madonna images rose in Forest's mind. He could imagine too well the way she would stroke her hand over Joey's curls, drape the blanket over him, being careful to leave his feet uncovered the way he preferred.

Paula had struggled with motherhood right from the start because of Joey's blindness. She'd traded Forest in for another model, a high-powered international attorney. She'd never even asked for custody of Joey, and now her weekend visits had dwindled to accommodate those European jaunts. After the divorce, Joey's pleas for his mama had just about torn Forest's heart to bits. Now Joey never asked for her. Somehow that hurt more.

Anna's voice continued to drift down the hall, "Sweet dreams. You're going to feel better in the morning."

Forest feared his world wouldn't settle quite so quickly. He glanced up to find Anna standing in the doorway, quietly, so somehow he must have sensed her presence.

She tilted her head toward Mt. Washmore. "What did you think I was hiding in the laundry closet?"

He tugged his ear. "Nobody."

"Nobody? *Nobody!*" She headed for the kitchen, indignation sparking from her. "You actually thought I would bring a man over while I was watching Joey? You should remember enough about me from that year we dated to know I'm not like that. Just because I don't live by your uptight rules doesn't mean I don't have my own moral code."

She dashed out the door.

Forest panicked. He sprinted after her, bounding down the steps. "Anna, I was just jeal—" No way would he admit that to her. *Swap tactics, Counselor.* "You can't quit."

She yanked her helmet off the handlebars. "I didn't say that. I finish what I start. But I have a problem coming here if you think I'm not trustworthy enough to watch your son."

"Don't be ridiculous. I know how much you care about kids." If he kept her talking, she wouldn't take off and he could sort things out.

"How big of you to concede that." She spun to face him, helmet clutched to her like a shield. "Did you or did you not think I had a paramour perched on top of your perfectly matching washer-dryer set?"

"Well—"

"Quit tugging your ear." She crinkled her nose. "It gives you away every time."

Damn. He hadn't even realized he was doing it. His hand fell to his side. "The thought may have crossed my mind."

"Apparently we don't know each other at all anymore."

With that, she launched her bicycle into motion, her hair sailing behind her as she made her way down the street. She pedaled slower than in the morning, her energy obviously depleted from taking care of Joey.

Forest kicked himself for not offering her a ride—not that she would have accepted it. But seeing her weary pace reminded him of how much she'd already given to his son.

And if for no other reason than that, he would keep his libido zipped up tight so she would stay.

ON FRIDAY EVENING, Anna stood by her front door and watched Forest park her bike beside the vegetable patch. Since he'd had to work late, past dark, he'd given her a ride home.

What a week they'd had. She'd gotten a Braille label maker and labeled everything in the house. After all, sighted children were exposed to words right away even if they couldn't yet read them. Why shouldn't children who were blind have the same experience?

The labels were clear, with Braille bumps, like the see-through sheets Seedlings used in their toddler books. When Anna read to Joey, she was still able to see the words, but Joey could run his fingers along the raised bumps, working to heighten his touch sensitivity.

Forest had been surprised at first, then embarrassed not to have started to do this himself. She'd reassured him it was easy for her to step in and point things out when he'd been mired in the day-to-day routine of raising a special needs child alone.

Any young child was tough work.

Mostly she'd done her best to keep up with a very active little boy who wasn't being challenged enough intellectually. She couldn't fault Forest as a father. He'd arranged his whole house and yard so Joey could run off all that energy.

But their house was sadly devoid of a variety of children's books. She'd found some fuzzy-textures board books for preschoolers. Most of the time Forest made up stories to tell his son. That was wonderful, too. Joey could create images in his mind. He didn't "see" the world the way his father or Anna did, but he had a vision all his own.

What was missing was reading. Forest hadn't been doing much with Joey, and Anna hoped that would change now.

Sheesh, the little stinker surely was working his way into her heart. The father wasn't too far behind.

Maybe she was coming down with Joey's virus.

She needed to get inside fast before she did something reckless like ask Forest to come in for a while. "Thanks for driving me home. That really wasn't necessary. I ride around at night all the time."

Leaving Joey snoozing in the truck, Forest ambled up the steps and leaned on the porch post with a weary sigh. "You've had a long day. We both have. It was the least I could do."

Anna fidgeted with her key ring. "You're such a nice man. You would probably rather be anywhere than here with me, yet here you are, doing the polite thing. When are you going to do something *you* want?"

Forest gave a half smile. "I already did that once earlier this week, and we almost ended up making out on a pile of laundry."

Anna gulped. Having the kiss hang between them all week had been tough enough. Flinging it out in the open sent her stomach into a somersault.

And they were alone. "Uh, Forest—"

"Don't worry." He grinned. "I've used up my supply of impulsive moves for the year."

She relaxed. A little. "It would be nice, wouldn't it, if we were the types who could do that."

"Do what?"

"Roll around in the laundry, get it all out of our system and move on with life."

His blue eyes swept over her. "Yes, it would."

"But we're not that way, are we?"

"Afraid not."

"Can we be friends?" she asked.

"I think we already are."

"Then why didn't you write me after you moved away from Oscoda all those years ago?" The words tumbled out of her mouth without her permission, but she couldn't bring herself to call them back.

His eyes turned sad even as he reached out to tuck a stray lock of hair behind her ear. "Because I was certain back then I wasn't good enough for you. When I left town, I figured a clean break would be best. It was better to let you lead your own life than string things out."

He'd broken her heart because he'd decided he wasn't good enough? Hadn't he seen how special he was then? Even her father thought he'd hung the moon. She'd even been a little jealous, feeling as if Forest was the son her father had always wanted.

"And now?" There she went again, blurting out words without thinking.

"Now? We're too different, and I have Joey to think of."

"Right. So we're friends." She stuck out her hand.

"Friends," he agreed, clasping her hand in his.

Why couldn't he have argued with her? And why couldn't she let go of him? "Then it's all settled."

Forest leaned toward her until Anna could feel the whisper of his breath against her skin, see every sweep of his long, black lashes.

Closing that last inch between them, he gripped her shoulders and pressed his lips to her forehead. Anna didn't move, merely held herself still just as he did, and breathed in the delicious, tangy scent of him, Forest, her high-school ex, who was fast becoming her grown-up friend.

He stepped back. "See you tomorrow at the recycling drive."

Forest pivoted away and loped back down the stairs to his truck. She watched him leave and wanted to cry with frustration. After this weekend to regroup her defenses, she still had one week left to fill out her contract.

Why did that scare her more than any extended stint in jail?

THE NEXT MORNING, Forest stared out over the library's parking lot. Suburbans, minivans and trucks were parked at odd angles while people unloaded bags and boxes full of recycling. Brown bins were parked near the tables for a recycling drive to earn money for the library—in particular, the children's section. Anna's doing, no doubt, after less than a month in town. He wove around the clusters of people. Smitty the cop held one of his daughters and a clear, blue plastic bag full of cans.

Forest tugged Joey forward, his gaze darting from group to group. Geez, was he really scouring the area for a simple glimpse of Anna?

Yep. He sure was.

Then he found her. She stood behind a table, clipboard in hand, directing the flow of activity. The sun glinting off her hair and the pencil tucked behind her ear. Forest's grip tightened around the twine binding his stack of newspapers.

They'd made it through their first week together with ease. Anna fit into his life so well it scared him. But people in town reminded him of the intense passion she'd shown for her various causes over the years—a passion that sometimes landed her on the wrong side of the law.

He welcomed the reminder. These people had known Anna longer than he had. It was tough seeing her smile when Joey brought her a flower. Hearing her laugh as they watched Joey soar down a slide.

Feeling the air crackle when they accidentally brushed against each other.

But right now, he needed to turn in his contribution to the recycling drive. Glancing down at his son, Forest straightened Joey's train conductor cap. "How about a treat? They've got cookies and juice."

"Cookies?"

"You bet. A whole tableful." Right next to Anna.

There wasn't any need to beat himself up about joining in the recycling effort. He had just as much right to be at the drive as anyone else. Like a good friend, he was supporting Anna's pet project. Why then did he feel like a teenager changing his route between classes so he could catch a glimpse of the new girl in school?

Joey tipped his ear to listen more closely, then a smile illuminated his round face. "Anna!"

He yanked his father's hand, pulling him toward the sound of her chiming laugh. With his other hand he waved the piece of newspaper he held. "Anna! I brought a 'cycling for you!"

Anna looked up from her clipboard. A grin spread over her face, brighter than the sun glistening off the asphalt as she took his lone flyer. "Hey there, Joey. What's this?"

"A recycling paper." He stuffed his hand in his pocket and pulled out a mangled dandelion. He lifted it toward her the way Forest had seen her do when Joey and Anna were playing "Name That Flower." Except Joey waggled it closer to her chin than her nose. "And a flower!" he announced.

"Oh, what a charmer you are!" Anna knelt eye level and received her presents as if they were bounty from a knight.

She pressed a kiss to his cheek. "Thank you, sweetie, these are absolutely the best gifts ever."

Forest lifted his neatly bundled stack. If Joey got a kiss for a scrap of paper, how would she react to a week's worth of *The New York Times?* "Joey and I wanted to do our part."

Joey gripped the edge of the table, stretching up on tiptoe. "Where's the cookies?"

Anna looped an arm around his waist and hoisted him level with the table so he could smell the cookies while she patiently identified each one. Finally, he settled on peanut oatmeal raisin. "Help yourself. There're plenty more."

Forest lifted his bundle of papers. "Where should I put these?"

She glanced over, her smile widening. "Toss them into the marked bin. We'll get a total weight at the end of the day."

If he got such a pulse-kicking smile for a measly week's worth of *The New York Times* and some old issues of *Sports Illustrated,* he could hardly wait to see her reaction to his bag of milk jugs.

Geez, he was worse now than during his teenage year when he'd tried to win her over with candy and meals out. "How much do you expect to raise today?"

"Not a whole lot. But that's not the point. If we earn enough to add a few books to the library while doing our bit for the environment and strengthening the community bond, then it's worth the effort."

"Well put." Forest untied the twine and pitched his offering in with ease. Ready to receive more praise for doing his part in saving natural resources, he pivoted to Anna. "I've got some free time this afternoon. As long as Joey cooperates, I'd be happy to help out, if you need an extra pair—"

He stared at the back of her head.

She was already preoccupied answering questions, offering directions to a group of people. He shuffled from one foot to the other, waiting for his turn.

It was an odd thing, being low on her list of priorities. And Forest was seeing a very different side of Anna. She was in her element, the undisputed queen of the day.

Accustomed to thinking of Anna as quirky and unconventional, he was startled to glimpse this smoothly efficient woman. Not even Judge Randall could accuse her of being disruptive today. She directed the whole event, armed only with a pencil and clipboard.

She didn't need him at all. Here, Anna was the cool, efficient professional, and he was just another guy with a pile of garbage.

CHAPTER FIVE

Monday morning, Anna pedaled up Forest's driveway and parked her bike where he wouldn't see it when he left. She had a surprise for him, and she didn't want him spotting it on his way out to work. They both deserved a reward for surviving the past week together.

And he had contributed to her recycling drive.

The image of him striding across the parking lot with his neatly bundled newspapers still warmed her. His offer to help had come as a shock, probably to him as well. He really could be sweet when he dropped the uptight act.

She rapped on the door, shrugging her backpack off her shoulders. No one answered, so she knocked again, harder. After another minute passed, she stepped halfway inside. "Good morning! Forest? Joey? It's just me."

"Hang on, Anna!" Forest shouted. "We're running late."

Late? Forest? She breezed into the house, through the

masculine living room with its big brown corduroy sofas and chairs, but little else for Joey to trip over. His toys all stayed piled in the same corners so he could find them. A few more steps took her to the breakfast nook.

Forest plowed into the kitchen, briefcase in hand. He scooped Joey up, gripping him by the back of his overalls and carrying him like a lunch box.

Joey squealed, "I'm an airplane! Flying high!"

"In for a carrier landing!" Forest skimmed his son to a stop on the tabletop. "Okay, kiddo. I have to get moving."

He plopped Joey into his booster chair and glanced over his shoulder at Anna. "Hope you don't mind feeding him breakfast. We lost track of time playing this morning."

A single lock of hair brushed his brow, just tapping the top of his glasses.

"Anna?"

"Huh?" She'd been totally focused on those baby blues. "Breakfast! Sure, I'd be happy to feed him. Cheese toast, right? No oatmeal."

"Are you all right?"

"I'm fine. Just thinking about all the money we raised at the recycling drive."

Anna had to make herself remember why she should keep her distance. Forest was too much like her conservative father. She was a free spirit. She would drive him nuts, and she truly believed this wonderful guy deserved happiness.

Bottom line, she'd had a lifetime of gentle censure from

her father. She didn't want to deal with it in any of her other relationships. Anna blinked back tears. *Think of your plans for Joey today, not Forest.*

She had dominoes in her backpack to help Joey work on numbers. He would be able to feel the indentions—almost like reverse Braille. She'd also ordered a few more Seedlings print-and-Braille books, even though he always wanted to end every reading session with *Seymour the Sea Turtle Snaps Up Lunch.* Good thing these books were so affordable because her budget was tight and she hated to ask Forest for money. Whenever she mentioned trying new things with Joey, a look of guilt crossed Forest's face as he blamed himself for not doing more for his son.

Forest knotted his tie. "I've never been to a recycling drive before. You really did a bang-up job organizing it."

"Thanks." Why did he have to be so nice?

"Okay. I really do need to go." He launched into motion again, snapping his briefcase open and dropping files inside. "I caught up with laundry over the weekend. That isn't in your job description here and I apologize for taking advantage. There's plenty of Joey's favorite juice in the fridge. And he has a new train set he really likes if you want to pull it out. Careful, though, because those pieces hurt like crazy if you step on them barefooted."

He grabbed the briefcase and his coat.

"Bye, son." He dropped a kiss on Joey's forehead, then turned to Anna.

Ohmigosh! Was he going to kiss her, too? He stood so

close, and Anna held her breath. She wanted to kiss him more than she wanted air.

He stepped back.

She must have imagined the whole thing. Good thing he couldn't see what was inside her head?

"Bye, Anna."

"Goodbye." It took every ounce of restraint she had not to smooth that lock of hair back from his forehead. She bit her lip, mumbling, "Nothing in common, nothing in common…"

Forest stopped at the door. "Did you say something?"

"Nothing important."

Friday couldn't come fast enough.

"HOLD STILL, sweetie!" Anna struggled with the chin strap of the helmet. She hoped she'd bought the right size. The box had said it would fit a four-year-old. The buckle clicked into place. "There! Ohhh, you look so cute!"

Joey stood in the middle of the kitchen, a neon-blue bicycle helmet in place. His head looked twice the size of his body, kind of like an alien child. He was all set for his first ride in her newly installed kiddy bicycle seat, complete with all the latest safety features.

She'd bought it over the weekend as a gift to herself after learning that hours alone in a house with a four-year-old could give a person an incredible case of cabin fever. Joey could only walk so far. The last thing she needed was more time to sit around and moon over Forest Jameson.

So why was she going to see him for lunch? *Just for Joey.*

The little guy would enjoy seeing his daddy. She latched on to the logical explanation with desperation.

"We're going to have such fun cycling around town today." She tucked the rest of their lunch in her backpack. "Ready to go? Do you need a potty break first?"

Much as Anna loved the kid, if she didn't get some adult conversation soon, she'd be a prime candidate for a strait-jacket.

"Let's go see Daddy." Joey waddled around the kitchen with a wide-legged cowboy swagger.

"Balancing that head must be quite a challenge, huh?" Anna knocked on his helmet. "Time to roll if we want to get that picnic lunch to your dad before noon. Daddy's going to be so proud to see his little boy in his very first helmet."

Twenty minutes later, Anna stowed the bike behind a row of bushes outside Forest's office and clasped Joey's hand in hers. "Ready to kidnap your dad, sweetie?"

Her heart beat faster with every step she took toward Forest's office door. She forced herself to walk slower along the cracked sidewalk, keeping more in step with the leisurely pace of her hometown.

The park loomed at the end of the street. At least she had memories of the time spent there. She was happy in her hometown, and if she wanted to continue to live here, she had to keep her job at the library. That meant no more protests, even if her park became a strip club. She shuddered. There had to be something she could do before time ran out.

Sighing, she pushed through the front door into the reception area of her father's old office, still featuring the same old-time trio of leather, mahogany and wainscoting.

And the Big-Hair Brigade.

Of course, these weren't the same women she'd seen in her father's office over the years, but they were carbon copies, and no fewer than five of them were wedged into the burgundy leather sofa and chairs. Ceiling fans clicked overhead, stirring the scent of furniture polish and hair product. All that gel should be considered a fire hazard. If anyone lit a cigarette, the whole place could go up in flames.

Anna strolled toward one of the women, an old classmate of hers. "Hi, Shirley."

Shirley Rhodes stuffed a tube of bubblegum-pink lipstick in her purse. "Good afternoon, Anna." She glided to her feet and pinched Joey's cheeks. "You are just the cutest little thing! You look just like your daddy-waddy."

Joey squirmed away, clinging to Anna.

"Sorry, he's just shy around strangers." Anna made a mental note to give Joey three treats later for his loyalty. She turned to the grandmotherly receptionist who used to work for her father before he retired. "Kay, is Forest free?"

Leather crackled as four women scooted to the edge of their seats.

The receptionist glared at them, then gave Anna a genuine smile. "He's tied up at the moment. But I'll let him know you and Joey are waiting."

"Thanks." Anna set Joey down and watched him scamper

over to the receptionist's desk. He felt his way down the drawers as if counting, until he pulled open the bottom one, where Kay apparently kept toys for him. Once he was settled with a pile of race cars, Anna turned her attention to Shirley. "What brings you here?"

"Another one of those blasted unpaid parking tickets. I don't know why I keep forgetting to mail the money. So here I am back in Forest's, I mean, Counselor Jameson's office." Shirley arched her back, making the very most of her chest. "Aren't we lucky to have such a smart young lawyer in Oscoda?"

"Hmm."

"Why are you here? Did you handcuff yourself to something else?" Shirley glanced back at her cohorts. Four compacts snapped closed, in synch.

"You heard about that?" A tic started right in the corner of Anna's eye.

"We're a small town of caring people," Shirley answered with ill-disguised insincerity.

Anna knew she should turn and walk away. A mature woman would smile politely and leave. She should ignore the spiteful bimbos and take Joey back to see his daddy-waddy.

Revenge was petty.

Joey tipped his face up from his Tonkas, grinning. She would have sworn his sightless expression said, *Go get 'em, Anna!*

If Joey insisted, who was she to argue? A wicked and

wonderful plan took shape in her mind. She could help Forest *and* her park without whipping out cuffs.

"Well, Shirley, actually, it's a rather sensitive matter." She paused for effect. "It's about Forest."

"Forest?"

"Oh, never mind." Anna pressed a hand to her cheek. "You're probably not interested in all this."

She didn't have a chance to pivot more than halfway around before Shirley grabbed her arm in a death grip.

"Spill it!" Shirley cleared her throat. "I mean, I would love to hear. Poor Forest may need a sympathetic shoulder."

He would probably asphyxiate on her perfume. "I'm sure he could use some friendly support."

"Well?"

Anna noticed that she had the attention of all five women and moved in for the kill. "It's about his park."

"His park?" Shirley arched a penciled brow.

This was too easy. "Remember the old park by the library?"

They frowned. Okay, maybe not as easy as Anna had thought.

"By the lake."

The women nodded in unison.

"It's slated to be a strip club."

Shirley shrugged. "So?"

Anna exhaled. They must be too busy time-sharing a brain cell—or maybe they actually cared what happened in this town after all. "That's where Forest's parents got engaged."

"Oh!" Shirley's hand fluttered to her chest. "How romantic."

"If it weren't for those oaks, Forest wouldn't be alive today." Anna shook her head slowly. The women were hooked. Now to reel them in. "He told me it's his fondest wish to find the woman of his dreams and propose beneath those branches."

"Oh, wow!" Shirley glanced back at her wide-eyed friends.

Anna sighed. "Too bad nobody's willing to help out with, maybe, marching in a picket line."

Shirley was first to the door.

Her cohorts weren't more than two steps behind her. The five frantic women pushed through the entranceway.

The door banged shut behind them.

Anna smirked, dusting her hands. She turned to the receptionist and shrugged. "Well, Kay, I had to clear them out so Joey could have some time with his daddy-waddy."

Kay winked. "Nice work, kiddo."

"Is he free yet?"

"He was hiding from the vultures, but I buzzed him when you arrived. He should be out in a minute." Kay winked. "I'll have to call you when the next batch flocks in."

Her stomach constricted. "Next batch?"

"There are plenty more where they came from." She shrugged. "Word gets around. At least he doesn't have to worry about ulterior motives with you."

"Of course not." She wasn't like *them*. She'd merely

helped Forest, with the side benefit of offering her park another shot at life. She couldn't have acted out of… jealousy?

Horror-struck, she gulped. "Uh, Kay. I just remembered something back at home I need to check on." She reached for Joey. "Come on, sweetie. We've got—"

"Kay, are they gone yet?" Forest asked as he stepped from his office. "Hi, Anna. I'm glad you're still here." He knelt and ruffled his son's hair.

He was? Anna stopped breathing. Their faces weren't more than six inches apart. If she breathed in even a hint of the spicy aftershave he wore, she might very well find herself staking out a spot for herself on the sofa.

She smiled weakly. "We stopped in to take you on a picnic."

"A picnic?" He looked wary. Was he remembering that almost kiss? With any luck, it would be the fastest lunch hour in history.

More importantly, they needed to finish before Shirley organized her troops.

"I loooove going to Anna's park," Joey squealed from atop his father's shoulders. He grabbed fistfuls of dried leaves from swaying branches while Anna and Forest strolled down Main Street.

Forest clutched Joey's feet to steady him as they walked past the row of lampposts. What a great small town. He'd have given anything to grow up in a place like this. Of course, that was why he'd chosen it for his son.

He'd almost kissed Anna again this morning at the house. Not some impulsive, hormonal kiss, but one of those "see you later" kisses. Those were the dangerous sort. They implied an ease with each other that went beyond just attraction.

After this week with Anna, he knew he respected her too much for a fling and he'd vowed he didn't want to get married again. What a mess.

Still, he owed her so much for all she'd done for him and his son. "Thanks for bringing lunch over."

"No problem." She clutched her sweater to her chest, the insulated food sack dangling from her elbow.

"It's nice to see Joey in the middle of the day."

"You can come home, you know. You don't have to hide from me in your office like you do from those other women. I'm not out to cuff you to the altar or anything."

The determined thrust of her jaw shouldn't have stung his pride, but it did. "I lose track of time at the computer."

"Then it's good we made you take a break." She hip bumped him. "You need to lighten up a little bit. Relax."

"I'm not that uptight." He felt relaxed—perhaps too relaxed. Maybe he should rile her a little and put some much-needed distance between them. "What's on today's menu? Any tofu in that sack? Nothing like a big slice of bran cake to stick to a man's ribs."

When she didn't answer, Forest glanced down at her. He couldn't have hurt her feelings, could he? He sometimes forgot how tenderhearted she was. She had one of those personalities that filled a room, even knocked down a few walls. "Anna?"

She nibbled her lip, staring straight ahead. The park loomed ahead, complete with her favorite bench. If he wasn't careful, Anna would have him cuffed to a parking meter while she sprinted over for an impromptu protest.

He needed to get her talking, fast. "You could have called me to come get you. It's a long way for you and Joey to walk."

"Oh, we didn't wa—"

"What the—?" Forest squinted, tipped his head to the side, then squinted again. Sure enough, a small crowd had gathered around an old oak, chanting and marching.

It was his waiting-room regulars, Shirley Rhodes and her pals. "It's our park! It's our pride! Those bulldozers better run and hide! It's our park…"

He turned to the woman beside him. "Anna!"

She blinked up at him with overly innocent eyes. "What? I'm not protesting. I'm having a picnic. I even brought Joey's jingle ball for you two to play catch."

Forest looked from her to the bizarre march. He knew she must have orchestrated it, but damned if he could figure out how. Which made him nervous. There wasn't a chance he could let her out of his sight now.

Worse yet, he didn't want to.

Grinning, Anna tugged him by the elbow, walking backward. "Come on. Don't let *them* ruin this for Joey."

Lord help him, she was beautiful. Radiant. The sun glinted

off her hair like fire. She had just the kind of body he liked, with soft, womanly curves.

Why was he supposed to resist her?

Oh yeah, their differences and his determination not to marry again. Funny how often he forgot about all that lately. "Okay. Whatever you did, I don't think I want to know. At least you're not dancing with that cheering squad."

She gazed longingly at the picketing bunch. "They're cheerleaders. Apparently they knew how to organize that sort of rhyming demonstration with a speed and ease I could learn from."

Shirley waggled a wave at Forest before resuming her hip-twitching strut and upping the volume. "Take your saw! Take your chain! Take them and go home again! Take your saw…"

The whole town had gone nuts.

Forest looked away from Shirley and her pals, not a difficult task, and focused on Anna. Her wide eyes blinked up at him. Tears glinted. Ah man, he was a sucker for tears.

He stroked a knuckle along her jaw. "Why is the park so important to you?"

Her eyes widened. She blinked faster. Anna dodged his touch and walked ahead.

He caught up, ducking to look at her. "Anna?"

She took her time answering as they padded across the park lawn. "You're the first person to ever ask me why."

"Huh?"

"No one ever wants to know *why* I protest. Not even my

father. I always thought that even if he didn't agree with me, maybe he would want to know why." She slumped back against a tree. "It hurts to think he doesn't care enough."

"Anna, of course he cares." Forest stopped in front of her and hefted Joey from his shoulders to the ground. "Your dad worries himself crazy about you."

"That's the whole point. He worries because he doesn't trust me. Strange, huh? I'm twenty-five years old, self-supporting, and he doesn't trust me to have enough sense to manage my life."

His heart thumped, and it had nothing to do with Joey's tennis shoes drumming against his chest. "Tell me, why is the park so important? I want to understand."

He really did want to know. A good attorney would have dug for the reasons the first night. An honorable man would have had the patience to listen. He'd let her down on both counts.

She traced her toe through the dirt. "My mother and I spent so many hours here. After she died, Dad packed picnics and brought me here so we could feel close to her. We'd sit under that tree with our PB&Js and root beer. He would ask me about my day and help with my homework. Silly memories, huh?"

"Not at all." Forest looked at the crown of her bowed head and wanted to hug her.

His throat closed. There was his reason for never asking. A vulnerable Anna was impossible to resist.

She flicked her braid over her shoulder, the old spunky

Anna seeming to have returned. Maybe it was just a woman thing, attaching so much sentimental value to a park. Women kept scrapbooks and pressed flowers. Definitely a woman thing. Even Shirley Rhodes and her pals had joined in the effort.

The former cheerleaders broke from a huddle and stood in a chorus line. "It's no joke. Save our oaks. It's no joke…"

Anna's shoulders slumped. The old Anna would have been joining in the march and scripting better lyrics.

Had he and her father done this to her? Dimmed the spark that made her so special?

Forest knew he was in deep trouble. With half a nudge, he could find himself painting signs and joining the march to save a bunch of trees with root rot.

CHAPTER SIX

Heart lighter than she could ever remember, Anna skipped over a root jutting from the sidewalk while Forest carried a sleepy Joey back to the office.

It meant so much to her that Forest had asked her about the park, and in talking, she had come to realize part of her reason for hanging on so tight. As long as the park was here she had hopes of healing the distance between her and her father. Odd how acknowledging a problem somehow eased its weight. Forest's logic had helped her with that.

"Be honest, now," Forest said. "You set up Shirley."

Anna enjoyed a much-needed grin. "I'm not admitting anything until I speak with my attorney."

"Your attorney needs the truth to properly represent you." He lifted a brow. "The truth?"

"They were driving Kay crazy. I told them how your mom proposed to your dad under the old oak tree and that you'd always wanted to propose to your bride beneath it." She shrugged. "And voilà, they called up their old cheer-leading skills in a heartbeat for an instant big-haired riot."

"You did it because Kay wanted them gone?"

Anna tugged at her turtleneck. "Maybe they were bugging me a little, too."

He grinned. "You were jealous."

Why lie? "A smidge."

Forest reached across to stroke a windswept strand of hair behind her ear.

Grinning back, Anna kicked a rock along the sidewalk as they walked to Forest's office. Lunch had been nice, but it would have been so much better without Shirley and Company. If Shirley Rhodes had thrust her chest under Forest's nose one more time, Anna would have gagged.

Then there was her own attraction to Forest mucking up everything. They couldn't keep jumping ten feet every time they accidentally rubbed against each other.

Accidentally? Or were those toe-curling moments in-tentional? At least she would have the bike ride home to clear her head.

Once outside the office, Anna reached to take the droopy Joey from Forest's arms. "Okay, kiddo, nap time."

Forest passed his son over. His broad hand skimmed her neck. Anna forced herself not to jerk away. If she moved, that would only make matters worse, because then they would look at each other. Aware.

She swallowed the lump in her throat. "Uh, thanks."

His brow furrowed, then smoothed. "Do you have a minute? We could set Joey down on the bench while we talk."

Talk? Oh Lord. He was going to harp on the Shirley debacle again.

"Sure," she said with little enthusiasm, gently settling a snoozing Joey on the bench. She shrugged out of her sweater and draped it over him. Bracing herself, she turned. "What do we need to discuss?"

"This." He dipped his head and brushed his mouth over hers, once, twice, before pulling away.

Breathless, she flattened her hands to his chest, grateful for the privacy of the overgrown hedges. "I thought you said we were going to talk."

"I lied. Do you have a problem with that?"

She couldn't deny the obvious. "No problem at all."

He took off his glasses and lifted her against him. Anna could only hang on, her toes off the ground, the delicious rasp of his afternoon beard against her skin reminding her they weren't in high school any longer.

She stroked the hair at the base of his head. How odd that she'd always preferred longer hair on a man. Not now.

Easing back, Anna looked up at him. "Wow."

"Ditto. Lady, you pack quite a wallop."

He set her on her feet again, not that it eased the feeling of floating.

She gulped. "I should take Joey home now."

Slowly he nodded. "Hang on a second." He wouldn't meet her gaze. "I'll check in with Kay, then drive you home. It's too far for you to carry Joey while he's sleeping."

"Oh, uh, I didn't walk. I started to tell you before we got sidetracked with my park. I have a little surprise."

"Surprise?" he said, voice tight.

"A kiddie bike seat." She slipped behind the row of bushes and returned with her bike. Joey stirred when she set him in the seat and adjusted his helmet, then settled back into slumber as she buckled him in.

"Cool, huh?" she said. "We had a nice little ride over."

Anna turned to look at Forest. He stood as still as the biblical Lot's wife when she'd taken that fatal peek over her shoulder.

Wow! She'd rendered Counselor Jameson speechless for once. Of course, Joey was mighty cute. "Maybe you could look into buying one for yourself, take father-son weekend trail rides. Oh, and I bet he would enjoy camping trips when he's a little older."

Why couldn't she stop babbling? So he'd shown an interest in her feelings, her concerns. That didn't mean anything. But Anna didn't even wait for his reply. She needed to get home before Forest did something sweet again. She did not need to have her heart trounced.

She swung her leg over the bike, ready to forget all about the man with the tender blue eyes. The first man to care enough to ask about her day since she'd gobbled PB&Js under the oaks twenty years ago. With a quick wave goodbye, Anna pedaled off, Shirley's taunting chants drifting on the breeze.

"We'll keep the park! We'll keep the land! We don't need no strip-club band!"

STANDING OUTSIDE his office, Forest watched Anna cycle away, his son's helmeted head bobbing from side to side.

And he just couldn't stop thinking about all those years riding in the side car of his parents' motorcycle, helmet in place. He winced at the memory of other kids in station wagons pointing and making faces, while he'd clutched his baseball and mitt. After graduating from law school, he'd bought the biggest truck he could afford.

He realized his knee-jerk reaction to seeing Joey in a helmet was silly. His adventurous son would enjoy the free-flying sensation and Forest wanted him to live life to the fullest.

For someone who'd known Joey only a week, Anna was doing an amazing job of introducing him to new experiences. After he'd finished reading the judge's proposal for his old congressman friend last night, Forest had spent hours on the Web site for Seedlings Braille Books for Children.

He'd been so focused on making sure Joey's physical life was unhampered, he'd missed other needs, assuming they would be addressed at school. Anna had simply smiled and said the two of them had everything covered now. That he was a loving, proactive father and Joey would have a rich life because of it.

Her praise meant a lot to him when every day he questioned whether he'd done enough for his son.

He was starting to care about Anna, too much, and that was dangerous. He just wasn't ready to think about relationships, especially marriage.

A long shadow stretched on the sidewalk in front of him, and someone tapped him on the shoulder. Just to be safe, Forest checked the shadow for big hair, then turned to find the judge. The father of the very woman Forest was all but panting after.

Forest swallowed heavily. It didn't help. "Hello, sir."

"Good afternoon, boy!" The judge snapped his plaid suspenders. "I hear you've been out for a little picnic."

"Word sure travels fast."

"I stopped in at the office and Kay told me."

Forest gestured up the steps toward the office door. "Why don't we head inside, where it's warmer."

The judge shook his head. "I only wanted to congratulate you on making it through the first week without any hardships."

Friday seemed five years away, rather than five days. "We're…managing."

"Thank you for keeping her out of trouble."

Forest bristled. An image of Anna's sad eyes as she stared at *her* park stabbed him. For the first time, he looked at the judge and found himself questioning his mentor's judgment. Were they right to keep their proposal to the congressman a secret from her? Her father swore it was best not to get her hopes up. "Actually, she's been a real godsend."

"Sure, she's good with kids. But those meals of hers." Judge Bonneau shuddered, a hint of a grin peeking through.

Forest resented the way the judge seemed to put down Anna. She was an amazing woman. Sure, her style was different, but different could be good. Exciting. Fun. "Her spinach lasagna's actually not half-bad. It's the first time Joey ate vegetables without flinging them across the room—"

Had the judge actually chortled? Forest frowned, certain he must be mistaken.

Judge Bonneau cleared his throat. "That's quite gentlemanly of you, son. But you don't have to defend her to me. I understand my daughter, faults and all, and she's going to need extra watching until I can persuade my friend in the House to get behind an injunction."

She needed watching? Damn it. There the judge went again, treating Anna like a child. "Sir, with all due respect, I think you need to spend some time with Anna and get to know your *adult* daughter. She's a bright, funny woman."

Also a beautiful woman who turned him inside out with her unreserved smiles.

The judge's bushy brows rose up to his receding hairline. "You can't actually be having, uh, feelings for my Anna?"

"Of course not." Maybe. A distinct possibility. Most likely.

"Now, don't get me wrong, I love that daughter of mine, but you two are oil and water and I really want you both to be happy."

Forest studied the judge, then realized that he himself might have spouted the same pompous-sounding bull a week ago.

Forest climbed the first step toward his office. "Think about what I said. Consider it the student passing along advice to the teacher for a change. Stop in and talk to your daughter sometime when you haven't been called by the police station."

"Sure, boy." The judge thumped Forest on the shoulder.

Forest felt oddly lighthearted as the wind spiraled autumn leaves down the sidewalk. But one fact clanged loud and clear in his mind. He could lighten up on his uptight ways, but he couldn't change who he was, and didn't really want to. Anna was special. He'd only just begun to realize how special. A man like him would take all that spark from her, just like her father was trying to do. That would be a real crime.

She needed someone with an adventurous spirit to match her own. He wanted peace and his *Sports Illustrated* subscription, for himself and Joey. Forest didn't like surprises, and Anna was like a magician's sack full of them. He never knew if he might get a cute rabbit, or if she would saw him in half.

Where did they go from here? Friendship?

At least it was something, a relationship of sorts, because he couldn't bring himself to tell her goodbye altogether. But he needed to make their friendship work.

If he'd learned nothing else from his debacle of a marriage, it was that relationships required compromise. He almost shuddered at the thought of more scenes like the one they'd just endured at the park. Protests and sit-ins and handcuffings. Somehow, he would have to convince her to compromise, as well, starting with throwing out those cuffs.

Forest stared at his mentor and resisted the urge to snap at him. The judge hadn't made his life one bit easier by throwing Anna and him together. He might as well have tossed a match onto a puddle of gasoline.

Anyone with sense could have seen how attracted Forest was to Anna back in high school. And the judge was too smart of a man to have missed that.

Forest thunked himself on his dense, hormone-fogged forehead and sank down onto the step. "You set us up."

The judge raised a bushy, red brow.

It suddenly made sense. "You orchestrated all of this. You knew full well that tenderhearted Anna wouldn't be able to keep herself from offering to help with Joey."

Forest sifted through the obvious, all the while kicking himself that he'd missed the signs earlier, including his nanny's abrupt departure. "Mrs. LaRoche's resignation seemed to come out of the blue. You sent me to help Anna with the handcuff deal and brought her those clingy clothes the day Joey was sick."

"Guilty as charged." The judge smirked, apparently not ashamed of being caught in his cupid antics. "You two were both so stubborn back in high school, too prideful to write to each other over the years. Trudy LaRoche and I decided to give you a little help this time."

Forest had a clear image of the judge and Mrs. LaRoche plotting his downfall. Who else was in on their scheme? "Judge Randall?"

"That part's real, and convenient timing."

"Why should I believe you now?"

"You should be complimented! I'm offering you my greatest treasure, my daughter."

"Sir, she's not yours to give." And perhaps not Forest's to have. The thought wasn't as comforting as a confirmed bachelor should have wanted. "Anna has a mind of her own, and a lot more sense than you give her credit for."

Wasn't the irate father supposed to be coming after him with a double-barrel shotgun? This kind of endorsement was too weird, and distinctly uncomfortable. Worst of all, he hated the sense that he'd been played, Anna, too, for that matter.

The judge chuckled. "I do so enjoy being right. This is perfect for everybody. You get a new wife, a keeper this time, because I didn't raise a quitter. Even that cute little boy of yours comes out a winner with a full-time mama."

Wife? Mama? The judge had blindsided him with the shotgun after all.

Forest gasped for breath. Of course the judge was thinking rings and weddings. Anna was his daughter.

But Forest had screwed up his first marriage, and he hated making mistakes. He wouldn't make the same one twice. He loved his son too much to put him through that again. He lov—

He *liked* and respected Anna too much to offer her anything but honesty. For now, he wanted picnics and friendship. They could continue or call it quits anytime. It wasn't as if he couldn't live without her.

Why then did he know without question that he planned to let Mrs. LaRoche finish her "vacation" just so he could have a few more days to play house with Anna?

ANNA TURNED the last page on the Seedlings Braille book she'd been reading to Joey. "The end."

"Again! Again! Again!" He bounced on the sofa.

"You've already memorized the words to this one." As well as the feel of the bumps, she hoped. "How about we try a new one. It's about a fire truck."

"A fire truck?" He tipped his head in concentration. "I like trucks."

She heard the rumble of Forest's truck outside. "Oops. Daddy's home. Maybe he can read this one to you."

The front door creaked open.

Joey's face lit up. "Daddy!"

He catapulted off the sofa and ran across the room, his tiny boot catching on a wrinkle in the rug. But Forest hefted him up just in time. What an amazing man. He'd been there in so many ways for Joey. Her heart ached a little more.

Joey plastered a big wet kiss on his father's cheek, then pulled back. "Guess what, guess what, guess what?"

"What, big guy?" Forest gave him a bear hug hello before

letting him slide back to the ground. The two held hands as they made their way toward the recliner chair where they always sat to share reviews of their day.

"Anna is teaching me to read."

Forest settled, half in, half out of his chair. "Could you explain that to me again?"

Joey squiggled and squirmed to get more comfortable in his father's lap. "Anna's teaching me to read bumpy books. I don't got it all right yet, but I like feeling the words while she tells me the story."

Forest's eyebrows met in the middle of his forehead.

Anna rose, raced over and knelt in front of him, giving him the small stack of books from her most recent Seedlings order. She placed them in his hands. "You have to let go and enjoy the books the same way you enjoy Joey's baseball-beeper." Her hands fluttered to rest on his knees. "Besides, you can't expect to think of everything yourself."

He covered her hands with his. "Thank you."

The connection crackled between them, until she wanted to crawl up in his lap and kiss him until they both couldn't think, much less talk, but Joey was in the room. And yeah, when it came to her shifting feelings for this man, she was a bit of a coward.

Anna slid her hands free, standing. "Well then, I guess I'll leave you two to your supper."

"Anna, do you want to—"

"I'll see you tomorrow." She cut short his invitation to join them before she caved and accepted. It would be too easy to let herself become a part of their evening routine and then be crushed when he found her unconventional ways unsuitable for a lawyer's wife—much less the mother of his child.

UNWILLING TO END this time with Anna and not sure why, Forest slid Joey off his lap and picked up her backpack for her. "Don't forget your bag."

He tried to close the bag, but the zipper kept hitching on something. By the time he caught up to her on the porch, he had figured out the problem. He pulled out a crumpled piece of paper that was part of a stack of letters held by a clip. He took them out to straighten the top paper.

Across from him, Anna froze.

It was a letter to the editor about saving the park, with copies to be sent to everyone from the governor to the garden committee. The letter bordered on libel, and violated their agreement for Anna to lie low.

How odd that he felt more betrayed than mad, Forest thought.

He passed her the backpack and her letters. "What an interesting definition you have of lying low."

She took the items solemnly. "People in this town express their displeasure about the part right and left, but no one else seems interested in doing anything about the situation."

Forest cocked his head. "How can you be so sure?"

"I watch. I listen."

"But you don't know all that's going on. Your father has a pal in the House of Representatives who owes him a favor. We've been working toward an injunction for over a week now."

Her features froze. "It would have been nice if you'd told me."

"The last thing your father wanted was you handcuffing yourself to the man's waiting-room sofa."

Her fists were clenched, her eyes wounded. "That's not only unfair, it's hurtful. I may not do things your way, but I am an intelligent adult."

She was right, and just like her father with Mrs. LaRoche and the congressman, he'd gone behind her back without asking for her input. He was just as guilty as her old man, whom he'd condemned a few hours earlier. "Wait, Anna, I'm sorry."

She backed away down the steps, toward her bike. "Sorry may not be enough if that's really how you feel about me."

He didn't want to let her go, ever. But what about her penchant for protesting? Would it increase over the years? Aside from giving him an ulcer, what kind of example would it set for Joey and any other children he and Anna might have together?

Other children. An impish little girl with freckles, red pigtails and stars in her innocent green eyes. The image was so distracting he almost walked into a ditch.

Not that Anna would agree to make babies with him anyway. She was looking at him as if he'd locked up Santa Claus on Christmas Eve.

Damn. There had to be some way to convince her to lighten up on the protesting, because he couldn't imagine letting her walk away from him. Or rather pedal away.

She climbed onto her bike and raced down the sidewalk before he could blink. Even if her views differed from his, he'd always loved the way she—

Loved? Hell, yes! He loved *her.*

Forest rested his forehead against a porch post. How was he ever going to win her back now? She would probably slam the door in his face.

Turning to go inside, he noticed she'd left some of her books behind, which gave him a perfect excuse to show up on her doorstep.

Somehow that seemed a little too obvious, and she had said the books were for Joey. Forest needed something big to snag her attention. His hand gripped her purse, the spare set of handcuffs poking the canvas.

Inspiration hit. He had a pretty good idea how to make sure she listened. "Hang on, Joey. We've got a few errands to run."

And he knew exactly where to go for mentorship.

CHAPTER SEVEN

The next morning, Anna stuffed her backpack full of the supplies she needed for the nature-walk activities she had planned for Joey—presuming Forest still let her in the house after their argument.

After stomping around her cottage for an hour, then tossing and turning half the night, she'd finally called her father. He'd surprised her by simply including her in the endeavor to appeal to his congressman friend. Pop asked her to stop by the park on her way to Forest's home this morning and snap some photos to go along with the paperwork he would be sending up to his friend in the House.

She tucked her digital camera into her backpack and zipped it closed before heading out. Pedaling over, she envisioned the different angles that would best show off the park's beauty and community appeal. She even considered moving benches around. Or what if she had time to add some of the equipment Forest had in his backyard?

Forest's backyard.

A vision began to form in her mind of a whole different park altogether—or rather a section of the park devoted to children with special needs.

Her excitement level rose as she envisioned a summer camp run in partnership with the library. It would offer activities for special-needs children that would give them the opportunity to stretch their legs, minds and emotional wings. Now, wouldn't that put little Oscoda on the map faster than any strip club?

Of course, the cool, collected Forest would be the best front man for her plan. They would be working together, combining their individual strengths. Just as they'd worked together to give Joey everything he needed. Why couldn't she have thought of that before?

Partnership. Passion. And love. The perfect blend.

After the way she'd dashed out yesterday, she had some apologizing to do. She thought about the photos she was going to take for her dad.

Working with Forest and her father. How funny. It was something she would never have considered less that two weeks ago. But then without Forest's influence, she would never have been open-minded enough to envision this park idea at all. What an amazing man.

Her heart filled with a love for him bigger than Lake Huron.

So why had she run from him last night? Time to start taking some risks in her personal life as well as her professional life. Starting today—after she finished these photos for Pop.

Anna fished around inside her backpack and pulled out the digital. She aimed, focused, took one shot after another, figuring she could weed through the pictures and choose the best later. She would definitely have to stop by again this afternoon with Joey and snap more photos when the park was full of people. She wondered why Pop had insisted she come now, when it was so darn chilly the mist hadn't even burned off the lake yet. A couple of joggers circled the perimeter. A lone man sat parked on the bench reading his newspaper.

Well, she could at least take some pictures of him to show the diversity of people who enjoyed the park. And it did make a romantic tableau—a handsome man, the Great Lake stretching out beyond him.

Handsome?

Her mind snagged on the shape of his head, the color and texture of his hair. It couldn't be. She moved closer.

It was.

Deep breath. She inched nearer as the park slowly came alive with morning activity. A dog walker headed for the lake. Three mothers appeared, pushing strollers. Anna stopped in front of the man just as he folded his paper and draped it over his arm.

"Hi, Forest," she said, her voice a breathless whisper. She glanced around. People were out for a stroll or a bike ride. "Where's Joey?"

"I have a friend watching him while I came looking for you." His wary blue eyes glittered behind his glasses.

She'd do anything to erase that wariness. "You were? I was just about to come over to your place so we could talk."

"Good." A lock of hair slid free and brushed the top of his glasses. "What did you want to tell me?"

"Not here," Anna said. "Too many people, and this is kind of private."

He clasped her hand in his and tugged her over beside him. "What's wrong with a little audience now and then?"

Could that really be her reserved attorney talking?

Snap. Forest clicked a handcuff around her wrist.

Anna stood frozen with shock.

Snap. He closed the other around his wrist until they sat side by side, the chain looped through a bar on the same park bench where she'd staged her protest.

"Forest!" Had he gone nuts? She tugged. "Forest! Unlock us. Stand up!"

"Nope."

"Have you lost your mind?"

"Nope." Her uptight lawyer had never looked more at ease. He was even grinning.

What did he find so amusing?

Clusters of people gathered around them. Forest's secretary, Kay, wandered over with a few of her friends from the garden club, and Shirley Rhodes and her friends waved from the beauty salon across the street, clutching their morning lattes from a nearby coffeehouse.

"Forest, you're really causing a scene here." Frantically, Anna looked left and right, expecting a police officer to appear. "Quit this! Now, before somebody calls the cops. You're a lawyer. You can't afford to be arrested."

He didn't budge.

"Be reasonable! What do you think you're doing?"

Forest gripped her hand in his. "I'm protesting the way you walked away from me without giving us a fighting chance at working things out."

His words sunk in, and her knees folded. She wilted down beside him. "Oh!"

From behind a dilapidated visitors' center, her father stepped out with Trudy LaRoche, who held Joey by the hand. Edward Bonneau winked at Anna as he slung an arm around Trudy's shoulders. "Hello, Anna."

"Pop?"

"I love you, daughter dear." He smiled at her with an openness she hadn't seen since her mother was alive. "I just want you to be happy."

Anna smiled back, but she was beginning to understand how Alice had felt in Wonderland. Just what was going on here?

She looked around at the familiar faces and realized their presence here couldn't be simply coincidence. Had her father and Trudy been matchmaking?

Anna turned to Forest. "You planned this, for me?"

He nudged his glasses. "You of all people should know you can't have a protest without an audience. So I'm making my statement."

Something warm and wonderful unfurled inside her, a renewed flicker of hope. "You are?"

"You bet."

While she told herself it shouldn't matter after he'd made such a grand gesture, she couldn't help asking, "What about last night and your disapproval of my protest methods?"

His thumb caressed the inside of her wrist. "I started thinking about that after you left, and letters are a perfectly acceptable means of protest. You were right. I was just... uh..."

"Hurt?" she dared ask.

"I thought you would have come to me for help with something like that. But then I realized your father and I should have trusted you as well with our congressional plans. My only excuse is that I can't think when you're around."

She understood completely, since she couldn't form coherent thoughts around him most of the time either. "You do say the sweetest things, Counselor."

"No, I don't, but I'm going to try, because I happen to think we've got something pretty special going between us."

Could this be real? "I agree. I want to work with you, and today I had a great idea for this special park. I want us to work *with* each other."

"You do?"

She gestured to the crowd and tapped the cuffs. "You sure know how to get your point across."

He smiled that wonderful lopsided grin. "All in the name of love."

Anna sure hoped she'd heard right. Just in case, she needed to hear him say it again. "For love?"

"For love. Isn't that what it's all about?" Forest linked hands with her. "Anna, marry me. Not because you're great with Joey or because we're attracted to each…" He paused, glancing at the crowd gathering around them. "Marry me because I love you."

Anna cupped his face with her free hand. "Those words beat a bouquet of flowers hands down, Counselor."

"Wait, I'm not finished yet." Forest stood, dragging Anna up with him. He turned to Trudy LaRoche and the judge. "Did you hear that? I love her! Did everyone hear me? I love this incredible woman. And if she'll have me, I'll even buy a tandem bike—with helmets."

Applause broke out, echoing up through the trees speckled with autumn leaves.

Forest rested his forehead against Anna's, creating a bubble of privacy in the overpopulated park. "Let's plant our own seedlings to grow into trees that we can sit under for picnics with our children and grandchildren. What do you say? Will you marry me?"

"Yes." She whispered the word, hearing it echo in her heart. "Yes to you, Forest, and yes to Joey."

She extended her arms for Joey, the precious child who'd really brought them together. "Joey?"

"Anna!" he shouted, arms outstretched as he launched himself toward Forest and her.

"She said yes!" Mrs. LaRoche squealed.

A rousing cheer filled the park. Anna eased away with a laugh just in time to see her father kiss Trudy LaRoche. She hoped he was feeling as happy as she was.

Shifting her attention back to Forest, Anna caressed his face. "I love you so much."

He gave an exaggerated sigh. "Thank heaven. Now I can cancel the circus that was going to perform on your lawn if you'd said no."

"Well, in case you're in doubt, my answer is yes! Forever." What a perfect team they would make.

Forest nuzzled her ear. "Are you ready for a family breakfast picnic? I've packed all your favorites."

She rattled the cuffs. "Shouldn't we ditch these first?"

"Good idea," Forest agreed. "Hey, Judge, pass me the keys."

Anna's father searched one pocket, then another. "Uh, hold on, son. I'm sure they're here somewhere."

No keys?

Forest cradled Anna against him. "No rush." He gazed down into her eyes. "This is exactly where I'd like to be for the rest of my life."

Dear Reader,

I am honored to have had the chance to work with Harlequin's More Than Words program, and I appreciate the serendipity to have been paired with the Seedlings Braille Books for Children project in particular as it's a subject very near to my heart. My youngest sister, Beth, suffered an accident at the age of six that left her partially blind. Due to therapy in conjunction with one of her many surgeries, she spent a summer completely blind. I was her "seeing-eye sister," helping her find her way around the world, reading to her for hours on end.

So you can imagine my heart swelling all the more when I heard from Seedlings founder Debra Bonde about the amazing tribute she has built in honor of her daughter Anna. After Anna died in an accident on her way to New Orleans to tutor disadvantaged children, Debra began "Anna's Book Angel Project," which donates at least ten free Seedlings books a week. I knew right away I would want to name the heroine in my story after this awesome young woman.

To learn more about Seedlings Braille Books for Children, check out their fabulous Web site www.seedlings.org. I hope you will consider purchasing a book to donate to your local library or making a donation directly to Seedlings to help fund their efforts to bring the gift of words to all. The quote on their Web site says it best...

"By the touch of a finger behold the world."

Many thanks,

Catherine Mann

http://catherinemann.com

Kathy Silverton

Stitches from the Heart

A tiny newborn baby sent home from the hospital wearing little more than a diaper. That's the image Kathy Silverton couldn't let go of eight years ago when her twelve-year-old daughter, Shane, told her about an article she'd read claiming many American babies born into poverty begin their lives without even a shirt on their little backs.

The story touched something deep inside the California mom, who immediately picked up her knitting needles and began to knit. Whenever she had a moment to spare, Kathy crafted booties, blankets, sweaters and hats for the babies and sent the tiny items to hospitals, hoping they would reach the families who needed them most. Soon she was recruiting her friends to further the cause.

But it wasn't until a short blurb about her charity work

ran in the *Los Angeles Times* that Kathy's mission took on a life of its own. Within days after the story hit the stands, over one hundred women contacted Kathy asking to help.

A dream was born.

It's ironic that Kathy has no time to knit anything these days. She's too busy. That one tiny spark of caring back in 1998 set off a blaze of generosity that has spread throughout the United States and into Canada and England. Today Kathy is the founder and president of Stitches from the Heart, a recognized 501 nonprofit organization whose main mission is to help families in need.

The organization now boasts a whopping ten thousand volunteers, who send their handmade baby and toddler items to Stitches from the Heart, based in Santa Monica. The items are packed, fifty to a box, and sent to over 432 hospitals and charities across the country. A quarter of a million hats and booties have been sent to needy kids.

"I look back and I cannot find the words to describe my amazement at this whole thing," says Kathy now. "I'm just so happy because so many good things have come from it."

Special delivery

In its formative stages, Stitches took over three rooms in the Silvertons' home. And no wonder. The charity was shipping and receiving approximately two thousand baby items a *week*. Not only was finding space a problem, but running the thriving organization in a residential neighborhood meant logistics dilemmas, as well.

"My postman was ready to kill me. I mean, he was *really* ready," Kathy says with a laugh.

Determined to find a better place to conduct business, Kathy subleased a storefront and opened the Stitches from the Heart Yarn Shoppe on April 1, 2004, on a wing and a prayer. The little shop initially even used free supermarket cardboard shelves to hold the merchandise. But now, with ample help from Stitches volunteers, the store has become a success story, helping to defray the overwhelming cost of shipping the donated items out to hospitals and charities. The volunteers help price and sell yarn, teach knitting and crocheting classes and pack boxes there, as well.

But there has been a downside to running the store. Barry, Kathy's ever-supportive husband, who initially convinced her she could turn her dream into reality, says he misses having all the women in the kitchen and around the house.

The other winners

Although the babies and their families are the obvious beneficiaries of Stitches from the Heart, Kathy says she's convinced that the volunteers receive something even more profound when they knit a tiny cap or sweater: a sense of accomplishment and purpose knowing they are contributing to a better world.

"I know the babies get the benefit, but think of all the givers," Kathy says.

Because of this unexpected offshoot, Stitches from the Heart donates yarn, needles and supplies to over ninety-two retirement communities for seniors who cannot afford to purchase their own materials. Yet the money to provide the supplies is getting harder to come by in the past few years, Kathy says. In the beginning, yarn retailers and manufacturers often donated crates of yarn, but now with the recent crafts and knitting boom, the stores are selling more and donations are drying up. Last year Kathy was even forced to dig into her own pocket to buy supplies for the seniors. Needless to say, Kathy still counts on individual donations from women willing to reach into their personal stash of unused yarn.

"I probably have enough yarn to last me five lifetimes," she jokes. "Knitters are like that."

While running a charity as busy as Stitches from the Heart has its frustrations and challenges, it's the letters from volunteers and the hospital nurses that help Kathy stay focused. Over the years she has received letters from elderly women who felt the world had forgotten about them but have since found new hope and purpose through Stitches. She has also received letters from cancer survivors who tell her their volunteer work for Stitches from the Heart helped them face their darkest days while in treatment.

But there is one letter that stands out and allows Kathy to understand the impact of her vision on the lives of real people across the country.

A traveling nurse in New York recently wrote a thank-you note saying she visited a small trailer where a woman and her children lived. The trailer, ice-cold, was without heat. Quickly realizing she had to warm the children up, the nurse ran back to her vehicle and pulled out the big box of knitted clothes she'd received from Stitches from the Heart. The youngest baby's tiny lips trembled from the cold as the nurse fitted it into a sweater and wrapped the children in blankets.

When Kathy hears these stories—and she admits she receives "tons of them"—all the hard work coordinating shipping, running the store and spending hours in front of the computer writing the organization's newsletter seems worthwhile. And she admits Stitches from the Heart never would have happened without the dedication of her volunteers, some of the "nicest people in the world."

"Here are women who spend hours making these little items for babies they'll never know and never see. Now, is that not giving from the heart?" she asks. "It's a wonderful thing. I just can't tell you how wonderful it is."

For more information visit www.stitchesfromtheheart.org or write to Stitches from the Heart, 3316 Pico Boulevard, Santa Monica, CA 90405.

TORI CARRINGTON

A Stitch in Time

Tori Carrington

National bestselling, multi-award-winning husband-and-wife duo Lori and Tony Karayianni aka Tori Carrington have published over thirty romance novels for Harlequin Temptation and Blaze, Silhouette Special Edition and Signature. With their Sofie Metropolis, PI hardcover series, they've also ventured into the mainstream mystery realm. They call Toledo, Ohio, home base, but return to Tony's hometown of Athens, Greece, as often as they can.

PROLOGUE

———————

Being a single mom introduced me to levels of exhaustion I hadn't known possible.

Not to mention the havoc it's wreaked on my love life.

Love life? What is that? I haven't had one since my louse of an ex-husband left me for a woman half my age four years ago. Shoot me, but something like that is capable of undermining women far more confident than me. And while I've found the strength I needed over the years, none of it's been applied to any romantic aspirations. Besides, my experiences with my ex make it damn hard not to hate the male population at large.

Not that I'm bitter or anything. Okay, maybe I am. A little. But I figure I'm entitled. After all, I'm the one who's spent the past four years raising three kids my ex takes complete credit for during his two weekends a month.

So normally I stick to the facts. Like my name—Jenny Smith. A thirty-nine-year-old mother of two daughters and a son. I'm also a soccer mom, resident car pooler, dedicated niece to a spinster aunt, all-around problem solver and an emergency-room nurse at an inner-city Detroit public hospital, in that order. At one time, I would have liked to become a doctor but never had the chance because of the aforementioned exhaustion. I don't know. Maybe one day when my youngest, seven-year-old Daisy, gets her driver's license and is able to transport herself to her dozen extra-curricular activities I might look into medical school again. But right now it's all I can do to complete half the items on my daily list before conking out upright in bed with my reading glasses perched on the edge of my nose, a procedural manual poking into my ribs, our family dog drooling onto my pillow. I don't have time for a love life even if I had the requisite man.

Of course, my three children would probably lock me in my room if I even breathed the word *date* around them.

Welcome to my life.

CHAPTER ONE

I could have done without this particular rainy morning in October. There I was, standing in my youngest daughter's doorway, staring at her as if she'd lost a few marbles on the way to the bathroom that morning.

If things were only that simple. If only I could retrace her steps, scoop up the marbles, then place them carefully back where they belonged inside her pretty, blond head.

But things were never simple. At least not when it came to my life. So I tried to wrap my brain around the sight before me and scrambled to find the words with which to deal with it.

"What?" Daisy asked, hands on hips.

I figured she must have adopted the stance from me. Lord knew I found myself doing it often enough. I looked down to find my own hands planted on my hips and consciously dropped my arms to my sides. I reached for a pair of discarded jeans on Daisy's white dresser.

"Change. Now."

"But, Mom…"

If ever there were two words in the English language I could do without, it was those two. "But, Mom, everyone has a pair of these shoes," complained my fifteen-year-old son, Jonathon. "But, Mom, Kaylie had purple streaks put in her hair last year and she's only ten," whined my twelve-going-on-twenty-five-year-old daughter, Meaghan.

And now my seven-year-old wanted to wear her belly dancer's outfit to school. An outfit that her father's new girlfriend thought would be "cool" for her to dress up in for Halloween, a little over a week away.

I turned and walked from the room, picking up the wet towel I had little doubt Jon had left in the hallway on his way to get dressed, and a hair clip that belonged to Meaghan. Spot, the dog—a shaggy golden retriever mix with no spots—was following on my heels, tongue out, panting. I'd figured out awhile ago that he probably did this because walking behind me was the safest and most exciting place in the house. He didn't have to worry about getting his tail stepped on by one of the kids, and more often than not if I was near any kind of food, he'd get a nibble or two.

Of course, by trailing behind me today he ran the risk of my stepping on his tail.

"And you," I said, bending over to shake my finger at him. "No more tracking mud in the house. You go out, do your business at the edge of the patio, and come right back in, do you hear me?"

He tilted his head and whined, then licked my fingers.

I tousled the damp mop on top of his head.

"Jon? Meaghan? The bus will be here in ten minutes," I called.

Meaghan's head popped around the corner of her open door, a straightening iron clamping down on her dark hair. "But, Mom, it's raining."

"Don't worry. You won't melt."

"But my hair will," she complained. "Come on, Mom, you always drive us when it rains."

And I was always late for my shift at the hospital when I did.

Daisy bounded out of her room with the belly-dancer top still on, now paired with her studded jeans. "Yeah, Mom. You always drive us when it rains."

Jon leaned against his doorjamb and crossed his arms, his grin reminding me of the man he was turning into rather than the towheaded little boy I was used to.

"Oh, all right. Downstairs in two minutes. Two minutes, do you hear me? Or else you'll all miss my ride *and* the bus and you'll have to walk to school."

They all stared at me like I was nuts, then Daisy gave an eye roll and stalked back into her room, probably to put the belly-dancer pants back on.

My life. I couldn't seem to keep up with the basic agenda, let alone the countless little extras that seemed to pop up unexpectedly. Just when, if ever, would I catch up?

"Never."

I swept toast crumbs from the counter into my palm then

dumped them into the wastebasket. A banana peel followed, then I rinsed out a nearly empty milk bottle and put it in the recycling bin.

I'd like to blame my ex for the chaos of my life, but the truth was that, aside from a few months off after each of our three children was born, I'd immediately returned to work as a nurse, needing to keep in touch with the outside world to keep me balanced. So even when I was married, my life had been a nonstop flurry of activity. Bill had never helped much. He'd brought home the larger paycheck in his job as a vascular surgeon, and since he had never had to lift a finger to do anything as an only child, he'd figured the house and kids were my responsibility.

But at least then I'd had something of a personal life. Aside from having him around to talk to, I could leave the kids with him to go to the grocery store or to stroll through my favorite bookstore, without worrying that they would kill each other while I was gone.

Too bad Bimbo Barbie—oh, I'm sorry, Susan—had caught his eye and showed him that she was very interested in taking care of certain physical needs that he hadn't been aware needed taking care of until she'd suggested it. Bill had been involved with other women since, but it was Susan who had brought our marriage to an end.

I twisted a bread bag with more force than was necessary, probably smushing the slices inside, and put it in the bread drawer. After checking the toaster for heat with the back of my fingers, I picked up the latest crocheted toaster cover, compliments of my aunt Precious—a fluorescent green work of art festooned with pastel yellow flowers—and yanked it down over the toaster. I considered exchanging it for one of the ten other toaster covers in various colors that were stashed in the towel drawer. When she'd given me this one the week before, I'd nearly had to bite my tongue to keep from asking if she was serious. In the past ten years, since she'd moved into the nearby seniors' retirement village condos, I'd had to ask her not to knit us any more scarves or ill-fitting sweaters. So she'd taken to making me tissue-box and toaster covers and pot holders instead. *Ugly* tissue-box and toaster covers and pot holders. Which was strange, considering I supplied her yarn needs. Somehow the pretty yarns I gave her were never used for the items she made me. She'd once said something about an in-village swap, but I'd held up my hand to ward off the explanation.

The woman had bad taste. That was that. The pieces she gave me were more suited for a dollhouse or a baby's room than a modern, stainless-steel kitchen decorated in blacks and reds.

But I always made a point of having at least one of her creations visible when I brought her home for Sunday dinner twice a month.

I looked at my watch and then let Spot back in from the yard.

"Jon, Meaghan, Daisy!" I called as I walked into the hall.

There they were, all waiting for me in their coats near the door.

"Maybe I should drive you every day," I said as I shrugged into my own jacket.

"Yeah!"

"Not a chance," I said, opening the door and edging them out to the porch ahead of me.

"I COULD JUST eat him up with a spoon," Francesca, one of the station clerks, said as I filled in an emergency-patient chart then slid it into the file holder.

"Spoon? Who needs a spoon? I could inhale him in one breath." Latesha, a fellow E.R. nurse, reached over me to put her own chart in behind mine.

I didn't need to ask who they were talking about. A new doctor had transferred from a Cleveland hospital to Detroit Community General a month ago, and that's all the female staff talked about these days.

"You two ought to be arrested for lewd gossip unbecoming to a hospital professional," I teased.

"Hell, woman, how else we going to blow off a little steam in between pileup accidents on I-75 and gang activity on Six Mile?" Latesha asked, giving me a nudge with her elbow.

She and I wore our turquoise scrub suits while Fran wore a white smock over a navy top and slacks. My blond hair was pulled back into a ponytail for work, but the last time I'd gone in for a trim, the stylist had taken a little more off than I'd wanted and I had to tuck stray strands behind my ears until it grew back out.

Dr. Harry Gordon. The new head pediatrician's periodic presence in the E.R. was enough to make everyone—including the female patients—go slack-jawed with undisguised lust.

Oh, all right. I guess the guy was hot. While George Clooney had played the role on TV, this guy was the real deal. And Harry Gordon could give Clooney a run for his money in the looks department any day of the week.

Merely watching the big hunk of a man cradle a tiny, ill baby in his large, capable hands was enough to make anyone's knees melt.

"Two more days and he hits the one-year mark," Fran said.

"Ooooh," Latesha moaned. "The official mourning period is over."

"Mourning period?" I asked, even though I knew I probably shouldn't.

"Yeah, you know. One year since his divorce became final."

"And that matters how?" I asked.

"Come on, Jenny, if anyone knows the answer to that one, you should. Being of the divorced persuasion yourself."

I shook my head.

"What it means," Latesha offered, taking over from Fran, "is that there will be no more rebound relationships. That what happens from here on out has to do with the future and not the past."

I squinted at her. It had been four years since my divorce, and I still didn't feel free from the past.

"Too bad that little resident has her eye on him."

Latesha sighed. "Yeah. Don't none of us stand a chance with her aiming those big, soulful green eyes his way." She leaned forward and whispered, "Word has it that they were both seen coming out of the linen closet together yesterday afternoon. She had her top on inside out and his hair had that telltale tousled look."

I rolled my eyes. "You two really need to find another topic to discuss. Like which character on your favorite soap opera is about to drive off a cliff. You know, that's something I feel like doing right now, listening to you two."

I moved off in the direction of examining room five, where a thirteen-year-old boy's younger sister had added insecticide to his breakfast cereal because she was upset with him. Essentially I was going to give him ipecac syrup to induce vomiting.

Definitely preferable to listening to Fran and Latesha go on about the dreamy new doc.

CHAPTER TWO

"Um, hi."

How was I to know that the minute I turned down the corridor I would run into Dr. Harry Gordon.

Okay, so the guy definitely rated the attention the hospital gossip hotline gave him. He had big brown eyes, neat dark hair sparsely shot through with silver, and a great build.

"Hi, Jenny," he said, giving me a grin that eclipsed all grins.

Oh, we'd met. Almost exactly a month ago after he'd come to work at the hospital.

"Pretty quiet so far today," he said.

I nodded. "Thankfully. I don't know if I could survive another shift like last Friday."

"Be glad you weren't here on Saturday."

"Saturday?"

"The casino bus accident on I-94?"

"You were here for that?"

He slid his hands into his pants pockets. "I come in to check on my patients."

"Of course. Well, um, I'd better get to room five."

I brushed past him, trying not to notice that he smelled like baby powder and lime. Still, the instant I passed him, I briefly closed my eyes and hummed as if somehow I'd been given a jolt that energized me down to my toes.

"Jenny?"

I turned around to face him even as I kept moving toward the examining room.

"How about I buy you a cup of coffee next break?"

I nearly stumbled. Which wasn't a good thing since I was walking backward. "Coffee?"

His gaze moved to my "sexy" white orthopedic shoes.

"Or tea, or soda. Your choice from the hospital cafeteria."

"No!"

His brows rose, making me aware that, yes, I had indeed nearly shouted the refusal.

"I'm sorry. It's just that you, me and the hospital staff in the cafeteria equal a lot of gossip. I prefer to avoid that if it's all the same to you."

A simple coffee with the handsome doctor would make it through the grapevine even before we sat down.

He grinned. "So it's like that then."

"It's definitely like that," I said. "No offense. It's just that...well, because of your being new to the hospital, you're the subject of a lot of attention."

"Attention you'd prefer to avoid."

"Thanks for the offer, though." I reached the door to the examining room and opened it.

I eyed the teen, who looked a little green around the edges. He sat on the bed, his skinny legs poking out from beneath the paper hospital gown. I could relate. While I wasn't at risk of poisoning, I did feel like I might be sick.

I took the patient's wrist in my hand and checked his pulse. "How are you feeling?" I asked unnecessarily.

"Like death warmed over."

"Can you be more specific?"

"Like I'm about to puke up my entire guts."

I smiled at him and ran the back of my knuckles across his forehead. "Vivid."

"You asked."

That, indeed, I had.

What I hadn't asked for was unwanted attention from Dr. Harry Gordon. While the jury was still out on whether it was welcome—it had been a long, long time since I'd felt the thrill caused by a fine-looking man's interest in me— any potential change in my personal life had to include my three children. Three children who would likely take duct tape to any man I brought home and stick him in the back shed for the rest of his natural life.

Or at least until they all turned eighteen.

Besides, I didn't have time for a man in my life. Much less one as hands-off as Harry. As a rule, I didn't date anyone from work. Of course, that rule had yet to be tested.

As I readied a tray with the ipecac syrup I'd have to give to the patient, along with countless plastic cups of water, I found the doc in question walking back down the corridor. He paused in the doorway, looking at me in a way I didn't quite know how to respond to.

He disappeared.

And the kid in question vomited what did appear to be his entire guts all over the front of my scrubs.

"MOM, I CAN'T BELIEVE he's doing this! You've got to talk to him."

Meaghan had never learned that the way to deal with her brother's pestering was to ignore it. "Meggy, you're just exacerbating the situation by reacting to it."

"Well, what am I supposed to do? I need that hair clip."

Meaghan didn't need the hair clip. She needed to talk to me and wanted me home. I glanced at my watch. And I wouldn't be home for another half hour or so.

"Find another one, Meg."

"You always let him get away with this stuff."

"You always rise to the bait."

We spoke for another couple of minutes then I clicked my cell phone closed and continued working on the reports I'd accumulated during the day. Normally, I'd have asked Meg to put Jon on the phone. But today was turning out to be anything but normal, mostly as a result of Dr. Gordon's surprise coffee invitation earlier.

Were Fran and Latesha right? Was the doctor now officially available because the one-year anniversary of his divorce was coming up?

And how did hospital personnel acquire that kind of information anyway?

I cut my finger on the edge of a report. "Ow." I shook my hand then stuck the finger into my mouth, sucking the blood away before it smeared over everything.

"Do you know how many germs you just transferred from your mouth to that open wound?" Latesha said, slapping a file down onto the counter alongside my paperwork.

"Do you have a better solution to a paper cut?"

She scribbled something inside the file. "I heard you and Dr. Harry exchanged words earlier."

I jerked my arm, nearly sending the reports I was working on over the side of the counter. I slid a glance at her. "Yes, it went something along the lines of 'How are you doing?' and 'Fine.'"

"I heard it was much longer than that."

Who passed around such meaningless details? And who had seen them?

"Then you heard wrong."

This was just what I didn't need. It was one thing to listen to the hospital grapevine. It was quite another to be a topic of discussion.

"You knocking off now?" I asked Latesha.

She glanced at the clock over the nurses' station. "Yes. You?"

"I have a couple of things to follow up on before I go."
She stared at me.

"What?"

She shook her head. "I didn't say nothing."

No, she didn't have to say anything. It was right there on her smiling face for God and everyone else to see.

"See you in the morning," I said, picking up my paperwork and walking toward the corridor to the examining rooms where the next shift had already taken over. But I didn't stop there. After filing my reports, I headed for the elevator and pressed the button for the third floor.

I needed to see Dr. Harry Gordon.

All afternoon I'd been distracted. I figured the reason was that I couldn't make sense out of his invitation. If I had encouraged him with anything I'd said or done, I wanted to make sure our signals didn't get crossed again. I'd seen other nurses dismissed for crimes far less serious than dating the new doctor on the block. And I needed my job. As much for my peace of mind as the money.

Not that I thought my job was at risk. I'd been at the hospital for four years after transferring from the private one where my ex had also—and still—worked. But setting things straight might stop me from considering the many annoying shades of "what if."

I stepped out of the elevator and walked toward the nurses' station on three. Even though I didn't think it a good idea to announce to the staff there that I was looking for Harry, trying to find him in the mazelike corridors of the old hospital would be akin to finding which hole the rabbit had disappeared into.

Besides, there would be no more fuel for gossip because I didn't intend to give anyone anything to gossip about. And as soon as I told Harry the same…well, the sooner I could get home and move on with my romantically deprived life.

I paused before talking to the single nurse's aide at the station. Had I really just thought that? Yes, while the sorry state of my nonexistent love life had always been fodder for jokes among my friends and sometimes even my colleagues, I'd never thought of myself as being deprived of anything.

Until this morning.

The memory of Harry grinning at me materialized in my mind and I nearly groaned.

Just looking at him made me feel romantically deprived.

And that was the way I would remain.

"Could you tell me where Dr. Gordon is, please?" I asked the aide.

"He's left for the day."

"Oh." I felt deflated. I hadn't considered that he might not be there. I'd assumed that, like me, he usually stayed a few minutes longer than required to make sure the next shift had everything they needed.

"His son had his final peewee football game today."

No matter how hard I tried to keep my brows where they belonged, they were just as determined to try to hit my hairline. "He has kids?"

She nodded, stapling a stack of reports together. "Two."

Divorced with two kids. Young, if the peewee part was any indication.

I resisted the urge to press the aide for more information and turned from the station.

"Shall I take a message for him?"

"No, no. I'll catch up with him tomorrow."

More like never. From here on in, I didn't plan on saying any more than what was politely required in the presence of Dr. Harry Gordon, one-year divorcé and father of two.

Don't get me wrong. I've nothing against single parents. As we've already established, I'm one myself. But while I'd loved the movie *Yours, Mine and Ours*—the original, starring Lucille Ball and Henry Fonda—life as a single parent had taught me that two single parents and three-plus-two kids equaled disaster. Something similar had happened to my sister when she'd moved from Detroit to San Diego to marry her college sweetheart. They'd split after graduation, married and started families with other partners, then come back together. And life, as she constantly put it, had been a living hell ever since.

So I'd surmised that there was a reason why movies like *Yours, Mine and Ours* were stocked in the comedy section at the video store, even though the horror aisle would probably be more fitting. I'd also seen firsthand what Tonya was talking about when she and her new husband and their combined seven children had come home for Christmas last year. It had been all I could do not to lock the hostile terrors in the garage for the duration, sliding whatever food they needed under the door three times a day.

I was still replacing things in the house that they had broken or destroyed to prove how much they were against this new family unit.

I stopped and blinked. Despite the cynical direction of my thoughts, I'd walked to the nursery window rather than the elevators. As I stood staring at the tiny pink- and blue-wrapped bundles in their acrylic cribs, I felt a nostalgia I hadn't experienced in, well, longer than I could remember. Usually there wasn't much reason for me to come up here. Any infants or toddlers or expectant mothers that came through the E.R. were a blur of faces before they were rolled up here.

I shuffled to the right where the neonatal intensive care unit stood separated from the rest of the nursery, essentially reserved for those babies that needed extra attention, like infants born prematurely.

I spotted a young African-American woman in a wheelchair accepting a small blue bundle from a nurse just inside the NICU window. I smiled. Time to go home.

An aide wheeled the woman and baby out. They passed me without looking in my direction, and I was about to turn back toward the window, when a blanket fell from the woman's lap onto the floor. No one seemed to notice.

I picked it up. "Excuse me, but I think you dropped this."

The aide stopped and I rounded the chair, looking down on the mother and child. I held out the blanket…only to realize that it wasn't a blanket at all, but rather a pillowcase.

She smiled up at me as she accepted it.

"Thank you."

The aide began wheeling the chair toward the elevators and I stepped aside, watching the young mother wrap the pillowcase around her child, who was swaddled in a hospital gown. Such feeble protection against the autumn air outside.

As the young mother was wheeled into the elevator, quietly talking to her new baby, sadness mingled with the joy in my chest, robbing me of breath.

CHAPTER THREE

Among my favorite things to do with my kids, reading with my seven-year-old daughter, Daisy, was a hands-down winner.

It was eight-thirty Monday night. The dishes were in the dishwasher, Meaghan and Jon were in their rooms either studying or on the phone with friends, and Daisy and I were curled up in her white princess canopy bed, three books laid out in front of us.

"So which one do you want tonight?" I asked.

We'd finished one of the adventures of Narnia the night before, and the next was among the three, along with a copy of *Little Women* and the first Harry Potter adventure, which I'd lifted from Jon's room. Daisy was at that age when she could easily move between *The Secret Garden* and Berenstein Bears without blinking. I'd been encouraging her to read chapter books lately, mostly because I was getting tired of oohing and aahing over cartoon illustrations.

Tonight, instead of choosing any of the books I'd suggested, Daisy slipped out of bed in her little white pj's with
pink bows all over them and picked out a fourth selection,
dropping it on top of the others before climbing back into
bed.

I put the other books on the nightstand, lifted my left arm
for her to snuggle in next to me, then considered her choice.

"Girls Hold Up This World," I read.

It was a title Meg had bought for her little sister while
we were out shopping for school supplies the month before.
We hadn't had a chance to read it yet.

Or at least I hadn't had a chance to read it. Daisy, it
appeared, had already been through it.

"It has nice pictures," she said.

Even though she was seven and had long since stopped
sucking her thumb, I noticed her edging her hand toward her
mouth before she caught herself and lowered it to the
blankets.

I smiled. "Well, then, let's see what else we like about the
book."

A huge plus about simpler books was that Daisy could
read them herself. And she did so now with guidance. The
book was a long poem about girls from different cultures
and how we were all connected as sisters. And as such, it was
our responsibility to help each other out, to elevate one
another to a greater understanding of love and of the world.
Pictures accompanied the poem.

As Daisy read, I was reminded of a woman who could

use a hand up: the mother of the baby who had been going home from the hospital earlier.

I'd seen my share of heart-wrenching situations over the years in my job as an emergency-room nurse, but this one…I don't know, this one stayed with me. Perhaps because I sensed there might be something I could do about it.

Before I could blink, Daisy had finished reading the book and sat looking up at me.

"Very good," I said.

"Yeah," she sighed. "I like this story."

I kissed her forehead again, then slipped from the bed, putting the book on the nightstand with the others.

"Good night, sweet pea. Sleep tight."

After switching off the lamp, I walked over to the door. Daisy had already closed her eyes and was well on her way to meet the sandman. But even as I stood gazing at my sleeping daughter, who had more clothes than ten seven-year-olds, all I could think of was the young mother in the hospital who had brought along a pillowcase to use as a blanket for her premature baby.

An hour later I sat in the family room by myself in front of the computer, decorated with Meg's butterfly decals and Jon's NASCAR stickers, doing a search for organizations that provided clothing not only to needy babies, but premature ones. There seemed to be little available…until a Web site scrolled up for an organization called Stitches from the Heart in California.

I sat back and read the story connected to the organization. Immediately I knew that this was something I wanted to be involved in. No, *needed* to be involved in. While I gained a great measure of satisfaction from my work, I was paid for that, so in essence it was my job. But this felt like giving back, and I realized it was something I needed to do, even if it just meant one needy baby leaving Community General with a new set of clothing and a blanket made especially for him.

I took down the listed contact information for Stitches from the Heart, and then sat back, reflecting on my day. Spot had his head on my right foot, which had fallen asleep along with him, and the house was quiet. I should have been tired but wasn't. By now I was usually in bed with my latest novel of choice—I was in the middle of a great action-adventure starring a kick-ass heroine—but for some reason the thought of going upstairs alone didn't appeal to me. Not tonight.

What was worse was that I knew it was because of Dr. Harry Gordon.

I was never one for self-delusion. My sister, Tonya, called me Polly Practical—never one to see bunnies in the clouds but looking instead for which direction the wind was blowing, and whether or not it would bring a storm. So I knew that a fantasy of a relationship with Harry wasn't what had slid under my skin, but the awareness that I was still very much a woman.

Funny, in the four years since Bill had left me, this was

the first time I'd felt that way. Could it be true that there was some sort of internal clock that let you know when you were ready to continue with the next stage of your life? Much like what Fran and Latesha had said about Harry and the one-year anniversary of his divorce?

If so, what was the normal waiting period for women? My sister had been divorced for eight months when she'd met up with her college flame and moved on to a new relationship.

Maybe it depended on the individual. I mean, I crossed paths with single dads every now and again as I took my kids to school and various other activities, and one or two had hit on me, but I'd never been tempted to take them up on their offers.

Harry, on the other hand…

Harry, on the same hand, was exactly what I didn't need in my life now. Not when I had a seven-year-old who still liked to be read to, and a twelve-year-old on the verge of adolescence. And Jon would start taking driver's ed classes next month.

My kids needed me. And I needed to be there for my kids. A man would upset that balance. Especially a man who could be nothing but a temporary fling, given that we worked together and he'd just come out of a divorce and had kids of his own.

Okay, I sighed. This called for drastic measures.

I shut down the computer, let Spot out for one last time, locked and checked all the downstairs windows and doors, then made my way up to my room, where I kept a private stash of horror movies to take my mind off almost any worry…and would put me to sleep in no time flat.

But fifteen minutes later, as I was snuggled up in bed in my old Tigers T-shirt, it wasn't the image of a murderous madman that flashed across the back of my eyelids every time I blinked, it was Harry's handsome face.

CHAPTER FOUR

I was running late for lunch the following day so I grabbed the quickest choices in the cafeteria line—half a tuna-fish sandwich, an apple and a single-serve carton of low-fat milk—then paid for them and headed for my regular table near the door, where Latesha was sitting along with two other nurses.

"You got caught on that emergency run, huh?" Latesha said as I sat down.

"Yeah. The medics had restarted the patient's heart but he arrested two more times on the table." I shook my milk then opened the container. "It's fifty-fifty whether or not he's going to make it through the day."

"How old?"

"Fifty-one."

Latesha groaned. "Those are the tough ones. Too young to be facing that kind of battle."

I agreed.

The other two nurses started to get up. "We need to get back."

We chatted for a couple of moments about what was going on in their wards, then they headed back to work.

"I should be getting back, too," Latesha said, looking at her watch.

I opened my mouth to ask her to sit with me for five minutes while I finished, when a familiar man in a neat white coat came up from behind her.

"Hi. Do you girls mind if I join you?"

Dr. Harry Gordon.

Latesha's eyes nearly bulged from her head as she looked at me. My cheeks burned as I focused on opening my sandwich wrappings.

"No, no, we don't mind. In fact," Latesha said, getting up and lifting her tray, "you can keep Jenny company. I've got to get back to work."

Looking up at Harry, I tried to communicate what a bad idea it was to sit with me, especially when half the room was already staring in our direction.

Over Harry's shoulder, Latesha lifted a plastic spoon and waved it at me. Then she left, and Harry sat.

I wondered how rude it would be if I leaped up and took my lunch with me.

Ruder than I knew how to be.

"Hi," he said once we were alone.

"Hi, yourself."

He had the same items on his tray that I had on mine, except that his milk was chocolate.

"I heard you were up on three looking for me yesterday afternoon."

"You heard that, did you?" I looked down at my ID tag. Seemed I hadn't given the young aide enough credit. She'd remembered my name when I hadn't offered it.

"Did you want anything in particular?"

"Pardon me? Oh. No." I couldn't tell him what I'd intended to tell him the night before. Not here, anyway.

"Do you have children?"

"Three." I took a bite of my tuna fish, hardly tasting it. "You?"

"Two. Hilary's nine and Ben's seven."

"Daisy's age." I cleared my throat. "My youngest daughter is seven."

"I'd guessed that."

I stared at him.

He chuckled. "No, I didn't find out via the hospital grapevine, no matter how well informed it appears to be." He eyed a resident who was walking by a little too slowly, waiting until he passed. "Ben and Daisy go to the same school. I saw you there yesterday morning dropping her off. Ben pointed her out to me and told me they're in the same class."

"We live in the same neighborhood?"

"It's a pretty good guess that we live in the same school district."

The thought that he could live nearby made my stomach bottom out. It was difficult enough having to pass him in the halls without having to pass him outside my front door, as well. After all, there was only so much one romantically deprived single mother could take before she spent hours glued to the front window hoping to catch a glimpse of him.

"So," I said, "how often do you see them? Your kids?"

"Every day. They live with me."

I noticed that he didn't say "I have custody," the more legal description. And for some reason I was impressed.

"You?"

"I have custody of all three," I said automatically, then frowned. What did my using legal jargon to describe my connection to my children say about me?

Probably that I was more than a bit bitter. Not an attractive trait in any woman.

"How long have you been divorced?"

I raised my brows. This conversation was getting more personal than I was comfortable with.

I crumpled the plastic wrappings on my tray around the remainder of my sandwich. "Oh, look at the time. I really must get back on the clock."

Then I remembered what had happened during my visit to his floor the day before. The dropped pillowcase and the tiny preemie going home with Mom. I put my tray back down.

"Actually, there is something I want to ask you."

"The reason you stopped by yesterday?"

"No. We can talk about that another time." If ever. "But the visit did motivate my current question. Does the hospital have any program to provide needy families with clothing for their newborns?"

"Not that I'm aware of. But I can ask."

"Okay."

I got up from the table with my tray, hesitated, then smiled at him.

"See you later then."

"Mmm. Later."

Had I really just invited the dreamy doc to a future chat session? Yes, I realized as I made my way toward the door, I had.

And a traitorous part of me was happy. Very happy, indeed.

"YOU DON'T STOP by nearly as often as I'd like."

That night after feeding the children and asking Jon to look after Daisy, I made my way to Mount Carmel Retirement Village with Meaghan to visit my spinster aunt Precious. The woman was sometimes more trouble than she was worth, but she was a fixture in my life, particularly after my parents had moved to Arizona the previous year, leaving me as Precious's only nearby relative.

Not that I minded. Precious was a tough old broad (her words, not mine) who shocked for pure shock's sake—garish crocheted toaster covers included.

"Actually, I'm a day early for my midweek visit."

My aunt's blue eyes twinkled at me as I kissed her cheek then took a chair opposite her, Meaghan doing the same.

"Does that mean I can look forward to another visit tomorrow?"

"No, that means we're visiting today instead of tomorrow."

She straightened her jacket. "Well, then, it's lucky for you both that I decided not to attend the watercolor class in the great room tonight or else I wouldn't have been available."

"Watercolor class?" Meaghan said. "I love painting."

I smiled at Aunt Precious. Both she and I knew that no matter what she was doing, she would leave it to be able to dish with me.

My mother often said that we were like two peas in a pod. That somehow I had come out looking less like her and Dad and more like her maternal aunt. And while everyone agreed I was practical to a fault, they also argued I had a sense of humor that sometimes rubbed the wrong way.

Not unlike Aunt Precious's.

"So to what do I owe the pleasure?" she said, folding her gnarled hands in her lap.

She had to be in her nineties by now, that much I knew. But the old woman refused to say exactly how old she was. Claimed that was nobody's business but her own and her doctor's. Sometimes I wondered how she could still crochet.

But since she did…

I handed her a bag of yarn, much larger than what I usually brought. One by one she took out the pink and blue selections, staring at each of them before reaching in for the next.

She stared at me. "Good Lord, Jenny, are you trying to tell me you're pregnant?"

Meaghan gave a gasp that could have been heard around the world as she turned to stare at me. "Mom!"

"No, I am not *pregnant*. I'd actually have to have a partner to achieve that goal." I reached into my purse for the items I'd printed off the Internet the night before. "Do you think you could crochet these patterns?"

Precious glanced at one. "They'd be awfully tiny."

"That's because the outfits are meant for premature babies."

She looked at the yarn again. "How many do you want me to make?"

"Actually, I was hoping you might be able to enlist the help of other residents in this task." I sat forward, warming to my subject. "You see, I came across information on this wonderful organization called Stitches from the Heart last night. They collect handmade clothing—you know, knitted and crocheted items—from people just like you, and then distribute them to hospitals for people who can't afford to buy clothes for their babies to wear home, especially the preemies."

"Stitches from the Heart," she said aloud.

"Yes. They pack boxes of fifty items—hats, booties, sweaters, blankets—and then ship them off to volunteers, who then distribute them to the families."

"And you're involved how?"

I sat back. "I've volunteered to be the hospital contact."

Harry had called me at the E.R. station that afternoon to tell me there was no such program at the hospital. But the

tone of his voice when he said he'd welcome my spearhead-
ing something of that nature seemed to imply that it wasn't
the only thing he'd welcome.

Aunt Precious looked up from the patterns, silent for
long moments as she considered me. "Are you sure you
have the time?"

I thought about the young mother I came across the
other day, then the million demands that were crammed into
each and every one of my days. I smiled. "All the time in
the world."

"Well," she said, "if you have the time, then I certainly have
the time." She held up the patterns. "Do you have more copies
of these? Oh, and this yarn won't be nearly enough. You may
want to bring along more during your weekend visit."

I nodded, the warmth expanding in my chest.
"Anything you want."

"I'd like to help," Meaghan said.

I looked at my daughter. I'd told her about my wish to
become involved with Stitches from the Heart, but I hadn't
considered that perhaps she'd like to take part.

My little girl was growing up.

I hugged her. "I'd like that."

She might be growing up, but she wasn't too old to blush
at my unexpected display of affection.

"Can you show me how to crochet, Auntie?" she asked
Precious.

I sat up. "That goes for me, too."

Precious looked through the items that I'd brought, took out two crochet hooks and handed us each one, along with yarn. I was thankful she didn't mention that she'd already taught me once. Back when I was about eleven or twelve. Meaghan's age, I realized.

I decided that this time the lesson was going to take.

CHAPTER FIVE

"It's the hospital, isn't it?"

I jumped at Harry's voice. I'd been checking the chart of a patient in examining room two and hadn't seen him approach. The same thing had happened a half-dozen times in the two days since our "lunch" together. Which hadn't really been together-together, as I kept telling myself and my coworkers, who would not give up on the possibility that the handsome doctor and I were romantically linked.

"I don't know what you're talking about," I said as I moved toward the examining-room door.

He blocked my escape and I was forced to look up into his smiling brown eyes. I caught a whiff of his lime after-shave. "The reason you're avoiding me. It's the hospital, right?"

"Has it crossed your mind that I'm simply not interested?" I challenged.

His grin widened. And to my chagrin I found myself smiling back.

"Not for a minute," he said quietly.

A resident hurried past. I realized with a start that it was Angela, the resident the gossip hotline had linked Harry to. She smiled at Harry then openly considered me as she passed.

I crushed the chart to my chest. "All right, so I'm attracted to you. Along with every other woman under the age of fifty in this hospital. For all I know, even the older ones drool over you the minute you turn your back."

"You drool over me?"

"You know what I mean."

"Actually, I hadn't a clue. Until now."

He appeared to look around him in light of the new information, as if maybe he should reassess his options.

"Cute," I said.

"I was trying to make you jealous. Did it work?"

Unfortunately, it had.

"Have coffee with me."

"I can't."

"Then have lunch with me."

"Lunch is over."

"Tomorrow."

"I have plans."

"Dinner, then."

I suddenly found it hard to swallow.

Was he inviting me on a date outside the hospital?

He was.

I considered him. "You know, what you're doing could be considered by some as sexual harassment."

The smile disappeared from his face.

I touched his sleeve. "That was a joke. Admittedly, not a very good one, but a joke."

"Go out with me to make it up to me."

Another resident walked by, then one of the nurses, both obviously trying to catch what was being said. I quickly removed my hand, looked around Harry toward an open examining room, then pulled him inside and closed the door.

He leaned against the table and crossed his arms. "You realize you've just made things worse."

"I hadn't until you mentioned it." I groaned inwardly.

I'd worked hard to keep myself above hospital gossip, but this man seemed to be testing that resolve.

"You don't seem too concerned," I said to him.

He shrugged. "That's because I don't care what they say. And neither should you."

"And if I do? Care, that is?"

"Then I'll have to try my damnedest to convince you otherwise."

I opened my mouth to respond. When no words came out, I discovered it wasn't because I had nothing to say, but rather that the words had been stolen from me by the nearness of Harry's mouth.

Oh, dear God.

Was he going to kiss me? It looked like he would. His gaze seemed focused on my lips, his pupils dilating. He didn't seem to notice that I'd gone silent, and that he wasn't speaking either.

I wasn't sure how I felt about the prospect of his kissing me. I take that back. Despite the suddenness of the possibility, I wanted him to kiss me. A lot.

It had been a good long time since I'd been kissed.

Mmm…

I wasn't aware I'd hummed aloud until he finally blinked, then smiled down into my eyes.

"Come on, Jenny. Have dinner with me."

"What you seem to be proposing has nothing to do with dinner."

"Depends on your definition of dinner."

I began to pull away.

He held me still.

"I think my bad joke tops yours." He lifted his hand and lightly stroked my jawline with his thumb. I shivered from the simple yet exquisitely intimate contact. "You can choose the place. Mexican, Italian, you name it."

I dropped my gaze to the front of his neat shirt. "Okay."

A rustle of a lab coat against scrubs as he leaned back to stare into my face. "Okay?"

I nodded, amused by his surprise.

"How about tonight?"

His eager question made me laugh. "How about this weekend?"

"Saturday night."

I nodded. The kids would be at their father's for the weekend. Saturday would be perfect.

The door opened and Latesha stuck her head in. I jumped away from Harry even though we weren't touching.

"We need the room for a patient," she said, waggling her brows. "So unless one of you plans on stripping down and getting on top of that table and feigning an illness, I'm going to have to kick you out."

BY FRIDAY NIGHT, a day and a half after closeting Harry in the examining room, I was ready to jump out of my skin.

Well, all right, maybe I was exaggerating. A little. But I bore all the telltale signs of a woman a day away from a hot date. Fluttery stomach. Damp palms. Stupid grins. Latesha had followed me around all day, trying to get the scoop on the change in my demeanor. As she'd said, "You can't put one over on me, Smith. So you might as well tell me what I already know."

But to tell anyone would be to ruin the secrecy of it all.

I gave a decadent little shiver as I tucked the folded clothes into the crook of my arm and headed upstairs from the laundry room off the kitchen. I put two shirts on Meaghan's bed. She was talking on the phone and simultaneously straight-ironing her hair. Then I knocked on Jon's door and held out a couple pair of underwear that disappeared from my hand without my really seeing his. Then I walked into Daisy's room to find her trying to zip half the contents of her closet into her Hello Kitty wheeled case. I sat down on the bed with her favorite pj's on my lap, along with three pairs of lace-top socks.

"Need any help?" I asked.

She shook her blond head, her face scrunched up in concentration. "I can do it."

I tucked a woefully wrinkled shirt into the side of the suitcase closest to me. "I brought these up. Are you going to pack them?"

She stopped huffing and puffing long enough to take the clean items from me, fling open the suitcase, then put them inside. The zipper war restarted again in earnest.

I knew better than to ask if she needed everything she was taking to her father's house for the weekend. I could spend the next hour before Bill came to pick them up talking her down to three changes of clothes, only to have her change her mind and want to start all over again. Better to let her do what she needed to do.

Besides, I was in too good of a mood to tussle with her.

So instead I thought about the night of pure pampering that lay before me. A long soak in the tub with the Jacuzzi jets at high speed while Norah Jones crooned on the stereo. A manicure and pedicure. Shaving my legs. A chick flick that I'd rented from the video store on my way home.

And lots of daydreaming about tomorrow night and my date with Harry.

"Are you sure you don't need help?" I asked. "I have a lot of experience with closing stubborn suitcases."

Daisy tried a couple of more times on her own, then

sighed heavily and threw up her hands. Trying to hide my smile, I carefully tucked in the material that impeded the zipper's progress and pressed down the top.

"Voilà," I said.

"Thanks."

She immediately tugged the case from the bed so it hit the floor with a thud, nearly shearing off Spot's tail in the process. The retriever squealed then moved to stand on the other side of my legs, well out of the determined seven-year-old's way. Daisy pulled up the handle then half dragged, half wheeled the tiny suitcase toward the open door.

"Are you sure you have everything?"

Daisy appeared to think about it, then she nodded. "Yep. I think I have everything."

My ex had grumbled that all of Daisy's things were wrinkled when she visited and asked if there was something I could do about it. I'd merely smiled and told him that maybe he would have more success in that area than I did.

The telephone rang. I could identify the four different tones from the various extensions. Since Meaghan had turned twelve, she'd commandeered the line, so a ringing phone wasn't something I heard often. More often than not, she'd pick up the second line while talking, then yell for me to pick it up, making sure to remind me that she had someone waiting for her.

"Mom! It's for you."

I got up from the bed, edging my way around the Hello Kitty suitcase. "Don't you want to take any books?"

I watched Daisy's blue eyes light up as she considered this new mission.

I held up two fingers. "Two nights, two books," I said, even though I knew the words were merely a suggestion. But at least book choosing would keep her from thinking of other things she'd like to take with her that would require a house-wide hunt or a speed load of laundry.

My sister said I indulged my kids too much. Between you and me, I'd take my slightly spoiled but well-behaved children over her four hell-raisers any day of the week.

I headed toward the extension in my bedroom.

"It's Dad," Meaghan said quietly from where she stood in her open doorway.

Jon's door opened and he stared at me as well.

Only Daisy appeared to miss the change in atmosphere as I heard her opening her bag again, probably to force her book choices in along with her clothes.

I crossed the length of my bedroom and picked up the extension on the other side of my queen-size bed.

"Bill," I said simply.

"Hey, Jenny. I'm sorry to be calling so late. I know I'm supposed to be on my way to pick up the kids now, but…"

I closed my eyes and absently rubbed my forehead.

"Look, I don't know how to say this any other way, but Tiff surprised me with a romantic weekend trip up north to do some leaf gazing. It was a special deal and the arrangements can't be canceled."

"Unlike your weekend with your kids. Those plans can be canceled."

"It was an honest mistake, Jen. Tiffany forgot that this was my official weekend."

Hard to do, considering that every other weekend was his weekend.

I noticed his choice of words, so unlike Harry's "they live with me." "My official weekend" sounded as if having his kids was a court-assigned chore or little more than a baby-sitting job for Bill.

I opened my eyes to find Meg and Jon standing in my open doorway. Daisy had apparently caught on that something was happening and forced her way between her older siblings.

I crossed the room, then quietly closed the door.

"You can't just do this, Bill—cancel out at the last minute," I whispered into the receiver even as I moved away from the door, hoping the kids wouldn't hear me. "For God's sake, they're already packed."

"I know. I'll take them next weekend. I promise."

"Next weekend is Daisy's school play. You know that."

I sank down on top of the bed. If ever there had been a sign that dating with children was dodgy, if not downright reckless, this was it.

One minute you could be nominated parent of the year, the next your mind was on your love life and you were choosing trips up north to canoodle with your latest squeeze over time you could never get back with your children.

"I'm sorry, Jen," Bill said.

I could no longer remember how many times those three words had gotten him out of trouble.

"It's not me you should be apologizing to."

"I know. I'll call the kids sometime tomorrow. I've got to go now. Thanks, Jenny."

I listened to the dial tone in my ear and sat for long moments staring at nothing and everything.

A sound outside my door alerted me to the fact that I had three children waiting in the hall.

I took a deep breath, got up from the bed, then stretched the kinks out of my neck. I opened the door so quickly, all three nearly tumbled inside.

"Did I hear anyone say pizza and a movie?" I said with enthusiasm.

"Yeah, pizza!" Daisy cried, clapping her hands.

"He bailed, didn't he?" Jon asked.

I looked at him. "Something came up."

"Yeah, Tiffany's silicone breasts."

I gasped, Meaghan laughed and Daisy blinked at the three of us, as if waiting to be let in on the joke.

I turned him around and urged him toward the stairs. "Tiffany's breasts, silicone or otherwise, are none of your business. And certainly nothing I want to hear about."

"What's silicone, Mom?" Daisy asked.

I did the same turnaround bit with her. "Never you mind. Just go put your shoes on and meet me at the front door in five minutes."

It was then that I realized I had a phone call of my own to make. To Harry to cancel our plans for tomorrow night. I watched my kids walk down the hall. I already had a date to spend time with three of the most important people in my life. Harry and romance would have to wait.

CHAPTER SIX

So instead of a night spent indulging myself, I indulged Jon, Meaghan and Daisy. We went to our favorite pizza place and gorged ourselves, leaving just enough room for popcorn and drinks at the movie theater. We'd chosen a movie that would please all four of us, even if Daisy did fall asleep with her head on my arm before the opening credits finished rolling.

The following morning, while Meaghan window-shopped with friends at the mall and Jon locked himself in his room with his latest CD, Daisy and I ran errands that previously hadn't been a part of my schedule. As I listened to her litany of things she could be doing that moment instead of being majorly bored driving around with me, I wondered if my new volunteer activities were worth the effort.

I looked over my shoulder at the crocheted baby items, compliments of my aunt Precious and friends, and smiled. Yes, definitely worth it.

Of course, being the overachiever that I was, I didn't stop there. I'd contacted other area Stitches volunteers and placed an ad in the paper advertising for help. I had also designed and printed up a flyer to take to other retirement and nursing homes. All this with complete cooperation of the home office of Stitches from the Heart in Santa Monica, California, and the local area volunteers. In fact, the main office was sending me supplies I could distribute to seniors who wanted them.

"Mommy, are we done yet?"

"Almost, sweet pea, almost." Daisy sat buckled into the passenger seat beside me and I patted her hand. She sighed for the third time in as many minutes. We'd already listened to her Kidz Bop CD twice, and I couldn't go another round with the kid-vamped pop songs. So instead, the radio was tuned in to a soft-rock station in the hopes that the mellow songs would relax my irritable passenger.

"Are we going to visit more old people?"

I couldn't help laughing, even though I knew I shouldn't show amusement at the inappropriate question. I cleared my throat. "No, we're done visiting seniors for today."

She rolled her eyes. "Good. That last woman hurt my head."

You had to have been there. An elderly resident of Sunny Side Retirement Home had patted Daisy's head, and the rings she wore had done a little damage.

"Where are we going then?"

"To the hospital where Mommy works."

She'd been to Community General with me before,

usually on my days off when I stopped by to pick up my paycheck or have a prescription filled with my employee discount. But today we were there for a different reason.

When we got there, I parked the car in the underground garage and reached across to free Daisy from her belt. "Okay, let's see how fast we can get this done so we can go home and have lunch."

"Hot dogs and macaroni and cheese."

"Hot dogs and macaroni and cheese," I agreed, even though the sandwiches and soup I'd had planned would have been easier.

When we walked through the doors into the E.R., I was surprised to see Latesha working. Because of seniority and family concerns, both of us worked pretty much nine to five, Monday through Friday.

"Hey," I said, stepping up to her at the station, holding Daisy's hand tightly.

"Hey, yourself. Don't tell me you got called in, too?"

I shook my head.

Latesha said hello to Daisy and handed her a sucker from her pocket. "Half the damn nursing staff came down with the flu," Latesha said with a sigh.

"More like they came down with World Series fever," I suggested.

"Tell me about it. Anyway, I decided I could use the extra hours, what with Leila's needing braces and all." She passed off her paperwork to the clerk. "So if you're not here to work, what are you doing?"

"Just some follow-up on that volunteer thing I told you about."

"That baby-clothes thing?"

"Yes."

Latesha's eyes sparkled. "Uh-huh."

I opened my purse and took out a dozen or so of the cards Stitches from the Heart had mailed to me along with their welcome and introduction package. "Here. Pass these around to anyone you know who knits or crochets."

Latesha looked at them. "I've been known to knit a mean baby blanket in my time."

"How much would it take to get you to pick up the hobby again?"

She put the cards into her pocket. "Oh, I don't know." She took the new chart the clerk handed her. "The true scoop on what's going on between you and Hot Doc."

I smiled. "Nothing."

And that was true enough. I'd called him that morning to cancel our date, before the kids could get up and overhear.

"Uh-huh." Latesha wasn't buying it. "You know where to find me if you decide you want to fess up."

"See you later," I said, then started walking toward the examining rooms.

Her response was to call goodbye to Daisy and wave her chart at me.

"Come on," I said to Daisy. "We need to go up to the third floor. Which means an…"

"Elevator!" she said.

If only my other two kids were as easy to please.

TWENTY MINUTES LATER I finished up with the head nurse in NICU. I'd already touched base with several nurses and residents and passed out informational flyers to the rest, letting them know what I was doing and asking them for recipient recommendations. I'd already received half a dozen and had yet to put together a single gift package. The main office was sending me what they could next week—I'd get more regular shipments once we had an idea of the demand we were looking at. Considering I worked at one of the busiest public hospitals in Detroit, the anticipated need was great, thus the reason for my pounding the pavement for local donations. But this week people would have to go without.

Of course, there was one person I wanted to make the first recipient of my efforts.

"Here you go," the clerk said as she handed me a note with an address on it.

I looked at it then put it in my purse. "Thank you."

"Look who's here, Ben," a familiar male voice said from behind me.

I turned around so quickly Daisy complained that I'd nearly twisted her hand off.

"Harry," I said breathlessly.

He grinned in a way that made my toes curl in my loafers.

"One minute I was thinking about you, the next you're here in front of me," he said. "I had to look twice just to make sure I wasn't imagining things."

"Hi, Ben," Daisy said.

"Hi," Ben returned.

I looked down to realize I hadn't seen the two kids Harry had with him.

It was easy to tell that they were his. Nine-year-old Hilary and seven-year-old Ben both had his dark hair and good looks. The difference lay in their eye color. While their father had brown eyes, Hilary's were blue, and Ben's were green.

Out of my three kids, only Daisy looked remotely like me with her blond curls and blue eyes. Jon was the spitting image of his father with dark hair and eyes, while the family joked that Meaghan had inherited all of the Irish genes the family spent generations denying with her deep auburn hair and green eyes.

"Well, hello," I said to them both, extending my hand. "I'm Jenny Smith. It's nice to meet you, Hilary and Ben." They gave a hesitant shake then I put my arm over Daisy's shoulders. "And this is my daughter Daisy."

"I already knew that," Ben said in the same easygoing manner as his father.

Harry chuckled. "Is there any specific reason you're on three today?" he asked me.

"I had an address I wanted to get."

"I could have gotten it to you."

"That's not necessary. It's Stitches business, not hospital business."

"Ah." All three kids started to look restless. "Hey, we were just about to head out to lunch." He looked at Hilary and Ben. "Do you think we ought to invite Jenny and Daisy to come with us?"

Hilary shrugged, as if it was no concern of hers. Ben looked at Daisy as if afraid she might bite.

"Yeah!" Daisy said, completely oblivious.

"That's nice, but I'm afraid we really can't accept," I said.

"Why?" Harry asked.

Daisy tugged on my hand. "Yeah, why?"

"Because we've already got plans," I told her, tugging on a curl.

"That's too bad," Harry said. "We were going for pizza."

"Pizza!" Daisy said.

"Well, we'll take a rain check. Besides, we just had pizza last night."

It seemed as if Harry was going to offer another choice, but he'd probably already promised his kids pizza.

By now, Hilary was watching us both closely, as if trying to figure something out, and Daisy had begun chatting with Ben, who looked deathly afraid of being contaminated with girl cooties.

I wished I felt the same way about Harry.

Truth be told, even before I'd finally agreed to this date, he'd ignited something within me that refused to be put out. Simply stated, I wanted him as much as he apparently wanted me.

"Harry! I didn't know you were on today."

Angela the resident came up to join the group and was looking at Harry as if the sun rose and set on him.

I grimaced. At least my ex was attracted to blond bimbos

with implants. Angela, to her credit, was a first-year resident with a brilliant future in medicine.

"I'm not on today," Harry said, indicating the kids at his side, making me wonder if childless women purposely made a point of not seeing the offspring of the men they were after. Ignore the kids and maybe they'd go away.

I hoped that she would insult them with some inane comment. Instead, she did the same thing I did by shaking hands with them and immediately turning her attention back to Harry.

"Angela," Harry said. "You've met Jenny?"

"Oh! Yes, of course, I have," she said. It appeared Angela also had a penchant for not noticing other women who didn't figure into her plans. "Hi. Is this your daughter?"

I'd half expected her to point out that I was a nurse, but was thankful she didn't.

She took the stethoscope from around her neck and put it into her lab coat. "I was just about ready to head out to lunch. How about you guys?"

"We're going for pizza," Ben said.

And there you had it. Harry's son had just picked his favorite of the two women in front of his father. Of course, Angela didn't come with a cootie-ridden girl like I did. Hey, to be honest, I'd probably match Harry up with the outgoing resident myself. Lord knew she had way less emotional baggage than I did.

Still, I noticed the way Harry frowned at Angela…and

kept looking at me as if he hoped I'd change my mind about the pizza.

He couldn't possibly want me over the perky resident, could he?

Yes, I realized, he did.

The problem was, he couldn't have me. Partly because of the aforementioned emotional baggage. Mostly because of my kids, his kids…and, well, at least half a dozen other reasons I couldn't list just then. Not when he was looking at me as if we were alone.

"Well," I said, "you enjoy that pizza. Daisy and I have to be going to see about those…plans we have."

I said goodbye to Hilary and Ben, then navigated Daisy toward the elevator.

"What plans?" my clueless daughter asked loudly.

I merely turned in the elevator so that I could see Harry waving after me and smiled, not letting down my guard until the doors had closed.

CHAPTER SEVEN

The following night, long after I'd read Daisy to sleep, looked in to find Jon asleep with his headphones fused to his ears and discovered Meaghan spilled over her bed, still dressed and softly snoring, I started a fire in the chiminea on the back patio, a University of Michigan stadium blanket over my legs as I concentrated on following the lessons Aunt Precious had given both Meaghan and me. Aunt Precious and my mother had always made it look so easy. Even my sister, Tonya, could turn out a blanket or two, although it might take her a couple of years to finish. Me? I couldn't seem to crochet a straight line if my life depended on it. Practice, Precious had said, it took practice. And I determined that I would practice.

It didn't help knowing that Meaghan had taken to crocheting as if she'd been born to the task, and was already halfway through a blanket.

Picking up on my frustration, Spot lifted his head from my blanketed feet and gave a soft whine.

I held my pitiful excuse for crocheting out for inspection. "You could probably do a better job than I can," I grumbled.

He barked and I shushed him, not wanting to disturb the neighbors.

I put the yarn on the table beside me. I prided myself on calling a spade a spade, and in this case I knew that it wasn't lack of skill that prevented me from picking up my crocheting but rather thoughts of Harry in the company of pretty resident Angela. I mean, how long could a man resist a young woman with her good looks and smarts? Especially when said young woman in question would gladly be naked waiting for him in bed if given half a chance?

I closed my eyes and sighed. Remember the emotional baggage I'd mentioned before? Well, I haven't been entirely truthful as to its origin. Oh, sure, I admitted I'm divorced and that I harbor some healthy bitterness regarding it—that is, if bitterness can be referred to as healthy.

You see, there were a few details I left untouched for simple survival's sake. But yesterday…well, yesterday had brought it all rushing back to me.

So you knew that my ex-husband left me for a woman half my age four years ago. Well, nearly half my age. What you didn't know was that she was an intern at the private hospital where we'd both been working.

Sound familiar? Maybe a little too close to the Harry and Angela scenario?

I wasn't much in favor of letting history repeat itself. Fool me once, shame on you. Fool me twice, shame on me.

I heard the sound of a car on the street in front of the house and tried to concentrate on that rather than the painful memories of the past.

Probably a neighbor, I guessed.

Spot lifted his head again, then got up at the squeak of a gate being opened. Not just any gate, but the gate to my backyard.

I bolted upright as well, the stadium blanket sliding to the patio as I reached for the cordless phone on the table.

Bill?

I watched as the shadowy figure of a man neared us. Spot barked once. I grabbed the back of his collar to stay him, ready to release him if it wasn't someone I knew.

"Harry." The name came out as a hyperrelieved sigh.

Spot barked again and I patted him, letting him know that everything was okay. At least I thought it was. While Harry posed a risk to me, it wasn't the life-threatening kind of risk.

"I'm sorry if I startled you," he said, coming to stand in front of me on the patio. He wore a suit, but his tie was loosened and the top couple of buttons on his shirt were undone. His grin told me he was anything but sorry. "Is this okay? My stopping by like this? I had a charity event tonight, so the kids are with a sitter and…well, I didn't much like the way things ended yesterday at the hospital."

"Fine. Your stopping by is fine." No, it wasn't. I must have looked like death warmed over in my ratty old sweats and fluffy pink slippers, and I was pretty sure I hadn't combed my hair since this morning, much less had any makeup on. I made a point of using the blanket to hide behind as I folded it then put it on the back of my chair. "Can I get you something? Coffee? Something stronger? I think I have a beer lurking in the back of the fridge."

"Water's fine."

The minute I moved toward the patio door, Spot decided to engage in one of his favorite pastimes. Namely, sniffing out visitors' crotches. The dog and my ex hadn't gotten along all that well because of this particular habit. Bill used to ask me to let Spot out whenever he was in the same room.

Harry evaded the crotch sniff like a pro, then crouched down. He let the mop of a dog smell the back of his hands, then Spot welcomed a hearty scratch behind the ears.

Huh. He'd passed the Spot test. What did that mean?

Probably that he had a dog of his own.

Even though the kitchen could be seen from the patio, I ducked quickly into the downstairs bathroom, squeezed a bit of toothpaste into my mouth and swirled it around, then washed up as best I could and ran one of Daisy's combs through my hair by way of a brush. I sighed at my reflection. I was thirty-nine, not nineteen. And unfortunately I looked it.

I filled two glasses with water from the refrigerator door then rejoined Harry on the patio. He'd sat down in the chair next to mine and was still petting the dog.

"Come here, Spot," I said.

"Spot?"

"Yes," I confirmed, deciding not to comment on the dog's solid color.

He leaned back in the chair and crossed his legs at the ankles, looking altogether too handsome in the navy blue suit and crisp white shirt. And far too comfortable. I looked up to find him watching me.

"This is nice," he said. "I've been thinking of getting one of these." He gestured toward the chiminea. "But I can't decide on it or one of those open fire pits."

I smiled, then frowned, then narrowed my eyes at him. "Is that why you came over? To talk about my chiminea?"

His chuckle warmed me more than any ten chimineas. "No."

"Then why did you stop by?" I slid my feet out of my pink, fuzzy slippers and crossed my legs on the chair. "I mean beyond your not liking how things went yesterday." I tilted my head. "And how did things go?"

"You thought there was something happening between Angela and me."

I raised my hand. "None of my business."

He said nothing for a long moment, then he leaned forward. "Sure it is. If I hold out any hope of getting you to agree to setting another night for a date."

I laughed. Not because he didn't stand a chance, but because he wanted one. "Despite my temporary moment of insanity, women my age really shouldn't date," I said.

I took a long sip of water, hoping the cold liquid would cool my heated blood. The way he was looking at me…it was far too intimate for a casual conversation.

"So you've decided on the spinster route, then."

"I have three kids, so I don't exactly qualify." An image of Aunt Precious alone at the retirement home came into my mind and I shuddered.

"You were also married."

I nodded, keeping my gaze focused ahead of me.

"Is that why you're reluctant to date me? Because your divorce went badly?"

"My divorce didn't go badly. It was the marriage that was a wreck."

That wasn't entirely true. I'd been very happy up to the point where Bill had decided he wanted something more. And that something more didn't include me.

I discovered I was staring at Harry. And he was returning my stare without blinking.

"How about you?" I asked. "Word has it that you're coming up on…no, wait, you've hit the one-year anniversary of your own divorce."

"Hospital grapevine working overtime." He held his water glass in both hands between his knees. "But I suppose in my case, the information is true enough. It's been a year since Karen and I officially admitted that what we'd thought would happen when we married and what had actually happened were two different things."

I watched him closely, trying to figure out how he felt

about that. I didn't detect an ounce of animosity in him. "And those expectations were?"

He shrugged. "Well, two children in, Karen decided she didn't have what it took to be a mother."

I raised my brows. "Hell of a time to figure that one out."

He gave me a half smile. "That's what I thought at the time. But now…I don't know. I guess I'm relieved. It wasn't until she said something that I realized we were just going through the motions. Pretending to be the perfect husband and wife and parents. When in reality both of us were miserable. And so were our kids. So we agreed we'd stick it out until the kids started school and then we went our separate ways."

I remembered the serious, somber faces of Ben and Hilary and wondered what life had been like for them. Never once had I not wanted my children. In fact, it would take an act of God to pry any of them away from me.

"Karen comes to pick them up from Cleveland one weekend a month, and takes them to dinner once or twice between visits when she can. But otherwise she's focused on her career as a U.S. attorney."

"And it took you only a year to recover from the blow?"

His smile was easy. "What blow? Sure, I'll be the first to admit that I was shocked when she mentioned divorce. But after everything had sunk in, I knew she was right. Divorcing wasn't wrong. Staying together would have been wrong."

Too philosophical as far as I was concerned. I'd taken

some comfort in keeping my bitterness close to me at all times. I'd been betrayed on so many levels, I couldn't count.

But if what Harry was telling me was true, so had he. And he seemed okay with it. More than okay, he appeared to be happy.

"Do Ben and Hilary know why their mom left?"

His gaze shifted to his glass. He took a sip, and then put it next to mine on the table. "They know enough. Although not about Karen's feelings that she isn't mother material. I don't ever want them to feel unwanted."

The backs of my eyes burned.

"So…" I said, clearing my throat. "Since you appear to have experienced a successful divorce, what would your advice be to me?"

His eyes appeared even darker in the shadowy light. "Forgiveness."

I felt as if he had put me into some sort of mesmerizing trance.

"And to go out with me."

WHOEVER HEARD of going out on a date on a Monday night?

The night after Harry's patio visit, I rushed around trying to pick up after the kids, put dinner dishes in the dishwasher and make sure the lists of things for the babysitter were out in plain sight along with my cell-phone number. And I kept thinking how ridiculous it was that I was going on a date at all, much less on a Monday night.

"Mom…" Daisy tugged on my blouse, dislodging it from

the waist of my skirt as I stood in front of the bathroom mirror. The arm holding my mascara brush dipped and I nearly put my eye out.

"What can I do for you, Dais?"

"Who's going to read to me tonight?"

I'd long ago figured out that guilt pretty much went along with the role of parenthood. I bent down to her level and straightened the top of her pj's. "Heather is going to read to you, sweet pea."

"But I don't want Heather to read to me. I want you to read to me."

I refused to look into her sad blue eyes, which were sure to be bright with crocodile tears, and kissed the top of her head. "Hey, I've got an idea. Why don't *you* read to Heather?"

"Me?" Daisy sounded surprised.

"Yes, that's exactly what you should do. Pick a book you can read and read it to her. That way you'll get a chance to practice your reading, and Heather will love being read to."

Meaghan appeared in the open doorway. "Heather's here."

"Thanks, Meg. Tell her I'll be down in five."

My tween daughter didn't budge.

"Where are you going?" she asked.

I'd begun applying mascara again and purposely stilled my hand to prevent another eye incident. "I'm not sure yet. Harry hasn't said."

"You're going out with a *man?*" Meaghan made it sound as if I were committing the ultimate sin.

"Would you prefer I went out with a woman?"

"Well, yeah," she said in that cocky manner that sometimes bugged me. "Like with Janice or Kathy or one of your other friends."

"It wouldn't be a date, then, would it?"

"Date?"

Jon had been passing in the hallway, putting his earbuds in so he could listen to his music even in motion. He left one hanging across his shoulder and stopped to stare.

"You're going out on a date?" he asked incredulously.

As I stood looking at my three children, I wished I hadn't been such a coward and had told them about my plans that morning. In all honesty, it would have been nice if I'd given them at least a month's notice. But Harry had asked and I'd accepted and that was that.

Only I'd known it wouldn't be that simple, hadn't I? I'd seen this showdown with my kids coming from a mile away. And I had purposely avoided it. Until now, when avoidance was no longer an option.

"But you never date," Jon stated the obvious.

I put the mascara brush down. "I decided to break that rule just this once with Harry."

"Harry?" Daisy repeated. "Ben's dad Harry?"

"Exactly that Harry."

"What's he do?" Meaghan asked.

"He's a doctor at the hospital."

"He has kids?" Jon followed up.

"Two. There's Ben, who goes to school with Daisy. And Ben's sister, Hilary. They live with him."

"You mean he lives in our neighborhood?" Jon didn't sound happy.

I remembered that was my reaction when I originally heard that Ben went to the same school as Daisy. "I don't know." I crossed my arms. "Hold on a minute here. If I didn't know better, I'd think you didn't want me to go out on this date."

All three of them had the good grace to look down at the floor.

The doorbell rang, and a few moments later, Heather called up from the bottom of the steps.

"Ms. Smith, there's a guy at the door. Should I let him in?"

"Yes, Heather. Tell him I'll be five minutes." I turned back to my children. "Now, I insist that since you're all responsible for my being late, the three of you have to go down and say hello to Harry, then keep him occupied until I'm ready."

Meaghan's eyes nearly popped out of her head. "I will not!"

"You will so. He's a guest in our house. You'll treat him with respect and generosity. Offer him a glass of water or something." I turned back toward the mirror to gauge how much time I had and what I could do with it. I also wondered where the duct tape was and whether or not the children had access to it. "By the way you're all reacting, you'd think I'd invited the devil over for supper."

They hadn't budged.

"Go," I told them.

They went.

CHAPTER EIGHT

"Are you enjoying yourself?" Harry asked an hour into our dinner.

I sat back and considered the question, along with the decadently handsome man across from me. He'd surprised me by taking me to Greektown. It had been a long time since I'd been to the ethnic area and even longer since I'd had such a decidedly Mediterranean meal.

Still, I suspected he could have taken me to a fast-food restaurant and I would have enjoyed myself just as much.

"Yes," I finally answered him, mildly surprised by my simple answer.

After I'd finished applying makeup and made my way downstairs earlier, I'd found Meaghan and Jon staring at Harry with barely concealed contempt, while Daisy kept trying to pull him into the family room to show her her toys. For at least the twentieth time since I'd agreed to this date, I'd wondered if I should cancel. My kids were more opposed to my indulging in something of a romantic nature than even I'd imagined.

Then Harry had looked at me and I'd known I had to go out on this date.

Now I was awfully glad that I had.

"Uh-oh," he said, thanking the server when he removed our empty plates. "You've got that look on your face again."

"What look?" I slowly sipped my wine, careful not to imbibe too much. I didn't want alcohol to interfere with whatever was happening between us. And I was pretty sure something was happening. What it was, I didn't know. But for the first time in a long time, I was merely going with the flow.

"The one that says you're trying to figure something out."

I put my glass down. "Maybe that's because I am."

He folded his hands on top of the tablecloth. "So why don't you just ask me?"

"Because you'll interfere with my thought processes."

He chuckled softly. "Are you saying I'll lie?"

"No, it's not that at all, really. It's just that when you're speaking…well, I can't seem to concentrate on what you're saying."

"What are you concentrating on then?"

I shrugged, knowing that I really shouldn't be sharing this, but helpless to do otherwise. "The way you smile when you look at me. The way your eyes crinkle at the corners." How much I wanted him to kiss me.

He was looking at my mouth, then seemed to catch himself. "I'm sorry. What were you saying?"

I laughed and sat back. "Tell me, Harry...why me? Why pursue me so doggedly when I made it clear I had no interest in being pursued?"

"You mean beyond your obvious attractiveness?" he asked. "Have I told you that you look great tonight, by the way?"

"At least five times. And thank you." I shifted in my chair. "But there are lots of attractive women around the hospital that you could have chosen instead."

His eyes darkened slightly. "Are we talking about Angela again?"

"No, no," I said quickly. "Not her individually. But as part of a group...well, yes. I mean, if your attraction to me is based on a physical level, then another woman could hold the same appeal."

He looked at me for a long moment, then shook his head. "It began with physical attraction. But that's not the extent of my feelings for you."

"Do tell."

He sat back. "Actually, I'm not all that clear about it myself yet, but..." He cleared his throat. "I suppose your not saying yes right away had something to do with it."

"Ah, playing hard to get."

"No. We're both beyond that stage now, aren't we?"

"I know I am."

He took the napkin from his lap and put in on the table.

"I don't know…the way you handle yourself at work. I've watched you with patients when you don't know anyone's around, and there's such a generosity about you. A commitment to that one person you're with. Beyond that room and that patient, nothing else exists. And you're damn good at your job."

I realized I was tracing circles on the tablecloth with my thumb.

"And if I'd had any doubts about your kindness—which I hadn't—they would have been put to rest the minute you started organizing this Stitches from the Heart effort."

What he said touched me more profoundly than a physical caress. In that one moment in time, I felt connected to him in a way I hadn't felt connected to a man in a very long time. I understood that he saw me—the real me—and that he not only got me, he…well, he liked me.

Suddenly I became aware that he'd put his hand over mine on the table. His skin was hot and rough from frequent disinfectant scrubs. Tiny tendrils of sensation curled up my arm.

I laughed quietly. "And here I thought it was because I was irresistible and you couldn't go one more minute without kissing me."

I tried to take my hand back and he held tight. "And then there's that."

ONE MINUTE WE WERE at the restaurant waiting for our Greek coffee, the next we'd skipped the coffee and were at Harry's house. His kids were at his sister's for the night, and the door barely closed behind us when I finally got that kiss I'd been looking forward to for so long. Since the moment I'd met his eyes in the E.R. his first day on the job.

I couldn't seem to get enough of his lips on mine, his tongue inside my mouth, his hard body pressed against me. Even as I stepped out of my shoes, I pushed his suit jacket down over his shoulders, then went to work on the buttons of his shirt.

He pulled slightly away so that he could untangle his arms from his jacket. The instant it hit the floor, I pushed his shirt down his shoulders to follow it.

I gasped when he turned me around and pressed me against a foyer table, clearing the top then lifting me to sit there.

Then we both stilled, looking at each other in the soft glow of the front porch light through the beveled windows.

I knew a want for this man that went beyond the physical. I yearned to know everything about him. I wanted to share his mind as well as his body.

I also wanted to give to him. Open myself up to him in a way that I'd been unable to do with another human being for much too long.

"You know, experience tells me that if we sleep together now, odds are we never will again," he said quietly.

I lifted my hand to the side of his face. "The too much too soon school of thinking?"

"Maybe. But I can't bear the thought of not seeing you again."

I leisurely kissed him. "Let's see how you feel in the morning."

He ran his thumb along my bottom lip. "It's not me I'm worried about."

I squeezed my thighs against his hips, drawing him closer, the bone-deep desire in me pulsing with a life of its own. "I'm here, aren't I? And I haven't tried to rebuff your attentions for, oh, at least a half hour."

He grinned, then kissed me so deeply he took my breath away.

THE FOLLOWING DAY after work, I became painfully aware that going without romance made people do stupid things.

And that finally inviting that same romance into your life made people do even dumber things.

It appeared Harry had been right in his too much too soon take.

Oh, don't get me wrong. I wanted Harry as much, if not more, than I had the night before. The problem was that everyone but Daisy seemed to know that. And they were now going out of their way to make sure it never happened again.

As I put a platter of chicken and a bowl of mashed potatoes on the set kitchen table, I faced the fact that I had one teenage son and one nearly teenage daughter who were having a very hard time adjusting to the fact that their mother was dating. If their somber silence wasn't enough to get the message across, then the resentful gazes they sent zinging my way when they thought I wasn't looking certainly were.

I'd somehow talked myself into thinking that their glum behavior over breakfast that morning had to do with it being a very chilly Tuesday morning. But I wasn't allowed that luxury now. It was very clear that the weather or the day of the week had absolutely nothing to do with their attitudes. Rather, their simmering sullenness was focused solely on me.

"It's not exactly lamb chops and spinach pie, but I guess it'll do," I said, referring to my dinner with Harry as I sat down.

"Spinach pie?" Daisy said as I spooned mashed potatoes onto her plate. "Sounds yucky."

"Oh, no, it's very good. Harry took me to a wonderful restaurant in Greektown last night. And you know what they do with the cheese? They set fire to it before putting it on your table."

Daisy frowned. "Don't you get burned?"

"No, silly. They put the fire out first." I added chicken and corn to her plate as well, then went to work placing food on my plate. I noticed neither Jon nor Meaghan had made a move since I sat down. "And it was very, very good. I was thinking the four of us should go together sometime."

"Four?" Jon said. "As in without Harry?"

My movements slowed. "Unless you'd like him and his kids to come, too."

He snorted. "Yeah, right."

I remained silent until he met my gaze. "Is there a particular problem you have with Harry? Or is it just the idea of my dating in general that has you upset?"

Meaghan answered. "What did you expect, Mom? I mean, you've never, ever brought a boyfriend to the house. Then— *bam!*—one night this Harry guy shows up from out of the blue. What, did you just expect us to start calling him Daddy?"

My throat tightened at the angry display. Part of me wanted to send them both up to their rooms without dinner. But I suspected that's what they were hoping for. Their sulking was geared to get a rise out of me, and the guilt I would feel would perhaps go a long way toward forcing life back to the status quo.

"I don't understand," I said carefully. "Your father's dated several women since the divorce. You don't seem to have a problem with that."

"Yeah, and he cancels visits and forgets to show up for ball games and calls on our birthdays…"

I knew that Bill's behavior had affected the kids, but until now I'd had no idea how much.

And I couldn't help wondering if my own bitterness about the divorce had negatively influenced my children's perception of their father.

I sat back, giving up any pretense of eating, although I motioned that Daisy should eat everything on her plate. Thankfully she did, content with watching what was going on around her, even if she didn't understand all of it.

Then again, maybe my kids understood more than I gave them credit for.

"And you're afraid that's what will happen if I continue to see Harry?"

"I'm not afraid it will happen," Jon said. "I know it will."

As I looked at the two older children across from me, I realized that I was seeing a side of them I wasn't familiar with. One that had no doubt developed as a result of Bill and my divorce, and had evolved without my ever truly knowing it existed.

Then again, maybe I had known. I just hadn't wanted to acknowledge it. Because by not acknowledging it, I was allowing their acrimonious feelings for their father to grow. Which suited me fine. Because, after all, he was a bimbo-loving heel who deserved to pay for what he'd done to me.

I wasn't positive, but I was pretty sure I winced.

"Is this how you act when you're with your father?" I asked quietly.

Meg and Jon stared down at the table.

Oh, God.

All this time I'd been making myself out as the perfect parent, when I'd probably been doing irreparable damage to them. And now I was being made to pay the price.

I was desperate to set things right…

But I hadn't a clue just how to do that.

CHAPTER NINE

T wo days later, as I helped Daisy get ready for Halloween trick-or-treating, I still felt a sadness so pervasive that it seemed to have bled into every other area of my life. It was more than the late-night telephone conversation I'd had with Harry following the children's revelation when I told him I couldn't see him for a while. Perhaps never again. It had to do with the way I'd allowed my own bitterness to spill over and poison my children's lives.

Daisy put her hand on my shoulder as I bent to tie her shoe, even though she could do it herself. "What's the matter, Mommy?"

I smiled at her. The first honest-to-God smile in two days. I'd poisoned everyone but this precious little girl before me. I didn't know if it was because she'd been too young to remember what I'd been like after Bill had left. Or if she'd just adapted naturally. But for some sweet reason I'd managed not to taint her. She loved me. She loved her daddy. There was nothing beyond that.

Nor should there be.

"I hate him sometimes," Jon had admitted to me the night before when I'd knocked on his door and asked if I could talk to him. He'd been speaking about his father, of course. And had demonstrated just how far I'd let this whole thing go. "How could he just...leave us like that?"

His words left me feeling as if Bill had moved out yesterday instead of four years ago.

And the realization came like a fist to the gut that I'd been so obsessed with my own pain that I couldn't help Meaghan and Jon deal with theirs. So they had never dealt with it.

I felt a sharp pang of guilt for what my ex must have gone through over the past four years. If the rancorous expressions he faced were anything like those I'd seen across the table from me the other night, and still saw now, two days later...well, I'd say he'd been punished plenty.

Unfortunately, I couldn't help feeling that it was our children that had been dealt the harshest punishment.

Bill wasn't a bad parent. Despite what he'd done to me, I knew he loved our kids. Too bad it had taken four years for me to get back to the point where I could view him as a father rather than a rat.

My children needed their father as much as they needed me. Somewhere down the line, I'd forgotten that. And I knew that Bill was capable of being the type of father the three of them needed—if he was given a fair chance.

Fair hadn't played much of a role in our nuclear family since the day we broke up.

Forgiveness.

I remembered Harry's words—or rather word—of advice on the back patio such a short time ago. I thought he'd meant that I had to forgive my ex. And while I'm sure that was part of it, I hadn't known that forgiving myself would also be a part of the bargain....

EVEN THOUGH MEAGHAN and Jon no longer dressed up for Halloween, I'd asked them both to come with me and Daisy as we made the trick-or-treating rounds. Most of Daisy's belly-dancer costume was covered up by her winter coat because the temperature had dropped during the day, autumn having officially settled on Detroit and the surrounding suburbs. An hour and a half later, we were walking back up our block on the way home when Meaghan spotted a car in the driveway.

"Dad's here," she said.

"Yeah, Daddy!" Daisy shouted, spilling some of the candy from her jack-o'-lantern bucket as she ran for the house, where her father waited inside.

"He's probably here to cancel this weekend, too," Jon mumbled just behind me.

I slowed my step so that we were even. "No. He's here because I asked him here."

He looked at me, curiosity in his dark eyes—eyes that mirrored his father's. It hurt me in that one moment to look into them because of the bitterness and hate that were also there for the same man.

I didn't kid myself into thinking that what lay ahead of me was going to be easy. Far from it. It had taken me four years to do the damage I'd done. And I had to face that it might take me nearly as long to undo it.

But I had to try. And tonight was as good a night as any to start.

THE FOLLOWING MORNING at the hospital was brutal. It was one of those days when I couldn't seem to catch my breath as urgent-care patient after urgent-care patient was wheeled into the E.R. I'd already changed out of one blood-covered scrub shirt, compliments of a gunshot victim who'd suffered a wound to the right femoral artery. My white shoes were spotted with fluid from a woman whose water had broken while I helped her up onto the examining table. And my mind was crammed with a seemingly never-ending stream of pain-filled faces all looking to me and the hospital staff for help.

"What a day, huh?" Latesha said as she came to stand next to me in the staff locker room, where I was wiping the fluid from my shoes.

"You can say that again."

"Actually," her voice went quiet, "by the looks of it, I'd say you've been having quite the week."

I smiled softly at her. "You can say that again."

She opened her own locker. "Anything I can help with?"

"I wish there was. But this mess...I'm the one who made it and I'm the only one who can clean it up."

She nodded, took something from her locker, then closed the door and told me she'd see me later.

I stared after her. There existed an understanding between Latesha and me that we would be there for each other if we wanted to talk, but if not, we would respect each other's privacy. I was glad for that.

I sat down on the bench and rubbed the back of my neck. I needed to get down to the cafeteria for something to eat, but I yearned for just five minutes to gather my thoughts.

Actually, I felt that even if I could have the next twelve months, I still would not have enough time for that monumental task. I'd have to make due with the five minutes.

All day my ex's face had haunted my thoughts. The expression he'd worn as he left the house last night had almost knocked the air out of my lungs.

He had been grateful. And for a moment I actually thought he was going to hug me by way of thanks.

Not that the night had been easy. Sitting next to Bill and addressing our three children had been difficult for me. And confusing to our children.

What I had made clear was that now that I understood what had happened and was still happening...well, no way could I sleep easy until I righted it.

And merely by opening up a dialogue between the

children and Bill and me regarding our responsibilities as their parents and our lives outside parenthood, I'd finally managed to do what Harry had suggested. I'd forgiven Bill.

And myself? Well, I still had a long way to go in that regard. But my ex's expression of gratitude, and Meg's and Jon's puzzled but hopeful faces, told me I would achieve it. Someday.

How did a person forgive herself for making her children choose between their parents? Allowing personal hurt to cast their father in the role of bad guy? A role he had no hope of changing because only I had the power to do that.

There was a light tap on the door. I got up and turned to close the locker. There was an intern down the row, so I wasn't the only one in the room. Surely the knock had nothing to do with me.

But when I saw Harry standing just inside the door, I realized it had everything to do with me.

My heart plunged to somewhere in the vicinity of my feet then bounced back up again, taking what seemed like a full minute to move back into its normal position.

"Hi," he said.

"Hi."

God, but he looked good.

Of course, I'd seen him countless times over the past few days since my late-night phone call. But I'd made a point of avoiding him. And he'd made a point of respecting my wishes. And this morning we'd both been so busy we hadn't a chance to blink, much less talk to each other.

Now I remembered every moment of our time together Monday night—had it really only been four days ago? And I yearned for him to touch me again.

My feelings must have been written all over my face because he narrowed his eyes at me, mystified.

"You know, when I said I was afraid that Monday night might be the last time I saw you…I was only joking."

I smiled. "I know."

He stepped closer. I tensed. He kept his distance. "I miss you."

I looked up into his handsome face, fighting the desire to reach up and run my fingertips along his strong jaw. "I miss you, too."

Had things between us really gotten so serious so fast? I recognized the metallic feeling in my stomach and knew that they had. What I was experiencing wasn't the infatuation of a woman who had gone too long without romance and latched on to the first opportunity for it.

"No, don't say anything," he said, doing what I couldn't by lifting his hand to my face and stroking my cheek. "I see it all in your eyes. I…" The sound of him swallowing filled the room. I was aware of the intern's attention on us, but couldn't have cared less. "I just want you to know that when you're ready…well, I'll be there. Waiting."

I easily slid into the cradle of his arms, absorbing everything that was him as his hands pressed against my back. I rested my cheek against his shoulder and bit my bottom lip to keep tears at bay.

I didn't know what I had done to deserve Dr. Harry Gordon. But whatever it was, I planned to make sure I kept on deserving it.

CHAPTER TEN

And so began a long journey, sometimes lonely, most times happy, as I worked to repair the wounds I had helped create. I was surprised by how open both Meg and Jon appeared to be at the prospect of a closer relationship with their father, and a more honest connection to me. Although Daisy had her school play on Saturday night, with the new openness and cooperation between me and Bill (I'd determined not to call him my ex anymore), we both realized he could still take Meaghan and Jon for Friday. In fact, it might even be better if he spent some time with them alone. And without Tiffany, who, Bill decided, came a distant second to his need to repair his relationship with his kids.

After the performance, which Bill, Meaghan and Jon all attended, I sent Daisy off with the three of them and spent the night alone, thinking about everything that had happened in the past two weeks.

When the telephone rang around ten that night, I immediately picked up, thinking it could be one of the kids or perhaps even Bill. Instead, I heard Harry's voice.

"What are you doing?" he asked.

I didn't know what to say, so I said nothing.

What did it mean, his calling me? That he wanted to see me? That he wasn't going to honor my request that we not see each other until I sorted everything out?

"I'm not asking you on a date, Jenny. I'm a friend sitting at home with his kids, who are both conked out in front of the TV with popcorn in their hair, and I thought I'd call to see how you were."

I smiled at that and burrowed more deeply into the couch, putting my crocheting aside. "I'm okay. I guess. Wiped out, but okay."

He'd been at the school play earlier. Ben had played the part of a butter squash in the Thanksgiving production. When I saw Harry come in with his daughter, for a split second I'd thought he'd come for me. Then after a brief wave and a smile, he'd moved with Hilary to the opposite side of the auditorium. I'd caught glimpses of him throughout the play, but we'd never come closer than a couple of rows apart.

Still, I'd felt as if he'd been standing right next to me.

"Oh, and I wanted to tell you that your daughter played her role as a pumpkin perfectly. I think you have a star in the making."

"Ben wasn't so bad himself as a singing squash."

I could hear him smile over the phone. Was that even possible? Maybe not with anyone else, but definitely when it came to Harry.

"I won't pretend to understand what's going on in your life right now, Jenny. And I'll respect your need for distance. But I…"

His words drifted off and I reached for the remote to mute the sound from the television.

"I want to know if it's all right if I call you every now and again. You know, to see how you're doing. Hear your voice."

I clutched the receiver that much tighter. "I'd like that."

"Good."

And then I spent the next two hours explaining exactly what was happening, the realization I'd come to and what I felt I needed to do. And he'd listened. Just listened. Interrupting only once as he woke his kids to send them up to bed.

By the time I finished, my ear hurt and I felt…lighter somehow. As if I'd shared a burden I hadn't known I'd wanted to share.

Harry had yet to say anything to fill the silence I'd left. So I sighed. "I'm amazed by how together you are. How do you do it?"

"I take it day by day."

"You mean you have problems?" I asked, frowning.

"Not quite as complicated as yours, but yes. And thankfully I've had my family here to help me keep things in check. It's one of the advantages of being from a big family."

I rubbed my forehead. Maybe that's one of the ways I'd gone wrong. Oh, I couldn't change the family angle, but in the wake of my divorce, I'd rejected Bill and our shared friends—convinced they had rejected me and my new single status—and collected those who shared my same cynical views on men and marriage.

"It looked like your ex-husband might be making some headway," Harry said thoughtfully.

During the play, I'd sat with Bill, Meaghan and Jon between us. Bill and Meaghan had gone over the program together before the opening scene, sharing a warm, affection-filled laugh at something Jon and I hadn't been privy to.

"I'd like to think so," I said quietly. "Normally, I would have sat at one end of the auditorium with the kids, and he would have sat on the other side alone or with his girlfriend du jour." I cringed, realizing how stupid that had been. As if in public I'd claimed the children as mine, and by doing so, I'd forced them to take sides.

"Jenny?"

I recalled a conversation I'd overheard between Jon and Bill on the way out of the auditorium. It seemed there was some sort of father-son baseball league that Bill suggested they join in the spring. Jon had shrugged as if it made no difference one way or another to him, but there must have been something in his face that I couldn't see because Bill had smiled as if he'd just made an important connection with his son.

"Hmm?" I said in response to Harry's question.

"Thank you."

Had I missed something? "Thank you for what? For un-burdening all of my problems on you when you clearly have enough of your own? For talking your ear off for the past two hours? Yes, I can see where you would be thanking me for that."

His soft chuckle filled my ear. "Thank you for letting me in."

HIS WORDS and the meaning behind them stayed with me throughout the following morning as I saw to chores around the house. And while I hadn't taken up volunteering with Stitches from the Heart for that reason, I'd found that working toward a goal outside my immediate situation provided me with a perspective that helped me keep on track. No matter how bad things might appear, my family had everything they needed. The same couldn't be said for others.

After lunch I put on a pair of slacks and a blouse, then climbed into the car to make a trip I'd been looking forward to since collecting enough materials to fill a special Stitches from the Heart bag a couple of days ago. From now on, the items would be presented to the families when they left the hospital, but I was compelled to make this particular delivery myself.

I drove out of the neighborhood, merged from I-75 south onto I-94 into the city proper, then consulted the address I'd gotten from the third floor nurse's aide last week and exited the highway.

I was in a part of town I rarely ever saw except when

passing by on the highway. Grand old single-family homes sat next to those that had been chopped into apartments and had fallen into disrepair. I pulled into the driveway of one of these buildings then shut off the engine and reached for the bag that sat in the passenger's seat before getting out.

It was a clear, cool November day and the first snowfall of the year was forecast for later in the day. But right now the sun shone brightly, if weakly, and the air was crisp and clean. I walked up the sidewalk then climbed the steps to the house, checking the names on the mailboxes for the one I was looking for. I pressed a doorbell button, then stood back to wait.

Two kids about Daisy's age ran from the side of the house, playing. I smiled at them and they resumed their game of tag as the door in front of me opened and I stood looking at the young mother I'd seen at the hospital nearly two weeks ago.

"Hi," I said. "I'm from Community General Hospital—"

"Sure, sure," she said. "I remember you. You're the one who picked up the baby's blanket."

It had been a pillowcase, but I wasn't going to correct her. Mostly because to her it had been a blanket.

I smiled. "I'm glad you remember. It's because of you that I've started this project…" I drifted off, realizing that I was making this about me when it was really about her. "How's the baby?"

"Winston? Fine. Fine." She grinned, pulling her sweater tighter around her slender body. "Growing every day."

"Good. I'm happy to hear it."

"I'd invite you in, but I just got him to sleep. You know how it is…"

"Yes, I do. I have three of my own at home." Remembering the bag, I held it out to her. "These are just a few items for Winston. Things people have crocheted and knitted especially to fit preemies from an organization called Stitches from the Heart. I thought you might like to have them."

Looking from me to the bag, she hesitantly opened the handles and peered inside at the tiny items. From the cap and booties to the blanket and sweater, every piece had been crocheted or knitted by people—including myself—in the hopes of making one person's life a little easier.

"Thank you," she said, fingering a blue cap. "Thank you very much."

"You're welcome."

I turned to leave.

"Wait," she said. "Wait a minute."

I put my hands in my pockets as she disappeared inside the house. She came back out a moment later with a picture of Winston. She held it out to me. "I thought you might like to have this."

I stared down at the tiny little baby in a hospital shirt and smiled. "Thank you."

The picture would go up on a bulletin board I'd installed in the staff locker room at the hospital…and would be joined by countless others in the months to come.

EPILOGUE

One year later...

"Over here," Meaghan said, leading the way toward the front of the elementary-school auditorium, where in just twenty minutes, third-graders would be presenting a special performance of *Peter Pan*. Daisy had fussed all day over the new nightgown she was to wear in her part as Wendy. And Ben looked cute as a button in his green leotards and cap, taking his role of Peter very seriously.

Meg said, "I think there's enough seats for all of us."

And we needed a lot of them. Eight, to be exact. Directly behind Meaghan was Hilary Gordon. Then Harry, who was now my fiancé, and I. Behind us was Bill, who was talking to a now sixteen-year-old Jon about the World Series, while Jon steered Aunt Precious in her wheelchair. And behind them was a very pregnant Tiffany, who was now Bill's wife, and, well, my friend. She was smiling and absently touching the baby bump that would increase our number by one.

As we took our seats in one row to watch Daisy and Ben perform, I realized we looked like one great big family. And we were. An extended, happy family. Oh, we still ran into problems. But with all of us working together there were more happy times than sad. And I figured anytime you could say that, well, you must be doing something right.

I shrugged out of my coat and Harry adjusted it around my shoulders. I'd just celebrated my fortieth birthday, and on that day realized that I'd finally graduated from busy single mom with an ax to grind to a much happier adult with a tighter grasp on reality. Part of that happiness came from my work with Stitches from the Heart, which had expanded to include over twenty area nursing homes and fifty additional volunteers, whose numbers were growing every day. We were getting enough knitted items to cover not only our hospital, but two additional ones, and we even had items left over to send to the main office in Santa Monica to be distributed where needed.

The personal rewards were priceless. While my efforts might only be a mere drop in the bucket, they meant that a few babies wouldn't need an old pillowcase in order to keep warm.

The auditorium went dark and Daisy and Ben's teacher appeared before the curtains to welcome us and introduce the play we were about to see.

Harry leaned in closer so he could whisper into my ear. "Have I told you how beautiful you look tonight?"

I smiled and whispered back, "At least five times. Thank you."

"Marry me?"

I stared at him and laughed, ignoring Aunt Precious, who shushed me so she could hear the teacher. Harry had already proposed a month ago, with all five of our kids in attendance, at our usual Friday-night pizza outing. He'd placed the ring under a piece of pepperoni in the middle of the pizza. I looked down at the ring now—a two-carat sparkler that I only wore on nights like this because I was afraid of losing it.

"When?" I asked.

"Tomorrow."

"But our daughters won't be able to be bridesmaids if we do that."

"We can still have the regular wedding in the spring. I just want...no, need to know that you're my wife now. Always." He kissed my lips, then kissed my nose. "Marry me, Jenny. Marry me now. Even if we can't let anyone know. Not at work or at home."

I looked into the eyes of the man who had opened my eyes to so much. Understanding. Forgiveness. Love.

"Name the time and the place and I'll be there."

And we both knew that I would....

Dear Reader,

We hope you enjoyed Jenny and Harry's journey to happy reality-ever-after, and the fictitious role Jenny played in heading up an additional Detroit-area contingent of Stitches from the Heart. Out there are the real people responsible for making this incredible endeavor such an ongoing success. Our hats are off to each and every one of them.

Handy with knitting needles? A crochet hook? Know someone else who is? Push the boundaries of your own life by getting involved with Kathy Silverton's Stitches from the Heart by visiting www.stitchesfromtheheart.org or calling 1-866-472-6903 today. You won't regret it.

Truly,

Lori & Tony Karayianni

aka Tori Carrington

www.toricarrington.net

www.sofiemetro.com